Simon Eady

The Teenage Spy

by

A. Monico

Cover by Sandra Nooke

Marmolada

Although the characters within this book are fictional and do not specifically relate to any one culture, the story is intertwined with anthropological information, beliefs and legends from the people who still inhabit the islands of the Pacific.

First published 2016 by Marmolada Pty Ltd
Copyright © Adrian Monico 2016
The moral right of the author has been asserted.
ISBN: 978-0-9873544-2-6

In memory of my loving grandmother

Author's BIO

Adrian Monico was born in Australia to Italian parents. His family returned to Italy when he was 2 years old where he was raised in the Alps until the age of 14. On returning to Australia, Adrian was required to learn English in order to complete High School and pursue his interest in Physics at University. At the completion of his first year at University, Adrian decided to join the Australian Defence Force (ADF) as a Commissioned Army Officer. During his 15 years of service Adrian reached the rank of Major. The ADF sponsored Adrian to return to university and study Information Technology. He also commanded Surface to Air missile systems and saw active service in East Timor. Adrian is currently a successful IT and Telecommunications Service Delivery Manager.

Contents

Acknowledgements

Once again I feel fortunate to be able to release a book that has been possible due a the number of family and friends that help me get it published.

My gratitude goes out to Penny and my kids for all of their love and support, my mother and TuQuan for the time spent editing the book, Sandra (Sandra Noke Illustration) for the beautiful artwork, Kevin for the editing and suggesting great storyline ideas, and Caitlyn (Artful Words) for the final proofread. Finally, I would like to take the opportunity to thank Adam (Plunge Publishing) for offering a partnership with his company to publish and promote the Simon Eady series.

Other Books By Adrian Monico
- Simon Eady.

PROLOGUE - Next In Line

Despite the fact he was about to launch himself out of plane without a parachute, Agent 2C was feeling at ease. He was quite pleased with the run of recent events and had done a similar night jump out of a C130 military cargo plane five years before. Back then, he was referred to simply as Trooper Bernie Keen and was serving Queen and country as a member of the elite 22nd Special Air Service (SAS) Regiment. Although not well remembered or widely known today, the 22nd SAS Regiment, gained its greatest notoriety in August of 1980 when it heroically carried out hostage extractions from the Iranian Embassy in London. The hostages had been held captive by terrorists. In a total time of just seventeen minutes, the mission had been executed flawlessly and a majority of the hostages were safely rescued. That had been before Bernie's time, but for years, the name of the regiment was often cited, especially amongst young British men like Bernie who aspired to become one of its members.

Among his Special Forces colleagues, Bernie stood out. The reason for this was precisely because he didn't want to stand out. Most of his comrades were confident soldiers who strived to be seen as suitable for promotion. In contrast, Bernie was a 'Grey Man'. Neutral as the colour itself, he was someone who, despite his achievements, kept himself away from the spotlight. In the regiment, Bernie was known as a very competent operator who preferred his own company. His long list of accolades, together with his no-nonsense countenance, chiselled physique and brooding impenetrable eyes, meant that Bernie was rarely the target of friendly banter. In fact, most of his peers and superiors saw Bernie as stealthy, even dangerous, and best left alone. Perhaps it was this, alongside his consecutive and successful participation in multiple missions, that brought him to the attention of MI6 as a potential candidate.

During a review of several SAS members' dossiers, MI6 noted that little was said about Bernie, even though he had multiple combat operations under his belt. What stood out most was that Bernie had a very high IQ. He was on track to complete his Masters degree in International Relations at the top of the class. He also did not appear to be romantically involved, which suited MI6. Although his initial psychology report flagged him as being potentially unstable, subsequent assessments disproved the original analysis. Bernie duly joined MI6, where his success continued and resulted in his recent promotion to the codename '2C'. After tonight's mission, he was looking forward to a paid holiday in the Maldives.

It was a simple drop in, that was all. Just camera work, no play. The location was a remote area of Columbia and the target was a financial advisor. He was the only person who knew the identity of the dangerous and elusive drug lord who was the focus of MI6's current assignment. The advisor was called the 'Consigliere' – a term commonly used by the Italian mafia. Bernie's task was to conduct surveillance on him and report his findings back to MI6. As the plane neared the drop zone, the loadmaster shouted for Agent 2C to take his position. The rear ramp began opening as he stood. Once the green cargo bay light showed, Agent 2C leapt, without hesitation or parachute, into the black abyss of the night.

For the first few minutes, Agent 2C plummeted through clear sky. Below him, no ground was visible. Although he completely trusted his instruments, the fact that he could not see any lights from the village that was supposedly beneath him made him a little nervous. He switched on his night vision goggles and allowed his eyes to adjust. All he could see was a green wall. It took a few seconds before it made sense. He was about to punch his way through an ocean of clouds. As he entered and was enveloped by the clouds, Agent 2C's vision filled with multiple bright flashes. His well honed instincts took over and he reacted defensively, throwing his hands over his face and holding his breath. Then, almost immediately, he felt a bit silly. A lightening storm had erupted. The impact points were akin to the flashes caused by exploding bombs. Agent 2C quickly recomposed himself and acknowledged that he couldn't always command his instincts. Within seconds, he was back to where he desired to be: in control and focused.

He straightened his body to accelerate his descent out of the clouds, getting thoroughly wet on his way through. Moments later, back in the dark abyss, his instruments signalled the landing point. Agent 2C fanned his body into a starfish shape. In doing so, he exposed the material that stretched between each of his limbs. The latest version of the 'wing-suit' Agent 2C was wearing allowed him to navigate towards his final destination. Even though he was still falling at a rapid rate, he was able to manoeuvre through the air, prolonging his free fall time, rather like a flying squirrel.

The wing-suit was not the preferred option among most of the agents. First, it had no ability to guarantee a safe landing. Second, it was not considered a safe alternate to parachutes. However, when a case study article about the suit was published by MI6 in an article detailing the latest essential accessories for operatives (a.k.a. 'spy toys'), Agent 2C immediately registered for a course on its use. What appealed to him most was that the wing-suit reduced the time agents spent exposed in the air. Over a period of six months, executing several jumps per week, Agent 2C became proficient in using it. He would often jump off cliffs to fly at the nap of the earth. It was during one of these jumps that he was captured on video by local teenagers who promptly uploaded the images to the internet. As he soared toward the earth, Bernie briefly recalled the hot water that the unwanted popularity of that had landed him in. He quickly dismissed such thoughts from his mind and focused his full attention on the task at hand.

What made his current jump tougher than any previous ones was that he was navigating with night vision goggles. The night vision technology, although having advanced in the past few years, still did not provide an accurate reflection of the depth of field. This meant Bernie found judging the distance of tree tops quite challenging. He likened navigating with night vision goggles to driving a fast car at high speed with one eye patched. It is difficult in such circumstances to judge how soon one will reach the chicane, with the result that one is very likely to miss the turn and end up crushed in half against the roadside barriers or rolling down the cliff.

Below the cloud base, the evening was eerily calm. The air was so humid it felt like a brick resting on Bernie's lungs. Despite his comfort with free falling, his muscles tensed as he gilded into a mountain crevasse. Bernie's mind, as a reaction to his increased personal risk, restricted to a single point of concentration which was the flight path ahead.

"Status of Agent 2C?" the Head of MI6, codenamed 'Beta', demanded as he entered the control room.

"Right on schedule, sir," replied the mission controller.

"Have we got direct satellite data feed?" asked Beta whilst scanning across the frameless flat screen monitors that displayed information and live footage of the several missions that were currently running. "Which screen?"

"First screen on your right, sir," replied the controller.

Beta's eyes were instantly drawn to the footage captured by a camera attached to Agent 2C's helmet. Although the screen showed predominately green and black images moving towards the camera at significant speed, it contained sufficient detail to allow Beta to make a brisk assessment.

"Has the area been scanned?" enquired Beta.

"Satellite thermal scan is almost complete. So far, only wildlife has been detected." Just as the controller uttered these words, a high-pitched tone sounded, accompanied by flashing lights on one of the monitors.

"What is it?" snapped Beta.

"Sir, it looks like the satellite has identified a human presence near the landing site," said the controller, loud enough for his second in command to hear. The controller brought the satellite image onto the central monitor and readjusted the focal point to increase its sharpness. The screen clearly showed three small human shapes were walking towards the landing point.

"You have got to be kidding me!" exclaimed Beta.

"Patching you through now, sir," replied the controller, as he frantically typed.

"Blue Moon, be advised, three Charlies are heading home," a metallic voice squawked in Agent 2C's earpiece.

"Roger. Out!" replied Agent 2C. He was frustrated by the thought of having to deal with children in the jungle at this time of the night. He heard the beeping sound that informed him the recommended altitude had been reached. It was time to terminate the

Adrian Monico

free fall. Agent 2C pulled a metallic pin located on his left shoulder. Within seconds, the wing-suit sections stretched between his legs peeled off. They dropped a few metres behind him before being pulled together by nylon ropes attached to Bernie's body harness. The wing-suit material, now resembling the shape of a rectangular parachute, instantly created sufficient drag to slow his fall to a manageable speed.

Four minutes later, Agent 2C pulled another metallic pin located on his right shoulder and the wing sections located off his arms detached, snapping back as extensions to the previously released material. This increased the size of the parachute to three time its original area. The drag from a chute this size would usually be sufficient to slow the landing to the same impact as most adults would feel from jumping off a bar stool. Smooth and gentle. However, this time Agent 2C had waited too long to release his arm wings. He slammed into the ground with the same speed as he would have generated had he jumped off the first storey of a building. Recognising his error, Agent 2C instinctively diverted some of the force of his impact into carrying out a 'para-roll'. Although his quick thinking ensured he did not acquire any physical damage, he did succeed in winding himself.

"Some plans are obviously better on paper!" Bernie murmured as he struggled to regain his breath. "I've got to find a way to get extra material into the wing-suit to increase the size of the final parachute."

"Blue Moon, be advised. Charlies ten metres from your loc," the metallic voice advised.

"Roger. I see them. Out," replied Bernie.

"Blue Moon. Bedtime stories. Over," ordered the mission controller.

"Negative," replied Agent 2C. "Bedtime stories can lead to nightmares. Over." He was fully aware that the effect of the Mosquito sedative darts known as 'bedtime stories' could result in cardiac arrests in people with a body weight of less than forty kilograms. The three teenagers he had seen through his night vision goggles were now only a few metres from him.

A new voice now crackled in his earpiece. "Blue Moon. This is Sunray. Bedtime stories. Over!"

Even without knowing that Sunray was the codename Beta used in radio communication, Bernie could hear the anger in his voice and understood this last communication was a direct and definite order. He did not respond. Instead, he decided to retreat into the forest, hoping that the cover of darkness would keep him out of sight.

"Back in the control room, Beta was not fooled. "Damn it!" he growled. "I know what you're doing, Agent 2C. Or rather, what you're not doing."

Oblivious of the irritation his actions were causing his superior, Agent 2C quietly slipped into the darkness of the forest and started jogging along the uneven ground. After travelling for a few kilometres, he looked at his Global Positioning System (GPS) and changed direction towards his target area. The three hour hike brought Agent 2C to within a few metres of the compound. He traversed this remaining distance on his belly, slithering to safety in a hidden location behind a dense bush. Bernie took out his telescopic lens and attached it to his camera. Fifteen minutes later, he watched a sleek Mercedes SLK drive into the compound.

Agent 2C did not know what the Consigliere looked like. From certain reports, he was believed to be Caucasian with blonde hair and blue eyes. As Bernie knew, however, appearances could be easily changed. He was not leaving anything to chance, so he photographed any person he could see within both the vehicle and the compound. The tinted rear window of the Mercedes opened just enough for the passenger to look out, but not enough for anybody to peer back in. Agent 2C took a photo, just in case digital editing could improve the image.

"Come on! What are you waiting for? Get out and let me see you," whispered Bernie. The words had only just left his lips when he was surprised to feel the cold steel of a rifle barrel suddenly resting on his ear.

"Levantarse!" came a voice, speaking in Spanish with a strong Austrian accent.

"Ok, ok", replied Agent 2C, surrendering.

"Ahora!" ordered the guard, demanding greater urgency.

Bernie stood up with his hands raised above his head. He was then handcuffed and directed to walk down the hill towards the house. Once he reached the car parked at the front door, he felt, without warning, a hard blow to his head and his world went black. As he lay unconscious on the ground, he was kicked several times for good measure. Satisfied their victim was unconscious, his assailants proceeded to search him. He was then dragged to a cellar deep underground.

Some time later, Bernie regained consciousness. He felt a sharp pain in the side of his head and struggled to stay on his feet due to severe dizziness. The pain in his head intensified to the point where he could only take short sharp breaths. His ribs were, without doubt, broken, and his hands were cuffed and chained to a rustic ceiling. The place smelled mouldy. He scanned the room with unfocused eyes. He was able to make out old wine barrels and bottles scattered around a small, dark space. His instincts told him he was not alone.

"How are you feeling, young chap?" asked a quiet voice from behind him.

"Peachy," replied Agent 2C sarcastically.

"You made a grave mistake, you know. You should have sedated the teenagers."

"So, my twinkle toes are rusty."

"Those teenagers know that sharing information pays well. I am very generous."

"What's next? Interrogation, torture, terminating me?" asked Agent 2C. He gave up trying to put a face to the voice. Being cuffed and chained, his movement was limited. He reverted to closing his eyes now and then to heighten his other senses.

"How barbaric! Bernie, Bernie, Bernie, you have such a low opinion of this organisation. We are no different from any other capitalist company. At times we may be a little heavy handed, but that's not unlike from companies using corporate espionage and legal battles to achieve their ends, or governments sending the military in to defend their national interests," continued the voice from the shadows.

Agent 2C realised his identity had been compromised. "Since you know my name, it's only fair I know who I'm talking to," he challenged. He was impatient. He wanted the voice from the shadows to confirm he had made contact with his target. "You seem to have the inside running on who I am," he continued. "That means you probably also know who I work for and that they know where I am." He tugged again at his restraints.

"No use, Bernie. You'll find those handcuffs and chains are unbreakable. There is also no point in buying time. There is no escape route. But don't worry. You have my word that no harm will come to you. Just follow all of my instructions and you will be fine."

"So, what is the point of all of this?" asked Bernie genuinely confused.

"Simple. My interest is in someone else. For my plan to succeed, I need you to be my guest for a while. If you behave, you only have to worry about explaining yourself to Beta."

Bernie felt a chill at the casual use of the codename for the Head of MI6. The Consigliere , who Bernie correctly assumed was talking to him, must have an informer who had infiltrated the organisation.

"Shortly, you will be moved to our 'guest' room. Be warned, my men don't feel the same way as I do about your wellbeing. Take my advice and don't test their patience," warned the Consigliere.

"Guest room, huh? Do I get a toilet break and all?" enquired asked Agent 2C in the hope that an escape opportunity might present itself.

"An en suite is located in the cellar guest room. Don't insult my hospitality by trying to escape. Just behave and enjoy your stay. I trust you will like your dinner. It's your favourite, lamb shanks."

Another chill ran through Bernie. He was now feeling very uneasy. "Is there anything that you don't know about me?" he demanded.

"I could go through your dossier," the voice said with dry amusement at Bernie's discomfort. "However, I have a prior engagement. Ciao."

Bernie already knew the reason for this sudden departure. The MI6 satellite was moving across into the Arctic zone which meant that the Consigliere had limited time to make his exit, undetected. Before Agent 2C could ask his next question, he felt a small prick at to the base of his neck. His last clear visual image as his head was falling forward was of large pair of military boots approaching.

CHAPTER 1 - A New Moon

A sliver of sun broke through the curtains and forced its way through a million dust particles before landing on soft skin. Although the warmth was only slight, Simon Eady was fully aware of it and decided that he was not getting out of bed. Of course, this was what Simon decided most mornings. These few moments before getting up was the time he spent remembering his mum while they were living in Malaysia. Only six months had passed since her death, but Simon still remembered the pain he felt when she died. His life had changed dramatically since his mother was first diagnosed with terminal cancer. After believing that his father had died when Simon was young, he was shocked to find out that he was actually still alive. His search for his father had taken him to Europe. There he met Signor Beppe and together they faced dangerous pursuit from unknown killers. His journey then took him to London, to the headquarters of MI6, where he was asked to join a special team of teenage recruits.

Simon was still only 17. As he lay comfortably nestled under the blankets, he reflected on how much his life had changed since joining the special MI6 team. His blonde hair was now shorter and his tall physique had filled out. Only his intense blue eyes remained unchanged. That, and his need to prove himself and continue his search for his father.

"Wake up, sunshine!"

The words were yelled at him by drill instructor who seemed to have expelled all the oxygen in his lungs in just those three words. Sergeant Ketchesky stood in the doorway and glowered at Simon. The man looked like a second rower in a rugby union team. He had no neck, his ears looked like they had been remoulded by a blender, and his thighs were the size of a large tree trunk.

"What are you waiting for?" he roared. "Do I have to flip your bed again?" Sergeant Ketchesky's his nostrils flared like a raged bull.

Simon, motivated by the threat of getting thrown off the bed again, quickly jumped to his feet and raced to the bedroom corner where his military running gear was laid out ready for him. He could not remember how long he had been at the British Commando base in Portsmouth. Although English winters were supposed to be cold and wet, he had spent most of his time at the base outdoors, running, jumping and swinging off ropes, with the result that he usually uncomfortably hot. In fact, he figured that of all the time he had been here, half of it was spent sweating and the other half showering the sweat off.

To most people, life on the base would not be considered fun, but for Simon it was just that. He viewed it all as an adventure and it had become his whole life. He often felt that he was in a movie like Heartbreak Hill. In that film, the sergeant, played by Clint Eastwood, had the same temperament as Sergeant Ketchesky. There were certainly few words of appreciation and praise coming out of his sergeant's mouth, but his eyes conveyed fairly regularly his satisfaction with Simon's achievement. Right now, however, they were narrowed with displeasure.

"Please don't tell me that we are daydreaming again, young fella! You got that glazed look again! I'm seriously worried that you are falling in love, and as I'm the person you spend most of your time with, it's making me nervous. Fortunately, regardless of your preference, the military has had years of experience in knocking such emotions out of young lads like you and getting them focused on the task at hand. The only love you're allowed is with the army and your rifle. So, MOVE IT! You're going to do double the distance this morning."

Simon flinched slightly to avoid getting hit with the usual tsunami of moisture that burst from the sergeant's mouth every time he opened it. He cringed at the mention of his morning schedule. Doubling everything meant running ten kilometres instead of five, swimming four kilometres instead of two, doing the suspended obstacle course twice, and carrying the truck tires twice up 'Gravity Hill' The only part he thought was a treat in all of that was the extra long swim.

"WHERE DO YOU THINK YOU ARE GOING?" barked the sergeant.

Simon had spent so many years jumping out of his bedroom window the second he woke up that he often forgot that hygiene came first in the British Army. Before anything else, he had to shower, brush his teeth and, if he had any time left, shave.

"You have five minutes to be ready outside the door!" Sergeant Ketchesky yelled.

Adrian Monico

Simon rushed to the shower. In three minutes he was out again, attempting to dry himself in seconds. The reality on most days was that he was still quite wet when getting dressed.

"Brushing teeth ain't the same as applying makeup, sweetheart!" called the sergeant, still standing outside the bathroom door as he did most mornings. Simon groaned. It was going to be another one of those days. The sergeant would trail him around, snapping orders, expressing disapproval and even monitoring his toilet breaks. Simon brushed his teeth quickly and spat out the water. He wondered briefly if the speed with which he brushed matched the frequency of an electric toothbrush. Maybe he'd try it sometime to see if it was any quicker. He grinned as he glanced up at the mirror.

"Oh, here we go!" came the sergeant's voice. "You've got those dreamy eyes again! Perhaps adding another log run at the end of today's exercises might help with your concentration?" A faint smile line was creeping in at the edge of his lips. He was now standing inside the bathroom door, observing Simon. This latest threatened punishment did have the desired effect on Simon's expression. He grimaced and his eyes slightly rolled upwards, landing directly on the sergeant's image in the mirror.

"Well, well, well. What did I just see here? We seem to suddenly have a bit of attitude from this young gentleman!" continued Ketchesky, satisfied that he finally got a reaction from Simon, even if only a small one. "My mother always said that a young man showing attitude was taking a step towards manhood. But unfortunately for you, my mother isn't your drill sergeant! I find attitude a sign of disobedience and freethinking. Last time I checked, our Majesty's government didn't ask me to make you into a freethinker."

Simon felt the urge to make a joke about the sergeant's ability, or his lack thereof, to think freely, but thought it better to bite his lip instead.

"Smiling are we?" observed the sergeant sarcastically. He had guessed exactly what Simon was thinking. "Well, since we feel like being entertained, I think I should also join in the club and get you to do another submarine emergency exist test." Ketchesky's smile stretched from ear to ear.

Simon froze. For an instant, he hated being there. The submarine emergency exit test was a simulation of a submarine sinking. Simon would be required to sit in a steel room until a siren rang out, at which point the room would be flooded and he would need to open a hatch to escape. However, the second that the hatch started to open, water would flood into the room at such a high speed that Simon had to hold his breath as the room completely flooded. Then he would need to swim through the hatch and up a flooded, pitch-black pipe for twenty metres. Although pipe was wide enough for him to use his arms to assist with his ascent, the darkness of it pushed Simon to the extreme boundary of a claustrophobic panic attack. He understood the purpose of the test but that did little to help him appreciate it. He hated it when Sergeant Ketchesky made him complete the exercise at least once a week. Now it looked like he would be required to complete it twice this week.

"Great," the sergeant beamed. "I see that you are fully focused at last. So what are we waiting for? Let's get going before the start of a full moon!" He bellowed the last words, obviously aware that the next full moon would rise that night.

Within seconds, Simon was running out of the door. As always, he found it extraordinary that he was dressed only in runners, shorts and a t-shirt, while the Sergeant was running beside him wearing heavy boots, camouflage pants and a matching shirt, and bearing a loaded military pack. The ten kilometres run was arduous and the sergeant expected Simon to keep up with him. Sergeant Ketchesky was in his mid forties, but looked more like he was aged in his seventies. His fitness level, however, was that of an elite athlete and was far greater than Simon's own. To further test – or as the sergeant said to "build" – Simon's fitness, every kilometre he was required to stop and carry out five activities, comprising twenty push-ups, thirty sit-ups, forty star jumps and fifty military lunges which consisted of taking an exaggerated step forward on one leg then standing back up and taking another excessive step on the opposite leg. To round out his exercises, Simon had to do sixty rapid steps on the spot, raising his knees above his waistline every time.

Of the whole morning routine, the swim was Simon's favourite part. For one thing, the sergeant would wait for him on the beach, as he found the idea of swimming in cold water quite ridiculous. This made it virtually the only time of day during which Simon would be left alone with his memories. The English Channel was eerie in the morning light. There was a thick fog that restricted visibility to only ten meters. There were no people on the beach. The locals, in all likelihood, did not find the idea of a morning stroll appealing in this kind of weather. Simon pulled his clothing off in mid run and, wearing only his Speedos, dived into the water. He gasped as the cold water hit his body, making him take quick, short gulps of air. For a moment, his mind jolted back to the time he and his dad were confronted by a shark. It was one of the few memories he had of him.

Today, Simon decided to avoid swimming along the coastline. Instead, he swam towards the centre of the channel. He did not need landmarks to determine the distance he travelled, as he simply used his watch to calculate it. The first few kilometres were perfect and he quickly settled into his normal cadence. His body adjusted to the cold temperature and the fog created an atmosphere of isolation that ensured no images distracted him. Four kilometres into the swim, a subtle slashing sound started slowly infiltrating Simon's mind. At first he ignored it, but after a few minutes, he found he could not think about anything else. Simon was completely baffled about the origin of the sound. The fog was still too thick to see its source and he struggled to believe it was caused by another swimmer this far out from the beach. The noise was not caused by waves thrashing against a floating object, he decided, for the swishing sound was not sharp enough. Nor could it be any wildlife swimming by, as the sound was too staccato, and it certainly was not a boat. The faint sound was not a continuous rhythm, but instead stopped and started at irregular intervals.

Feeling inquisitive, Simon changed direction and swam towards the source. Every so often the noise would stop, and so would Simon. This short sequence of swim-stop-listen continued for five minutes. It was as if someone were mimicking him. Whenever he swam, the noise would start, but when he stopped, so would the noise. Even so, Simon found after each swim that he was getting closer and closer to the sound. Suddenly, out of nowhere, he spotted the silhouette of a man in the water, about ten metres away. He seemed to be staring back at him. Simon immediately stopped swimming and peered, dumfounded, at the man. His heart started thumping so hard that it became the only sound he could hear. Straining his eyes, he tried to make out the face of the person staring back at him. He felt paralysed. Maybe, just maybe, this was the moment and he would finally see his dad again. However, he was also petrified by the idea that moving any closer to the figure could ruin his dream. In a daze, he remained where he was.

Simon did not know what to do. The man staring back at him also appeared indecisive. Both remained still, bobbing slightly in the water, each unable to decide on their next move. Then suddenly, the man waved. Not knowing how to respond, Simon instinctively waved back.

"Dad?" he heard himself call out.

The person in the hazy shadows did not respond. He looked to his left then, he shouted. Simon at first heard the words only as jumbled sounds bouncing around inside his head. Then they slowly started to make sense to him, but he still felt lightheaded and confused.

"Simon!" came the voice, followed by muffled sounds. "Simon, swim! There…" His voice was lost and more muffled sounds followed before it came again, more clearly this time. "Simon," the man yelled. "Swim! The ship!"

This last urgent cry broke through Simon's astonishment. He immediately snapped his gaze to the right and saw the bow of a fuel tanker looming dangerously over him. Simon and his enigmatic companion immediately freestyled with all of their strength in opposite directions, away from the path of the oncoming steel beast. Unfortunately for Simon, his reaction was too slow. Before he knew it, he felt himself being dragged along the port side of the tanker. His body scraped against the rusty hull, and just as he started registering the acute pain, he found himself sucked under the water by a powerful invisible force. Unable to swim against the current, he turned in its direction and kicked with all his might with the hope of leveraging the drag to slingshot himself back to the surface, but to his horror, Simon suddenly realised that he was being sucked towards one of the gigantic propellers. Unbidden, his mind instantly conjured up images of his body being carved into pieces by the powerful blades. He knew he had only seconds to react. The adrenalin pumped through his bloodstream and he kicked to the left of the propeller with all the strength. His reaction proved just sufficient and he was able to escape the metal guillotine, narrowly avoiding a bloody end. His relief was short-lived, however, as the water churning behind the propeller sent his body spiralling under the water.

Simon once again kicked hard to stop himself from plunging deeper down. He was quickly losing strength and his body cried out in pain. With his lungs feeling as if they were about to burst, he offered a silent prayer for help. A few seconds later, Simon broke the surface of the water and took in a long, deep breath. He was only moments away from passing out. His next reaction, as he expelled the air from his lungs, was also instinctive.

"DAD! DAD!" he screamed, then paused and listened. He tried to hold his breath again in an attempt to quell any possible noise that might interfere with a response. "DAAAD!" he yelled again, using all of the air in his lungs.

The world stopped. The only sound was the distant noise of the fuel tanker and the soft wash of small waves in the wake of the ship. Simon strained to detect any other noise. Very faintly, he began to make out the subtle slashing sound of someone swimming. He immediately launched himself in the direction he thought the sound was coming from, but after swimming for only a few metres, he realised the noise had stopped.

"I know you can hear me! Please come back! I need you!" shouted Simon in desperation.

Silence.

"I am doing everything you expect of me! I just need to see you. I can't do this alone!" he cried out into the fog, but the only sound he heard was the pounding of his own heart. Simon felt a rush of anger surge through him. "Don't you get it? I am scared! Why don't you care!" he called out in exasperation. He had not cried since his mother's death, but now he felt his eyes burn with unshed tears. Then, from out of nowhere, he heard a clear, calm response. It was almost as if the person who was speaking was standing shoulder to shoulder with him.

"Simon, you know why this is not the right time. Don't be afraid. I'll be always in the shadows, watching over you." There was a pause. "I love you." Then there was silence.

Simon waited. He felt as if he were in a vacuum, like an astronaut drifting in space. There was nothing but a depressing eeriness surrounding him. Simon waited a while longer. Although he wanted to call out again, he knew it would be futile. Forcing aside the wave of emotions that rose up in him, Simon instead focused his mind on treasuring the brief encounter. It had happened at last. He had finally met his dad again. His swim back to the beach was slower than usual. The tears he had held back for so long now flooded down his frozen cheeks. Again and again he fought against the feelings that threatened to overwhelm him. He had seen his dad again. He wanted to savour that. But a loud voice infiltrated his thoughts.

"Simon. SIMON! Where are you?"

Simon looked at his watch, suddenly realising that his swim had taken him thirty-five minutes longer than usual.

"SIMON!" the voice boomed again across the water. This time Simon recognised its source.

"Here, Sergeant," he yelled back. Surprised, he heard the splashing sound of the sergeant swimming in his direction.

"Are you ok, son?" the sergeant asked between puffs as he drew near Simon.

"Yes, Sergeant. I'm sorry. I ran into a bit of trouble," replied Simon, feeling guilty at the expression of worry he saw on the man's face.

"Trouble? Are you ok?" Ketchesky asked again. He was genuinely concerned.

"Yes," Simon reassured him. "I decided to swim out towards the middle of the channel instead of along the coastline. Bad call. I almost got myself run over by a fuel tanker."

The sergeant felt his blood boil. Close enough now to see Simon's pale and troubled face, he decided to hold back his anger. He would simply reserve the lecture, and physical punishment, until Simon had a chance to regain himself.

"You're not saying anything," Simon ventured, as they started swimming back to shore. "I know I deserve to be punished."

"Punished?" replied the sergeant. "Don't worry about that, young man! I had to take all of my clothes off to come and find you. Once we get out of the water, the sight of my ghost-like skin should be punishment enough." They both chuckled.

Adrian Monico

Once on the beach, Sergeant Ketchesky decided to call an end to the morning's exercises and head back to base for a hot shower. Years of experience told him that his trainee was considerably shaken and in need of a dose of comfort to regroup himself. Simon did not talk during the light jog back to the barracks. Upon his return, he took a very long, very hot shower. He took his time getting dressed, eventually presenting himself an hour later at the sergeants' mess, where the sergeant said he would be waiting. Ketchesky decided that Simon would spend the rest of the day doing light training, comprising night navigation theory, small arms drills with pistols and rifles, camouflage techniques, and preparation of field rations in ways that made them almost edible. Late in the day, upon seeing Simon's more customary insouciant attitude return, the sergeant spoke seriously to his charge.

"Simon, I know you are still shaken by what happened out in the channel. But it's moments like these that tell us what kind of men we are." He looked closely at Simon to make sure he was listening before going on. "I was in Afghanistan when my patrol was ambushed. Thousands of rounds came raining down on us from nowhere. Half of my guys died in the first few seconds of the attack. The rest of us sustained enough injuries bad enough to make us incapable of fighting back." He paused, remembering the sense of panic and desperation. "The only sound you could hear other than the thudding of bullets was the men screaming in pain or crying out for the enemy to spare their lives. I myself was frozen, just waiting for the bullet with my name on it. I'd already been hit in the shoulder. Perhaps it was the pain of that bullet, digging its way into me, that woke me up at last. I stopped feeling scared and started firing back. Once I did, four of my men also started firing back, even though they too had multiple wounds. I don't think any of us managed to kill anyone, but I believe that our show of defiance made the enemy withdraw."

"Where... where did you find the strength?" Simon asked quietly.

"I honestly don't know," Ketchesky said, looking away from Simon's face for a moment. "What I do know is that the second I fired that first shot back, my body spontaneously cast aside its fears and simply obeyed the instincts embedded in it over all my years of military training." He gazed intently at the teenager as he spoke his next words. "You see, Simon, what I'm teaching you here is not what's going to save your life. What will save you is the number of times you repeat what you learn. If I show you how to strip a weapon, from that moment onward you need to spend all of your time stripping and reassembling that weapon. If I teach you how to navigate at night, from that moment on, you must spend every spare evening going on short navigations. If I tell you to set aside your emotions and focus on the task at hand, then you must fight against letting those emotions control your decisions and expressions."

Simon nodded slowly. "I understand. Everything you teach me, I take seriously. I know that everything I'm learning here will make a difference."

"I've got to be honest with you, Simon," the sergeant said. "You are not the most naturally talented recruit I've ever had, but you are the most focused. Keep it that way and you will be one of the best soldiers I have ever trained. Although..." He trailed off. Sergeant Ketchesky was under strict orders not to speak about Simon's background or his future employment within her Majesty's service. He ignored the quizzical look Simon gave him and hurried on. "Although standing around talking like high school girls will only make us soft," he said, recovering from his near blunder. "Kid, I've got word from Crystal Palace that tonight you are doing a night jump and navigation exercise."

"Crystal Palace?" enquired Simon.

"Long story," he said with a wave of his hand. "It's the name I give to headquarters. Anyway, you'll be dropped in a pine forest and you'll need to navigate to the first checkpoint ten kilometres away. Once there, a further kilometre to the north will be your target. The target will be a post with a few glow sticks attached to it. If you can tap the post without getting caught by a few well-placed sentries, you win!"

"Win what?" Simon asked, without any real interest.

"A week off. Apparently you'll immediately be flown somewhere on a holiday," grinned the Sergeant.

"If I win, that is."

"If you win," agreed the Sergeant, still grinning.

"What time do I leave?"

"Be on the tarmac at 17:00." As Simon walked back to his room, he heard his instructor quietly wishing him good luck.

At the tarmac, Simon was pleased to see that his aircraft was a C130 Hercules. This was the same aircraft that took him from Malaysia to Italy. Although the cargo aircraft was noisy, smelled of jet fuel and was very uncomfortable, it reminded him of his mum and the reason why he was undergoing this invaluable training. The journey took a few hours as they were flying tactically at night. At every opportunity, the aircraft dropped between hills in order to keep below the horizon and therefore too low to be detected by radar. They were following the nap of the earth, so it also regularly banked from one side to the other, or gained and dropped height with no warning. Simon was surprised that the continuous movement did not cause him motion sickness.

Two hours into the flight the cargo master approached Simon. He was very tall, with fiery red hair, against which his complexion appeared colourless. He looked to be in his mid fifties and strong enough to bench press the cargo plane itself. All in all, Simon decided, the cargo master was someone he did not want to argue with.

"Fifteen minutes to destination, young man. I've been instructed to hand over this backpack. Was told it's got everything you'll need. Any questions?" yelled the cargo master over the engine noise.

"Where are we?" inquired Simon as he accepted the small black backpack.

"I've been instructed not to answer any questions!" replied the uniformed giant with a big smile.

"So, why did you ask me if I had any?" Simon yelled back. Then he shook his head. "Never mind, I get it!" He found the joke at his expense to be in poor taste.

The cargo master grinned again. "Back in ten minutes to open the cargo door!" he called as he started walking back to the front of the aircraft.

Not wanting to waste any time, Simon opened the backpack and found a photocopy of a map with no roads shown on it, an emergency whistle, a small torch with a red filter, a pocket knife, an aerial photograph with the words "landing site" handwritten across the top, a water bottle, night vision goggles, a compass, a pistol and a note. He read the note.

"Simon, this is the final test of your basic military training. It has come to my attention that you are now ready to move to your next phase: urban training. If you get caught on this mission and cannot manage to touch the post, you will return to Portsmouth for another three weeks of basic training. Three sentries are deployed in the area and a two week vacation in the Canary Islands has been promised to the one who finds you first. The rules for tonight's test is don't get caught! Good luck." It was signed "The Director."

Simon had met the Director back in London on the day he agreed to join MI6. That occasion was the first and last time he had seen him. He wondered briefly if the Director knew his father, but returned his focus to the mission at hand. Without wasting any more time, Simon used a permanent black marker to copy the map onto his handkerchief. This would ensure that he would not make any noise when he had to look at the map. The other benefit of this technique was that, apparently, a handkerchief would burn faster than the paper. That at least was the claim made by Signor Beppe, and one never knew if the need to do this would arise. Simon assumed that 'need' in this situation meant he was about to be captured and his priority would be to burn any evidence that indicated he was a spy. Just as Simon finished his careful copying, the cargo master returned.

"I see you've wasted no time and are eager to go!" he called out, checking that Simon had placed the parachute on himself correctly. "Well done. Let's get you on standby to jump." He directed Simon towards the rear ramp.

Within a few minutes the ramp opened and Simon felt a chill as the outside cold air came rushing in. Much as he disliked the submarine emergency escape exercise, Simon hated night jumping, or parachuting at any time for that matter. He was not afraid of heights, but hated knowing that his life depended on equipment which did have a risk of failing. He took in a deep breath.

"Ready?" called out the master, signalling with a thumbs up. Simon simply responded with a thumbs up of his own as he hooked his tandem line onto the aircraft. The cargo master then counted backwards, "Three, two, one," before slapping Simon on the back as he called out "Go!"

Simon stepped out the aircraft into complete darkness. The first few seconds were, as always, terrifying. He felt again the dizzying rush of free falling whilst hoping that the parachute would open. The fall felt extremely long and Simon was aware of a sense of panic beginning to set in as he tried to get some control over his fall. A few moments later, the parachute deployed without a glitch and Simon immediately felt at ease. Once his parachute had opened, the descent became more tranquil and less nerve racking. Simon was unable to clearly make out the ground below him, but he knew there was supposed to be a clearing somewhere. As far as he could make out, the whole area was covered in pine trees. He scanned the gloom beneath him intently.

About twenty metres from the ground, Simon suddenly spotted his landing point. It was about one hundred metres to his left and far too distant for him to guide his parachute in that direction. He steeled himself for the only alternate option, which was to get ready for a very rough landing. Simon dropped amongst very tall pine trees, hitting enough branches on the way down to feel his skin getting ripped open, though this did little to slow his decent. Once the parachute dropped between the tree line, it too started getting snagged. Each time it caught, his descent would be momentarily jolted for a few seconds, until a branch would break or the parachute would tear, allowing Simon to continue his fall. After four such jolts, he came to a complete halt, hanging approximately five metres above the ground.

At first Simon remained still, waiting for the parachute to dislodge so he could hit the ground. Then, as he realised his descent was not going any further, Simon decided to keep quiet for a few more minutes and listen out for any other noises. He wanted to make sure nobody heard, saw or was looking for him. Once Simon was satisfied that he was alone, he started swinging from side to side in the hope of eventually catching a branch. His plan worked. Within two swings, he managed to grab hold of a branch to his left and use it to pull himself closer to the main trunk of the pine tree. He then undid his parachute harness and let it swing free. Only belatedly did Simon realise that he was supposed to retrieve the parachute and hide it to make sure nobody would accidentally stumble onto it and raise the alarm. Simon, having let go of the harness, had lost the opportunity to pull the parachute free. He had no choice but climb the tree and try to grab parachute's canopy.

After fifteen minutes of strenuous work, compounded by a general aching caused by the bruising and small lesions that resulted from the branches whipping and snaring him during his original descent, Simon reached the closest point to the parachute's canopy. He then proceeded to walk to the outer edge of a thick branch and yanked at the parachute until it came free. Simon took advantage of his height to look around for any landmarks he could used to aide his navigation. Unfortunately, as there was insufficient ambient light, he could see very little. He wondered if it was better to do these activities on the night of a full moon or with no moon at all.

Simon rolled the parachute into a ball and shoved it into his backpack, although some of it still hung out. As he slowly climbed down the tree, Simon decided to pause once more to make sure that there was no one below waiting for him. He tried his best not to breathe, as he did not wanted anything to interfere with his hearing. After a few minutes of silence, comforted by the notion that he was all alone, he looked down to see which branch to place his next foot on. It was at that moment that he saw a shadow moving within the thick vegetation. At first Simon thought he had imagined it, but a moment later he saw the shadow move quietly forward once more. The silhouette was undeniable that of a tall man. Whoever he was, he moved cautiously amid the scrub to minimise any noise he might make. With a jolt of disappointment, Simon worried that his test would be over even before it had started. Then he saw a sight that enveloped him in horror. The stranger below carried a high-powered rifle.

As Simon watched, the shadow looked through a scope on his weapon and scanned the surrounding area. Whoever it was down there, he was looking for something or someone. Maybe he was a hunter? But Simon quickly disregarded that thought, as the person below gave the impression of being military trained. Noticing that the person was heading in his direction and was now only a few metres away from his tree, Simon considered his options. At first he thought he might jump on top of the man and disarm him. However, as Simon was approximately seven metres above ground, he came quickly to the realisation that he might hurt himself in the attempt. Alternatively, he could take a chance and call out to the person. If he were a friendly hunter, he might even be able to help Simon reach his destination. This seemed an unlikely prospect, though. Regardless of the options that came to Simon's mind, he knew the person below looked dangerous and his best course was to avoid being seen. He decided to keep still, hug the tree and avoid making any sounds.

Down below, the silhouette continued to scan the terrain. He was definitely looking for someone or something. Every so often, he would freeze and look fixedly in the direction of any new sound. All the while, Simon remained frozen against the tree. His legs had started to go numb. He would need to move soon. With a sense of dread, Simon watched as the man below the tree took off his backpack and removed a few items from it. The first was clearly a map, which he examined using a small torch with a red filter. Simon knew from his training that the red filter made the light more difficult to spot in the night, compared with the white light of standard torches. He himself had a similar filter on the torch tucked into his own backpack, although he actually preferred a green filter as he found the red light made it too challenging to see the brown colours used to mark contour lines on topographical maps. In either case, such equipment was used by most modern armed forces. Feeling his dread increase, Simon knew without a doubt that this was not some friendly hunter lost in the woods.

Wincing as the numbness crept further up his legs, he watched as the stranger took out some night vision goggles, placed them over his eyes and switched them on. He then scanned the area again, every so often pausing and staring into the distance. Then the hairs at the back of Simon's neck stood up, as the person raised his eyes and started staring into the sky among the tree tops. With no moon to give light, the person did not have to contend with any overbrightness through the goggles. Simon knew that his time was just about up. There was no way that the person was going to miss seeing him.

Moments before the man's gaze reached the location where Simon stood exposed and clinging to the tree trunk, Simon's hand closed around his trusty pocket knife. He waited in silence, ready to react to any hostility. With a sudden rush that started approximately ten metres away, a third person began sprinting away from their location.

Simon was so startled by this unexpected movement that he almost lost his footing. A few flakes of bark dislodged and drifted down towards the person underneath his tree. The man down there also appeared to have been caught by surprise. The moment the third, unknown person started running, the man with the night vision goggles snapped his head in the direction of the noise whilst lowering his own profile by dropping himself onto his knees. The small pieces of dislodged bark fell slowly. Simon held his breath as they landed softly on the shoulder of the man underneath the tree. He hoped that the man would not notice, but this time, although unbeknown to Simon, he had no such luck. The person below the tree quickly stowed the items he previously taken out of the backpack and removed a spray can instead. With it, he commenced spraying around the tree twice before proceeded quickly in the direction the third person had run.

Once both strangers were out of sight, Simon pulled the parachute from his backpack and reached for the cords. He cut them and placed them in his backpack, deciding to leave the parachute itself behind as it could fit easily into the backpack. He then lowered himself to the lowest branch of the tree and, before jumping onto the ground, scanned the area which had the man had sprayed. He could not see any colouring, but he knew something had been applied onto that area. Deep within him, he knew too that if he ignored this, he would pay for it later. With an effort, he tried to remember the dimensions of area that was sprayed. Then, using all of his strength, tried to leap beyond it.

Once he had landed, Simon made a quick examination of the sprayed area. He could not see any wetness. There was no unusual colouring, and nor could he smell any odours. However, Simon had recently become aware that anything used in the world that he now operated in tended to either work for him or against him. In this case his gut feeling told him it was the latter. The strange spray did in fact work against Simon. He did not realise that the man had sprayed two rings around the tree, around thirty centimetres from one another. This mean that while Simon was focusing his attention on what he thought was the only sprayed area, he was standing on the outer ring. Oblivious to this, Simon reassured himself again that he was alone, before proceeding to his destination which, fortunately, was in the opposite direction to the one the two strangers had gone.

Simon was pleased he was in a pine forest. The millions of acidic needles underfoot made his movement easier as there was little undergrowth to get tangled in. Furthermore, although there was no brightness from the moon, the tree canopy was open enough to allow in sufficient ambient light for him to make out the terrain and avoid using his night vision goggles. Simon decided to take his time walking to the destination. Only when he was a few hundred meters from his target, would he drop on all fours and crawl the remaining distance. Every fifteen minutes or so along the route, Simon moved in a U shaped pattern until he found a place to hide and check whether anyone was following him. He would wait silently in this spot for five minutes before recommencing his travel in the original direction. Simon walked cautiously in this manner for thirty minutes. So far, nobody seemed to be following him, but he remembered what Signor Beppe had once told him: "Even if you can't see anyone following you, whoever it is might simply be good at hiding. So always think that you are being followed." Simon missed the old Italian man. Although his military training in Portsmouth had been great, he felt he had learnt far more from his time with Signor Beppe. The U shaped technique to check if he was being tailed was one such valuable lesson.

As Simon continued towards his destination, he was unaware that one hundred metres behind him, Sergeant Ketchesky was using high powered night vision binoculars to track his trainee's progress from a distance. The sergeant was dressed in a yowie suit, also known as a ghillie or camo suit. specially constructed to allow military snipers and hunters to blend in with the surrounding environment. Ketchesky's suit was comprised of lots of foliage and coloured strips of a sandy coloured material that looked like fallen pine branches. It was not only effective in camouflaging him with the local flora, but it also broke up the recognisable outlines of his body. Like Simon, he made regular checks, turning around and using the binoculars to ensure that the person who had previously chased him was not still in the area. He had been completely surprised by the presence of a non-authorised person in the midst of the operation, where he had been deployed earlier to assess Simon. This was a military range and the only staff sanctioned to be here were the young guys located near the final destination, who were charged with spotting Simon and preventing him from reaching his target. Whoever was the person the sergeant had spotted earlier on was, he had been trespassing.

Moreover, to Ketchesky's eye, he looked unfriendly and smelt like trouble. Usually he would have detained him, but in this case he did not want to spoil Simon's test. That is why he had broken cover when he saw the person standing underneath the tree where Simon was stuck, thinking his movement would draw the stranger away. Had the man not taken the opportunity to chase, Sergeant Ketchesky might have believed his suspicion was wrong and the person might simply have been a hunter or someone who was lost. Instead, his ploy had worked, confirming that person was not 'friendly'. The sergeant had already alerted the exercise controller by radio and the military police were on route. After checking back over his shoulder again, he advanced forward quietly, maintaining a consistent distance as Simon crept closer to his goal.

Back amid the gloom of the forest, the agent known as Shadow lay completely motionless as he noted the sergeant looking back towards him. Although he had expected the young student would be assessed by hidden eyes, he was nevertheless still taken by surprised when the figure had appeared so suddenly near the tree and sprinted away from him. With grudging respect, Shadow had to admit the sergeant was certainly great at camouflage. He had initially thought about sedating him, but then decided to use the opportunity to have a little fun. Besides, the chase would allow Simon to move from the tree he had become stuck in.

As he lay behind a fallen tree trunk and watched the sergeant scanning the area, Shadow glanced down at the ground between himself and the instructor. He allowed himself a tight smile. Although he did not like the idea of carrying an aerosol can, the odourless radioactive spray worked like a charm. Through the special glasses he wore, he could see every step Simon had taken. The radioactive footprints appeared yellow through his lenses, but remained invisible to the naked eye. The glasses were also great as they amplified light at night and automatically shaded it during the day. It was true that the radioactive technology did have a few limitations. The footprints could easily be washed away in the rain, the aerosol can did make a noise when used, and it could get a bit confusing if several agents used it in the same confined area. Even so, Shadow was satisfied with its performance this evening. It had made it so sweetly easy to track his prey.

Ahead, Simon lay hidden. He waited. Around him he could only hear the whistling of the wind blowing through the pine trees. There was no movement anywhere to be seen, but still he could not shake off the feeling of being watched. Beppe's words of warning were reverberating in his head. Even so, he decided to move on, conscious that any spotter might be aware of his direction where he parachuted in. He decided to undertake a large circumvention of the destination area, even if it took him longer to reach his target. Once he had reached the opposite side of the area, he could then approach his destination from a hopefully unexpected direction. As he swallowed a mouthful of water and commenced his trek again, the image of the person spraying something undetectable underneath the tree came to his mind. That event was still unexplained and it made Simon feel uneasy. Why had he only sprayed around the one tree where Simon was stuck? The single distinguishable difference between that tree and all of the others surrounding it was Simon himself.

He knew I was up there, Simon thought grimly. So what was it with the invisible spray? Why spray all around that tree? The questions were now chasing one another in his head. Even if he knew that I was up there, what did that spraying achieve? Another voice echoed in his head. "The best way to understand your enemy is to put yourself in their shoes." It was Sergeant Ketchesky. Simon recalled him shouting this out during one of his military tactics classes. Ok, what would I do if I were looking for someone in the forest? Simon asked himself. If I wanted to just follow the person, I would do it from a distance and try not to be seen, he continued, trying to think through all the basic points. If I meant to harm or capture someone, I would either climb up the tree or wait for the person to come down. If I meant to follow him, I would hide, unless I accidentally got spotted and then I would try to create a diversion to give the impression that my being there was a coincidence. He thought hard. But since I am most likely in a military owned forest, creating a convincing story like that would be tough. So instead, I'd make like I was following the person, but give them a way out. I'd let them think they had lost me even though I still had them in my sight. Simon frowned as ideas sped through his mind.

Was the chase of the second person a set-up? Are the two people working together? he wondered. But if I was just following someone in a forest on a moonless night, why have a second person to help me out? Unlike in the city, where population density can work against mobile surveillance, one person should be enough in a forest, he reasoned. Even so, the spray is obviously some form of tracking device. Just because I couldn't see it, doesn't mean it wasn't there. And why be seen doing it? Twice? The question burned in Simon's mind. Twice! He almost whispered the word aloud before resuming his speculations. The person would naturally jump from the tree past the point where I sprayed, unless... Unless I covered a large enough area that it would be physically impossible to jump over it. So why would I spray paint around the tree twice?" Then it clicked. So there would be two rings of paint. That allow a wider area to be covered. He nodded, certain now of his conclusion. Of course! I would paint two distinctive rings, but make it look like one, so the person in the tree thinks he avoid stepping on the single line. I can pretty much bet that I stepped on the second ring, he decided, as he stopped and sat down.

Simon carefully removed his shoes, being careful not to touch their soles. He then placed the shoes in his backpack.

"Just as well I'm wearing thick army socks. They should provide me with some padding so it doesn't feel like I'm walking barefoot across the pine needles," Simon mumbled. He glanced back in the direction he had come from. "Now for the second question: why use two people to track one teenager in a dark forest?" Turning his gaze forward again, he stepped cautiously in his socks across the forest floor.

If they're out here to help one another, what is the correlation between my pursuer and the other man? he wondered. They couldn't have been together, or else the second person would have remained hidden and followed me from a distance, while the first person would have found a way to make it look like I lost his trail. The conclusion was obvious. There are two people trailing me then. That would explain why Mr Spray Can looked so startled when Second Person appeared. He sighed. As if the night hadn't been annoying enough already.

Mindful of what little time he had left to lose his two trails, Simon wiped all thoughts from his mind and proceeded to head directly east, in an attempt to change the direction of his approach. His idea was to switch from an anticlockwise circumvention of the target area to a clockwise circumvention. However, he knew that he had little time left, if any, before whoever was following him would possibly see him. Once he reached the point for starting his new circumvention path, Simon again made a U shaped turn and watched silently to see if he was being followed.

His switch worked. Sergeant Ketchesky did not see Simon change direction. Although his night binoculars were in range to see his trainee, the sergeant failed to scan the forest and simply concentrated on the direction Simon had originally taken. Unable to see Simon, he simply assumed that the teenager must have picked up pace. He would have to do the same thing now. A little further back, Shadow was surprised to find the radioactive footprints had disappeared. He realised that either Simon had been abducted by aliens or he had worked out that the spray was tracking him and had taken his shoes off. Having lost the tracks, Shadow contemplated which direction to take next. He could follow the same direction Simon had been taking and try somehow to get past the other person who was also trailing him. Or he could take the most direct route to the target area and simply wait there. But if he could circumvent to the left instead, he might be able to get into a suitable position to wait for Simon's arrival. Shadow pondered his options. He only had one chance to get this right.

Simon was feeling tired. He had been walking for hours and his body was screaming for a rest. He felt that he was against the clock, although he was unable at present to recall his given deadline. The forest was now very dark and with the exception of the odd noise from nocturnal animals, its silence was surprisingly soothing. Despite the limited ambient light, Simon's eyes had quickly adjusted to the dimness and he could make out most large objects in his proximity. He paused to again practice some of the 'night ops' techniques he had learned during his recent training. He particularly tried the scanning technique of casting his eyes from left to right and from top to bottom in the area he had just come from. He was told that not looking directly at a location in the darkness made it easier to spot moving objects. It was something to do with the sides of the eyes having the ability to detect movement better than the centre of the pupil. Simon understood the theory and knew that this technique took practice to perfect.

His scanning technique paid dividends almost immediately. At first, he did not know what it was he saw moving, but he identified the direction fairly accurately. He stared at the location, but could not spot what had moved. He tried to looking slightly to the left. Within a few seconds, he again detected the movement and this time more accurately. Upon further close scanning, he was relieved to see an owl staring back at him from a tree branch a few metres above the ground. The owl, almost in recognition of Simon's achievement in sighting it, commenced hooting. Simon found the sound soothing. The owl also seemed to be relaxed, despite its close proximity to a human being. Every so often, it would twist its head to check the area to its rear.

Simon, realising that any more time spent sitting down with his back against the fallen trunk would lead to him into sleep, decided it was time to move on. As he was summoning the energy to stand up, however, he was startled by the owl suddenly changing its soft hoot into a bark. Simon thought it was he who had alarmed the bird. However, looking up at it, he realised that it was staring in the opposite direction. Simon could not tell what the bird was staring at, but its call sounded like an alarm. With a slow realisation, Simon noted that there were no longer any other wildlife sounds around him. Cautiously, he slowly lowered himself onto his stomach and silently slithered around to the opposite side of the tree. Whatever was approaching from the distance had concerned the owl. Simon was instantly suspicious.

Shadow was always amazed that after years of training to become invisible, he still never managed to fool animals. Earlier on, he had been startled by the statute pose a fox had frozen itself into so as to avoid detection. Shadow was surprised that the fox was caught off guard and had to resort to this defensive mechanism to avoid detection. On the other hand, Shadow himself had missed the fox until he was almost on top of it. Trying not to panic the fox, he had decided to slowly move away from it before continuing on his same course. He was just as startled by the bark of an owl. It was obviously caught off guard by his movement and had reacted with a warning call. Unlike his response to the fox, Shadow was concerned by the sound of the owl as the rest of the wildlife surrounding it reacted to its cry and instantly went silent. If this were a mission in which he was approaching a guarded site, he would be worried that the sudden environmental change would alert any professional guard.

Simon, seeing the same person who sprayed around the tree, felt his heart miss a beat. The hair at the back of his neck stood up. Whoever this person was, he looked very dangerous. His movement was completely controlled and lithe like a panther. As Simon had no luck in the 'being followed' department, this slick, dark panther was unlikely to be a friendly person with good intentions. A flash memory of Whisper distracted Simon for a moment. The unknown person, who Simon now mentally referred to as Mr Spray Can, kept moving toward the teenager. Simon lay motionless. He could hear the pounding of his heart and had difficulty breathing as he watched the man come closer and closer. He silently wondered if he should ambush the man and challenge him? He knew that he had only a split second to decide on his next move. Ambush him, he thought. However, something about Mr Spray Can told Simon that this was the last person in the world he would want to challenge. Simon took a deep breath and closed his eyes, ready to spring up and defend himself.

One of Shadow's reasons for his survival over the years was his sixth sense which always told him when something was not right. Although he still didn't know what exactly it was within him that could detect danger, after all these years, he knew to completely trust the feeling. He could tell now that something was wrong. He was not alone. He didn't know what it was, but trusted his instincts and dropped down on one knee. A quick scan of the immediate area revealed that everything was deathly quiet. Even the owl looked like one of the marble statues on the rooftops of Notre Dame. Not yet spotting the threat, Shadow commenced analysing the area for likely spots where a person could hide. His eyes worked like a lens, zooming in on different zones around him. He took note of a few larger trees with trunks wide enough for someone to hide behind. He also noted a clump of berry bushes that could be used as a place of concealment. He scanned each location attentively. Nothing moved. By a process of elimination, he analysed the areas he had identified as possible danger points.

He decided that the bushes were a bad hiding place as they provided no protection from bullets, and in certain areas the branches were so sparse he could see light filtering through them. The wide trunks of the trees were better to hide behind, but to remain concealed from searchers, a person would need to keep moving around the circumference of the trunk and the movement would always create some sound. Trees were never an ideal place to hide. Therefore, if anyone was hiding nearby – and Shadow's gut feeling was still telling him they were – then behind the fallen trunk was the most likely place they would be hiding. Not only did it provide good coverage, but it also made for an ideal firing position. Shadow stealthily removed a hand grenade from his backpack. He had deadly enemies and was not about to take any chances.

From his crouched position, Simon became aware that

Simon Eady - The Teenage Spy

Mr Spray Can had suddenly stopped moving. His heart beat even faster and the pounding was now echoing in his ears, as adrenaline pumped into his blood stream. Something was about to go terribly wrong. Alarm bells were sounding throughout his body and he felt a cold shiver down his spine. Simon had no doubt that conflict was unavoidable. His only hope was that Mr Spray Can was purely here to tail Simon and had no intention to engage with him. But Simon's past experience with furtive followers like this man had always proven to be deadly and he knew he had to be prepared. Cautiously, he peeked out of a small hole that had been eaten through the trunk, either from natural decay or possibly by termites. The forest was dark and it was difficult to distinguish details in the distance that stretched between the two of them. Even so, he recognised with a sick feeling the outline of the frisbee hand grenade that Mr Spray Can was now holding in his hand. It was the same one Simon himself had used by a few months earlier in the ambush in Malaysia. Simon closed his eyes, and took a deep breath, knowing he was about to die.

Shadow, although still unsure if there was someone hiding behind the trunk, was not going to take any chances. He looked down at the new model of the Frisbee hand grenade and made sure he had picked the correct one. Unfortunately, the different types of grenades were differentiated by a coloured strip. He made a mental note to tell MI6 to use bold letters or distinguishing markings like Braille instead, as colours at night were too hard to distinguish.

Simon's eyes flashed open again. He knew he had only seconds to act. He was not going to give up this easily. As quietly and as quickly as possible, he unclipped the pack off his back and reached in for the only weapon at his disposal: the Mosquito pistol. As he gripped the pistol, his heart stopped at the sight in front of him.

Shadow suddenly heard a sound from behind the trunk. Knowing that the difference between life and death could be down to a split second, reached back with his left hand, grenade ready in his palm. At the same time, like a cat, Simon sprang to his feet, bringing the pistol up with both arms extended until it reached eye level. Shadow's arm, without conscious instruction from his brain, responded automatically like a mediaeval catapult to the sudden movement behind the trunk. It launched the grenade. Simon's thumb and forefinger worked in unison, flicking the safety mechanism to fire and pulling the trigger. Shadow, horrified by the sudden realisation of who was staring back at him through the sight of the pistol, heard the 'click' sound of the hammer striking the primer of the bullet. For a moment after pulling the trigger, Simon stood there paralysed. In horror he watched the grenade making its way as if in slow motion in his direction. A split second before the bullet struck, Shadow managed to say, "Not this way." He felt a prick sting his face and his world immediately turned black.

Simon, driven by a survival instinct, dived as far as he could away from the direction of the grenade. However, as he hit the ground, the grenade infrared sensor picked up his body movement, tilted on its side and exploded. Surprised by the muffled sound of the blast, Simon at first thought that the grenade must have been a dud. With his body was full of adrenalin, he didn't feel several needles penetrating his thighs. A second later, his world too turned black.

CHAPTER 2 - Crossing The Starting Line

The stairs were causing a burning sensation in the thighs that was both welcome and hated. The race had only just started but the body was already calling out that it had reached its limits. This early in the morning, very few people were up and about. It meant that Deepa could see into the distance and track Stephen's progress. She still found it funny that she had taken an early lead in the run. Only an hour before, they had left the apartment near Sagrada Famiglia on a race that would bring reward to the winner and earn extra homework for the loser. Stephen, as expected from a boy, believed he had the physical strength to beat a girl. The moment the race had begun, he had immediately sprinted off in the most direct route to Stadium Olympico. So confident was he about his speed and stamina that he didn't even look back to check the distance he was gaining against Deepa.

Deepa herself had started the race by heading slightly away from the final destination, as she sprinted to catch the 06:25 Catalonia bus. Once aboard, she travelled comfortably across the city and disembarked at the Placa D'Espana, near the modernised Arena of Barcelona. She then proceeded to jog between the two Venetian towers and up the very wide avenue called Avinguda de la Reina María Christina. Spanish names were still a challenge for Deepa. At the first opportunity after she got off the bus, she purchased a map from a tourist souvenir shop that was just opening for the day's trade.

As he ran, Stephen realised that felt somewhat robbed of the opportunity to enjoy his win. Indeed, he felt almost insulted at being asked to race against a girl. Within seconds of the start, he left Deepa a long way behind him. He had enjoyed his spy training so far, even if he had to undertake it with someone else who, worse still, was female. He didn't know much about Deepa. She simply turned up the day after he arrived in Barcelona, just minutes after Whisper had to suddenly take off to "attend to some urgent matters". These were the words Whisper called out to him as he was walking out the door without any forewarning. The unexplained disappearance didn't bother Stephen as he did not particularly like Whisper.

Still feeling that he had plenty of energy left in him, Stephen, arrived at the big roundabout next to the Arena. He really liked this city. Every corner seemed to contain beautiful buildings and gardens. He could not help taking a moment to admire the long avenue that started with two domineering towers and a set of steps and gardens leading up to the exhibition centre called Palau Nacional. The roads were still fairly empty, although the odd shop was starting to open its doors. The air was crisp and cool enough to prevent his body overheating, but not too cold to require any additional clothing to a t-shirt and shorts. Stephen cut through a big roundabout with an eye-catching fountain at its centre. Once he reached the other side of the roundabout, he continued his run toward the exhibition centre. Looking ahead, he noted another person jogging towards the striking Centre. Whoever it was had almost reached the top of the stairs, a good kilometre from him. As he watched, the person stopped at the top of the stairs and turned back, possibly to admire the view. For a split second, Stephen thought the figure into the distance looked it might be female.

"No way in hell that's her! It's too far for someone to that far in such a short time!" The words escaped from Stephen's mouth, but he instantly dismissed the possibility that the figure on the stairs could be his rival.

Deepa paused for a second, taking in the beautiful view. She smiled at the sight of a runner making steady progress in the distance. It could only be Stephen. Grinning, she turned and continued her run towards the Olympic Stadium. Although Deepa had taken a few opportunities to do some sightseeing around Barcelona, this was her first visit to the Olympic Stadium. As she reached the gates of the Olympic Park, her jaw dropped. To the right were two long rows of very tall, menacing columns that reached high into the air. They seemed to Deepa like an army of concrete guardians, charged with protecting the park. Controlling this army of towers was its general: an exquisite white telecommunications tower that stretched towards the sky as the gateway to the universe beyond. Deepa couldn't help thinking that the tower looked like had been designed by aliens, perhaps as a portal to other planets. In the middle of the army of concrete columns was a pristine modern garden that cleverly balanced a combination of Spanish design and Japanese Zen concepts. To her left was the stadium, which was distinguished by the unusual construction that was the Olympic torch.

Deepa was speechless. She could not take her eyes off the park. Every inch of it presented a unique and mesmerising feature. She walked very slowly to the stadium steps, keeping her gaze on the park to her right. She sank down onto the steps and, mouth open, soaked in all the beauty that surrounded her. Stephen, however, was too distracted to admire the aesthetics. As he approached Centre, he felt like a complete fool. He had no idea how Deepa managed to beat him to the stadium stairs. She must have cheated. Although shocked by the sight of her, Stephen continued running all the way to the steps without losing his rhythm.

"You are a cheat!" he called out as soon as he was in earshot of Deepa. Completely lost in her own world, Deepa did not respond. "The least you can do is to give me the courtesy of providing an explanation," continued Stephen, feeling pride and anger choking his words.

Deepa was completely in love. She had never felt so emotional about such beauty. Until this moment, she never understood how people fell in love with buildings.

"Well! Are you going to answer me?" yelled Simon. He was looming above her now, sweating and angry.

Finally Deepa, still sitting frozen on the concrete steps, moved her eyes away from the smorgasbord of beauty around her and looked up at the red faced boy who was almost standing on her toes. "Stephen," she said gently. "Turn around."

Stephen felt an urge to spit out more fierce words, but feeling somewhat hypnotised by Deepa's soft tone, he held his feelings back and hesitantly turned around. The unexpected sight of the park hit him like a slap across his face. He felt himself being emotionally drawn to the concrete pillars. He could not have said why, but these monolithic structures touched something deep within his heart.

"Come," invited Deepa, now standing next to him. She held out her hand. Stephen permitted himself a quick glance down at her outstretched palm. There was no way he would let himself be seduced by offer. "Scared?" Deepa asked in responded to Stephen's cold stare. "Fine! If you aren't interested in finding out how I beat you without cheating, feel free to stay here." With that Deepa, withdrew her hand and without another glance walked down towards the pillars.

Stephen hesitated for a second then followed her. The walk to the concrete pillars was slow, with both teenagers mesmerised by their beauty. Halfway along the rank of pillars, Deepa stopped and lay down on the concrete, looking up. Although the ground was cold, it also accentuated the faint warmth of the rising sun.

"Lay down," called out Deepa. This time it was an order, not an invitation.

"No!" Stephen's response was instinctive.

"Wow! Did you know that today is the first time in weeks you've actually said something to me? Even if it is just accusations and monosyllables," grinned Deepa.

"What do you want?" snapped Stephen.

"I want you to lay down next to me. It's the last chance for you to find out how I beat you and how I'll most likely do it again," shrugged Deepa.

A flash of anger rose again in Stephen. Although bitter about the loss, he just wanted to turn around and run back to base. But he was also curious. He looked down at Deepa. Hesitantly, and feeling rather foolish, he lay down next to her. Immediately, he could see why she had insisted that he do so. From this position, the cement pillars appeared even more domineering.

"Beautiful, aren't they?" whispered Deepa in awe. Stephen remained silent. "But also very sad," she continued, ignoring Stephen's reticence.

"How?" he burst out abruptly.

"How what?" asked Deepa innocently, taking the chance to force Stephen to speak again.

"How did you…" he paused, "get here first?" He refused to use the word that almost did not exist in his vocabulary. Deepa guessed straight away what he had been about to say.

"Ah! You mean how did I BEAT you? Because you were BEATEN by a girl, after all. That must hurt," she teased with a big grin.

Stephen's body jerked as he started to stand up. He'd enough of this stupidity. As he shifted his weight onto his right arm, he felt a sudden grip on his wrist. Deepa, in a flash motion, had taken hold of it.

"Please don't! I'm sorry. Stay." Deepa's apology was sincere. She stared into Stephen's arctic blue eyes. Stephen, feeling completely unsettled by the attention and touch of another person, hesitated. This whole situation was unfamiliar and destabilising to him. He looked at the girl beside him. She was smiling a little contritely now, waiting to see how he would respond. Stephen knew that if he allowed anyone to get close to him, he could no longer remain detached and concentrate on his plan. Whisper had taught him that 'feelings' were a weakness. They would work against his becoming the top MI6 spy. He looked down at his hand and was surprised to see that Deepa was still holding his wrist. He took a deep breath and, without entirely knowing why, lay back down beside her.

Deepa's smile relaxed as Stephen reclined. "The mission was to be the first to get here," she recounted. "We were told only that we were having a race and the first one to get here would be rewarded, while the last one would get punished. We were then lined up like at the start of a sprint race and ordered to go." She paused.

"And you cheated, Deepa. You must have used some form of transportation to cover the distance in such a short time." Stephen's accusation was immediate.

"Stephen, I never lie or cheat. We were never told that we had to run the distance. You just assumed that we did, possibly because you were blinded by your competitive nature," declared Deepa. She was starting to lose patience.

Stephen didn't speak. He was still angry, but he also knew that Deepa was right.

"And just so you know, next time I'll take offence at being accused of lying before even being given the opportunity to explain! I've been nothing but nice to you, Stephen. In all these weeks you have never once spoken to me. Even when I greet you in the morning, you don't even give me the courtesy of looking at me. I've always respected your need for solitude. I've left you alone and haven't barged in on your privacy! I've spent day after day studying next to you, doing training alongside you, attending the same lectures as you, without ever imposing on you or judging you! So, I think it's not unfair of me to ask for the same consideration," stated Deepa, irked by Stephen's conceited attitude.

Stephen cleared his throat. He was taken aback by Deepa's tirade. "I'm sorry Deepa," he said at last. "I'm... not good with people," he admitted, catching Deepa by surprise.

The two teenagers lay silently on the ground looking at each other, both relishing the truce that had arisen between them. Deepa realised that she still held onto Stephen's wrist. Embarrassed, she let go. She wondered why Stephen had not pulled his hand away before. Stephen was strange, she decided. For weeks he ignored her, behaving as if her mere presence was intolerable, and now he had apologised to her and was lying down beside her letting her hold his wrist. Strange. Deepa was the first to break eye contact. She turned her gaze back towards the columns.

"Why do you think such simple construction has us both mesmerised?" she asked to break the silence.

Stephen, still deep in thought, remained silent for a while longer. After looking at Deepa for an extra second, he slowly turned his eyes to the closest column.

"I see me. Or at least what I want to be," observed Stephen, almost to himself.

"I don't understand," said Deepa, perplexed. Stephen was becoming more of a mystery to her now than he was when she first met him.

"To be honest, Deepa, I don't quite understand it myself," replied Stephen after some thought.

"Ok. Let's try this. What words come to your mind when you look at the pillars?" asked Deepa, looking again at Stephen. She was glad to be finally conversing with this enigmatic person.

"Mmm... Solid, engineered, reliable, resilient. Firm, strong, striking, intimidating," answered Stephen forcing himself to smile. He could not remember the last time he had done so. The action had become unfamiliar to him. "You?"

"I agree with you up to a point," replied Deepa slowly. "But the words solitude, desolate, stuck, beautiful, misplaced, sad, also come to mind,"

The conversation paused for a few moments. Both teenagers seemed lost in their own thoughts as they lay still on the cold concrete, staring up at the closest cement pillar.

"Alone, misplaced, sad, solitary," echoed Stephen. He spoke so softly that Deepa barely heard him.

Unsure as what to say next to help Stephen with what appeared to be some kind of internal turmoil, Deepa simply lifted her left hand and, like a snowflake, let it fall onto Stephen's again. The touch shocked Stephen, opening up a torrent of unfamiliar sensations. The warmth from her hand seemed to escalate until it became a hot stream flowing through his veins and up into his arm. When it reached his chest, it felt like it exploded. The heat then travelled up into his brain. Once there, like a lighting flash, the rest of his body was instantly awash with heat waves. He began to perspire. He felt paralysed and overwhelmed with fear. Instantly suspicious, he thought at first that Deepa must have had some sort of chemical on her hand to trigger this reaction in him. He felt confused. Unable to react, he closed his eyes and concentrated on his breathing. Deepa, was oblivious of the response she had just caused in Stephen. She was just pleased that he did not pull his hand away. The two of them lay there in silence, unaware of the other's thoughts.

"I didn't outrun you, Stephen. Not really," explained Deepa. "I simply took the bus most of the way. The mission was to be the first one to get here. There was no mention of having to do that by running. So when we got to the end of the countdown, I went to the nearest bus stop and caught the bus that would take me the closest to the final destination."

Distant sounds started penetrating Stephen's concentration. He slowly became aware of his surroundings. Perspiration was trickling down his face and his head was thumping. Above him, the towering pillar reached up into the sky.

"So you see, I didn't cheat. It's just that your competitive nature took over and you assumed this was another opportunity to excel at a physical event," continued Deepa.

Stephen's breath became short as he attempted to regain control by injecting extra oxygen into his lungs veins. No longer did he hear any of the words coming from Deepa's lips. He turned his head to look at her, trying to make sense of what was happening to him.

Adrian Monico

"Sorry, Stephen. I don't want to make you feel bad. It's just that I don't want you to see me as a liar."

He could see Deepa's soft, red lips moving. Her deep hazel eyes looked up at the sky and he observed the unusual and mesmerising reflections within them. All along her neckline was the perfect, clear, dark bronze colour of her skin. On her cheeks were tiny dimples and her long, wavy, black hair was perfectly laid out around her as if in a scene from a photo shoot with a model floating in water. Stephen felt dazed. What was happening to him?

Deepa was still speaking. "I don't want for you to distrust me at a time where I'm here alone and would love your friendship." She wasn't looking at him, but there was a note of urgency in her voice.

Stephen's breath was getting increasingly shorter. A flutter of panic also started setting in, as it would for someone who was drowning or having an asthma attack. Feeling completely suffocated and unable to last much longer, he tried using all of his willpower to control his breathing again. Each minute particle of air that reached his lungs was registered and celebrated. After a few small breaths, he felt a tiny sense of relief settling in. As his panic subsided, he suddenly registered some of what Deepa had been saying. The words "I'm" and a bit later "alone" came through to him. Did she drug me? Stephen thought angrily. He was familiar with anger, more so than he was with these strange sensations, and so he lashed out.

"How would you know about being alone? You? You can always run to your mummy and daddy," he yelled, glad to be back in control, even if it sounded to him like some third person was talking. The heat that had invaded his body instantly disappeared, and a glacial sensation filled its place. Oddly, his body seemed to scream for the heat to return, in the same way that only a moment before, it screamed because it was unable to cope with the warmth.

It took only a few moments for Stephen to snap out of his trancelike state and identify the cause of this change in body

Simon Eady - The Teenage Spy

temperature. Deepa's hand was no longer resting on his. In fact, Deepa was no longer lying next to him at all. He sat up quickly and scanned the surrounding area. Within seconds, he spotted her running away. Perplexed, he tried to remember what had just happened. Then his angry words came back to him. He did not know anything about Deepa, or her family. He felt a little guilty about his outburst, but sat there silently and watched her go. He just could not deal with any more emotions.

Deepa felt crushed. She let herself become vulnerable and was rewarded with a harsh reminder of the death of her mother. The pain of it lanced through her. It was still a very deep and open wound. She ran through the Olympic Park gates and turned left towards the bottom of the hill. With tears streaming down her face, she could barely see the footpath. As she swiped angrily at her eyes one more time, she ran into a man stepping out from a side path. So as not to lose her balance, she instinctively held onto the stranger with both hands.

"I'm sorry!" apologised Deepa, still struggling to focus through the tears.

"Deepa! What's the matter? Why are you crying?" The man sounded alarmed.

At the sound of the voice, Deepa looked up in shock. It took a second to verify that she was not dreaming. "Dad!" she cried and threw herself forward to hug him.

"Sweetie, calm down. What's wrong?" asked Inspector Lau. He spoke in Malay, the language of her childhood.

"Nothing, Dad. I'm just a silly girl who'll never learn," replied Deepa, also in Malay, not wanting to burden him with her troubles.

"Have you had breakfast, sweetie?" asked her father, content not to dig any deeper into the cause of his daughter's tears. There would be time later when she had calmed down.

"N-no," hiccuped Deepa.

"Ok. I need to buy some food to cook for you kids for lunch. How about we get breakfast along the way, lah?" smiled Inspector Lau.

"Us kids? Are you staying? Why are you here?" asked Deepa, feeling confused.

Adrian Monico

"Sweetie, I'm the instructor for the next phase of your training. Surveillance, counter surveillance and tracking. Let's get breakfast and I'll explain."

Twenty minutes later, Deepa and her father were seated in a small, secluded restaurant that had opened for breakfast. Although neither could speak much Spanish, they found gestures proved to be the true international language, especially in restaurants.

"So Dad, please fill me in," said Deepa, once they had made their order to a patient waiter. "It was only a few weeks ago that you told me that you used to work for Interpol and that I could be part of an international team too, if I wanted." She sighed. "To be frank, Dad, I'm not really sure what I'm doing here. The training is a bit full on. I pictured myself joining an academy with lots of other students. But there are only two of us, and the other guy is such a misfit. I cannot understand why Interpol would want him."

"Before I answer you, sweetie, let me start by saying that I only have your best interest at heart." Inspector Lau remained silent for a moment, remembering his past. "I started my career many years ago in the 69th Commando Battalion in the Malay Army. I quickly became very efficient in special investigations and counter-terrorism. During these years, I often found myself being sent to train with foreign nations or training Malay troops. But my breakthrough came when a terrorist group assassinated a British politician in Kuala Lumpur. I was asked to assist Interpol with the investigation. Before too long, I tracked the killer down in Denmark and alerted Interpol headquarters." He paused while the waiter arrived, depositing coffee and plates of food before them. Once the waiter was out of earshot, Inspector Lau continued.

"On my way back home, I found myself invited to dinner as a thank you. When I arrived, my Interpol 'handler' revealed himself as an agent for British MI5. Although I did not believe it at first, I went along with him. That night I was made an offer to have a permanent role within Interpol, with the understanding that at times I would also be needed by MI5. I was given a new mission that took me six months in twelve nations, and opened many doors to the espionage world. I was asked to track down all seven remaining members of the terrorist group who had a hand in the assassination of the British politician." He took a sip of coffee and bit into his breakfast

"Dad, can I ask you a question?" Deepa had barely touched her own food and was looking a little perplexed.

"Of course."

"Why didn't you believe the agent belonged to MI5?"

"MI5 are an internal group and usually don't operate outside of the UK, lah. Although they'd hate for me to say this, you might think of them as being the same as the American FBI. This person, my handler, was present at most of the locations around the world where I had to travel to before landing in Denmark. Each time I found a terrorist, he was the one who I handed over to, to 'take care' of the remaining 'work'."

"Ok. Keep going." Deepa was satisfied that her question had been sufficiently answered for now. She realised she was starving and started hungrily eating her breakfast.

"In the course of my mission, I met several MI5 agents. Every time I tracked down another terrorist, I would call a number and within fifteen minutes an agent would turn up. Each time, I would hand over the details of the terrorist's location and walk away, never knowing what would happen to the terrorist. Each time, I also found that my tracking skills were improving. I was becoming faster and better at finding the next terrorist."

"Weren't you curious about to what happened to the terrorists?" asked Deepa. She knew she would have been and she wondered why her father did not obtain more information about the cases he was dealing with.

"Of course," replied the inspector. He hesitated. "I asked once." A long pause followed.

"And?" Deepa asked, starting to feel impatient.

"And the agent in question changed his expression and essentially told me that he was happy to answer, just as long as I was I happy to risk the consequences of knowing. I would myself become a target of the terrorists' accomplices. He went further and highlighted that most likely 'they' would go after anyone I loved and cared for. I still remember how smug I felt. For a split second, I was confident enough to challenge the agent," smiled Inspector Lau.

"What happened?" Deepa had stopped eating again. Her eyes were fixed on her father as she awaited his answer.

Adrian Monico

"The agent smiled and placed an envelope on the table. He told me that every agent, including himself, had a right to understand where they stood in the big picture. He then slid the envelope across the table to me." He swallowed another mouthful of coffee, well aware of the effect his story was having on Deepa. "In the envelope was a photo of a girl I had just met at the Interpol office. Nobody knew about her and me. The agent calmly went on and told me her full name, the place and date of her birth, her passport number, where she went to school, where she got her degree and in what, and where she was at that exact second."

Deepa was horrified. "That's terrible, Dad! Why would they blackmail you?"

Inspector Lau smiled at his daughter. "My initial response was the same. But the agent was simply highlighting the consequences that come with knowledge. Needless to say, I no longer wanted to know anything more about the missions than what I was told. I was falling head over heels for that girl, and it would have been selfish of me to jeopardise her life."

"Was she…?" Deepa paused, unsure if she wanted to know the answer to her question.

"Yes, she was your mum."

"No! You're kidding me? Mum was an action woman?" Deepa cried out, feeling suddenly proud.

Her father glanced around the restaurant before replying. "Um, not quite," he admitted. "She was a liaison person. She managed agents who were assigned to other enforcement agencies."

Deepa didn't seem overly disappointed by this news. "You charmer!" she grinned at her father. "You swept your liaison agent off her feet!"

"Not quite. Your mother organised a briefing for me at a restaurant. Or so I thought. But once the main course had been served and she still hadn't mentioned about the next mission, I had to ask her when we would talk business."

Deepa laughed. "Let me guess. Mum looked surprised because she thought the two of had 'something' and she took a chance by inviting you out." She grinned.

"Apparently so. It seems that in this area I was a tad thick, lah," replied Lau. He was still solely speaking Malay.

"Poor Mum," replied Deepa in English. She knew that practice was the only way to improve her English pronunciation.

"She was very understanding, but also very embarrassed. At first she tried to brush the situation off by joking about it, but at the end of the main course, she apologised and stood up as she felt she could not continue the dinner."

"So what happened next?" Deepa had the feeling she was listening to a campfire story.

"She left the restaurant, got reassigned, and I never saw her again," replied the inspector with a melancholy look.

A moment of silence passed.

"Daaaad, can you stop kidding around?" exclaimed Deepa.

"Sorry, sweetie. I couldn't help myself," grinned her father. "What really happened is that she stood up, I placed my hand, almost as an instinct, on hers and I asked her to please stay."

Another pause.

"And?" Deepa asked, becoming increasingly frustrated with her father's long pauses.

"She stayed. From that moment onward we started seeing each other more frequently. All in secret, of course. Within a few months we came out and told our co-workers and managers. After six months, we moved in together."

"Were your managers ok with it? Isn't there some rule against fraternising or something?" Deepa was tucking into her breakfast again. She noted that despite doing so much talking, her father had managed to almost clear his plate.

"Fraternising is certainly frowned upon by many military organisations. But I was surprised to learn that organisations in the spy world don't mind internal relationships. It certainly makes it easier for them to manage the risk that intelligence could be leaked via spouses. I guess that when two agents get together, both partners are already closely monitored."

Deepa paused her questioning for a few minutes. She was imagining her mum as a young woman working in a spy agency. "What happened next?" she asked at last.

"We both continued working in Europe for another year, although my job took me to many countries. Then came the toughest assignment either of us had ever faced. It required our combined effort."

"Really?" Deepa was disconcerted. She felt a growing unease for the suspense her father was creating in the story. "What was it? Was Mum pulled into the field?"

"Parenting!" came the inspector's reply.

Deepa rolled her eyes. "Dad, can you stop it with the jokes?"

"Actually, it's true. Your mother became pregnant and our government gave us a break from our hectic lives and moved us closer to our families. At the time there were two positions opened in Hong Kong, which we gladly accepted."

"That's when you met Signor Beppe." Deepa knew a little bit of this part of the story.

"Yes. However, I honestly did not know what he really did for a living. Until recently, that is."

"So, how did we end up back in Malaysia?"

"In a way, it was because of Signor Beppe. You see, when I found out that he and his wife died in a plane crash, I reassessed my life and decided that remaining in my current role was a risk that I no longer accepted. So, your mother and I spoke to our managers and we both resigned. Our request was at first rejected."

"Rejected? How can they force you to stay?" asked Deepa, puzzled.

"Oh, I assure you, they can! Anyhow, a week later I was here in Barcelona chasing down a Russian spy, when I confided to my handler my wish to get out. Funnily enough, it was the same agent who many years earlier 'blackmailed' me," replied the inspector. He sketched quotation marks in the air with two fingers on each hand.

"That's kind of funny. What did he say?"

"He just sat there and finished, very slowly, the cup of tea he was drinking. The whole time, he was just staring at me. He then got up, paid the bill, and walked out without a word of goodbye. Rather rude of him, I thought."

"Dad, stop stalling!"

"I'm sorry, sweetie," her father smiled. "I'm just genuinely enjoying seeing your expression. It reminds me of when I used to read you bedtime stories and you got frustrated when I took too long to turn the pages." He shook his head slightly at the memory. "Anyway, about fifteen minutes later the handler sent me an SMS simply telling me that he would think about it."

"I don't understand. Why did you ask the one person that, in your story anyway, came across as cold and not very sympathetic?"

"I know what you mean, sweetie. Don't ask me why, but at the time I thought there was something about that young agent. He was closed to the world and, yes, not very personable. But he also had an aura about him that made me feel that nothing was impossible for him. And if there was one chance in a million that I could convince him to help your mum and I, then I figured it was worth taking."

"So, you told him the reason?"

"Yes. I told him everything. Including the plane crash being the catalytic factor for me wanting to get out."

"He obviously decided to help. How long did you have to wait?"

"A day. I tracked down the spy and called the agent for the handover. Once I showed him the whereabouts of the target, he handed me a yellow envelope and I walked away."

"What was in it?"

"A phone number. "

"You're still stalling," Deepa accused him. He gave a guilty wave of his hand and continued.

"An hour later, I called the number. It was answered by a Malay police commissioner. As soon as I introduced myself, he become excited by the prospect of me taking up a role as an inspector in the Malay police force. Apparently Interpol had organised the transfer and provided him with an impressive dossier on me. To this day, I have no idea what was written in it, but it did not matter. Twenty four hours later, I landed in Hong Kong and broke the great news to your mum, whose own resignation had also just come through. With an unexpectedly handsome payout, we bought our home and set ourselves up for a normal life."

"So cool!" sighed Deepa. The waiter came by again to refill their coffees and remove their empty plates. Deepa sipped the hot drink, absorbed in her own recollections. "Dad?" she said hesitantly. "Can I ask you a few personal questions?"

"You can ask me anything, sweetie," smiled her father. He knew what her next question would be, just as he understood his daughter would never be satisfied until she had the whole story.

"Did you regret leaving your other life for me?" Her voice was small but his answer was immediate and unequivocal.

"Best decision we ever made. I would do it again in a heartbeat. I have loved every single second of being a husband, a dad, and a police inspector," grinned her father.

"But," she persisted, "didn't you miss the action? After all, you went from a full-on military role to an adventurous career as a spy to just, you know, having a day job." She trailed off, hoping she hadn't offended him.

"Actually, I don't believe my job ever changed. Just the employer. In the military, with the exception of a few unusual missions, I spent most of my time tracking down terrorists. When I joined Interpol, and the other spy agency, all I did was continue tracking down wanted criminals. When I came back to Malaysia, again I spent most of my time tracking down more criminals."

Deepa nodded. "Ok. Thank you for saying that. On a different topic, when you worked for Interpol and the other agency, did you have to kill anyone?"

Inspector Lau exhaled, relieved that her question did not extend to his time in the commando unit. He didn't want to lie to his daughter.

"I rarely carried a weapon. And with the exception of when I practiced at a firing range, in those roles I never had to fire a round."

Deepa smiled. The idea of her dad killing someone was disturbing to her. She was glad that he had never done so. "Did you ever find out what happened to any of the people you tracked down?"

"Yes, once. But before I reply, you need to promise me never to tell anything we are discussing to anyone else. Ever!" stated seriously her father.

"You have my word, Dad."

"Remember how initially I was asked to track down the remaining members of the terrorist group who killed the British politician?"

"Uh huh," Deepa nodded.

"Well, I decided that the best way to find another terrorist, was to re-find that first terrorist who I located back in Denmark and then trail him to his 'colleagues'. It took me a few days of digging around, but I discovered that the first terrorist seemed to have been shot in his apartment. I say 'seemed to have been', as the body was never recovered. The only evidence I found was that the neighbours heard shots being fired the same night I reported him to my controller. When the police arrived, they found bullet holes in the wall, but no sign of the man. After a few weeks of being searched for as a missing person, he was filed as a cold case and the police moved on."

"Wow! You think he was assassinated?" whispered Deepa.

"Yes. It was then that I decided to simply bury my curiosity and move on."

"What makes you so sure that he didn't just run and hide? Or that someone else killed him?"

"When I left Denmark, I returned to my temporary apartment in Brussel. I walked in, dropped my bags, went into the bathroom via the bedroom and got straight into the shower. When I walked back out, I found a yellow envelope resting against the bed pillow. I immediately reached for my gun as the envelope had not been there when I first walked in and there was nobody else in the apartment. Whoever dropped the envelope got in and out within minutes."

"What was in it?"

"Two photos and a note. The first photo was of the terrorist looking like he was asleep on the bed in the same apartment where the shots were heard. The photo had the word 'terminated' typed across it. The second photo was of your mum sitting at a desk typing. The photo had a date stamped across it. It had been taken two hours earlier." The inspector paused again, feeling the same chills running down his spine as he did at the time he first saw the photo.

And the note?"

"It just said: Knowledge has consequences. Your friend is safe, but you are not helping her. I didn't know what to do. I panicked and dialled your mum. When she answered, I changed my mind about alerting her and simply convinced her to take an earlier departure and go away for the weekend." He stared momentarily into his empty cup. "That was the worst weekend of my life. I couldn't help looking over my shoulder. I felt that I was being followed the whole time and I didn't know who to trust. I was sure that the envelop came from the agent who used the same technique back in Denmark. It seemed that I was not trusted."

"So what did you do?"

"We went to Florence. On the Saturday afternoon, while your mum was having a siesta, I left the hotel and tried to verify that we were not being followed. As it turned out, nobody was watching us. Over the next six months, I taught myself to let go of that fear."

"But, how can you let go?" Deepa demanded. "I wouldn't be able to. I guess I could learn to live with it," she reflected, "but I could never let go."

"You are right, sweetie," her father agreed. "I never managed to completely let go." A silence fell once more across their table. It was broken by Deepa who glanced down at her watch.

"Sorry, Dad. I just realised that I'm taking advantage of you and keeping you from going back to start your lessons."

"Oops. Thank you, I have lost track of time. Let's go and on the drive back, you can tell me the reason for your earlier tears."

Deepa's face creased into an uncomfortable frown. The idea of spilling her guts to her father about the morning's discussion with Stephen was not a pleasant one. She still felt confused and hurt about what had happened and did not want to think about it, much less go over it again it with Inspector Lau.

Meanwhile, back in London, Beta, the Head of MI6, was completely engrossed in an End of Exercise Report, often abbreviated to an Endex Report or even just an ER, which had just been delivered hot off the press.

"Sir, your next appointment is here," a feminine voice called from the small speaker located underneath the desk.

"Very well, Carla. Please let him in," replied Beta via a hidden microphone. Within moments, Kevin walked in, looking very serious.

"Good timing! I was just reading the ER involving Simon. You know, there's not much that surprises me these days, but I have to say I was astonished to read that Simon achieved something that no other person has managed to do up until now. He took out Shadow!" Beta's tone was cheerful as he directed Kevin to a set of very old brown leather couches with a wave of his hand.

Kevin sat down and looked around Beta's office. "Well, you don't pack much, do you?" he observed. The office was the size of a bedroom that could fit a queen sized bed, a couple of side tables and, with a bit of luck, a tallboy.

"Why would I need more?" asked Beta, a little defensively.

"True, I suppose. And even when you do have personal belongings, it seems they remain stored in cardboard boxes," said Kevin, breaking into a slight smile.

"If you are referring to the cardboard box behind you, that is something that nobody to date has dared to smile about!" retorted Beta, exposing a full mouth of teeth.

"Oh, really? Do tell," grinned Kevin, enjoying the friendly banter.

"How are you Kevin?" said Beta, promptly changing the subject. "I am always so happy to see you. I was hoping that once I gave you the job of director of the spy academy, we would get to see more of each other." He extended his hand.

"I'm great, Bart," the other man replied. "I just had a long sleep and feel fully energised. Still avoiding the uncomfortable questions I see!" He shook Beta's hand.

"I tell you, if it wasn't for you, I would forget my birth name. Even my car licence has a fictitious name. Of course, people who do find out my real name seem to have a very short lifespan," joked Beta, although his words seemed to hold an element of truth.

"Let me guess, they get cut into pieces and stored in that box," winked Kevin.

"I see that you will not let go of this," sighed Beta. "No, I do not resort to such barbaric measures..."

"You get others to do it for you," finished Kevin, settling comfortably back onto the couch and crossing his legs.

Beta grinned and nodded. "Morning tea?" he asked as he returned to his desk.

"Of course. We are British spies after all. It is in our blood," replied Kevin, knowing that tea was not exactly what Beta was offering.

"One day this grappa will be the end of me, Kevin. And you will have to live with the knowledge that you introduced me to it. Or was it your old man?"

"We simply solved your problem. You did not want to lie to the new government ministers when they ordered not to keep scotch and cognac in the office because it gave a bad impression to staff and foreign visitors. We simply gave you an alternate," Kevin winked. He stretched his left arm across the backrest of the old couch.

"Mmm. I still think that my approach delivered considerably more benefits?" Beta mused as he collected a bottle of grappa and two small port glasses. He looked again in the direction of the cardboard box.

Kevin caught his glance. "Do tell," he said. Other than the two couches, a small coffee table, a framed picture of the queen, a large oak desk and matching swivel chair, the box was the only visible item in the room.

"Well, truth be known, whenever I meet the new Secretary of State or one of the new ministers, I always take it upon myself to educate them about protecting themselves from their indiscretions being uncovered," started Beta, with a subtle smirk on his face.

"Indiscretions?"

"Affairs, bribes, legal proceedings dropped despite a clear case of guilt, political contributions aligned to supported policies. You know, the usual stuff that we use to motivate people of interest to defect," shrugged Beta.

"Go on," said Kevin. He had a gut feeling about where this was heading.

"Well, they walk in here, I seat them on these couches and I commence my usual educational speech. I ask them if there is anything that I should know that needs to be taken care of. Naturally, they always deny that any such matters exist. That is when I present them with a yellow folder containing all the incriminating evidence against them that MI6 or MI5 have uncovered. I find that at that point, their ridiculous impositions on me – such as banning scotch from my office, for instance – seem to go away."

"Bart, that is blackmail!" cried Kevin, entertained at his friend's approach.

"I call it establishing boundaries of efficiency," smiled Beta in return.

"So, what happens if you have nothing on the new ministers and secretaries?"

"Kevin, unlike you and I who are solely accountable for our own actions, politicians are also accountable for their families, including their distant extended families, as well as their department, their employees, any companies they some point either owned or worked for… You see what I'm saying. There is always something that, if it gets in the media, brings the risk of dismissal just one step closer."

Kevin reflected for a moment. "Ok. But what has this got to do with the cardboard box?"

"Simple. Before they leave, I make sure that I place their files in that box."

"Are you kidding me? You store sensitive material like that in a plain cardboard box?"

"No. I initially place the file in there. Later on, I get it destroyed. After all, I am here to protect the British people, not blackmail them."

"But they leave here thinking that you will keep the file, and that it will be permanently stored in that box."

"Correct."

"Then every time they come and see you, they see the box too and it reminds them of what they think is stored in it and what you have over them."

"Correct again," beamed Beta. "Although the odd thing is that they never seem to want to meet me here. Which, incidentally, suits me to a 'T'. Meanwhile, their conscience gets a nudge every time they see a standard removalist cardboard box." Beta unscrewed the lid of the grappa and poured the liquid into the port glasses.

"Aren't you worried that they might want to even the odds and hire someone to get dirt on you?" asked Kevin.

"Worried? No. Does it happen? Yes. That's when I then pay them a special visit and explain that their 'not so secretive actions' should be 'boxed' away as a bad and risky idea." Beta winked and passed the small glass to Kevin.

"To Queen and country!" toasted Kevin, raising his glass towards the framed picture of the queen.

"To Queen and country!" echoed Beta. He sipped from his glass. "So, how is Simon?" There was genuine concern in his voice.

"The sedative knocked him out for a few hours. He is about due to finish his medical check-up and fly out to Spain," replied Kevin. He still felt some doubt about involving his son with MI6.

"Ah, yes. Before I forget, I've taken the liberty to upgrade his seat to first-class," grinned Beta.

"Really? Why? Isn't there a policy to reduce first-class flying?" asked Kevin, surprised by Beta's action.

"I thought I just covered my approach about policies that I don't believe are appropriate for MI6," observed Beta mildly. "Besides which, he deserves a reward for dropping Shadow which is not something anybody else has ever achieved before. And since it seems to matter so much to you, I used my own frequent flyer points for the upgrade. By the way, how is Shadow?"

"His pride is slightly damaged, but he'll live," replied Kevin.

"For a man who was supposed to have died, he has certainly been busy!"

"I've just heard about Agent 2C," Kevin inserted as a change of topic. Pleasant as it was to sip grappa and chat, he thought this may have been the real reason he had been summoned to meet Beta.

"Ah, thank you for reminding me. I assume you read the report?"

"Yes. He is being held prisoner at a small villa in the middle of Colombia. Satellite shows that his vital signs are all ok. Just some distress."

"Why do you think that is?"

"Whoever has him is interested in keeping him alive. My theory is that he is being used as bait and the kidnapper wants us to know his whereabouts. Otherwise, the body sensors would have been destroyed by now," replied Kevin.

"Go on," encouraged Beta.

"I think Agent 2C was given away by a mole. The report says that he exposed his presence by not sedating the teenagers, but I did some checking and there is no evidence of mobile phone calls in the area between where he landed and where he was captured. Unless those kids outran him to alert someone, I do not support our intelligence analysts' conclusions about the reason behind the mission's failure. We did not continue tracking the kids, which was a mistake. For the first few minutes after the encounter, they appeared to continue towards their original destination at the same pace. This suggests to me that they were not really alarmed. Then again, if you live in Colombia, seeing someone parachuting in the middle of the night might not seem as odd as it would be here in the UK," concluded Kevin.

"So, where does your logic about the mole come in?" Beta asked, who supported Kevin's observations so far.

"The last satellite image we have of Bernie, Agent 2C, is when he gets presented to the VIP at the entrance of the house. If you look carefully at a still image from the footage, you can see that he's got his hands over his head but they're both clenched into fists. His fingers are not splayed out you would traditionally, instinctively do."

"I don't follow."

Kevin withdrew a sheet of paper from his pocket and handed it to Beta. "This is a list of books Agent 2C has borrowed over the last six months. The one of note is the internal publication called Field Signals of a Spy. If you look at the photocopy I made of page 75, you can see that it says holding one's hands clumped into fists above one's head means..."

"Cover is blown. Target knows of my identity, the identity of the mission, or intelligence only known to those intimately involved in the mission," Beta read from the notes. He looked up. "It could be a coincidence."

"Yes, but I have the graphs of Agent 2C's biometrics sent by the device implanted in him. Have a look at the breathing graph," Kevin continued, handing over another sheet of paper.

"I don't see anything other than peaks, troughs, and varying frequencies," admitted Beta. He was unsure what it was he was looking for.

"Ok. To help you understand what I'm about to explain you, have a look at this." Kevin held up a clear sheet with a few marks on it. He superimposed it over the breathing chart. It indicated a line in the places where Agent 2C's breath was held and a dot at the points when he took a deep breath.

"Morse code! I'll be dammed," cried Beta. Before he could follow up with another question, Kevin handed him another a piece of paper. This one had a few words written on it with the same marker that was used to create the overlay. It read "T G T H E R E M O L E . T G T H E R E M O L E . T G T H E R E M O L E .

Beta stared at it. "Have I got this right?" he asked, although he already knew the answer. "TGT means 'Target'. So TARGET HERE and there is a MOLE?"

Kevin nodded. "There's more Morse code. I've got the analysts working on it as I ran out of time to do it myself and didn't want to keep you waiting."

"Kevin, how did you pick this up? Why didn't my brainiacs upstairs spot it?" His frustration was clear on Beta's face.

"Bart, I've told you before that MI6 needs to send our analysts out into the field more often. Get them to shadow one of our operatives for a few days. The problem we have is that doctrine is always a step behind operations. We constantly evolve. But because our doctrine writers can only capture new procedures and tactics after they happen and are reported, our documentation will always be one step behind. By sending analysts on regular field trips, they will learn lots of tricks of the trade before they end up in books or training manuals. In this case, though, we already had everything on paper. That book Field Signals of a Spy was written in the 1970s. Resourcing to Morse code as a way to communicate is a very old military discipline. I've asked the analysts to go back to the satellite images to check if they can see Agent 2C using his fingers to tap out messages in Morse code while he has his hands above his head."

"I support your idea about the analysts, but I still don't see that it would have made a difference in this case. How did you work it out?"

"It was luck, actually," Kevin admitted. "Last week, I borrowed the book as part of the course curriculum I'm building for the academy. In the inside cover, I noticed that Bernie is the only other person who has borrowed the book in the last four years. Not sure why we still use such an old librarian style record keeping, but this time I am grateful for it. Although I don't really know anyone in MI6, I recognised Bernie's name from his experimentations with the flying wing-suit. As you know, I have been contemplating teaching this new entry technique to the kids. In fact, I went as far as reading Bernie's dossier, as I thought he might be the person I will use to teach the teenagers. When I first heard that Agent 2C had been captured, I did not even make the connection. However, when I was in the control room, one of the analysts made a joke about setting up a bet about would be the next agent to get named with the unlucky 2C code. Someone else said that after what happen with Tom and now with Bernie, agents would rather get numbered as 13 rather than 2C. Once I heard the name

'Bernie', I remembered seeing it in the library book and, just in case, I started looking for signals. The message in the breathing graph was easy to find once I started looking. The fists on his head was more challenging. I only spotted it minutes before coming to you."

"Well done, Kevin," said Beta. As if thinking aloud, he added, "So now, I have a spy to rescue and a mole to find."

"Send Shadow to free Bernie. You concentrate on the mole. Maybe you could set a trap yourself," Kevin suggested.

"Shadow? You think he'll be interested in doing another mission after all the trouble we went to 'retire' him?"

A wide smile stretched across Kevin's face. "Right now, after by being taken out by Simon, I'm sure he is itching to recover some reputation."

"Good point. Let's make it happen," Beta ordered.

When Deepa and Inspector Lau got back to the apartment, they found Stephen sitting at the kitchen table staring at a cup of tea he held in both hands. Deepa avoided making eye contact when he looked up, instead passing right by him and heading for her bedroom via the second kitchen door. Stephen's gaze followed her. It was is if he wanted to tell her something, but the moment was missed as his courage was missing as well.

"Hello! I'm Inspector Lau," said the inspector, holding out his hand. Stephen looked first at the hand then at the small man standing beside him. A slight upward movement of his eyebrows was the only acknowledgement he made.

"Not in social mood, lah?" prompted the inspector. Stephen simply stared back into his cup of tea. "Young man, this is not best way to start. You know that I have an ability to talk until people give in, lah," he smiled, although his enthusiasm about the next few days was beginning to strain

Possibly driven by the guilt, Stephen rose in a single motion with his right hand spiralling upward. Without really thinking it through, he felt angry and driven to shove the small man who was making the annoying noise. As he stood up, his shoulders passed the top of the inspector's head. Unfortunately, Stephen's misjudgement of height meant that his hand was about to connect with the instructor's head instead of his chest. With quick reflexes, Inspector Lau arched backward and dropped just enough avoid contact with the flying hand.

His own left hand came up and pushed Stephen's right elbow, forcing his swinging motion to accelerate. Stephen was completely taken by surprise and, despite seeing everything in slow motion, felt incapable of influencing what was happening to his body. Not only did his right hand barely miss Inspector Lau's head, but it continued on its circular trajectory at a faster rate, causing his whole body to go off-centre and follow the swing. He looked like he was attempting a discus throw.

Having twisted around, Stephen now found himself facing in the opposite direction. A sudden, sharp force collapsed his left knee forward, making him drop to the floor on both knees. He had just enough time to prepare himself for the pain of feeling his knees collide with the hard terracotta floor. But that pain was never felt. In fact, all sense completely vanished as his body seemed to go into some form of paralysis. Then, without warning, an incredible pain shot from his shoulders, exploded into his brain and down his spine. He gasped and despite wanting to reach back to grab his shoulder, he found the pain was so extreme that he could not move. Inspector Lau stood calmly behind the young student with his hand placed on a midpoint between Stephen's neck and left shoulder. He was using a very old technique in which the pinching of a specific nerve paralysed an opponent. He felt very proud that after all of these years, he still had not lost his touch.

"Young man," he began calmly. "I am Inspector Lau and I am here for a few days to teach you kids about tracking, surveillance, and counter surveillance. I was going to go over a few rules later on, but since we have an opportunity to discuss some of them now, let me start by saying that I am not pleased with acts of violence between students or against staff. Understood, lah?"

Stephen refused to reply. He was angry at the small man who he believed had tricked him. A sharp increase in pain forced the words out of him. "Ok!" he screamed. "Understood."

Inspector Lau nodded. "I also Deepa's father. So if you hurt her again, I will show you the exact level to which this technique can trigger pain."

"Please stop!" cried Stephen. The pain was now pushing him beyond his endurance, but the small man seemed not to notice. He continued speaking calmly.

"I also empowered to throw off the course anyone I feel is not right to be spy, lah. I make a decision at the end of training. I already suspect that you no have place in MI6. So, for your sake, I hope the next few days will be sufficient to change my mind." With that, he released the pressure of his pinch. Although a few words were missing from his accented sentences, his message was clearly understood by Stephen.

"I'm sorry!" he said quickly, fearful of the setback that being kicked out of training would have on his mission and relieved by the sudden easing of the pain.

"Deepa is one you need to apologise to. Her mum died not long ago. At a time she emotionally exposed to try and befriend you, you hurt her very deeply, lah. I do not know who you parents are, but if you my son, I would not very proud of calling you that. The way you treat people is poor, lah. Now, please stand up and face me," ordered the inspector.

To Stephen's amazement the pain was suddenly completely gone. He staggered to his feet, using his right hand to massage the point that a few seconds before had triggered his agony.

"Good morning. I am Inspector Lau," the man repeated, holding out his right hand.

"Good morning, Inspector. I'm Stephen," replied the teenager hesitantly. He shook the instructor's hand.

The small man released Stephen's hand and glancing over his shoulder at a clock on the wall. "I am going to unpack and cook us lunch. We will start the classes after that. Meanwhile, please clean up the spilled tea and maybe go apologise to Deepa, lah."

"Ok," replied Stephen. He had only just noted some time within the last few minutes, he had managed to knock over his cup of tea.

Behind one of the kitchen doors, Deepa stood silently, having heard the entire incident as it transpired. Before she could be seen, she headed for her room, confused again about what to think of Stephen, and surprised by her dad's ability to defend himself against the 'jerk'.

Ten minutes later, Inspector Lau was back in the kitchen after unpacking his luggage. Stephen was also in the kitchen, sitting at the table with a fresh cup of tea. He felt awkward and did not want to make eye contact with the inspector. He did not know how to talk to this strange man, nor what to make him. Fortunately, his instructor did not have the same problem.

"Stephen, you help me cook, please? You have quick hands, lah! Good for cutting vegetables," smiled Lau.

"I guess," replied Stephen. Embarrassment over his earlier display of anger still prickled him uncomfortably and he wanted to prove to the inspector that he was not entirely lacking in social skills.

"Ok, you cut carrots like this," instructed Lau, as he efficiently sliced through the first one with a large stainless steel knife. He flung the knife into the air and caught the flashing blade in mid descent. "Here you go, young man. You cut now, lah." The inspector smiled as he handed the knife to Stephen, handle first.

"Th-thank you," stammered Stephen, politely accepting the knife. He was impressed by Lau's trick.

"Very good. If you no like being a spy, you always get out and be chef," the inspector joked.

Stephen did not reply and concentrated instead on cutting the carrots. At first, he wanted to see how fast he could slice them. Then he started competing against himself by seeing if he could do it faster. A few minutes passed, during which both were completely occupied by their respective tasks. The inspector felt like spaghetti and choose to cook a bolognaise sauce.

"Um, young man," he said after a time. "Only five of us eat. No need to cut whole bag." He pointed to the volume of carrots cut by his student.

Stephen, caught up in his competitive chopping, suddenly realised that he had sliced his way through two full bags of carrots. Feeling startled and embarrassed, he struggled to make eye contact with Inspector Lau.

"Sorry," he mumbled. "You must think I'm some idiot who is out totally of control. Can't keep my emotions in check, can't follow a simple instruction." After this morning's encounter with Deepa, Stephen had thought his day could not get any worse. Instead, he seemed to be coming across as moron to his new instructor. His future depended on his self-control and ability to stay cool in the face of unexpected events. Today he felt like he had completely lost any such discipline. Inspector Lau looked at Stephen but said nothing.

"Maybe it's true. Maybe I'm not cut out to be a spy. But it's the only thing I want to do. I need to do this because I've got nothing else." Stephen paused. This time he looked the inspector square in the eyes. Again, Lau did not respond. He simply turned his back to the teenager, and walked towards the pantry.

Stephen knew he was coming across like a lost cause. Not knowing what else to do or say, he stared down at the big pile of carrots he had sliced in only a few minutes. He was startled when another bag of carrots landed with a bang right in front of him.

"You think you good? You want to take on the champion?" asked the inspector.

Consciously trying to settle his heartbeat after the scare, Stephen looked up at the inspector who was holding up another bag of carrots and pointing at it with his spare hand. His grin revealed all of his shiny white teeth.

"Um…" Stephen heard him say. He was unsure how to read the situation.

"Scared to be beaten by old man?" challenged Lau.

"More like scared that people will ridicule me if they found out that I beat an old man. I should really see if Deepa is free, as she's a more realistic competitor," joked Stephen, finally settling into the moment.

The inspector cleared some space next to Stephen, found another chopping board and knife, and stood shoulder to shoulder with the teenager. He glanced at his rival. "Ready?"

At the same moment, Stephen yelled, "Go!"

Both of them began grabbing carrots and cutting them as fast as they could. At the start, Lau's speed was faster than Stephen's, but before long, the teenager was catching up carrot by carrot. It took three minutes for both bags to be emptied. In the end, the inspector beat Stephen, but only by a whisker.

"You were lucky," Stephen winked at his instructor. "One more carrot and I would have beaten you."

"Really?" replied Inspector Lau, walking back to the pantry once more.

"Really," said Stephen firmly. He was impressed by how quick he was becoming in the vegetable chopping stakes.

"Ok, let's put money where mouth is," challenged the inspector as he walked out of the pantry with a bag of potatoes in each hand.

Within a minute, the race recommenced. This time, both competitors were neck and neck for the duration. They finished their respective bags at exactly the same time.

"You still think you faster?" asked the inspector, sensing that his winning streak was coming to an end.

Stephen walked into the pantry and emerged after a few seconds holding up a bag of celery, a bag of tomatoes and a bag of mushrooms.

"Winner takes all, Inspector!" challenged Stephen.

"Ok, but I am worried you are fragile boy and losing again is not good," teased Inspector Lau.

Stephen moved back to his place at the table and they proceeded to evenly divide the contents of the bags.

"Ready, set," began Stephen.

"Go!" finished Inspector Lau, giving himself a cheeky half second lead.

"Cheat!" Stephen laughed as he tried to recoup his delayed start.

Both competitors cut at an incredibly fast rate, once in a while glancing at the thickness of each other's slices and keep their own at similar size. Throughout the contest, even when some chunks of celery were chopped bigger than others, both competitors remained within a few slices of each other. At times it seemed like the inspector was pulling ahead, but at other times Stephen appeared to have the advantage. The inspector finished the tomatoes first, but Stephen overtook on the celery. It was all down to the mushrooms. As he started to cut the last one, Stephen knew he had a chance to win. His knife hit the board for the last time, and he let out a triumphant yell.

"FINISHED!"

But even as he uttered the word, he heard an odd thud. Stephen traced the sound and stared. Inspector Lau had thrown the last slice of his final mushroom into the distance and with a swift motion, he hurled the knife after it. The knife penetrated the centre of the mushroom slice, pinning it the wooden frame of the kitchen door.   There was a momentary silence as man and boy examined each other's achievement. Then they looked at each other and burst into laughter.

"Great! Now you are on his side!"

The stern words came from Deepa who had witnessed the last few moments of the race from across the room. Before either of them had chance to reply, Deepa turned and took off for the front door of the apartment.

"Deepa, wait!" called Stephen.

Deepa, although feeling her blood boil, responded by freezing on the spot with her back to the kitchen.

"I'm… I'm sorry" he whispered.

"If you've got to say something to me, be clear about it, as I am over dealing with your spoilt, childish behaviour," snapped Deepa. Although she did not turn to look at Stephen, already a small sign of satisfaction had crept on her face.

"I am really so sorry, Deepa. I behaved inappropriately and completely unfairly to you." Stephen's voice was louder this time. "You're the only person in a long time that has bothered to make an effort with me," Stephen continued, feeling embarrassed but at the same time relieved. "I should have been nicer to you."

At last Deepa turned around. Trying hard to maintain an impassive expression, she walked up to Stephen. He mentally prepared himself for the slap across the face that he both expected and felt was warranted. When the two teenagers were standing almost toe to toe, Deepa flashed out her right hand. Unwillingly, Stephen flinched.

"Friends?" she asked.

Surprised, Stephen took her hand. "Friends," he replied, matching her sudden smile.

"Dad, you still are hopeless with quantities!" exclaimed Deepa, staring at the piles of sliced vegetables that lay on the kitchen table bench.

"Anyone for eating out?" asked the inspector. It seemed like a good opportunity for a team bonding activity.

Both teenagers nodded and burst into laughter.

"We only just had breakfast, and you are already cooking lunch?" Deepa asked.

"It was going to be slow cook sauce," he replied. There really was, he realised, quite a lot of chopped vegetables.

"Ok, if we go out now, it means that we are having lunch at 10am." Stephen was a bit unsure whether he should interject with such an obvious statement

"Then we go out for morning tea and start class at restaurant, lah?" the inspector suggested.

"I know a place!" called Deepa as she led the way to the front door. Behind her, she thought she heard her father murmur a quiet "Well done" to Stephen. Perhaps things were looking up. She reached to unlock the door and pull it open. As she started stepping forward, a tall figure suddenly materialised in front of her. She almost walked right into him. There was a pause as all three of them took in this unexpected appearance.

"Simon!" Deepa cried. She opened her arms and launched herself into him.

"Hello Deepa," replied Simon. His calm tone hid the fact that he was taken aback by the sight of Stephen. Suddenly not feeling very hungry, Stephen himself took one look at Simon and turned angrily towards his bedroom.

"Young man, stop!" ordered Inspector Lau, already aware of the history between the two trainee spies.

Stephen reacted to the order, but as Deepa had done before, still faced the same direction, keeping his back to the group.

"You two need to get along. You not get along, then I buy plane ticket for you to go home!" threatened the inspector, even though he knew neither boy had any real home to go to.

Stephen turned and stared at Simon, who returned his gaze with equal ferocity. Both refused to be the one to make the first move.

"I no ask you again, lah," Lau warned.

Still, neither of them flinched.

"Simon, please."

Deepa's whisper broke into Simon's concentration. He allowed himself to break eye contact with Stephen and glance down at her. Something stirred inside him and in a flash, his anger towards the other boy was gone. He tried to retain it, but he knew he was fighting a losing battle. His mind was already filling with thoughts about the cause of his real anger. For Simon, Stephen was just a stranger who provided another avenue for him to vent his sense of loss over the death of his mum. He did not really have a gripe against

Stephen making his life hell during the last few days of his mother's life. It is true that he did not really trust Stephen, but for the time being, he would make an effort. Besides, Inspector Lau was adamant that they should get on. Without a word, Simon extended his right hand.

Inspector Lau turned his eyes to Stephen. "I mean it, boy!"

Having already having come close to ruining his plan once that morning with his challenge to the inspector, Stephen finally conceded that pursuing the public confrontation was the fastest way to fail at his own personal mission. There would be times ahead when he could confront Simon again. He reluctantly took up Simon's hand and silently shook it.

"Good!" stated the inspector. "We now go eat and learn to get along. After all, today is first day of this team working together, lah." He started ushering the three teenagers through the door.

CHAPTER 3 - Back To Basics

"Bernie, are you awake?"

At sound of the eerie whisper, Bernie opened his eyes and found himself hanging from his wrists by a rope that was tied to a large butcher's hook implanted in the cement beams above his head. He must have passed out and his legs had collapsed underneath him. The dead weight of his body caused a painful rope burn. As his awareness gradually returned, he became aware that his hands were numb and he could only feel the burning sensation around his wrists. His head was pounding.

"Yes, I-I am," he said, trying to sound more alert than he felt.

"Shortly my men will come and take you to a room where you will hopefully have a more pleasant stay. I want to apologise in advanced for the measures that my team will take to ensure you don't feel motivated to try and escape," the cold voice explained.

Agent 2C knew what was coming next. He had been briefed during his training about what could happen if he got caught. He could not defend himself, even if he was not tied up, so he closed his eyes to block out the pain he was already feeling and gathered his inner strength to prepare for what was to come next.

A group of four men walked into the room and, without ceremony, threw a barrage of punches at Bernie, targeting his arms and legs. Bernie locked his mind in a distant place and tried to block out the pain registers in his body which were screaming out for help. He did not know how long the onslaught continued. His mind only started to notice his surroundings again when he felt his body being lifted and his tied hands were released from the hook that was holding him up. When his body collapsed, it was with a painful thump onto a rough surface. Face down, he could smell the dank, musty dirt of the floor and he slowly opened his eyes. In the dim light, he could see again the old wooden barrels and wine bottles that were stacked from floor to ceiling in the room.

He did not have time to orientate himself before two men lifted him to his feet and hauled him forward. He had no strength to walk on his own or try to resist being dragged along. His legs were numb with pain and he would have collapsed again if he had not been held up by the men. Even so, Bernie could not refrain from biting out some sort of retort.

"You know all of this was completely unnecessary. A pistol to my head would have given you my complete compliance," he rasped, trying to get a glimpse of the voice that had spoken before, but all he could see was an empty space.

The two guards dragged him out of the cellar into a nearby room that looked like it had been used for storage. The ground was compacted dirt, it had no windows and the walls were a dark grey cement. In one corner a single, bare mattress and in the other stood a bucket. Bernie staggered and tumbled as he was shoved inside. The steel door slammed shut behind him. He lay on the ground and tried to assess the damage to his body. Although he felt as if he had been run over by a herd of bulls, nothing seemed to be broken. His assailants were professionals. They did not want to kill or disable him completely, just give him a taste of what would happen if he tried to escape.

He lay still on the dirt floor until he felt his breathing ease and some of his strength returning. Then, slowly, using his teeth, he untied the rope that bound his hands and crawled over to the bucket. Using the wall to help him stand, he rose unsteadily to his feet. Nausea clawed his stomach and perspiration from the strain of moving ran down his forehead. Bernie closed his eyes and leaned his head against the cold wall above the bucket. As he stood with his back to the room using the bucket as a toilet, a hatch at the bottom of the door slid open and a picnic basket was pushed inside.

"My apologies for having taken a while to get the room ready. You have no idea how difficult it was to get the ceiling completed" the same voice as before called out from behind the door. Agent 2C looked up and noted for the first time that the cement was fresh.

"Lead lining. I think you've had enough conversations with MI6," the voice explained.

Bernie understood. They found out about his morse code trick. Despite feeling worried that this further proved that MI6 had a mole, his morale received an injection of energy from the knowledge that someone in London got his message. Although he was not hungry, he turned towards the door and unsteadily staggered to the picnic basket. Curious, he lifted the lid and found himself surprised by its contents.

Adrian Monico

"Bernie, despite the safety precautions that I take when moving you, I am not a barbarian. The champagne is an extra reward for your assistance with my plan," laughed the cold voice.

"Plan? Do you know who they are sending after me?" Agent 2C suspected that this mission was nothing more than an elaborate trap for someone else. He had no hope in succeeding at his task and now understood why he had not been instantly killed when captured. Live bait is better, after all.

"No, but I'm working on that. Meanwhile, enjoy your meal and rest. Also, when you've finished, make sure you put all the leftovers back in the basket and place it near the door. And just in case you think of being clever, we'll be counting all the non-edible items. If there is one thing missing, even a small chicken bone, my men will take whatever measures necessary to find it, and you'll be on water rations for the reminder of your time here," threatened the voice.

Bernie considered these words. The voice must belong to the leader, the Consigliere, he surmised. Perhaps his mission was not a complete failure after all.

"That's right, Bernie. The better option is to continue building your strength and resting your body so that you have the greatest chance of escape if the opportunity arises," called out the Consigliere, reading Bernie's mind from behind the reinforced door.

"Do you miss it, Consigliere?" asked Bernie, following a hunch.

"Miss what?" asked the Consigliere. Agent 2C now knew for certain that he was speaking to the infamous Consigliere. He continued to subtly discover more about one of the most wanted men in the world.

"Being part of the secret agency world," continued Bernie. He was not sure which agency his target was from, but with his well-articulated language and slight accent, Bernie's bet was that the answer would be MI6.

"It's funny how your mind cannot break away from its paradigms. You are thinking that I am MI6. But my accent is throwing you. You fail to grasp that MI6 has achieved great success by adapting techniques from other agencies. So yes, I know all MI6 procedures and protocols, but no, I have never belonged to it nor to any other secret agency."

A silence followed. Straining his ears, Bernie thought he could hear another voice whisper something to the Consigliere.

"Pleasant as this is, it seems that our discussion is making someone nervous. I will leave you to enjoy your meal. And remember, we will count every item."

Bernie picked up the basket and sat on the mattress. He was not hungry but knew the Consigliere was right; he had to eat. He felt exhausted and his arms ached as he lifted the food to his mouth. His mind was consumed with analysing the conversation that had just transpired. Who is the mole? Who is this Consigliere? And who is he really after? The questions continued to spin around Bernie's head as he chewed and swallowed the food.

In Beta's office at headquarters, the two men decided to go for a second glass of grappa. "So, my friend, is there something else you wanted to cover?" asked Beta as he sipped the strong drink from his glass

"Can't friends enjoy a quiet moment without talking about business?" asked Kevin. His face was completely straight.

"Kevin, the problem is that I have known you too long and that mumbo jumbo reply really does not wash," smiled Beta.

"Ok, you win! I wanted to ask you the reason that you felt I should be trailed throughout Tuscany," said Kevin, his forehead crunching into multiple waves of skin.

"Sorry, old friend, what are you talking about?" asked Beta.

"Bart, let's not play games. She was great but not perfect." Kevin knew he had just called the bluff.

"Ok, ok! I was trying to get Simon to you and needed to know where you were at all times. How did you pick it?" asked Beta. His top agent never failed to impress him.

"Beppe told me about the conversation between himself, Simon and Chiara. As a waitress, she knew far too much about me. I also found her a tad too interested in an old man's life," smiled Kevin.

"So, I guess that you have now filled in the gaps?" assumed Beta.

Kevin nodded and took a sip. "Her grandfather, Corporal Grant, was killed in the Falklands War while he was carrying a wounded lieutenant over his shoulders. Despite having a bullet penetrate his lungs, he somehow found the strength to get up and carry the wounded soldier another few hundred meters until he reached the medevac point. along the way getting another bullet lodged in his shoulder. By the time the helicopter arrived at the medical evacuation point, he was dead, but the lieutenant was not. Corporal Grant left behind a wife and a young son. The son, possibly because of unresolved anger, got himself mixed with the wrong circle of friends and might have been involved in some gang warfare. Although it is not confirmed, young Thomas Grant might have been the one to have harmed the leader of a rival gang. This is where the story gets hazy. But I did find a handwritten note in the archives that says T Grant to Oz." He sipped again from his glass and continued his narrative.

"After some digging I found out that the now not-so-young Grant was living in Australia, with a change of name to Anthony Frenzi. He was married to a Samantha Del'Capenna and father to a girl called Chiara. I also found out that Thomas, or Anthony, completed a few degrees and started his own consultancy company, although I can't tell what type of consultancy it was. Quite a few years ago now, whilst on a holiday in Spain, he was killed by a car bomb. There is an article in a local newspaper mentioning a witnesses seeing a foreign, blonde man diving on top of his friend as the blast went off and paying the ultimate price for his bravery. The article also mentioned the disgust of the witness that the blonde man's friend, who incidentally looks like he received some kind of facial wound, simply got up and walked away with no apparent concern about the friend who had just saved his life and lost his own. Did I miss anything?"

"I don't know what you expect me to say," commented Beta who had catapulted down into an abyss of his own thoughts.

"Then perhaps you can tell me again how you received that scar on your right cheek?" asked Kevin.

"Ok, ok! You got me. I was the lieutenant who was rescued by Corporal Grant. After Thomas was killed, I felt guilty for again being the factor that facilitated the death of a Grant family member. As Anthony, or Thomas, was dying, he made me promise to look after his wife and daughter. Since then, I have paid for Chiara's schooling and provided Samantha with an allowance. I also visit them once a year."

"Wow. Remind me not to become your friend. It seems far too risky!" joked Kevin.

"Last year Chiara wanted to know what happened to her dad, so I told her," continued Beta, ignoring Kevin's joke.

"Was Anthony on our payroll?"

"No, he was a professor of criminology at Melbourne University. I flew him to Spain to offer him a job. I think the bombing was purely coincidental and not targeted at me. Anthony watched the car do a handbrake turn in the square and as the flash of the bomb appeared, he dived on top of me. The rear door of the car blew off and hit him in the head. Glass shrapnel made a mess of his back. He died a few minutes later."

Both men sat quietly, contemplating the events.

Finally, Kevin spoke. "I often think that whatever the reasons we find ourselves in this secret world, they are often not the same ones that explain why we stay."

"I agree," Beta nodded. "We stay because we see what is out there and we want to make the world a better place. Even if that sometimes means we have to become as ugly as the part of the world we are trying to improve."

"So, Chiara is not on the books?" asked Kevin.

"Not really. She wants to be. She initially was driven to do law and become a prosecutor. But once she found out what I do – or at least sort of what I do – and learned the details about the terrorist group who detonated the bomb, she became quite motivated to join us. I sent her to San Gimignano as a trial mission. The reality is that I do not want her in harm's way. I have caused enough pain to that family. I do not want to add another person's name to the list."

"I understand," Kevin said. "I feel the same way about Simon. But they are their own people and have their own will. Chances are that there is nothing we can do to change their minds. It certainly seems that way with Simon." He sighed, reflecting on Simon's ordeal. "So we do the next best thing. We keep them close and try to protect them."

"So you think I should recruit her?" Beta asked.

Kevin had been impressed by Chiara's performance in Italy. "I am actually thinking of having her in the academy," he conceded. "But also keeping her off the radar. Don't register her as a member of MI6."

"You are really worried about the mole aren't you?"

"Bart, this is really serious. The details of Agent 2C's mission was on was strictly need-to-know basis. Either someone close to you is a mole or there is someone who has access to our missions vault," replied Kevin. His gut feeling told him a mole was the most likely explanation.

"I guess I could simply assign her to the academy," Beta reflected. "The existence of academy itself is only known to seven people, other than the teenagers, and it is completely privately funded. It would mean that she could feel part of the MI6 family, but be somewhat shielded behind the secrecy screen that we have in place."

"It will not be long before the academy gets noticed by our own and other agencies," Kevin warned, instinctively thinking of possible measures to delay such a revelation from happening. "Where is Chiara now?"

"Bordeaux."

"What is she doing in France?"

"Research."

"She's looking for the head of the terrorist group who detonated the car bomb?" asked Kevin.

"She's already found them. But she understands that she needs to do more than that."

"So now she is looking for the financier," reasoned Kevin.

"The organisation in question has legitimate businesses that are set up for money laundering purposes. One of these is the winery where Chiara is working as a casual employee."

"Is she getting anywhere?"

"Unfortunately not. The managers of the winery are completely oblivious about who the owners are. We struggled to find out as well. It is a waterfall structure of companies owning trusts that own companies. Took us six months to trace it back to the parent company."

"Do I know which syndicate is at the head of the organisation?" enquired Kevin.

"Yes. Want to take a guess?" asked Beta with a smile.

"Why do I think it is the very same as the one that was targeted in Bernie's mission?"

"Because, Kevin, you are a very intuitive operator and your instincts are remarkably accurate," grinned Beta.

"Can you relocate Chiara to Spain?"

"Your plan?" asked Beta.

"The two boys are still at each other's throats. I think Deepa has stirred a few emotions in them and might be adding fuel to the fire. Ideally, I need a fourth person there. That gives me the ability to set up two teams."

"Chiara could become an excellent mission controller," affirmed Beta.

"Yes. Problem is that the report shows both of the boys like both of the girls, so however I pair them up, it could lead to distractions getting in the way of missions."

"Anything on how the girls feel about the boys?" asked Beta.

"So far I only have psych evaluation on Deepa. I think she is very fond of Simon. But earlier on, Lau sent me a message saying Deepa and Stephen had some sort of an emotional clash. He thinks that with some mentoring, they might form a good partnership. But he is also Deepa's dad and I am thinking that he is subconsciously trying to create some distance between her and Simon. I can only guess why," shrugged Kevin.

"Either way, the two observations justify his recommendation," stated Beta.

Kevin reflected for a few moments before replying. Putting any four teenagers together was always likely to result emotional issues of some kind, but it was especially probably with these four in particular. It was a matter of trying to find the better options.

"I suppose pairing Deepa with Stephen could work. Especially if she has possible feelings for him, which means we have a natural emotional separation in place between her and Stephen. But what if Stephen develop feelings for her? That would surely trigger further aggression from him towards Simon," mused Kevin.

"What about Simon's relationship with Chiara?"

"That is hard to tell. Beppe told me that Simon acted like a little rooster around her back in San Gimignano, but he struggled to determine if the feeling was mutual. I think she is highly driven and not someone who lets emotions get in her way. Given that I really don't know anything about her, other than she tricked me, I think that pairing her with Simon is just the better option." Kevin looked expectantly at Beta. No matter what they decided, predicting how teenagers would act was almost impossible, he thought.

"I agree. She was able to fool you and will also keep the other three on their toes," winked Beta.

"Ok then, it is decided." Kevin did not sound totally convinced, but he did not have many choices.

"Look after her," Beta said unexpectedly.

A little puzzled by this unusual request, Kevin stood up. "I will," he promised as the two friends shook hands.

Brunch was a very quiet affair. Deepa and her father attempted to exchange a few words across the table, but they were mostly encapsulated by the silent conversation going on between Stephen and Simon, who sat on opposing sides and glared at each other. The atmosphere around the table was volatile and both boys seemed ready to exchange blows. Deepa and her father looked on, perplexed by the hostility that emanated from the two boys.

Stephen hated the predicament that he was now in. Since starting in MI6 not that long ago, he had though that achieving his secret mission would be 'a walk in the park'. Very soon though, his encounter with Simon turned his life into one source of frustration after the next, including almost plunging to his death from the London Eye. Stephen really did not know much about Simon. He firmly believed that he himself was much better than Simon and did not have much of an issue with competing against him. But Deepa thought Simon was a good guy. Actually, Deepa liked Simon, which made him even more insufferable in Stephen's eyes. Thinking about today's encounter with him, Stephen finally decided that he really did dislike him. Clearly, Simon was manipulating Deepa into thinking he was a nice guy, when in actual fact he was mendacious. In Stephen's mind Simon was also highly emotional, unreliable, deceptive and a risk to his own personal mission. The conclusion was simple. Simon had to go. The only problem was that Stephen's own recent emotional outbursts made him look like a questionable character. Stephen had to get rid of Simon, but subtly. These thoughts kept churning in his mind as he sat across the table from Simon.

For his part, Simon struggled to understand why MI6 was interested in training Stephen. He was highly emotional, driven by what appeared to be a hidden agenda, did not follow orders, was a careless and a bully, and, given that he tried to shoot Simon on the London Eye, apparently willing to kill without hesitation! Stephen could prove to be an impediment to Simon's ability to finally see his dad. He had to find a way to get rid of him, but in a subtle way. Any direct confrontation could result in MI6 getting rid of him instead of Stephen.

After watching the silent combat between the two boys, Inspector Lau finally had enough. "Kids, like it or not, you all got to make this work. If any of you fail, training program cancelled, lah? You about to go through toughest training. You will be put at harm's way. So, you fail, you will be looking for work, or feeding worms, lah.". He folded his arms across his chest.

"You are right, Inspector. Simon, I'm sorry. I'm happy to move on," Stephen suddenly stated, offering his hand across the table.

Simon knew with every inch of his body that this was a trick, but he also knew that he had no evidence against Stephen. Yet. "Agreed," responded Simon, playing along for the moment and shaking Stephen's hand.

When they returned to the apartment, they commenced their lessons. Surveillance was first, as the inspector felt that knowing how to follow someone made it easier later on to learn how to spot someone following them and thus be predisposed to understand the best way to lose a tail. The formal dining room of the apartment was converted into a lecture room. Other than the old paintings on the wall, the dusty smelling burgundy carpet and the wall unit, which were all left in place, the room was emptied. The dining room table was replaced by high school style desks and chairs. The desks faced the outer wall of the room, where a white board and projector were set up next to an external window. .

The classes ran similarly to academic lectures, with training objectives for each class outlined upfront and the learning outcomes covered at the end. Every fifty minutes, the teenagers were given a ten minute break. The pace of the lessons was very quick. The inspector explained that they had to train their brains to pick things up quicker than they had ever done before. The classes delivered the training material, while evening study periods allowed them to review and remember the information. They were also told that each night they had to memorise one hundred Spanish words and would be tested by their language instructor the following morning. At the end of the five days allocated to this phase of training, they would sit a practical test.

"Inspector, what will the test entail?" asked Simon a couple of days into the training. He ignored his grumbling stomach. It was early evening and they all felt hungry.

"You will work in pairs on a specific mission, where you'll be tested on what I've taught you," stated the inspector.

"Pairs?" sniggered Stephen looking around the room, wondering if this self-satisfied little man could really teach him anything.

"Are we rotating the partnerships?" interrupted Deepa before Stephen could make any more remarks. She thought switching the pairs was a good idea, as she would have a turn with each of the boys and they themselves would eventually be forced to get on in order to work together.

"No. You be setup with permanent partners. Until you prove good spy, you not have accreditation to operate alone," replied Inspector Lau in his broken English.

"Who is the fourth person?" asked Simon, frowning slightly as he glanced from Deepa to Stephen.

"That would be me."

Without turning, Simon immediately recognised the female voice from behind him. All three teenagers pivoted in their chairs to look at the speaker, who was leaning casually against the doorframe.

"Hey there," winked Chiara directly at Simon. "Bet this comes as a surprise!"

"A pleasant one," replied Simon with a smile that just managed to distract most eyes away from his blushing. Chiara was as attractive as he remembered her. Her long brown hair swung below her waist as she turned to Stephen.

"Speaking of surprises, I never thought I'd be running into you again. Stephen, isn't it?" Chiara took in Stephen's orderly appearance. His jeans and t-shirt were designer label, indicating that he had money.

"Hi," was the only word Stephen managed to say. Was it possible that he was blushing too?

The girl now turned her attention to Deepa. "Hi, I'm Chiara," she smiled. "I'm so pleased to see I'll not be the only girl in this course." It was true, too. Chiara was glad of Deepa's presence. She noted Deepa's very large brown eyes and long black hair tied back into a ponytail. At least I won't be the centre of attention here, she thought Chiara as she walked up to Deepa stood up to shake hands.

"Nice to meet you. I'm Deepa. That's our instructor and my dad." She gestured towards her father. "I'm relieved to get some added moral support in this testosterone overloaded group." Deepa's grin was genuine, but she had not failed to observe the blushing that Chiara's presence had triggered on Simon's cheeks. She tried to quell the sting of jealousy she felt.

"Good evening, Inspector. I have been given this package and a note for you from the Director," said Chiara, holding up a small paper-wrapped bundle and looking closely at Inspector Lau. She needed to know these people well if she was to succeed in her objective.

"Nice to meet you, and thank you," he replied, as he accepted the package and letter from her.

Everyone remained silent while Inspector Lau read the letter. Every few seconds, Stephen took a quick glance first at Deepa and then at Chiara. Deepa seemed only interested in Simon and kept glancing at him to check if his blushing was subsiding. She wondered why he looked so nervous in front of Chiara. Maybe there had once been something between them? Simon, in turn, pretended to look at the inspector, although his focus was slightly to his left, where Chiara was now standing. Although aware that she was being watched by her new peers, Chiara simply stood with her back to them and focused on trying to read the words of the letter through the paper the inspector held and attempting to interpret his expressions.

"Ok. Looks like you have new text books. You read cover to cover as you will be tested in two days. We are also having a guest visitor tomorrow. Let's break up for dinner, then continue with our classes, lah," the inspector finally said. He gave the teenagers a knowing look.

All four welcomed the break and walked quickly to the kitchen to see what was for dinner. When they entered, they found the table was set but instead of plates, there were recipes typed on A4 pages placed at each of their seats.

"You cook each night. Good time to think about what just learnt, and you get to know one another," smiled the inspector from the door.

Although disappointed about having to wait longer for their food, the four saw this task as another opportunity to prove themselves. They picked up the recipes and commenced the preparation of dinner.

"Master Stephen, maybe this time not so much carrots," joked Inspector Lau. He winked at the teenager, who winked back at him. Simon noticed this and wondered what had happened in the apartment before he had arrived. If Stephen was already chummy with the inspector, his task would become more difficult.

The teenagers quickly established that there were only two recipes on the table. This meant they had to work in pairs. Tonight, by pure chance, the boys had to work together.

"Before you start, I have little something to keep mouths busy," called Inspector Lau, who proceeded to the fridge and removed with a flourish a cheese and ham platter delivered earlier by a local catering company. "Feel free to nibble on this, lah."

"Thank you!" came the cry from Simon, Stephen and Deepa, who wasted no time in shoving ham and cheese into their mouths while Chiara silently continued her preparation.

Soon all the teenagers were busy cooking. They were tasked to prepare a traditional steak and salad dinner. The boys were in charge of the lettuce and potato salads. Over the course of cooking the steaks, Deepa could not help herself, and interrogated Chiara about her background, family, and most importantly, how she knew the boys. Despite feeling a streak of jealousy towards her, Deepa liked Chiara. She was friendly and did not seem to be overly interested in Simon.

Dinner was a silent affair, with only the two girls exchanging a few words. Each teenager was immersed in their own thoughts. After they had eaten, everyone retired to their bedrooms for some intense studying. After glancing about at the small room she was to occupy, Chiara made her way to Simon's bedroom.

"Are you ok? Anything I can help you with?" Chiara heard Deepa's voice behind her as she was about to knock on Simon's door. She turned, surprised not to have noticed the open bedroom door directly opposite Simon's. I really must be more observant, Chiara reprimanded herself.

Deepa was sitting on the floor with her back supported by a small couch. Around her were scattered notes, pens and her study book. Chiara walked in and looked around the room. Deepa had numerous family pictures on her bedside table and desk. In the middle of her bed she had a well-worn teddy bear.

"I was hoping Simon could spare some of his precious time to explain these lecture notes from the classes I missed today," explained Chiara, focusing her attention on the girl sitting on the floor.

"I'd be happy to help," offered Deepa. "Simon might also be struggling a little as he spent much of the class time daydreaming about something else." It wouldn't hurt to put some distance between Simon and Chiara.

"Oh? Is something up with him?" asked Chiara.

"Not sure. Well, actually, he just lost his mum and doesn't know where his dad is," replied Deepa. As she spoke, she felt herself struggling not to slip into depressing thoughts about the loss of her own mother. Still, she enjoyed the fact that she knew more about Simon than Chiara.

"Looks like that the two of us have come from similar situations. Poor Simon, he'll be stuck in that world for a few years," replied Chiara, almost talking to herself.

"Yes," was all that Deepa could say.

"What about Stephen?" enquired Chiara.

"I have no idea. He's a closed book. I think he does still have both of his parents, though. But good luck trying to get him to open up!" declared Deepa. Her frustration was clear in her tone of voice.

"Really? He doesn't even open up with you?" asked Chiara.

"What do you mean by that?"

"Well, I've noticed the way he looks..." She broke off. "Never mind! Let's study." The two girls had only just met and Chiara realised that embarrassing Deepa like this was not an appropriate way to begin their acquaintance.

"Oh, ok, let's," replied Deepa. She hadn't known what Chiara was about to say , but her gut feeling told her to go with the switch of topic. She glanced across the corridor towards Simon's door as she and Chiara settled in to their books.

The sun was barely up. Simon knew that the days ahead were going to be quite intense with little spare time. Today might be one of those few occasions when he would be able to go for a swim. He walked out of the apartment and took a few seconds to orient himself, then commenced the run towards the main beach. Glancing over his shoulder, he could see that he was not far from La Sagrada Famiglia, the famous large Roman Catholic church designed by Gaudi. The weather was perfect and the streets were quiet with only the odd car passing by. He found it surprising that the city was not already buzzing with early traffic. Then again, he also realised that he did not know what day of the week it was. Perhaps it was the weekend.

The run did not take him long. In just over thirty minutes, he arrived at the main beach. Apart from one person who was standing and staring out at sea, he had this jewel all to himself. Simon stopped a few metres from the sand and took off his few items of clothing off. He folded them and laid them neatly on top of his runners. Wearing only his Speedos, he walked to where the sand kissed the warm Balearic Sea.

"I see you are also planning to venture out into the water," called the man who stood quietly looking out to sea.

"Yes, while I can," replied Simon, feeling a tad surprise to have bumped into a fellow English person. He stared at the man for a second. He was wearing a thin black wet suit that looked like it was made of a material similar to Lycra with shark skin patterns all over it. A set of goggles rested on his forehead and his wrist bore a big diver's watch.

"May I join you?" the gentleman asked.

Simon found the idea disagreeable. This was the time of the day when he most wanted to be alone with the memories of his father. He was about to politely decline the request when realisation hit him like a tsunami.

"You don't have to agree, Simon," said the Director, reading the young man's body language.

"Actually, I would like to," Simon replied quickly, seeing an opportunity to spend time with someone who could perhaps tell him stories about his dad.

"Thank you. Are you planning to swim directly out to sea or along the coast?" asked the Director, although he well knew his son's swimming habits.

"Directly out. I enjoy the solitude. I like the small thrill of being left completely to my own devices. And it's sort of a tradition," Simon explained.

"Tradition?"

"I mean habit." He corrected himself, not wanting to explain that swimming directly out to sea was his way to get closer to his dad.

"Ok, then. Let's go! The water is not going to get any cooler," joked the Director as he headed into the waves.

Back on the sand, Stephen watched Simon follow the strange man into the sea. He had heard Simon leave the house and decided to follow him. He did not trust Simon and wanted to find out where he went this early in the morning. After following Simon all the way to the beach, he had watched him and the strange man exchange a few words before they ran together into the sea. He was sorry he not close enough to make out what they were saying. Maybe they are swimming out so they can't be heard, he thought. Stephen remained hidden for a while, looking out to the water, before he gave up and jogged back to the apartment. He may not have learned much this morning, but he would keep even a closer eye on Simon now.

Simon and the Director quickly broke into a freestyle stroke and swam straight out towards the big emptiness. Their rhythm was very similar and both gained energy from each other's presence. After about thirty minutes of strong, steady swimming, the Director conceded that he was getting old and called out for a pause.

"Sorry, Simon. If you want to continue, please go ahead. But I am afraid that this old body needs some respite!" he smiled, now floating a few metres from the teenager.

"It's ok. I was actually taking advantage of the fact that you're here and making the most of it. I was only going to have a very quick swim. But since you are here, I figured that Inspector Lau couldn't get too angry at me for being late to breakfast. So I was going to swim for as long as you did," laughed Simon. The Director joined in his

Adrian Monico

laughter.

"Can I ask you something?" called Simon, a few minutes later. He didn't want the opportunity to slip by.

"Sure."

"Do you know my dad?"

"Very well," replied the Director after a short pause.

"He's ok?"

"Yes," Kevin replied. He dropped his face toward the water as he struggled to hold back the emotion. He wondering how he could evade any of his son's direct questions without lying to him. Simon, however, remained silent, not knowing what to ask next.

Kevin finally broke the uncomfortable silence that had lengthened between them. "He knows how tough this is on you, Simon. He is very proud of how you are handling it." There was another pause.

"Do you have family?" asked Simon, taking a different angle.

"I did. But I am alone now."

"Oh, I'm sorry," Simon said. It was clear he just touched on a painful topic and he felt guilty for intruding into the man's life.

"It's ok. The sad truth is that we all volunteer to join the service, but we have no idea of what the service will take from us. There are very few of us who manage to maintain some form of family life. Many have tried, many more will try, but extremely few will succeed."

"So why do all of you stay in? Don't you value your loved ones more than the job?" Simon's questions came out abruptly.

"That is a good question," mused Kevin. "It starts as an adventure. But bit by bit you get to be exposed to a horrible side of humanity. At first, these criminals, we think of them as being inhumane. They walk our world and destroy families, communities, companies, countries. They tend to operate in the poorest parts of the world. They exploit the weakest, most desperate people. With each mission, you learn how they keep increasing their power bases in poorer nations. They themselves, however, have never been in the slums where these desperate people live. They have minions to do their dirty work. They stay in expensive hotels and live in the wealthiest places in the world. These same people who have the power to wipe out whole communities are presenting themselves as law-abiding citizens. Underneath this façade, they exercise their muscles in the UK as an act of defiance against our laws. It becomes more and more obvious the more you find out about them. Around this time, agents start to feel despondent. They begin to wonder if maybe it is time for them to get out, as they have already spent years away from their love ones. However, it is not so straightforward. They are faced with difficult other moral issues. They've spent years working in teams that have become like family. Agents worry that the people who stay behind will not be able to deal with these ruthless criminals by themselves. They'll become more vulnerable and be put at risk." The Director paused, aware of his son's gaze concentrated on him.

"Then there is also the fear that the family the agents want to go back are also vulnerable and at-risk. The worst thought is that they might one day die from an 'act of defiance'. So they spend many sleepless nights staring at their loved ones and contemplating if it is better for them to leave the agency and live with the idea that their family's safety is in someone else's hands, or to stay in and go after these criminals and try to protect their families from afar. In the end, most agents choose the latter. But the problem is that just as one criminal is removed, another takes his place. So, after many years spent believing that one more mission will finally make the world a better and a safer place, the few agents who do not die along the way go home to a family that has moved on without them. Not only that, the agent will never be able to tell their family why the years they've been away was a sacrifice worth making. In addition, once they leave the agency, they are also forgotten about by their other family, their colleagues and teams at MI6. Of course, there are also agents who simply love the thrill of being a spy. To them, it's all a game, played against spies from other countries."

Simon remained quiet for a moment, thinking that these words might one day be the ones his dad would say to him. He understood it all, but still felt angry and hurt. His dad abandoned he and his mum for a job that someone else could have done. He was never there when Simon needed him and he would never know the loneliness and desperation he had felt over the years thinking that his father was dead. He had to take on the responsibility of caring for his mother at a young age. In effect, Simon had lost his childhood because of his father's career choice.

A small wave slapped across his face, bringing him back to the present. "So... is that what happened with my dad?" he asked.

"Yes and no. Your dad was already in the service. In a way, he never chose to be part of it all. He was born into it. Also, if I'm not mistaken, he did get out and chose his family over the service. But your family were being targeted so he had to get back in. He really had no choice."

"There is always a choice! From what mum told me, he just decided he was going back. He might have made that choice, but we did not. I am 17 years old and all I have are a few fragmented memories of him. I was told that he was dead! I mourned him every day of my life. Do you know what that feels like?" Simon was shouting now. His anger carried across the waves.

"From what I understand, the sacrifice your dad made by going back into service allowed you to have some normality in your upbringing instead of your family spending all their time on the run, thinking every day that one of you might be killed," reasoned Kevin, a little defensively.

"Please don't take this the wrong way. I am grateful to hear what you have to say," began Simon. "But if you look into whatever file I'm sure MI6 has on my family, you'll find that we ended up spending our lives on the run anyway! We moved regularly at very short notice. I have spent my life being the new kid in the school, with no friends as we never stayed anywhere long enough for me to make any. I spent my youth jumping from school to school being alone. I was always the one who got picked on by a mob of kids who got a kick out of being bullies. I spent days trying to hide from them or hiding the bruises so Mum wouldn't see it. At one point, I even had some assassin sent to kidnap me! I was caught in a full-on ambush only a few months ago, where I almost died trying to find my father. I fell down a quarry at high speed. I got shot at by the same teenager that I am now supposed to get along with. I almost fell off the London Eye. So, please tell me how my father's sacrifice was the best choice for me?" he screamed.

Kevin waited, feeling the impact of his son's fury. "I think that if you were in your father's shoes, you would understand his choices," he said at last.

"Why are you defending him?" demanded Simon.

Simon Eady - The Teenage Spy

Why couldn't this man understand?

The two of them bobbed up and down in the water, neither saying a word. The only sound was the splash of the waves.

"You are right, Simon. You have been dealt a hard deal. So have your mum and dad." Kevin kept his voice calm. He wanted to end the conversation before his inner emotions gave him away.

"Sorry, Director, for my aggressiveness," muttered Simon. "We should probably head back." He would not feel sorry for himself. He was now on a mission and could not waste any time looking back at what could have been.

"Good call. I wouldn't want Inspector Lau to get angry with me," winked Kevin.

They eased into a synchronised stroke. The pace of their swim back to shore was considerably slower than when they first struck out. Despite the tension of their conversation, neither really wanted to end the swim.

"Why the weird wetsuit?" asked Simon, keeping his head out of the water as he swam.

"It's something MI6 made for me. It is made from an ultra-light material lined with very small electrical wires that generate a pulse to keep sharks at bay. If I need it to, it can also generate heat and self-inflate to act as a buoyancy jacket."

"Wow! That's cool. Where's the electricity coming from? I didn't see a battery pack."

"The electricity comes from very long, thin battery cells located in the lining along my arms and chest. They act as light shield in the event that agents get involved into a fight or get shot at."

"Like an armour-plated vest," observed Simon, feeling impressed.

"Yes, a very light version of it. We are currently working on using Kevlar as the lining of the battery packs, hopefully providing better protection."

"That is seriously a cool suit!"

"It's certainly one of the perks of the job," laughed the Director, pleased by Simon's excitement.

"Who comes up with these ideas?" asked Simon curiously.

"We have a very clever bunch of scientists. They get ideas from reviewing missions and identifying what equipment or innovations could have helped. Or they attend to ideas that agents themselves come up with."

"Really? So if I have an idea for a cool gadget, I can ask to have it built?" asked Simon. He already had a few ideas.

"Within reason. After all, we are limited by what science has discovered, and we do try to keep our research costs within allocation."

"How much money do we spend on research?"

"Sorry, that is a secret only known by a few. I wouldn't worry. The reality is that we never spend it. In the last three years we seem to have had a shortage of innovative ideas," reflected the Director.

"I've a few. Could you take them back for me?"

"Sure. I would love to. This is an area that I like to get involved in. I was the person who actually designed this wetsuit," responded Kevin.

"That's amazing! But why did you come up with an idea for a wetsuit if you don't really swim?"

"Good question,'" replied Kevin. Simon's question had him feeling like he was a fish caught in a net. "We had a few missions where agents found themselves confronted by sharks. Many years ago, I also had an encounter with a shark that completely scared me. So I decided to find a solution."

Simon thought about that and himself at the image of the Director panicking when confronted by the shark.

"Aren't you scared of sharks?" asked Kevin, remembering their shark encounter.

"The thought is there. But my father instilled in me a confidence about the matter that allows me to set aside fear," replied Simon shortly. He did not want to dwell on the topic and run the risk of getting emotional again.

"You are lucky, Simon. My fears are numbed by the toys that I carry," joked Kevin.

For the rest of the swim, both agents were quietly absorbed in their own thoughts, treasuring the time together for different reasons. Once they stood on solid ground again, the Director offered to drive them back to the apartment.

Chiara had woken up very early. The apartment was quiet as she walked to the kitchen. Everyone must still be asleep, she concluded. Simon's bedroom door was slightly ajar and peeked in. He was not there. His bed was made and his jeans and t-shirt were draped on top of his bed. Chiara entered and looked around. It looked like a typical teenaged boy's room. Some magazines lay on his bedside table and his study books sat on his desk along with other pieces of stationery. A framed picture of a family – mum, dad and a small boy – was also on his desk. Chiara opened a drawer and pulled out a handful of postcards. Tourist destinations did not interest her so she put them back. She looked around once more, then silently exited the room, leaving the door slightly ope.

Further down the hall, she stopped in front of Stephen's door. Chiara tapped silently and waited. Nobody answered, so tapped louder. No reply. She opened the door and poked her head in. This room was also empty, so she crept in. For a moment she was taken aback. Everything was in meticulous order. No article of clothing could be seen anywhere. The table beside the bed held only a lamp. Stephen's study books were neatly placed on one corner of the desk. Two blue pens, two red pens, a highlighter, a ruler, a black lead pencil and an eraser were all perfectly lined up in the centre of the desk. Nothing else was in sight as she looked around the room.

Curiously, Chiara opened his desk drawers. They were empty. No papers, no letters, no other stationery, no pictures. She then went to his wardrobe. Stephen's clothes were hung neatly. Money, she thought again, noting their quality. Chiara frowned. The room contained nothing personal. She found a couple of spy books in a small suitcase at the bottom of the wardrobe. Everything looked too perfect to be normal. She smiled to herself, reflecting on the differences between her three peers.

"Ah, you two just in time for my very popular eggs!" called Inspector Lau, as Simon and Kevin entered the kitchen a little while later. He was serving breakfast to the three teenagers who sat around the table.

"Popular? Really? Who told you that?" Kevin replied as he moved offering his hand to his colleague.

"Just about anyone who has had my eggs! Especially people that find out the alternative option is to cook their own!" winked Lau. He shifted the frying pan from his right to his left hand and accepted the handshake.

"Ah, those eggs. I've heard they are the best in Spain!" replied Kevin with a big grin.

"Would you prefer them after a shower?" asked the inspector. Both Kevin and Simon still had wet hair. Inspector Lau interpreted the wetness as sweat.

"If it's ok, I'll have breakfast now," replied Simon.

"We ran into each other at the beach. I asked Simon if I could join him for a swim," explained the Director.

Stephen looked suspiciously first at Simon then at Kevin. Simon was friends with the Director? This was not good news. Now it would be even harder to get rid of him. He stood up alongside Deepa and Chiara and shook the Director's hand. The older man greeted each of them by name. He spent much of his breakfast answering questions from Deepa and Chiara about the length of their training, the expectations he had of them, when their first mission would be, whether they would get the same scheduled leave at the academy as they would have at university, what salaries they would earn, when they would get to play with the cool toys agents were known to carry, if their training would take them to other countries, and how long before they would no longer have to work in teams. Stephen and Simon did not ask questions, but listened to the Director's responses.

"Ok, no more barrage of questions. Class in fifteen minutes, lah" interrupted the inspector, staring specifically at his daughter when he said the word 'barrage'.

"Ok, ok," replied Deepa with a big smile.

"I'll help with the dishes," offered the Director.

Inspector Lau nodded, "Thank you. That'd be great."

"So, already getting chummy with the Director?" joked Chiara, slapping Simon on the back as they were walking back to their rooms.

"Leave him alone, Chiara," grinned Deepa. "Simon needs all the help he can get to keep up with us." She put an arm around Simon's shoulder and stared back at Chiara with a big smile.

Stephen's eyes locked onto Deepa's arm as it curled around his rival's neck. Girls! He never had any time for them. They were so silly most of the time.

"Come on, don't be mean," laughed Simon. "I simply asked the Director to give you girls some concessions as I felt it was unfair that you had to compete against us boys."

"Oh, really?" replied Deepa. Her eyes were still fixed on Chiara and the two of them seemed to be having a silent conversation. With one movement, the girls peeled away from Simon and headed for their rooms.

Stephen waited until he was alone with Simon, then he hissed at him, "You think you're so smart, don't you? Sucking up to the Director, acting like an idiot with the girls. I'm here to join MI6 and you're just wasting your time fooling around. One day soon we'll finish what we started, only this time there will be nobody there to stop me!"

Simon was taken aback by Stephen's open hostility. He thought that they could keep their animosity hidden whilst in training. He was wrong. With narrowed eyes, he replied, "I don't like you and you don't like me. But I'm willing to offer a truce until we leave this place. Otherwise we may find that both of us get thrown out. Agreed?" He waited, observing the antagonism in the other boy's face. Finally, Stephen nodded once and pushed roughly past him.

Later, as Inspector Lau and the Director stood in the classroom, the girls walked in and sat at their respective desks. Both men looked up, expecting the boys to follow Deepa and Chiara.

"Girls, you lost someone?" asked the Director seeing the class half empty.

"Sorry, Director. Last time we saw the boys they seemed to be having a private D&M," shrugged Chiara.

"D&M?" asked Lau.

"Deep and Meaningful," said a male voice from the back of the class. Stephen and Simon both walked into the room, looking displeased.

"I see," said the inspector. "Got distracted along the way?" he asked, noting that Simon was still wearing his running gear.

Simon opened his mouth to reply but closed it again without saying anything. The Director interjected. "Ok, this next phase of your training will one day make the difference between your life and your death," he began.

For the next five days, the Director and Inspector Lau took turns teaching the classes. They continued covering theoretical and practical lessons in surveillance and counter surveillance, along with Spanish and the ongoing memorising of Field Signals of a Spy. The Director also took them to a nearby rifle range to practice their shooting and spent at least two hours a day teaching them unarmed combat. A morning run and swim session were added to their training. Although at first did not like the idea, Simon found himself enjoying the company for these activities. Deepa joined in on the run, but sat out for the swim. Already a good swimmer, she had a phobia about sharks and her instructors did not see any gain in pushing her at this point.

With so much to learn, the four teenagers did not have any time to think about anything else but their assignments. The shaky truce between Simon and Stephen continued and all of the agents-in-training seemed to become accustomed to be working in teams and relying on one another. Stephen's feelings for Deepa were still confusing. He still did not try to analyse these how he felt, but found himself sitting next to her in class and thoughts of her often popped into his mind when he least expected.

One morning, same as always, everyone was up early, ready for their run and swim session. The teenagers were a little sleepy after spending another late night memorising Spanish words and testing one another. Over the course of the past few days, Stephen and Deepa, and Simon and Chiara, were paired up as study partners. At first Deepa was disappointed that she did not have Simon as her partner. Stephen was still closed book to her, but every now and again she would get a small glimpse into his life. Her biggest surprise came when he had unintentionally mentioned that he came from a cold, loveless family.

"Good morning, all," called Inspector Lau, as he pushed a bicycle out of the front door.

"Good morning," they dutifully replied.

"Today we running twenty kilometres to another beach, lah," he instructed.

"We?" smiled Chiara, pointing to the bike.

"Right! By 'we', I mean 'you'," replied the inspector returning her smile.

"I tried to convince him to join you on the run, but he chose the easy way out," commented the Director. He was dressed in a suit and held a medium sized cardboard box.

"And I gather you are not coming either?" asked Simon, trying to not to feel disappointed.

"Sorry, Simon. I need to go and lead a rescue mission. If all goes well, I'll be back in less than a week," the Director explained.

"What's in the box?" asked Deepa, always curious.

"This, my dear, contains a gift from me to you. Actually, there's one for all of you. It's a special wetsuit I've had custom made for you. It has a unique technology built in it to keep sharks away." He looked at Deepa. "Today, I would like you to swim with your peers," he said.

Deepa felt her stomach lurch. "Ok," she replied hesitantly. She hoped the suit would work.

"Simon, I have implemented the modifications that you suggested. It now has a way to fold itself into a small backpack."

"That's great! Thank you, Director," replied Simon. Excitement was plain on his face, but he was still observing Deepa's concerned expression.

Stephen looked at Simon in surprise. He had also noted Deepa's worried look. "You can swim next to me if you'd like," he said to her. "I'm much more appetising shark bait."

"I'll be by your side as well. I'm not afraid to confront a shark!" added Simon quickly. Deepa seemed to relax a bit. She smiled at the boys, not noticing Chiara turn away to hide her own amusement at the exchange.

The Director handed over the wetsuits, which were cleverly folded up into backpacks. A black car pulled up next to them. "Ok, kids, this is my ride. I will hopefully see you in a week." He looked at Simon before adding, "Good luck!"

Moments before the car took off, Deepa walked up to the rear passenger door and knocked on the window. It lowering itself with a subtle hum.

"What is it, Deepa?" asked the Director.

"I'm not sure I can do this," she whispered.

Although Chiara, Stephen and Simon could all hear Deepa's words, they acted distracted and continued looking at their suits. Simon was the closest to the car and he turned his back so as not to accidentally make eye contact with Deepa. Inspector Lau also seemed preoccupied by something in an attempt to avoid adding any pressure onto his daughter.

"Deepa, you are a very determined young woman who is capable of anything. You may not think you can do this, but I know you can. The suit does work, I promise. I have tested it myself," the Director assured her. She continued to look doubtful and stared, embarrassed, at the ground. "If it's of any help, there is a trick to use when dealing with predators. Never show fear to them, as it will give them the confidence to attack."

Simon suddenly felt a cold chill crawl up his back.

"Ok. Thank you. Have a safe trip," replied Deepa dubiously.

"Take care," called the Director as he started raising his window.

Simon slowly turned toward the car. A second before the vehicle started moving, he looked directly into the Director's eyes. In that instant, Kevin knew the mistake he had made. The car moved away. Despite his urge to chase it down, Simon found himself completely paralysed by the shockwave of realisation.

The Director was his dad?

CHAPTER 4 - A Family Affair

The air was thick and sticky. A dark silhouette slithered between the shadows of the tall pine trees, wary of an ambush. Although he was almost certain that nobody had seen his entry into the country and forest, he knew that his arrival would most likely be expected. The mole in MI6 would have been busy. He trod cautiously, even though he speculated the noise factor was not a risk. A hand grenade could have gone off and not be heard above the ear-piercing song of thousands of cicadas. But experience had taught him never to be complacent. There could be sensors picking up different frequencies hidden amongst the trees. The forest was overcrowded by thick trunks and low vegetation, creating lots of dark areas for Shadow to slip into. He was now only a few hundred meters from the isolated Colombian house and needed to find a hideout to wait for the dusk.

So far, the mission had gone too perfectly. That always made Shadow apprehensive. He checked his automatic rifle and decided to leave the sedative needles as his primary defensive option. After all, this was a rescue and not an assassination mission. He extracted from his backpack a black aerosol can and proceeded to spray a white foam circle on a large bush that looked a bit like a blackberry. It only took a few seconds for the acid to eat a hole into the bush. He repeated the action a few more times until he had a cavity deep enough to crawl in. Shadow made a mental note to share with MI6 the new way he had found to use the acid foam. It was actually intended to cut through fences, non-reinforced doors and windows. He crawled in the opening and lay on his stomach with rifle in hand and an eye on his watch. He had three hours to wait until sunset. Three more hours to go over his plan again. That was plenty of time to go over numerous times every possible scenario he could envisage.

"How are you feeling Bernie?" asked the Consigliere's voice from behind the reinforced door. Bernie kept silent, looking fixedly at the chains that were shackled around his ankles and bolted to the floor at the centre of the room.

"Sorry about the chains, but you were warned and should not have tried to escape," the voice continued. Bernie wondered why he had been moved. He was, after all, the bait for a trap. It's true that he had tried to escape and warn the agent coming to rescue him, but his effort had failed. However, he was not beaten again nor killed. He was simply moved to another location. Why are they still keeping me alive? And what is the Consigliere up to? Bernie wondered.

"I see that you've moved me," Bernie finally replied in an attempt to gather information about his new whereabouts.

"I needed to set up a welcoming committee at the previous site," came the calm reply.

"But why move me to a location so far from the other one? Surely you realise the risks of being detected when moving hostages over long distances."

"Bernie, Bernie, Bernie," sighed the Consigliere's voice. "I know you are trying to get information out of me about your new location. How about you have a guess instead?"

"I was sedated. That means that you had to move me either through police or customs checkpoints. There is a certain familiarity about the smell of the air, which tells me that we now are in the northern hemisphere. Based on the time of the year and the current temperature, I'm guessing either in Europe or Russia. Looking at the amount of olive oil used in the food and the cold climate cheese and prosciutto that I just ate, I'm thinking that most likely we are either in Italy or one of the Baltic nations. I'm discarding Italy as their customs checkpoints have become more diligent of late. I can't smell salt in the air, so we are away from any coastline. I would take a guess and say either Croatia or Bosnia, with the latter being my gut feeling."

"I'm impressed. You have made several well-grounded assumptions. And I must say I do like your logic. But you will just have to wait and see if you are correct. That is if you come out of this alive," sneered the Consigliere as he sauntered away. He walked upstairs to his makeshift office. Deep in thought, he went over to the large window that overlooked the surrounding countryside. Green, undulating hills stretched into the distance, but the Consigliere did not stop to admire the tranquil scene.

"Are you going to change his meals around to confuse him?" a scratchy voice hissed from a dark corner of the room.

"Hello, Whisper. No, it would only verify that he was correct. But I was thinking to amuse myself and tomorrow serve him McDonalds," replied the Consigliere, turning to face the voice.

"Your gentlemen's code will be your demise. I would have gotten rid of him by now. Or just given him bread and water," criticised Whisper, although his repulsion towards the Consigliere was no worse than his feeling for most people.

"Maybe. But my code has given me considerable success to date. I believe that there is more to be gained by my methods than yours. Although, sadly, yours are also often required."

The two men stood silently facing one another.

"The trap is set?" continued the Consigliere.

"Yes. I'm flying out in two hours," replied Whisper.

"Where is he?"

"In the forest just outside the house."

"Tell me again why you are not already there?"

"Firstly, I dislike the weather in Colombia at this season of year, so the less time I spend there, the better. Secondly, he will be the most vigilant during the first 24 hours. By the time I'll get there, he'll be an easier target. Thirdly, I told you before that I had a prior engagement to attend to first," replied Whisper, annoyed that he had to justify himself. If the money was not so good and he did not have a personal interest in the mission, he would have left long before now.

"Will he still be there?" queried the Consigliere. He knew who Whisper was up against and wondered if the raspy voiced man had underestimated his opponent.

"Yes. I told you before, unlike you, I've been trained by them and know their tactics," snapped Whisper. It was always good to rub salt into the wound.

"Thank you for pointing that out, although it was unnecessary." The Consigliere's face remained calm but he could feel his blood start to boil. He hated being reminded of his past. One day he would ensure Whisper would regret that remark. His anger quickly passed, however. It was, after all, his past that motivated him to become the person he was now.

"So, am I ever going to meet your boss?" asked Whisper with a disinterested expression.

"I told you. You can do so anytime, but you will be killed immediately after. Nobody is allowed to see him and live."

"Except you."

"Not even me. Once my services are no longer needed, I will take my own life," revealed the Consigliere. Or others will, he thought.

Seriously?"

"Yes. In exchange, I have been given a very luxurious lifestyle. And obviously my wish for revenge."

"Each to their own. But you could have achieved your revenge by yourself. Just walk up to Beppe in the street and pull the trigger." Whisper gesticulated with his hand, pretending to shoot a pistol.

"I could have done so," agreed the Consigliere in a tone that indicated he never would. "I believe that you have a flight to catch."

Fingers of darkness were starting to spread through the forest. Shadow knew from his research that there was only one hour left until sunset. Using the high powered scope on his sniper rifle, he took a few measurements of the distances between himself and the guarded house. It was an old, run-down Spanish style hacienda. From the outside, it looked neglected. The formerly white stucco walls were now grey and in need of a whitewash. Shadow knew that this exterior appearance was only a smokescreen to mask the activities that went on inside it. He had originally planned to go in during that first night. Since arriving, however, he decided to wait. The guards' routine had changed and that made him apprehensive. In the time preceding his arrival, the guards would do a daily run to pick up rations, but over the last fourteen hours, none of them had left the building. This made no sense, unless MI6 surveillance failed to identify that on their last trip to pick up extra food. He doubted it.

Shadow quietly removed a small plastic case from his pack. Within the case were five long rifle rounds, each marked with a different number. These rounds were the latest in bugging technology. The rounds contained a listening device that would activate once it embedded itself in the targeted area. The device came in two designs. With one, the bullet would imbed itself into the wall and the bug would then start transmitting. The second type would magnetically attach itself to metal objects such as vehicles. The latter used a lower velocity when shot as it needed to fall onto the target rather than spearing itself into it. These sound bugs were old technology that had recently been upgraded. The microphones in them picked up and transmitted the vibrations caused by sound waves hitting against the wall. Once embedded, the microphones would be able to pick up fairly easily the conversations between people in the room. That was the old part of the technology. The new bit was the hyper-vibration technology that could turn the bug into a mini bomb. Instead of capturing soundwaves, it would generate them at such a frequency that would at first pierce eardrums, and then heat up to the point that it would explode like a hand grenade. The explosion would turn wall particles into lethal flying fragments.

After a moment's thought, Shadow selected the magnetic type first. He had memorised the specification table and was fairly confident that he could shoot the bug onto the corrugated iron rooftop. He waited patiently until one of the guards went to the external toilet. The toilet was made of aluminium and made a considerable metallic noise every time the door closed, perfect to disguise the sound of the bug landing on the house. Shadow did not have to wait long. The bullet initially travelled at high speed through the silencer at 50 degrees elevation. As it started to lose momentum, its climb also started rapidly decreasing. When it eventually landed on the rooftop, it bounced once but attached itself magnetically on the second contact. A few seconds later, both Shadow and MI6 started listening to the conversations within the house.

The run back from the swim was the toughest experienced by all the teenagers. Simon's leg muscles screamed in complaint. The burning sensation in his arms sent signals of pins and needles to his brain. His breathing was falling into a chaotic pattern, varied in frequency and duration. He had a splitting headache from the overexertion. Each step required a real effort as spasms of pain shot through his body. His motivation to go on was nowhere to be found. He just wanted to sit down, catch his breath and come to terms with his discovery.

Simon was the last in the group. He was trailing ten meters behind the others. They too were finding the morning's physical challenge especially arduous. Normally for Simon, both the swim and running distances were well within his fitness range. Today, however, his mind kept going over his last encounter with the Director. With... his dad? He struggled to concentrate and pace out the exercise, burning up far more energy than normal. Simon's emotions were all over the place. His stomach churned and knotted as he kept switching between the elation of finally having found his father, disillusionment that his dad had not trusted him enough to tell him the truth, anger that the man he thought was dead or absent had been there all along but chose to keep up his charade, dejection over all the years he and his mum had been neglected, more anger for all the hardships and pain and fear his mum had had to face without his father, sadness and a little shame that his first conversation with the Director was essentially criticism of his father, worry that something might happen to him on the rescue mission he was now on, and desperation at the though that if something did happen to his dad then their last encounter would be the last time they saw one another and there was still so much to say.

"Who in the hell cares? He abandoned us no matter what justifications he gives! He faked his death. He could have also faked all our deaths so we could have stayed together! I should just leave and make my own way like I always have," Simon muttered angrily to himself. He was enveloped in an emotional hell that had no exit.

"Come on, slowcoach!" called Deepa. Despite her exhaustion, she was feeling proud of having almost overcome her fear of sharks.

"Let him be," suggested Chiara from beside Deepa. "I think Simon has just slammed into some emotional wall."

"Maybe he is sick or something?" speculated Deepa. She did not want Chiara to know Simon better than her.

Stephen, running directly in front of the girls, picked up on the word 'emotional'. As he saw it, Simon was just pulling one of his stunts. It was clear he just wanted the attention of the girls and was making excuses for his lack of fitness. As she ran, Chiara continued thinking about Simon and tried to understand what had triggered his sudden change. She reviewed in her mind the scene from earlier in the morning. Simon had been so excited about the wetsuits, especially when the Director mentioned that the suits had been modified in accordance with Simon's own suggestions. But then, once they reached the beach, his whole demeanour had changed. She recognised the expression on his face. The only thing that could have triggered such a change in him was that he must somehow have realised that the Director was his dad. Chiara had no idea how that could have occurred.

She had been working in a trattoria in San Gimignano when Simon turned up looking for his dad. Chiara knew who Kevin was because he lived in the town, although he went by another name. The Director had met up with her again in France when he recruited her for the special MI6 course. He had explained why it was paramount that she kept his secret for the time being. Of course, she had intended to do so. What spurred the sudden recognition? she wondered to herself. Chiara recalled the final moments between the Director and Simon. He was still happy when the Director got into the car. Then Deepa went over to the car and explained her fear of sharks. What had that to do with Simon? She slowed her pace to let him catch up with her.

Simon was kicking himself that he had not seen the resemblance before. The Director's eyes were the same as his. They had not changed. His voice also had not changed. "I would never have believed that my dad would purposely deny me the truth, no matter what. Maybe I just built him up as my hero from my childhood memories. He really couldn't care less about me. Bloody hell!" he exclaimed.

"Simon, are you ok?"

Simon did not hear or see Chiara, who was now running next to him.

"Simon, are you ok?" Chiara asked again. She reached out and touched his shoulder.

A jolt ran through Simon as he felt the touch and was surprised by the sudden appearance of another person beside him.

"I... I... I'm fine," replied Simon, struggling to speak.

"You know," Chiara whispered.

Simon almost stumbled with shock. How could she know? Nobody knows! She must be talking about something else, Simon thought.

"You also know," he declared. His statement was an attempt to draw out what Chiara was referring to, but the girl remained silent. "The Director is my dad!" exclaimed Simon no longer able to keep silent.

Shadow took a sip of water. Although he was feeling hungry, he did not want to eat his energy bar. It was not still dark enough and opening it would require him to tear the wrapping. This was an unnecessary noise risk. He only had one food bar and he had to make it stretch for another day. He had come unprepared for all eventualities. It was yet another sign that he was getting old and starting to let his mind become distracted by personal emotions. He had presumed that he would complete the mission within 24 hours. As such, he travelled light and brought only two energy bars with him: one for himself and one for Bernie, in case he was malnourished. However, since Shadow decided to delay his plan by another day, he had to make his own food bar last another 24 hours.

The temperature was quickly dropping. Although the day was hot and humid, he was high up in the mountains and was starting to feel the cold creeping down from the surrounding peaks. The moisture from the forest floor created an uncomfortable dampness beneath him. Lying still for hours did not help, for it did not allow him to generate any heat through movement. To make matters worse, he was now resigned to the fact that his body was no longer pleased to sustain the physical discomforts imposed by these types of missions. Although Shadow's mind was as active as it had been in his heyday twenty years earlier, when he was known as the most notorious spy in MI6, he could no longer deny the discomforts of his age. He wondered how many years he had left before his body won the argument against the mind. With a despondent feeling, he realised that it would not take much longer at all.

"Sierra, Alpha 1, Beta Victor, Charlie 1, Delta Nil" came a message through his headphones.

"Sierra Ack. Out," whispered Shadows into a small microphone. He disliked having the radio silence broken, especially when he had to acknowledge the message. Yet if he did not reply, Command Centre would continue to contact him until he acknowledged the message.

Shadow thought about the information that had just been transmitted. He liked the fact that MI6 still used military-structured messages. It was the best and most efficient way to pass on intelligence without compromising the field agent. Almost without effort, he mentally decoded the message. Sierra was his designation. Alpha was the item that designated the message type. This was a slight difference MI6 had to what the military did, where they called out the message type by abbreviations or acronyms such as SITREP for situational report or CASAVAC for casualty evacuation request. In this case, the code Alpha 1 informed Shadow that this was an alert message. The word 'Beta' referred to the nature of the alert, while 'Victor' indicated one or more vehicles were approaching his proximity. 'Charlie' declared the number of vehicles and 'Delta' was the option for more information. In this case, there was none.

Within minutes, Shadow saw a vehicle approach the house. It was a black Land Cruiser. The 4WD drove directly to a carport to the left of the house where a driver proceeded to get out and walk towards the front of the house. Five guards exited the house and immediately formed a circle around the driver. Shadow watched the strange behaviour, but was not concerned. Then one of the guards turned around and gazed in Shadow's direction. He looked only for a moment before something occurred and he snapped his head back towards the house. The microphone on the corrugated iron roof could not make out the ensuing conversation, but Shadow could tell that the guard was currently being reprimanded by the driver.

"Sierra, verify Delta over" whispered Shadow into the microphone.

"Sierra, stand by. Over," came the reply.

Shadow felt a familiar tingling running up his back. Something was wrong. He could hear his heart beat faster and all his senses were on alert. He would not relax until MI6 validated that there was nothing else to report about the vehicle's arrival. The extra communication added to his risk of being detected, but right now it was worth it.

"Sierra. Victor slowed down under tree cover five hundred metres out. Over," squawked a reply.

"Sierra out!" acknowledged Shadow. Someone could have gotten out of the car five hundred metres back and could potentially be sneaking up on him from behind. He stilled himself and listened. Nothing. Not even the cicadas that had earlier filled the forest with their raucous noise now disturbed the stillness. Nothing moved, yet something was wrong. Shadow could feel it. The tingling sensation was growing.

"Freeze, Shadow!" came the order from a few metres behind him.

Shadow lay still, his mind racing.

Adrian Monico

"Before you do something stupid, just realise that I have a shotgun aimed at your head, ready to spatter your brains. Now, slowly crawl forward with your hands in front of you at all times!"

Shadow complied. He glimpsed the guards now running towards them.

"Keep your face down and place your hands behind your back."

Shadow obeyed, realising that unless the person made a mistake, he would soon join Bernie, if Agent 2C was still alive. The man behind him moved quickly, placing a knee hard on his back, while resting the hard metal shotgun barrel on Shadow's head. He then used plastic ties to bind Shadow's hands together.

"Ok, now stand up! Slowly!"

Shadow stood awkwardly and turned to face his captor.

Both men's jaws dropped.

"Whisper?" asked Shadow.

"Well, well, well," sneered Whisper. "I never thought that you were the famous Shadow! What alias do you go by now? Nicola, is it? No, that's not right. Ah yes. Kevin Black," he concluded triumphantly.

"I thought you never took missions against MI6," commented Shadow. Although his voice was steady, the shock of his capture and of seeing Whisper's face rang through his body.

"It might have been so once, but that was always my own rule and not an official agreement. Times are tough and this mission offered some great financial incentives for me to break that rule," smirked Whisper.

"Brother, if you are strapped for cash, you could have come and seen us," Kevin offered, still flabbergasted by the reunion.

"I'm not your lousy brother!" snarled Whisper "You and your family made sure I was reminded of that when you kicked me out."

"You threatened to kill Lucca. What did you expect? Even so, we all cared for you," replied Kevin, more calmly than he felt.

Whisper made an angry, dismissive gesture. "Love to chat, but we have an appointment with someone I know is dying to say hello to you," he said.

Before Kevin could say anything, he felt an explosion in his head, followed by a veil of blackness that rapidly filled his mind.

"Get him down to the house, strip him and get him into a new set of clothes," ordered Whisper to the driver who just hit the back of Kevin's head with the butt of his rifle.

Two loud knocks disrupted Beta from his work. Before he had the chance to reply, an agent from the control room walked in.

"Sir, he's been taken," the agent calmly declared as she reached Beta's desk.

"What!" Beta sprang to his feet.

"It gets worse, sir. Whisper was his captor," reported the agent.

Beta was stunned. Whisper had officially betrayed MI6. It was unbelievable. His mouth went completely dry. "Let's go to the control room! And get Beppe here ASAP!" ordered Beta.

"Yes, sir!" replied the agent in hurried pursuit of Beta.

"Simon. Simon, wake up!" A feminine voice came out of the darkness. Someone was gently shaking him.

Simon woke up, startled. "Deepa, what's up?" he asked. Adrenaline pulsed through his veins.

"Dad has asked us to meet him in the kitchen. It sounded urgent."

Still drowsy, Simon took a couple of moments to process Deepa's words. He rose and immediately headed to the kitchen. As he walked in with Deepa, he was greeted by the sight of the other two teenagers and Inspector Lau already sitting at the table.

"Please sit," the man said. Without waiting for Simon and his daughter to find their seats, he went on. "I have bad news. The Director has been captured."

Nobody spoke. Chiara instinctively looked at Simon. He sat there, pale and deathly still.

"There's more. Whisper betrayed MI6. He's the one who captured the Director."

With the exception of Deepa, every pair of eyes automatically glanced across to Stephen. She noticed the looks. "What? What is it?" she demanded, surprised by the reaction.

"He was assigned by the agency to be my mentor," replied Stephen. He looked dumbfounded, but was secretly pleased to learn he was not the only one wanting to bring MI6 down.

"He's also the man who attempted to kidnap Simon in Malaysia," added Inspector Lau to Deepa.

"Oh," whispered Deepa. She felt sorry for Stephen. It's not his fault! she thought.

Silence pervaded the room. Nobody spoke, all stunned by the news. The only sound that could be heard was the wall clock ticking off every slow second.

"There is something else you need to know," said Lau, finally breaking the silence and bringing the teenagers back from their thoughts. "You have been asked to help." He glanced at Deepa, already feeling worried for her.

"How?" she interjected impatiently.

"There is house where the agency believes the person behind the kidnapping is currently staying. You've been asked to go on surveillance mission only. But you are to keep out of harm's way. No risks are to be taken, lah. Hopefully you see the person that will lead us to Director," stated the inspector. Why, he couldn't help wondering, would Beta send these teenagers on this mission instead of more experienced agents?

"Isn't our identity already compromised? Whisper knows what we look like," Stephen pointed out. It was his attempt to highlight the ridiculous request about not taking risks.

"Yes. This mission is going to be risky," he replied. When he raised the same concern with Beta, he was simply overruled.

"Where are we going?" asked Chiara.

"Montenegro."

"Why wouldn't the agency just use satellites?" asked Stephen.

"Unfortunately our satellites travel can only see specific areas at certain periods of the day. Lah. So far the kidnappers have only moved during uncovered periods"

"When do we leave?" asked Chiara. She was aware that Simon had yet to speak and was still staring, frozen, at Inspector Lau.

"In ten minutes the car arrives to take you to airport, lah," came the reply.

"Dad, aren't you coming?" asked Deepa. Her mind was whirling but she fixed on the realisation that the car would only have enough room for the four teenagers.

"No, sweetie," he said gently. "I have to go to London. But you will be in good hands. Signor Beppe will be your handler, lah."

At the mention of the name, a memory of the fight back in Treviso between Beppe and Stephen flashed across Simon's mind. He stiffened, but Inspector Lau seemed not to notice and went on speaking.

"Ok. You go pack. Here are your tickets. Beppe will meet you at Podgorica Airport in Montenegro and brief you."

There was a scraping of chairs as everyone quickly got to their feet. As they hurried down the corridor to their bedrooms, Chiara caught Simon's arm. "Simon, I'm sorry about the Director. Don't worry, you'll get to be with your dad again."

"Thanks," mumbled Simon.

Podgorica Airport was busy with hordes of tourist arriving from a number of larger European countries. The overcrowding suited Beppe, who was sitting in the arrival area waiting for the teenagers. He had spent the morning being briefed about their mission. All the information registered in his sharp mind, and his calm demeanour belied the cocktail of emotions he was experiencing inside. To begin with, he struggled to come to terms with the fact that Whisper had seized Kevin. If he had not heard the voice recording from Kevin's hidden microphone and seen the satellite footage for himself, he would not have believed it. He also could not comprehend that, despite his shady list of clientele, Whisper had betrayed MI6. The only positive aspect about this insane situation was that he was about to see his grandson again. He missed Simon's company and the time he had spent teaching him the craft of spying.

He did not have long to wait. The four teenagers walked out of the terminal each holding a small suitcase. Signor Beppe walked up to Simon and threw his arms around him in an emotional hug. After a long moment, he broke from the embrace and apologised to the remaining teenagers and greeted each of them as long lost friends, including Stephen, who was expecting cold treatment from the older man. Simon felt the wash of Beppe's affection when he greeted him. He had missed Beppe and wanted to confide in him about his anger and confusion, but after the last few days, he felt he could no longer trust anyone. Did Beppe know Kevin was his dad? Did Inspector Lau know? Simon wondered how many more secrets were being kept from him.

On their way to their accommodation, an inconspicuous apartment in the outer suburbs of the city, Beppe took them on a familiarisation drive of the area they would be operating in for the next week. This included a quick drive-by of the targeted house. Simon listened to Beppe's explanations but remained withdrawn. Beppe glanced at him a few times but did not speak directly to him. It was clear something was wrong. He had never known Simon to be so despondent. Once they had arrived at the apartment, they were quickly shown the surveillance equipment issued to them for the mission and were briefed on their respective roles. As had been the case throughout their training, Stephen and Deepa would work as one team, Simon and Chiara as the other. Deepa still missed not working with Simon, but this was their first mission and she would not do anything to jeopardise the harmony of the group; there was already too much tension between Simon and Stephen.

After a quick lunch at a nearby restaurant, the pairs were dropped at their respective operational areas. Stephen and Deepa were situated in a small park that was a popular picnic destination for couples and families. The picnic ground was on the side of a mountain and was mostly surrounded by a dense pine forest. From its west side, however, there was the clear view back across the city. Fortunately for Stephen and Deepa, the city was not the only aspect that could be seen from the park. A few hundred metres below the park sat the villa that was under surveillance.

"Are you sure you know how to operate that?" asked Deepa, looking sceptical.

"Trust me, growing up I crashed many of these!" joked Stephen.

The model aircraft was a glider fitted with a small engine and a surveillance camera. The aircraft itself was fairly simplistic and carried no special technology. In contrast, however, the remote control was the outcome of a considerable investment from MI6. It was linked via satellite back to the MI6 control room. Primarily, it acted as a retransmitting device for video footage taken from the glider. It also served as an autopilot for the glider. This meant that once the glider was in the air, the small but powerful computer inside the remote could take over and automatically fly the glider in either a pre-recorded flight path or in a new flight path determined and recorded by its 'pilot.

Deepa watched while Stephen fiddled with the small aircraft. Within minutes the glider was in the air. Ordinarily, the presence of such an object would have possibly drawn the attention of those in the house that was under surveillance. However, this park was a popular site for model aircraft hobbyists. In fact, in two weeks' time a competition was planned that would see the park turned into a small airfield to be used by hundreds of enthusiasts who wanted to display their accurate replicas and show off their skills with difficult acrobatic flights. The small MI6 spy plane piloted by Stephen and Deepa would be relatively inconspicuous amidst the other craft already soaring in the air that day. Once their glider was in the air, Stephen followed the brief given to him earlier by Signor Beppe and flew the aircraft one hundred metres to the east of the villa. When it reached this location, the glider switched into a predefined path. It had been designed to look like an entirely non-suspicious flight whilst also providing the best opportunity to maintain a regular watch of the villa. Video footage from the glider soon started streaming to a small screen on the remote and was relayed to a monitor in MI6's control room.

Deepa's role in the mission was to act as a smokescreen to further reduce any suspicion. She would appear as if she were only there to keep Stephen company while he flew his model plane by laying on a picnic blanket with a magazine in hand. What she was actually doing was maintaining communication with MI6 control room and the second surveillance team of Simon and Chiara via a small microphone. Every now and then, she would look up at Stephen and give him an update. Stephen welcomed the interaction. Although interrupted by the odd glance down at the small monitor, pretending to fly the model aircraft turned out to be boring. Worst still, Stephen had expected that he would be allowed to fly the aircraft himself for most of the day, instead of pretending to fly it and simply watching it instead.

From Beppe's briefing, Stephen and Deepa knew the villa under surveillance was a modern house built on a block of land the size of a football field and surrounded by a three metre wall. Half of the outdoor area was covered by a small pine forest that made an impenetrable cover from inquisitive eyes from above but provided great visibility from within, as acidic pine needles completely covered the ground thus preventing the growth of any scrub, grass or weeds. All branches on the trees themselves had been symmetrically cut to a height of two metres above the ground. The villa itself was a two storey block of white rendered bricks. Numerous black tinted windows were placed at various inconsistent heights in the walls, instead of in the expected two tiers of the ground and first floor. Security cameras, which monitored every inch around the house, were covered by the same render used on the house, making them difficult to spot from afar. There were two pedestrian gates and a driveway gate, although they appeared to be seldom used. With the exception of the regular gardener and house cleaner, the house appeared to be inhabited.

Initially, MI6 had briefed Beppe to find a way to replace the existing gardener and fill the position himself, bringing Simon along as his apprentice. However, Beppe's suspicions quickly proved correct when he confirmed that the gardener and house cleaner arrived together because they were a husband and wife team. This most likely meant that they were directly hired by the occupants and were not provided through a maintenance agency. Replacing them would instantly make the residents of the villa suspicious. Although Beppe had seen these residents yet, he did not want to take any chances. In addition to the apartment in the city where he brought the teenagers from the airport, Signor Beppe also rented a three storey house a few hundred metres from the villa. The house offered no visibility inside the villa's walls, but it did have a direct line of sight to the front gates.

Simon sat at the back of the BMW staring absently gazing at Chiara and Beppe who were having a conversation in the front seat. He was not interested talking about the European economy and did not join their discussion. This mission was paramount to Simon and he could not understand how Signor Beppe and Chiara could waste time engaging in non-essential chit chat.

"Signor Beppe, why rent the apartment and the house?" asked Simon, emerging from his deep contemplations and inadvertently interrupting Chiara's and Beppe's conversation.

"The three of us staying at the house does not raise suspicions. There are lots of houses in the area that are up for rent. We do not appear necessarily out of the normal and could come across as a brother and sister coming on a holiday to Montenegro with their grandfather. If Stephen and Deepa also stayed with us, that might look a little odd. An old man with four teenagers does not really fit with the common make up of households around here. It could draw the wrong attention and any attention at all is what we want to avoid. So that's one reason for Stephen and Deepa to stay at the apartment. Secondly, we are supposed to be acting as tourists, so we cannot be cooped up in the house all day. But we also need to work on our surveillance. Having the apartment allows us to leave the house, giving the sense that we regularly spend the time sightseeing, but also having a location to go to work," explained Beppe.

"And why are we driving in such a luxurious car? Shouldn't we get something more discreet?" continued Simon feeling a bit too conspicuous in the shiny BMW.

"The car goes with the house. It's a very expensive house we are renting, so driving a cheap car would look out of place. Also, this is the 325i model which is very common around here. It shows that we have money, but we're not extremely rich," Beppe responded. As always, his spoken English was eloquent and his selection of words exact, but they were still spoken with a fairly strong Italian accent.

"So, other than looking out the window from time to time and flying a model plane around, what exactly is the plan?" asked Simon, giving voice to his impatience and frustration.

"Simon!" reprimanded Chiara with a parental tone.

"It is ok," Beppe murmured to her. He glanced in the rear view mirror at the face of his worried grandson. "Master Simon, I too am worried about the Director. I understand your frustration and I am also frustrated that we need to be sitting here watching a house because of some unconfirmed bit of MI6 intelligence. I believe we should go to the point where Kevin was captured, which incidentally is on the another side of the world, and start our search there." His words were reasoned and showed only slightly his frustration with his orders from MI6. Beppe was not a man who enjoyed sitting around and conducting surveillance 'just in case', but he could not let the teenagers know his true feelings. He looked at each of them in turn before continuing.

"But I trust Beta. And this is actually his mission, not one of his analysts. He feels that in this house is the man who has captured your father. So we need to all work together and trust Beta. In terms of the mission, I have no idea what we are going to do. But with this, I am ok. We will watch for a little while until the opportunity comes to for us to spot the person of interest and hopefully follow him to the Director, your father, or we wait until something else comes up that is the clue that we need."

Nobody said anything after that. They arrived at the rental house in silence. The rest of the afternoon was spent using high powered binoculars to watch the front gate of the villa, looking at a monitor relaying the footage from the glider, and checking in via radio with Deepa and Stephen. That evening, during the three hour period when the MI6 satellite was in range and could record the activities at the villa, the five of them met at the apartment and debriefed one another. As none of them had so far spotted anything unusual, the debrief took only a few minutes. Conscious of not wanting to do anything risky or different, Signor Beppe decided to take them all out for dinner and hopefully get them to wind down a little. He knew from experience that passive surveillance missions like this one, which essentially entailed lengthy periods of just sitting back and watching, tended to drag on.

Beppe's decision turned out to be wise, as it gave everyone time out from the monotony of watching the surveillance monitors. With the exception of Chiara, however, who was reading out to the others what the Lonely Planet guide had to say about Montenegro and Podgorica, the rest of the group remained subdued, absorbed in their concerns about the Director. Even Beppe was quieter than usual. After dinner, they headed back to the apartment where they sat around a monitor staring at streamed footage from the surveillance satellite. The satellite provided two identical images side-by-side. One was taken using an infrared telescopic lens, and the other was a new satellite technology which generated the image by soundwaves. The sound scanning carried out by the satellite was based on a similar concept as sonar pings. Soundwaves would be sent from the satellite and, depending on the way they bounced back, they would be interpreted as an image. Although the image was somewhat lacking in details and often blurred in areas where external sounds, like a car driving by clashed with the waves, it did provide a good understanding of where people might be located inside the house. Thermal imagery was dismissed as an option in this case as the house appeared to have been purposely insulated, thus appearing in such imaging as completely black. This in itself was considered suspicious as houses were not normally insulated against thermal imagery.

The daily routine of Stephen and Deepa going to the park and the remaining three staying back at the rental home continued for a week. Sometimes the teenagers swapped roles for the day in order to break the monotony. Everyone was becoming dispirited; they wanted to do more than just watch. Simon, especially, withdrew even further into his shell, confused, angry and afraid for his father. Only Chiara, who was always talkative, could distract him from his mood. While they all spent hours staring at monitors, Simon found a way to spend his time in what he considered a more fruitful manner. He used the hours to discover ways to improve the technology that was currently available. His approach was to look at all the phases of a surveillance mission and determine what technology would help to increase its success. Over the course of the week, two of his ideas were submitted to MI6. Both were accepted and development of them commenced immediately.

Simon's first idea was to tweak the sound bugging technology so that the bugs could be used to send a subsonic soundwave. The wave could then be picked up by the satellite and read as images of the internal house or – and this was the reason that MI6 immediately started working on the submission request – the satellite could find a way to decipher what Simon called the 'negative wave', which essentially meant that it could isolate the sound interference that caused by people talking and thus indicate their location within the house.

The second technology improvement idea was to update the current military night operations helmet. Simon thought of placing small infrared and night vision cameras all the way around the helmet. These already came with eye protection visors that acted as a heads up display, with the image was projected across the visor. However, the current view for the image was basically projecting the some span as the human eye. Simon's idea was to have an image that provided a 360 degree view. The displayed image would be projected either as a panoramic view across the eye protection visor or sized down into a section of the visor and superimposed over any of the other projected images chosen by the spy. The theory behind this was that if Simon or any other agent needed to gain access to a house, day or night, he would literally have eyes at the back of his head. Although coming up with these ideas did help the time pass by, Simon remained frustrated by the lack of action to find and free his father.

The first break in their mission came late one afternoon. Simon was walking back from the nearby shops when, lost in thought, he accidentally missed his street and turned into the next one along. It did not take long for Simon to realise his mistake, but as the street was just a block away from the villa under surveillance, he decided that it was safe to continue on the alternative route. The street was fairly busy, with cars passing by or leaving and arriving at the various homes. All the houses were of similar design. They had large external walls with garages built into them. Ensuring even more privacy, large pine trees the lined the internal walls and obscured the houses within.

As he walked, Simon started looking for the house that backed onto the villa under surveillance. He figured that if it was vacant, they could rent it to try to get a better view. After walking a little further, he identified the house in question a few hundred meters away. Unfortunately, as he watched, he saw a black Mercedes with dark tinted windows drive into the garage. The house was not vacant. A little time later, a van and a second car also arrived and drove into the garage. Simon found it difficult to comprehend how two cars and a van could all fit in one double garage. But after a few seconds of pondering, it finally occurred to him that the garage was simply a thoroughfare into a courtyard of some sort. Instantly, Simon's thoughts began a rapid race of question and answer.

Why would there be a van?
Maybe someone is getting a delivery.
Delivery of what?
Catering, furniture.
But why an escort car?
Maybe it has a precious package.
What could be precious?
Art, contraband.

Is this an area where criminals tend to come to?

Hard to say. I know of two houses in the same block and have noticed nothing to indicate criminal activity.

Is one criminal house backing another criminal house a good thing or a bad thing?

Possibly bad, as one criminal would not know what trouble the other criminal might bring.

Would the people in the villa know of any illegal activities carried out by their neighbours?

Most likely they're keeping an eye on my neighbours in case law enforcement agencies stumble into my activities as a result of investigating theirs.

So why take the risk of being in the vicinity of another criminal?

You wouldn't, unless... Simon's thoughts raced on. What if it is not another criminal, but both houses are owned by the same criminal or group? That would make sense. Especially if one house is used as the entry for the second house. That would explain why only the cleaners have been seen arriving and leaving the villa.

Excited his potential discovery, Simon crossed the street and continued to the house, anxious to tell Signor Beppe his theory. It was the first time since the first day of their surveillance that Simon felt motivated again. When he reached the house, he raced through the rooms, calling out for his mentor.

"Signor Beppe! Signor Beppe!"

There was no response.

"Deepa?" tried Simon. Again, no response. He could not see either of them anywhere. After searching the house, Simon headed to the kitchen to make himself a cup of tea and consider his next move. He noticed a handwritten note propped against an empty glass in the middle of the kitchen table.

Simon, we have gone to pick up the other two. On the way back we are also going to change our rental car and motorbike. Don't do anything silly. Deepa.

Simon could not remember he had been told about this before he went to the shop. He read the note again and laughed at Deepa's last piece of advice.

After he made himself a cup of tea, Simon went into the surveillance room to see if anything was happening. The monitors, as usual, showed no real activity at the house. Even the satellite image was useless. Simon pondered for a few minutes then sent a request through to headquarters to pan out the satellite view so he could also see the houses immediately surrounding the villa too. This proved to be an astute decision, as immediately he could see lots of activity at the newly discovered 'entry' house. Several guards were patrolling the yard and someone was using a water hose to wash out the inside of the van. Simon thought this was odd. Two German shepherds were strolling along the inside of the wall. He continued watching the activity on the monitor and after fifteen minutes, audio from the satellite started streaming through. The sound ran about a minute behind the image, but still provided great intelligence about their target.

"What do you think of ... package?" came the crackling voice of one of the guard.

"Yeah ... was told ... very important ..." was the distinct reply from someone else.

"... heard the boss ... him Director of ...6."

"Really? Man, everyone must ... looking for him."

"Careful, here co... Whisper."

Simon felt his heart beat faster as he registered the significance of the last comment. He leaned in close to the monitor and zoomed in on the small overhead view of a third man who was approaching the guards. From the satellite image, he couldn't tell if this person really was Whisper or not. A moment later, more sound came through.

"... huddle. You ... be patrol..." The words were barely audible.

"Yes, Whisper. We ... just handing over ... coming off shift," one of the guards said.

"...n't call me ..." came the stern reply.

My apolog... sir. I will not make that mi... again."

The satellite footage showed the third man walk to the back of then van that had just been washed and look into it. Thereafter, he returned to the house.

"I liked it bett... when he word for the oth... side," called one of the two guards as he started to walk toward the house.

"I agree. Don't like double agen...s. See ... later"

Simon Eady - The Teenage Spy

Simon felt the hair on the back of his neck bristle. A constant chill ran through his body and his hands trembled with excitement. Although he could not be one hundred per cent certain that Whisper or his dad were inside the house, every fibre in his body was telling him that it must be so. He knew what he had to do. The sun was sinking and it was almost dusk. He would not get another chance for another 24 hours. The thought that maybe he should wait for the others flickered briefly across his mind, but he preferred not to place them at risk. Besides, Beppe would probably not allow the four of them to go in. Other, more experienced agents would be called which would mean more time would be wasted. Better that he do it himself, and do it now. Simon quickly packed what he felt was needed for the mission. The thought occurred to him that this really was his mission. It was, after all, essentially a family affair.

Adrian Monico

CHAPTER 5 - An Act Of Foolishness, A Sign Of Courage

Kevin felt drained. He was not sure where he was, but knew that he was no longer in South America. Based on the smell of the air and the tiny glimpses he'd managed to glean, he would have to guess that he was somewhere along the Baltic coast, inside a cold room, most likely underground. His lip was still bleeding from the blow that had struck him during his attempted escape. Although he knew that being chained in the back of the van as he had been at the time made any escape virtually impossible, his attempt was really aimed at trying to remove the hood from his head and hopefully have a peek at his whereabouts. Even though the result was a split lip, the few seconds he'd been able to see the surrounding area made his effort worthwhile.

"Was that worth it?" came a hoarse whisper from the door.

"Yes, Whisper, it was," smiled Kevin, knowing he would leave some confusion in Whisper's mind.

"Why? Even if you got a glimpse at your whereabouts, the information will not help you."

"Perhaps," replied Kevin.

"It's nice to spend some time with you again, although the circumstances aren't ideal," Whisper observed. "I do have fond memories of our time together when I was being brought up by your family."

"You are one of us, Whisper. What are you doing? Get yourself out of this mess before it's too late. You don't have to worry about me. I'll be ok. But if you keep going with this, MI6 will come after you," Kevin warned him, feeling genuine concerned.

"Thanks, but I'm only here as an arbitrator. Nothing more."

"An arbitrator? For what? Who are the parties in dispute?" asked Kevin, perplexed.

"I'd love to be the one to tell you, but I've been specifically asked to leave the surprise to someone else," said a smug Whisper.

"Surprise? Whisper, this isn't a game. You've captured two MI6 agents, damn you!"

"Ah well, you see, Bernie is about to be set free. He was simply a pawn. Right now he's sedated whilst being taken across to Russia. He'll be released near the border."

"Bernie was a pawn? Then am I a pawn too?" Kevin was becoming more confused by the minute. What was all this about? How could they – whoever 'they' were – know he would be the one to rescue Bernie?

"This conversation has been nice. I look forward to the next one," Whisper said, then turned and walked out of the room.

Kevin's brain immediately started analysing the information he had just received. He was relieved to learn that Bernie was going to be ok, but it seemed as if he himself was going to step into Bernie's place at the centre of this plot. He had made many enemies during his life and felt as if his past was catching up to him. First Simon, now who?

"How is he holding up?" the Consigliere asked Whisper as he walked into the study.

"Tough as expected. He's a bit at a loss to understand what this is all about," replied Whisper.

"He'll learn soon enough."

"Where is Signor Beppe?" Whisper asked.

"We don't specifically know. He is in this city, but we lost his trail almost immediately."

"I guess we have to assume that he's somewhere nearby, watching the house," Whisper observed.

"I am counting on it."

"Aren't you worried that MI6 will send in the troops?" Whisper followed on.

"They will keep in abeyance until they have evidence that we have their Director. The only way that will happen is for Beppe to come and have a look for himself. Their surveillance will not be able to find anything. Besides, to a great extent, we are in control of MI6," smiled the Consigliere. He was quite looking forward to the anticipated confrontation.

"And what are the plans for the kids who are with him?" Whispered asked. A memory of the last coaching session he had with Stephen surfaced in his mind.

"To be frank, Whisper, I have plans only for one of them, as you know."

"And Simon and the girls?" asked Whisper genuinely curious.

"Don't know. Part of me feels that Simon has nothing to do with this. But part of me tells me that I should get rid of him too, as one day I might regret it if I don't. At this point, I am not really concerned about the girls, but if they get in the way, just get rid of them."

A very long moment passed by in silence, with both men quietly pondering Simon's possible fate. The only sound was the big pendulum clock that stood as a centrepiece in the study. The room smelled dusty. It contained shelves that stretched across two walls and was filled from floor to ceiling with books. A large oak desk and an antique leather chair that both looked to be about one hundred years old despite having been well looked after were placed a few metres in front a dark tinted window. Although anyone walking into the room would immediately be confronted by the large desk that faced their direction, the two metre tall clock that stood behind the desk near the window would be the object that captured their eye, with its somewhat hypnotising swinging pendulum.

"What do you think?" asked the Consigliere, being the first to break the eerie silence.

Whisper's response came spontaneously. "Simon is still young enough to be 'moulded'. I've been thinking of expanding my business, particularly as in the last two years I had to turn down a lot of work. I'd like to take him on as an apprentice." His attempt to potentially save Simon's life was not missed by the other man.

"My, my," mocked the Consigliere. "Whisper is getting sentimental."

Whisper said nothing. He stared at the Consigliere with a stone cold expression.

"Fine! If he doesn't get in the way and survives my plan, you can have him," the Consigliere eventually agreed.

Whisper nodded slightly and turned to leave the study.

"And Whisper... If in the future, he starts making me feel uncomfortable, I will make you personally accountable."

With his hand on the door knob, Whisper nodded once more before opening the door and exiting the room.

Simon was ready to go. He was dressed completely in black clothing and his face and hair were smeared with black camouflage paint. He equipped himself with a Mosquito pistol, his newly improved night vision helmet, and a few hand grenades. One of these was the same type that had been used against him in the forest. It was capable of tranquillising anyone within a three metre radius of its detonation. Throughout the afternoon, he had maintained surveillance on the villa. In that time, he had counted four different guards, including one he thought was Whisper. Of all the people he had seen on the small monitors, the latter was the only one he believed to be a worry.

He had been expecting Signor Beppe and the others to return at any moment and try to thwart his plans. But the time came for him to leave and still they had not returned. He left a note propped in the same place where he had found the one from Deepa. He did not know why they were taking so long to come back to the house, but was grateful for whatever had held them up. Waiting for darkness to fall had been agonising for Simon. He was anxious to get moving but understood the advantage that night would lend to his mission. Satisfied at last that it was dark enough, Simon silently walked out of the house and headed for the back entrance to the villa he discovered earlier. He was not afraid. Indeed, an odd sense of calm prevailed in him. Beneath his cool state of mind, however, his senses were on high alert and his body was ready to spring into action.

The two German shepherds were exceptionally well-trained guard dogs. They were able to pick up a foreign scent two kilometres down wind. Nevertheless, being in a suburban area that was full foreign scents, the dogs depended mostly on their acute hearing. Having the dogs proved a great patrolling solution, but it also meant that the ground sensors were ineffective as the continuous movement of the animals would keep turning the alarms on. Security was thus dependent as much on imagery from the innumerable cameras positioned both inside and outside the villa as it was on the dogs and guards. Night vision cameras had been installed around the villa, but were ineffective when used in areas illuminated by artificial lighting. Usually, the better option would have been to have areas lit up by large powerful lights, but this was not an option as it would have made the house stand out. This meant that at night, with the exception of a few door lights, the grounds were fairly dark. The dogs depended on their hearing and the guards depended on their night vision devices, as did the wall mounted cameras. This was the information that Simon surmised from his hours of surveillance.

One of the dogs was the first to detect Simon. It picked up the sound of Simon's backpack accidentally brushing the perimeter wall as he climbed over. Simon had wanted to wait for the dogs to turn the corner of the house before coming down the wall, but he lost his balance and came down prematurely, a split second too early. The first dog had already turned the corner of the house, but a growl emitted by its companion just behind him put him on the alert. Both dogs promptly backtracked along the wall, not yet pinpointing the precise position or cause of the noise. Years of training had them already salivating. Their veins filled with adrenalin, ready to attack. They closed in on the section of the wall where it seemed the noise had originated, prowling and sniffing, yet they were unable to clearly see through the darkness that pooled under the trees and shrubs growing close to the wall.

Behind one of these trees, Simon lay motionless, naively hoping that the darkness made him invisible to the approaching dogs. Just to be safe, he already held his Mosquito pistol in hand. The dog that initially heard Simon was also the first to pick up his scent. It launched itself at the dark corner where Simon hid. It took a few steps towards him before the needle penetrated its shoulder, sending it almost immediately into a deep sleep. The second dog paused for a second next to its companion, sniffed it a few times, then poised itself ready to charge. It never had the chance to take the first step, as Simon's second needle struck home and sedated it almost immediately.

Simon cautiously moved the sleeping dogs into a dark corner, hoping that nobody would come looking for them. His helmet was working well. His heads-up display was showing multiple, semi-transparent images before his eyes. The 360 degree view was projected as a landscape image covering the top third of the visor. His forward night vision device covered the bottom two thirds. On a small square section to the top right, Simon could see the live feed from the satellite. He switched his headset to stream the sound captured by the satellite and turned off the communication relay back to the MI6 control room. He did not need any distractions like receiving orders from London to get back to the house. Simon was impressed with the way his helmet was working. The only component that did not seem to be functioning was the thermal imagery camera. He assumed that the house was specifically designed to interfere with such technology.

"WHAT ON EARTH IS GOING ON?" yelled Beta as he rushed into the control room, having just been alerted to the protocol breach.

"One of our cadets appears to be breaking into the house that backs onto the villa under surveillance," replied the duty officer.

"WHY?"

"Sir, we believe that Sierra 2 has discovered, but did not report, that the rear house is a secret entry to the villa."

Sierra 2 was the codename given to Simon, using the international radiotelephony spelling alphabet for the initial of his first name. Stephen's codename was Sierra 1, Chiara's was Charlie and Deepa's was Delta.

"Have you ordered him to get back?" demanded Beta.

"Can't, sir. He has switched off our communication channel."

"What? Then send some text to display across his helmet visor."

"Unfortunately, sir, we can't do that either. Sierra 2 is wearing one of the new prototype helmets. We weren't able to have the communication text display feature built in, as we needed the majority of the computer processing power in the helmet to project the 360 degree image."

"Well, what can we do then? Tell me that you have a plan?"

"Sir, Team 12 is on route. They'll be there in fifteen minutes. We have no choice but to do a rapid deployment, as we believe the target is in the house. We thought of letting Sierra 2 continue his mission alone, but this might lose us the chance of capture."

"Ok." Beta closed his eyes as he accepted the decision. It too late now to alter the plan about sending in reinforcements.

Everyone in the room stared at the screens that displayed data from the unfolding mission in front of them. The main central screen showed the same images that Simon was seeing in his heads-up display, except on much larger scale. On the right, there was a separate set of smaller images that were showing the view of six special agents flying in a helicopter. The back cabin of the helicopter was illuminated by a low intensity tactical light and showed images of the agents looking at one another without speaking.

Oblivious to the consternation his mission was causing back in the control room, Simon approached the first door of the villa. With no real plan for how to get around the surveillance camera, he simply rushed passed it and sped on through the unlocked door. The two cameras and the trip switch on the door were all linked to a red light and a buzzer in the guardroom located within the house. As the guards were about to do their last patrol before locking up all windows and doors, most of the buzzers were still switched off. A small red light, situated amongst many others on a panel which showed a map of the house, started blinking. Fortunately for Simon, several other lights on the panel were also flashing. With people still moving about within and around the house, the guard on duty was not especially concerned. External security had never been breached before and flickering lights on the panel at this time of night were not uncommon. The guard was further distracted by the shift's roster for the night. He trying to work out who would be stationed on the various shifts and, more importantly, what time he would be finishing his.

Closing the door quietly behind him, Simon found himself in a long, dark, narrow corridor. After a few steps, his vision adjusted to the dimness and he realised that the first corner was so sharp it gave the appearance of a dead end. Once he turned that corner, he was again confronted with the illusion of a dead end by another sharp turn in the corridor. He continued to follow the corridor until he arrived at two doors. Before peering behind either, he placed sound devices against the doors and actively listened. Once again it seemed the thermal imagery was not working.

"Why he is waiting so long to move? It's obvious there is no noise coming from behind the doors," muttered Beta nervously. He was able to hear via satellite the sound emitted by the sensor.

"I don't know, sir. Maybe..." The duty officer cut short his observation as the answer became clear to him. He and Beta both stared at the screen as a black and white picture began to emerge. The sound device was using sonar technology to create an image of the rooms on the other side of the doors.

"I'll be dammed! Clever boy," commented Beta to himself.

The duty officer was similarly impressed. He was himself still learning about the capability of the technology. The satellite had picked up the sound signal, transferred it to a central computer in

MI6, processed it, and then transmitted an image back to Simon's helmet and onto the screens in the control room. Simon could see on the corner of his helmet two very small images that showed faint 3D portraits of the two rooms. The door on the left looked like it led to the main foyer of the house. He could see a set of stairs at the centre of the room, which he guessed were used to access the upper floors. He could also see two people standing together in the middle of the room. The room appeared to have minimal furniture, with two large pot plants being the main decorative features. Behind the door on the right was a set of stairs leading downwards. The image was not very clear, as the subsonic sonar waves simply disappeared at the bottom of the stairs, making it look like they led down to a large black hole. Simon paused for a second and then decided to head downstairs.

"Clever boy!" called out Beta.

"Sir?" queried the duty officer.

"Sierra 2 is there to rescue the Director, which means that he will be looking for a prison cell. If it were me, I would keep the prisoner someplace where the sound of screaming could not be heard. For that reason, I would keep the prisoner underground," explained Beta.

"But what makes us think that there aren't other downstairs areas accessible via different stairwells?" asked the subordinate.

"If I designed a safe house, I would make sure there was always more than one exit out of each area, otherwise you can be trapped. My bet is that downstairs is like a rabbit warren made up of multiple corridors with multiple entry and exit points. So, no matter which of the downstairs access point you find, it is likely to head to the same area."

"That would make it more difficult to defend. Castles and the like used to have limited gates that permitted entry behind their walls."

"Young fellow, castles are also known to have had secret tunnels," replied Beta, feeling suddenly old. He turned his full attention back to the screen.

Simon entered the door on the right and then cautiously proceeded down the stairs. As soon as he closed the door behind him, a guard entered the corridor via the door on the left. Again, Simon was fortunate that the guard was starting his patrol around the perimeter of the house and proceeded down the corridor leading towards the outside of the house instead of following Simon down the stairs. They were quite narrow and spiralled steeply downwards. As if on delayed reaction, Simon was starting to feel really nervous. He commenced his slow descending, gripping hard on his pistol. He pointed it straight ahead of him, keeping it close to his body. He was careful not to extend his arm too far, as he was worried that might give him away to anyone coming from the other direction. Every few steps, Simon would stop and listen for any suspicious sounds, but all he could hear was his heart pounding inside his chest. The noise felt magnified in the eerie silence that surrounded him.

After approximately forty tensed filled steps, he reached the bottom of the house. The stairs seemed to end right in the middle of another corridor at a T-junction. The corridor curved gently away in opposite directions. Simon immediately suspected that it acted as a continuous ring underneath the house in which both sides would eventually rejoin. Along the inside wall of the corridor were doors placed at even intervals. Simon turned left and moved to the first door. If his dad were held captive somewhere down in this warren, he needed to check each room.

The first room turned out to be an armoury. Racks of weapons were bolted onto the walls on either side. There were enough rifles in the room to equip a small army. In the centre, on top of a very large stainless steel table, lay numerous small crates. These had been opened and Simon saw they were filled with hand grenades. Simon, although already well-armed, grabbed a few grenades without thinking and clipped them onto his harness. He then moved to the rifle rack and strapped an AK-47 assault rifle over his shoulder. Although he had never fired this type of rifle before, his military training with other weapons was sufficient to help him understand how to use it. After filling his pocket with a few rifle magazines already loaded with bullets, he quickly left the room and moved down the corridor towards to the next door.

"Homestay, this is Margaret! Seven minutes out. Over!" came a voice out of the speakers in the MI6 control room.

"Margaret, this is Homestay. Ack. Out," acknowledged the

communications officer. Everyone in the control room now knew Team 12 were seven minutes away reaching from the villa.

Just as he placed his right hand on the next door handle, Simon realised that opening each door in turn was a dangerous way to determine what was inside. He took out a small sound sensor and placed it against the door, as done on the floor above. A few seconds later, a new image projected itself onto the corner of his visor. Simon felt instant fear. He was standing outside a dormitory in which what looked like ten or so people were asleep. The room seemed to be twice as long as the previous one had been with three-tiered bunks along each wall. Between each rack of bunks, he could see a set of personal lockers that reached up to the ceiling. Simon did not know what to do. He obviously could not take on ten trained men and a gunfire fight would alert the rest of the house. But he was also worried that at any moment, one of these men could come out into the corridor and spot him.

After a few moments of hesitation, he relocated the sound bug to the lock of the door handle. He then found the remote control in his pocket and pressed the self-destroy button. The bug instantly generated an intense heat. It liquefied into the handle and melted some of the handle itself. Not completely satisfied with the result, Simon repeated the exercise with another bug.

"Clever boy!" Beta whispered again, as he watched the events unfolding on the main monitor. "Send this footage to the Research and Development. I want those bugs to be perfected for this purpose and not solely set up to self-destruct," he ordered.

Satisfied that the door lock was completely melted and would take considerable effort to open, Simon moved to the next door down the corridor. He now had only two sound sensors left at his disposal. Using one of these, he could see this door led into a room filled with screens showing footage from around the house. It was clearly a control room. Inside it were two guards who were watching the screens. At first Simon thought of melting the door handle as he had done on the dormitory, thus trapping the guards within. Then he realised they could simply sound an alarm. He had no choice but to take them down.

Simon looked at his arsenal of weapons. He deliberated between using the tranquillising hand grenade, which was fairly silent when it exploded, or choosing the Mosquito pistol instead. The hand grenade had no guarantee of knocking out both guards, but Simon did not trust himself enough to be able to shoot both guards with the pistol before they would either fire back or sound the alarm. After debating with himself for a few seconds that felt like a lifetime, Simon placed one hand on the door handle whilst holding the Mosquito pistol in the other. He decided that he would fire two tranquilliser needles at each guard. His heart was racing so fast that the drumming noise pounded in his ears. He was so nervous about what he was about to do his whole focus was on the door, oblivious to the image updates appearing on his visor.

One of the guards inside the room stood up to go and get a coffee for himself and his colleague. As he reached the door and placed his hand on the handle, he looked back to his comrade while pulling the door open inwardly. Simon, caught in a panic, found himself staring at the guard whose face was still turned towards his colleague who had his eyes fixed on the monitors. In a split second, it all happened. The guard at the monitors turned around and, seeing Simon standing behind his colleague, quickly withdrew his pistol from the holster. Without thinking, Simon fired two needles him. The first needle hit the chair but the second one inserted itself into the man's arm. The guard closest to Simon, seeing his colleague's reaction, turned to face Simon and instinctively threw his hands at the teenager who had seemingly just materialised out of thin air.

Simon tried to aim the pistol at him, but found himself being flung across the room. He landed on the control dashboard and bounced downwards onto the floor. The guard leapt at him before he had a chance to get up off the ground. Forgetting about the pistol which he still had in his hand, Simon rolled to his right and barely avoided having the guard land on him. As he felt a grab at the back of his jumper, he reached out with his spare hand and seized hold of a swivel chair which he immediately launched at the person behind him. The guard, momentarily let go of the teenager to try and block the path of the flying chair. This gave Simon the opportunity for to roll once more and end up on his side with his pistol held towards the guard. Although still driven to neutralise the teenager, the man realised his defeat and raised his hands as a signal that he was giving up.

"Get up slowly," whispered Simon, confronted by the unexpected turn of events. Both he and the guard heaved themselves back onto their feet and stood only a few metres apart from one another.

Move and I'll shoot. Scream and I'll shoot. Look at me funny and I'll shoot," Simon threatened.

The guard nodded.

"Where is your prisoner?" Simon asked, trying hard to stop his hands from shaking.

"Cell 3," the guard replied. He cast his eyes at one of the monitors on the wall.

Simon followed the guard's line of sight and saw a monitor showing an image of a man standing with his hands tied to a chain hooked to the ceiling. He felt a jolt of excitement.

"Where is that?" Simon asked.

"Out of that door, turn right. It's the fifth door down the corridor," the guard replied. Simon paused, wondering what to do next. Noting his uncertainty, the guard spoke again. "You are a bit young. I have no idea how you got in, but you'll not get out of here alive." He moved ever so slightly forward.

Simon ignored the comments as he was too preoccupied with thinking about what his next actions would be.

"Kid, drop your pistol and I'll make sure that not too much harm comes to you," continued the guard, still edging forward. Simon noticed at a map of the house that was placed on the wall, and spotted what there appeared to be an underground exit.

"Shoot, kid! What are you waiting for?" cried the MI6 duty officer. Even he could see that the guard was about to pounce forward.

"Two minutes," called another MI6 officer, indicating the time Team 12 was due to arrive at the villa.

"Why aren't any cameras along the outside corridor?" asked Simon. None of the screens in the control room showed any footage of the corridor.

"What? Oh, I see. Only selected rooms then, as the boss was concerned that anyone tapping into our signal from the outside could use the cameras against him. I personally think that he is paranoid," replied the guard still slowly edging forward.

"Are there any other exits out of the basement or is it only the stairs opposite the dormitory?" Simon asked, pretending not to see the map.

"Yes. Via the garage," replied the guard, now glancing at where the teenager was looking, anticipating the moment when he would jump and disarm him.

"Where is that?" asked Simon. The idea of an underground garage surprised him.

"It is the only door on the outside wall of the corridor," replied the guard. He pointed at the exit door.

Simon kept his pistol levelled at the guard but his eyes automatically followed the man's hand and he looked toward the door. The attack caught him by surprise. In an instinctive reaction, Simon simply pulled the trigger twice even before his head turned towards his assailant. Although both needles penetrated the guard's skin, the two second period it took for the sedative to completely him knock was sufficient for Simon to a punch to head, sending him to the ground. The guard, after landing the successful blow, saw his world go first blurry then black. He lost consciousness, falling on top of Simon.

"That was close," quietly observed the duty officer, back in the MI6 control room.

"Sir, Team 12 has the villa in sight and will be doing a hot landing in forty-five seconds," reported the other officer.

Although two other surveillance missions were currently being run out of the MI6 room, most of the staff on duty were quietly focused on the footage transmitted from Simon's helmet and the ever-watchful satellite.

Simon stood up and searched the guard. He located the transmitter used for communication between the guards and placed the headset in his left ear, then switched on the transmitter.

"Alpha 1, this is Bravo 7. I say again, we found the two dogs sedated. We have an intruder."

Simon froze. He had been discovered.

"Sir, Team 12," called the duty officer, directing Beta's attention to the footage of the team in the helicopter.

Simon quickly left the control room and went back into the corridor.

Team 12's sharp shooter, referred to as Eagle Eye, was sitting on the floor of the Blackhawk helicopter with his feet hanging outside. His .50 calibre sniper's rifle was firmly locked against his shoulder with the barrel resting on a crossbar. He already had his first target in sight and was waiting for the order.

"Eagle Eye, free to engage," the Team 12 commander ordered from the second helicopter. It was positioned above the courtyard, ready for the team to drop from the helicopter via a set of long ropes hanging on both sides.

Eagle Eye's first round hit a guard standing near the sedated dogs. In the same moment, the team on the second helicopter slid towards the ground like spiders trying to escape from harm.

Simon moved along the corridor to the door where the guard said his father was apparently being held. Not wanting to waste another moment, he fired several rounds from the guard's rifle into the door lock. His first lesson for the night was that unlike in the movies, the bullets did little to damage the metal lock. The door was still unmovable. Swiftly, he employed his previous technique and used his last sound bug to melt the lock. Once he opened the door, he found the room to be some sort of safe. It contained several tables covered in money, jewellery and hundreds of bags filled with what he assumed to be drugs, although he had no idea which kind. He swore under his breath. There was no sign of his father here. The guard had lied to him.

"Alert! We are under attack!" Simon heard the call over the second radio. Unaware of Team 12's arrival, as he was too deep underground to hear the helicopters, he incorrectly assumed the call was in reference to his own presence in the basement.

Out of sound bugs, Simon retraced his steps back to the control room. If he was to find his dad, he needed the keys that would open the doors. He searched the two guards unsuccessfully, then started tearing open various console drawers. Thinking he had no time left before other guards found him and unable to see the keys, he slammed his fists on the control console in despair. Then, in a moment of clarity, he saw what he was looking for. The map of the house that he had previously referred to for orientation was actually an imprint on glass. He moved closer to the map and touched the diagram of the room he was in. A beep rang out in acknowledgement of his touch and a small pop-up window appeared over the map. It seemed the map was actually a touch screen. The pop-up menu had two options: one was labelled Cameras and the other one Security. He touched on the Security option and was presented with two buttons labelled Lock and Unlock. Jabbing his finger on the Lock button, he heard a click as the lock of the door behind him immediately apply itself. A very small padlock image appeared on the top right corner of the diagram of the control room on the map. Simon paused for a second to catch his breath. He scanned the map for all the rooms displaying the tiny padlock symbol.

Team 12 cleared the outside area within minutes and were already sweeping through the ground level of the house. So far, despite some intense fighting, the team only sustained a few light flash wounds. The wounded soldiers would need immediate evacuation once the mission was complete. Meanwhile, they would self-administer first aid and remain on watch for their comrades to rejoin them.

Realising that his father would be in a secured room, Simon started clicking on all the downstairs rooms shown as locked and selecting the camera option in each. He eventually found his dad in a room five doors further down the corridor, labelled as Room 8. Tapping the screen, he immediately unlocked that room along with the one he was in.

In his soundproof room, Kevin Eady was unaware of the assault by Team 12 or the presence in the villa of his son. He simply stood chained to the ceiling using the quietness of the room to try to understand all the events that led to him being there, including, most importantly, Whisper's betrayal. Even if Whisper did not truly belong to his family, Kevin had always looked after him as if he were his little brother. Kevin knew that Whisper was motivated by money, but he also knew that he had always been careful not to go up against the main NATO powers. The only thing that made sense to Kevin was that there must be some personal reason behind Whisper's actions and the most likely personal motivation was something against his own adopted family.

A faint sound and tiny movement interrupted Kevin's thoughts. His eyes flicked instantly to the slow downward movement of the door handle. When the door opened, Kevin smiled with delight.

"Well, well! I'm glad you're here. I was just thinking about you. I have a question to ask."

"It'll have to wait. Looks like MI6 has decided to try and rescue you. We need to go," replied Whisper as several guards followed him into the room.

Kevin ignored both the guards and Whisper's evasion. "So, this is personal, isn't it?" he observed. "You are specifically targeting the only family you ever knew." The chain that ran between his handcuffs and the ceiling was detached from the wall and relocked against his ankle cuffs.

Whisper simply stared at Kevin without giving any reply.

"What? Am I wrong? This isn't motivated by personal reasons?" asked Kevin. Guards held him by both arms and started shuffling him towards the door.

Whisper still stared silently.

"Oh, I see. It is personal, but not for you. Who then?" asked Kevin, thinking aloud.

"Shut your mouth or I'll do it for you!!" threatened one of the guards as all four dragged Kevin towards the downstairs garage.

Fully aware that the guards would follow through with such a threat, and needing to keep himself free of injury for as long as possible, Kevin stopped talking. He was rather pleased that in all the rush, neither Whisper nor the guards and Whisper had remembered to cover his face with a mask. Kevin counted seventy-five paces until they arrived at the first and only door on the left. Two more guards were waiting beside it. The corridor was quiet, allowing Kevin to make out the sounds of shouting and gunfire that was just audible through the earphones of the guards. A sudden shout reverberated along the corridor.

"Daaad!"

Adrian Monico

Kevin, Whisper and the guards snapped their heads back in the direction from which the shout came. All stared at an armed teenager dressed black. It took a second for Whisper and Kevin to recognise him.

"Simon!" they both called simultaneously.

Simon's heart was pounding the adrenalin throughout his body at a rapid rate. He could hear through the stolen headset that the fight with the MI6 team had now reached the stairs leading to the underground area. He knew he had a limited chance against the six guards and Whisper. Somehow, he had to delay their escape until reinforcements came. He thought of reaching for one of the tranquillising hand grenades, but he knew that any movement would most likely lead to a confrontation which he had no chance of winning. Fortunately, the corridor formed as a perfect circle. He needed only to take a few steps back and he would be covered by a wall.

Simon was just about to make his move when a hand grenade flew as if in slow motion from behind the group near the door and sailed towards the teenager. The grenade landed a few metres away from him, then bounced all the way to his feet. Acting purely on instinct, Simon kicked the hand grenade past him and threw himself to the ground. The grenade skidded along the outside wall and disappeared out of sight before detonating. Although Simon was shielded from the full force of the explosion because of the inner rounded wall, the airwave caused by the blast reached the teenager, along with some shrapnel which bounced off his helmet. As soon as he felt steady enough, Simon quickly stood up with his rifle in hand, ready to fire. He turned towards his father and the guards but saw only two men standing at the external door. Before he could understand where his father had gone, he pulled the trigger. Simon had grown so accustomed to the Mosquito pistol that was unprepared for the recoil of the normal rifle. As the barrel jerked upwards, so did all the bullets that were spewing from it.

The two guards, who dived inside the door at the sight of the teenager's barrel moving in their direction, had no such difficulty with their weapons. They both threw themselves to the floor in a firing position and commenced shooting. Simon, knowing what was about to head his way, leaped behind the natural curvature of the inner wall just in time to evade the supersonic bullets. He dropped onto one knee and peeked around the corner the moment the first wave of bullets ceased and then fired his rifle again, this time maintaining better control and accurately keeping the bullets in a tight grouping. The guards rolled behind the door as the teenager's bullets chipped concrete off the floor, door and wall next to them. Amid the wave of ammunition, the two men rolled back towards the door, ready to fire again. Just as they were about to pull the trigger, they saw a stun grenade staring back at them from the edge of the door frame. Their highly tuned instincts yelled at them to roll back away from the door, but their actions were not quick enough. The stun grenade exploded, momentarily neutralising all their senses.

Simon, trusting the effect of the grenade, was already on his feet and running towards the grenade a split second before it exploded. What never occurred to him was that the grenade would also impact on him. There was a bright light that exploded at lightning speed, blinding all within its proximity. The sound shockwave followed like a tsunami gushing from the door and slamming anything in its path. Burnt shrapnel scattered in all directions, like carnival fireworks. Although trained in the use of these weapons, Simon was still naive of their real effects when used outside a controlled firing range. He was prepared for the flash, turning his head and closing his eyes at the moment of detonation. Still, the sound wave knocked him off his feet and made his ears ring. The force of the wave was confronting. It dropped Simon to his knees and made him feel nauseous. As he collapsed, he was dimly aware of something wet and warm trickling from his ear.

CHAPTER 6 - In The Lion's Den

       The agent who had taken him to the local hospital and stayed while he was being treated left Simon at the front door of the house and drove off without a word. Feeling bruised, battered and dejected, Simon tucked his helmet underneath his left arm and winced slightly. In addition to the six stitches on his lower back, he sported eight more for a cut on his shoulder. He could not even recall when that injury had occurred. Hoisting backpack over his right shoulder, he stood for a moment outside and took a deep breath. Then he walked through the front door and braced himself for the lecture he was sure to get from Signor Beppe. He was not looking forward to it, but he knew he deserved it. After all, it was he who had caused the mission to fail.

       "Dinner is on the table!" called Stephen as he passed Simon with a plate of spaghetti in hand and walked to the communication room.

       "Thanks," Simon replied quietly, awaiting the stinging criticism from other boy. It never came. Stephen did not even pause as he headed into the other room.

       Simon slowly walked into the kitchen where he found a plate of hot spaghetti waiting for him. No other plates where on the table. He picked up the plate and the fork that lay beside it, and headed into the communications room as well. There he sank into a seat next to Stephen and quietly commenced eating, staring at the monitor showing satellite pictures of the house where the raid had just occurred. The silence dragged on.

       "You might as well have your say while you can," Simon said at last.

       After a long pause, and without looking at Simon, Stephen finally spoke. "You stuffed up royally. Learn from it."

       His words were without inflection and betrayed no hint of the pleasure Stephen felt about the evening's events. Simon's actions tonight would make him less of a threat to Stephen and hopefully less trusted by MI6. He had failed to follow orders and had made a mess of his whole mission. That wasn't all, though. Ten minutes earlier, Stephen had been informed that the incident would eventually help him with his own personal vendetta. He was especially glad of Simon's recklessness because it had triggered his father to secretly contact him. Stephen was on a real high and he did not want to spoil the feeling by getting into another argument with Simon.

After an extremely slow, strained dinner, Simon collected the two empty plates and went to the kitchen to wash them, hoping to avoid Signor Beppe. He knew that sooner or later he would have to face the consequences of his actions, but he felt drained and hoped the encounter could be deferred until later. After he finished washing the dishes, it occurred to Simon that he and Stephen were the only ones in the house. Filled with angst about Beppe's likely lecturing, he completely forgot about Chiara and Deepa. He returned to the communication room where Stephen still sat, eyes on the monitors.

"Stephen, where is everyone else?"

"Honestly, I don't know. Deepa and Signor Beppe rushed off together after we came back and saw what you were up to. I was told to stay put and report to them everything that was coming through the monitors. They called thirty minutes ago saying that they were ok, but they would not be back for a while and Chiara and I should maintain radio silence. About ten minutes before you got back I think I heard the phone ring. I went to find out who called and discovered that Chiara has also disappeared," shrugged Stephen.

"She didn't leave a message?"

"No, man, she simply left. I didn't even see her go, because I was glued to these monitors," lied Stephen. In truth, he had been upstairs in his bedroom, talking to his father.

"So, what are we meant to do next? Did you get any instructions about me?" asked Simon, feeling a tad concerned about Chiara's wellbeing.

"Signor Beppe told me that an agent would call when you were leaving the hospital. He asked me to tell you to stay put, as you've done enough for one day," replied Stephen, who was now looking sidelong at Simon.

"Ok," replied Simon. He was not sure what to do next. Maybe a cup of tea?

"We're being sent a babysitter," added Stephen as Simon was about to walk out of the room.

Simon turned back. "Inspector Lau?" he asked. Very few people were meant to know about the four teenage trainees, although tonight's event would likely change that.

"Don't know. Deepa didn't say."

"Deepa? You saw her as well?"

"I only spoke to her. The instructions from Signor Beppe came from her. Apparently he was occupied," replied Stephen, shrugging again.

Simon's eyes kept returning to the view of the silent house on the monitor. It made him feel uncomfortable. "Want a cup of tea?" he asked.

"I'll make my own," Stephen replied. "I'm sick of staring at these screens. It's all over now anyway." He stood up and gave Simon a sly smile as he walked past.

"Signor Beppe, do you think they know we are tailing them?" asked Deepa. She was feeling anxious about Signor Beppe's plan.

"It's always wise to plan for the worse," replied Signor Beppe, already contriving ways to keep Deepa safe. "So, yes, let's believe they're aware of us." If their quarry did indeed know that they were being tailed, they might act unexpectedly and thus place Deepa at risk. He couldn't let that happen. "We might have to get you a separate vehicle," he continued.

"How do you propose to get me a second vehicle without losing their trail?" asked Deepa. The idea of separating from Signor Beppe did not appeal to her at all.

"Good question. Let's have a think," replied Beppe. Perhaps catching a taxi was the only plausible idea.

Both boys sat at the kitchen table deep in their own thoughts. From the moment they walked into the kitchen, neither one had spoken. As they sat there, oblivious to their surroundings, a tall figure passed silently behind Simon and proceeded unnoticed to the kettle. It was only when the sound of the kettle boiling could be heard that Stephen looked up and saw the domineering presence.

"Who are you?" yelled Stephen, startled by the stranger.

Simon, a second later, reacted by jumping to his feet and twisting to see who had alarmed Stephen. "Aleks!" he cried, moving quickly from alarmed to excited. He mopped ineffectively at the cup of tea he had spilled across the table.

"Hey, Simon. Signor Beppe and Signor Stefano asked me to come by and visit for a while," Aleks replied calmly as he sauntered over to the sink.

"You mean you're here to babysit us," stated Stephen, still unsure about the stranger. The fact that Simon knew him was at least a little reassuring.

Aleks crossed the room and shook hands first with Simon and then with Stephen. In his other hand, he held a wet cloth.

"I'm Aleks. I'm one of Signor Stefano's bodyguards," Aleks informed Stephen.

"Signor Stefano is Signor Beppe's brother," explained Simon, trying to join the dots for Stephen, although he did not really care much about including him in the conversation.

"Two peas in a pod, I think the saying goes," continued Aleks as he wiped Simon's spilt tea.

"Aleks, I stuffed up. That's the real reason you are here," said Simon miserably, in case Aleks did not hear about this evening's events.

"I don't know, kid. That's not what I've heard. You definitely were a tad hasty, but I think you did more good than harm," replied Aleks. He had heard the full story of Simon's exploits from Signor Beppe.

"What do you mean?

"Kid, it was a trap. And you sprung it early on them." Alex smiled at the expressions on the two boys' faces.

"A trap! For whom? And by who?" interjected Stephen, wondering how much MI6 knew.

"That we don't know," replied Aleks.

Nothing in his manner betrayed the careful regard he was paying Stephen, but Aleks made a mental note to do some research on the teenager. He did not like working with people he did not know, and it appeared that nobody really knew that much about Stephen. Aleks had of course been given MI6's background check on Stephen and his family, but he had found it unsatisfying. There were just too many gaps, especially in his family history. It was almost as if the whole family simply appeared twenty years ago with barely any history going back further than that. MI6 accepted this because Stephen's parents apparently grew up in East Berlin, but Aleks was not so easily sold. He hated any gaps, no matter how insignificant or trivial they seemed, and resolved to find out more about Stephen in the hope of filling some of the ones in his past.

"They are stopping for petrol. This might be the only chance to get you a car, Deepa," Beppe said as he drove past the petrol station and looked for a good hidden spot to park.

"Chiara is only a few minutes behind us," said Deepa, looking down at the tracking software loaded on her phone.

"Bene, bene," replied Signor Beppe. "Remember, my dear, you and Chiara need to keep well behind me. Just track me via your phone and not depend on keeping me visual range."

"I still don't like it, Signor Beppe. When they catch you, they'll most likely move you into another vehicle and then search you. We could end up losing both the bug in the car and the one on you." Deepa's unhappiness with the plan was evident in her tone.

"True, my dear. But right now their car is full. So the chances are that they'll initially use this vehicle to move me. But even once they move me and take all my clothing off me, you'll still see me for six to eight hours after that."

"How?" asked Deepa. What other bug could Signor Beppe have on him?

"Simple, signorina. I'll swallow one," he smiled.

"Is it safe?" asked Deepa. The idea of swallowing a tracking device the size of a small coin did not sound very tempting.

"My dear, a bit of indigestion will be the least of my concerns. Si?" Signor Beppe replied with a loud laugh.

Deepa smiled back, but new images of what could happen to Signor Beppe filled her mind and made the plan even less appealing.

"Signor Beppe, how will we know if we need to come to your rescue? I still have no idea about the protocols in these situations. I'm afraid I don't really know what I'm meant to be doing as a spy," Deepa said, feeling really worried for the old Italian gentleman.

"Deepa, always go with your gut feelings. The only difference time and training will make is that you will become better at trusting your gut instincts," replied Signor Beppe, aware of Deepa's concern for him. "Just remember, the mission always comes first. You are not responsible for my wellbeing. So, don't compromise the mission for me. Si?"

"Yes, I understand," Deepa replied softly, hating the situation. She hoped that Chiara would be stronger and surer than her.

Signor Beppe pulled over between several cars parked parallel along the main road in front of a busy set of restaurants.

"Here? Really?" asked Deepa. It seemed a strange choice of location.

"Signorina, it is easier to hide amongst many cars than to stand out as the only car in some dark, abandoned laneway," smiled Signor Beppe. His young trainees still had so much to learn.

"I guess so," Deepa agreed uneasily. "But they can still spot us."

"That's not so bad. I want to be seen," responded Signor Beppe. He glanced across at Deepa, whose worries were clearly visible in her eyes. He couldn't help thinking that she was too young for this game. She cared too much and valued other people's lives too much. He wondered if he was making a mistake to put her through this, but it was too late for any such doubts. Any change in the plan would interfere with the mission, and as he had just instructed her, the mission always came first. If he survived it, he decided he would help Deepa and find a way for her to make an honourable exit from the program, if she wanted that.

"She's here!" Deepa said, seeing the red dot on her phone that showed Chiara was pulling up behind them.

"Ok, signorina. You know what to do. Be careful, my young princess!" Signor Beppe nodded towards Deepa's door as an indication for her to leave the car.

"Th-thank you. Take care, Signor Beppe." She put her hand on the door then turned impulsively turned back to him. "Forget the mission," she blurted out. "Your life comes first. Simon could not cope with losing you. He has come to consider you as his family, not just his mentor." She stared directly into Signor Beppe's aged eyes for a few seconds before getting out of the car and joining Chiara. Signor Beppe sat and watched as Deepa got into Chiara's car. For the first time in his life, he questioned the mission.

"So, Aleks, what's the plan?" asked Stephen.

"Not sure, buddy. I guess we just have to wait," Aleks replied, still unsure about Stephen. There was a lot of suppressed hostility in the boy. He could feel it.

A knock at the front door surprised the trio. They froze, staring in the direction of the front door.

"Were you expecting someone?" whispered Aleks.

"No," Simon whispered back. "Maybe it's Signor Beppe or one of the two girls?" He was looking forward to seeing Chiara again but still dreading the forthcoming lecture from Signor Beppe.

"Stay here!" ordered Aleks. With a smooth movement, he scooped up a kitchen knife and proceeded quickly to the front door. The knocking came again. Aleks took up a position to one side of the door in case someone was about to shoot through it. "Who is it?" asked

"Bernie. I'm expected," came the reply.

"Code?" asked Aleks. He had been informed that a second person would be turning up.

"Silver."

Satisfied with the answer, Aleks opened the door. He found himself facing mountain of a man, who looked like he might struggle to fit his broad shoulders through the door frame. "Come in," Aleks offered, keeping the hand that held the knife behind the doorframe and out of Bernie's sight.

"Certainly, once I'm given something," replied Bernie. He had not moved an inch forward and seemed to be fully aware that the person staring back at him most likely held a concealed weapon.

"Really? Oh, sorry. Nitrate," said Aleks.

"Odd code words, don't you think?" mused Bernie, holding out one of his giant hands.

"Signor Beppe is a pharmacist and obviously loves his chemistry," grinned Aleks. He shook hands with Bernie but kept his left hand hidden.

"You won't be needing that," said Bernie as he stepped into the house, one finger pointed at Aleks' hidden hand. Aleks simply smiled and lifted his left hand into sight, revealing the kitchen knife.

When the two men entered the kitchen, Simon and Stephen stood like frozen mullets gazing at the imposing presence of the stranger.

"Gents, this is Bernie. He's a field agent who's been sent across to help," Aleks said. He walked past the stunned teenagers towards the kettle and raised an empty mug in the air. "Bernie, a cuppa?"

"Love one. Thanks," replied Bernie, not taking his eyes off the boys.

Aleks took his time making the cup of tea. When it was ready, he moved to the table and placed it at the closest point to the new guest, who was still standing at the kitchen door appraising the teenagers. Aleks looked at him for a moment, then at Simon and Stephen. No one spoke. With a small shrug, Aleks went back to the kettle and poured himself another cup of Earl Grey tea. He sat at the kitchen table and looked again at his silent, staring companions.

"My, but you're a sociable lot," he said and chuckled. His mirth triggered small bursts of laughter in the other three, thus breaking the silence.

"So you're the agent who was captured that the Director came to rescue?" Simon asked Bernie. He was already fairly confident that the person in front of him was the same one he read about in the incident report a few days earlier.

"Yes," Bernie admitted. "Not my finest hour." Although somewhat embarrassed, he kept an emotionless expression on his face.

"Would it be ok if you could tell us all the details about your capture? It might help us track these people down," Simon asked, full of hope.

"Sure, kid. But you are actually not looking for 'people'. Just one person," replied Bernie as he sat down at the table and sipped his tea.

"The Consigliere," Aleks said with a grimace and Bernie nodded.

Over the next forty minutes, Bernie relayed every detail of his capture. Three times Simon interjected with a question. Both Stephen and Aleks simply listened attentively.

Signor Beppe kept a safe distance from the vehicle he was following. The traffic helped keep him inconspicuous. He was also pleased to note that the two girls were completely out of sight, although he knew they were definitely following him. The phone rang and the sight of the caller ID filled Signor Beppe with joy.

"Ciao, Stefano. Come stai?" asked Beppe.

"I am well, thank you, and you little brother?" came the reply from Stefano in Italian.

"So, so. Thank you for sending me Aleks," said Beppe, pleased of the opportunity to converse in Italian. In the last few weeks, he only had the chance of doing that when calling his wife and grandchildren or when Simon practiced his language lessons.

"It's ok. He was bored anyway and itching for an adventure. He also thinks fondly of Simon and was looking forward to running into him again. As a matter of fact, some of the others also often reminisce about Simon's heroic effort at the ambush in Malaysia."

"Yes, he has our family's blood in him: courageous and dangerous to himself," replied Beppe, thinking back to the risk his grandson had taken just a few hours earlier.

"Speaking of being dangerous to himself, what are you planning to do about Kevin?" asked Signor Stefano. He was fully aware that his brother would take great chances to free his own son.

Beppe sighed. "I have decided to finally face the person who for all of these years has kept you in hiding, put Simon at risk, and now captured Kevin. The thing I don't get is why, in all of these years, he hasn't tried to get at you, by going after me."

"Perhaps, all along it was not me that he has been after. Perhaps it was you," his brother replied.

"Stefano, due to the nature of the career I had, my enemies are all under six feet of ground. They were also not the type of people to be missed once they were gone, so I doubt there is anyone out there seeking revenge on me. If the plan was to get to those I love in order to wreak revenge on me, then this person have to be really upset with me. With exception of Whisper, who until now I thought had accepted of what has happened between us, there is nobody who comes to mind that could be driven by such a personal vendetta."

"Maybe so, little brother, but the tell-tale signs are there just the same," replied Stefano. Beppe thought about this for a moment. Both he and Stefano lapsed into silent reflection.

"I can't believe Simon took such a chance tonight," Chiara said out of the blue, breaking the silence that had hung in the air for the last fifteen minutes.

"He is certainly courageous," agreed Deepa. She wished she'd the opportunity to call him and check that he was ok.

"You know, it is very obvious that you really like him," Chiara commented, glancing over at Deepa.

"We're good friends," replied Deepa, a little defensively. "I worry about him as I would for any close friend."

"If you say so. But we both know that is not what I meant."

"Yes, Chiara, I know what you meant. Speaking of which, I actually thought that something might spark between the two of you. Simon does come across as being sort of infatuated with you," remarked Deepa. Her words were aimed putting the focus on Chiara, although saying them still tore her inside.

"I know," the other girl agreed. "But it's only a temporary infatuation. It will pass. I really like him, but I'm not interested. I guess the situation isn't that dissimilar as to what is occurring between you and Stephen."

"Men! They certainly have a way to get themselves set up for failure," declared Deepa with a smile.

"They certainly do." Chiara winked back at her before both girls erupted into laughter. "Let's call them!" Chiara suggested.

"Signor Beppe said I shouldn't," reported Deepa. Her longing to speak to Simon had not diminished, despite the instruction she'd been given.

"Ok, then. I'll call them," Chiara announced. "After all, the order was directed at you," she added cheekily

The two men and the teenagers were still discussing Bernie's unexpected release when Simon's mobile rang. He answered it, conscious of the full attention of all those around him.

"Yes, hello? Oh, hi Deepa." He noticed Stephen automatically sit up straight at the sound of Deepa's name. "I'm ok. Yes. I know, I know. Ok, I'll try to be smarter. I promise to try. Um, not much. Stephen and I are passing the time with our two babysitters. One is the agent who the Director was supposed to rescue and the other is some goon that Signor Beppe's brother sent." Simon looked at the others as he spoke into the phone and grinned at Aleks when he said the word 'goon'. Aleks gave him a friendly scowl.

"Simon, can I talk to her?" asked Stephen. He was eager to hear Deepa's voice.

Simon nodded but kept on listening to what Deepa was telling him about the events of her evening. "Hold on! Is Chiara there with you? Is she ok?" Simon felt suddenly relieved to know Chiara's whereabouts. "Oh, hi, Chiara," he said. "Sorry, I didn't realise I was on hands free." He felt his face grow hot.

"Simon, put your phone on hands free as well," Aleks ordered quietly.

"Hey, I'm putting you on hands free as well. Hold on a second," Simon said and looked for the little speaker button on his phone. "Chiara, Deepa, you're on hands free. Stephen, Bernie and Aleks are all listening in." Simon placed his phone at the centre of the round kitchen table.

"Hello, everyone," came Chiara's cheerful voice. "Aleks and Bernie, I don't envy your job!"

"No fuss. We'll have them in nappies and tightly tucked in bed by eight! And for the record, this is the handsome goon," joked Aleks. The two girls laughed and Simon looked at Aleks in surprise. On their previous encounter, he was a very reserved and much less sociable person.

"Deepa, where are you heading?" asked Stephen. He wanted to hear her voice but wanted to gather information too.

"Hi Stephen. I'm sorry but I can't tell any of you. This is on strict orders from Signor Beppe," replied Deepa, who had been coached on how to respond to anyone who asked her that question.

"Where is Signor Beppe?" asked Bernie.
"He drove off all by himself a little while back with the intention of getting captured," replied Chiara, alarming all those listening around the kitchen table.

"That's insane!" Simon burst out. "Why would he do that?"

"He hopes that he'll be taken to the lion's den," replied Chiara, not too sure what the phrase actually meant. She thought lions lived in the open or maybe in caves?

"Ha! You're quoting Beppe there," Aleks diagnosed. "He loves his biblical references." He laughed in an attempt to make the teenagers feel less panicked.

"What else did he say?" asked Bernie.

"Not much, other than to keep an eye on his signal and provide the location of his last whereabouts if the bug is discovered," replied Deepa in accordance with the words she had rehearsed with Signor Beppe.

"The bug?" asked Simon.

"Yes. He has a bug on him that is sending his location to my phone. He said that once the bug stops sending data, it has either been damaged or found. In either case, I'm to call you guys and then, and only then, report the last received coordinates," continued Deepa.

"Won't they easily find the bug if he does get captured?" Stephen demanded.

"I asked him the same question. He said that he has it located right next to where he keeps his emergency money. That way, if they take his socks off, they'll be more distracted by the money than the tiny microchip that's woven into the socks," answered Deepa. She wondered if Beppe's concern about a mole would turn out to be true.

"So what are we meant to do until then?" asked Simon.

"Signor Beppe told me you'd be asking that question," Deepa answered. "He said to tell you that the answer is for you to reflect about what you did wrong earlier on when you broke into the villa." She spoke quickly, hoping to lessen the impact of her words.

Simon felt instantly flooded by guilt. He shut his mouth and listened quietly. Aleks saw the change in him and knew that he would need to speak to Simon later about Beppe's answer.

"Ok, Deepa and Chiara, anything else?" asked Bernie.

"No, that's it. We need to get off the phone. We'll keep you posted. Bye," Chiara ended the conversation.

"Be careful, Deepa," called Stephen. "And you, Chiara," he added quickly, hoping no one noticed that he hadn't mentioned her at first.

"We will. Catch you later, alligator!" Chiara sang.

"In a while, crocodile!" replied Simon. He realised how much he missed Chiara's jovial company.

As soon as the call ended, Simon asked if they could go back to the villa to see if the MI6 investigative unit had found any clues about where Kevin might have been taken. A quick call was made to Beta and Bernie got the approval. During the walk to the villa, Stephen and Simon walked a few metres ahead of their two babysitters. The men used the opportunity of this distance to quietly discuss a plan.

Signor Beppe, comfortable that the girls were now back far enough to be out of direct danger, started making a few intentional rookie mistakes in his tailing technique, like changing lanes whenever the car ahead of him did. Usually this was unnecessary when driving on a freeway, as staying in the lane closest to the exits meant that whenever the trailed vehicle veered off suddenly from any of the lanes, the car trailing it would not necessarily give itself away by also taking the same exit. If instead, the trailing vehicle had to cross several lanes to make the same exit, it would most likely give itself away to those it was pursuing. Although Beppe would customarily stay in the same lane when tailing on the freeway, he now started moving across lanes just as the car he was following did.

His ploy worked. Within minutes, the driver of the car announced, "We are being trailed." None of his passengers, being professionally trained, turned to look at the vehicle behind them. "I've changed lanes a few times now and that car keeps following," continued the driver.

"How many?" asked Whisper. It was difficult from the backseat to get a glimpse of the car in the driver's side mirror.

"Difficult to say. The car is a hundred meters behind us and it's still too dark. So far I have only made out one silhouette," stated the driver. Whisper had no idea what the man's name might be. This was, in fact, the first time he had seen him.

"Keep steady. We don't want to force their hand and make them spring early whatever plan might be waiting ahead for us. With a bit of luck, they're simply following us to find out where our next hideout is," observed Whisper.

"MI6?" asked the guard sitting across from Whisper in the back seat.

"Most likely. If so, I'd say that their intent is to simply follow us until an opportunity presents itself to free our hostage," Whisper replied. Both he and the guard looked at the slumped form of the man who sat sedated between them.

Beppe noticed that seven minutes had passed since the car's last lane change. Up until that point, it had consistently switched at the five minute mark. Beppe deduced from this that he had been spotted. It seemed the driver too made rookie mistakes.

"You know they now know they've been seen." Kevin's words came unexpectedly from underneath the black bag that covered his head. He sat up, startling the guard on his left. The man cocked his right elbow in a reactive instinct to strike the hostage and hopefully knock him out again, but Whisper raised one hand as a signal for him to not to continue with the action.

"Welcome back, Kevin. I trust you had a good sleep. My friend to your left is inclined to knock you out again, but I thought that perhaps I'd leave you the choice first. If you give me your word not to attempt any escape until we get to our destination, then I'm happy to leave you sitting there quietly. Otherwise, I'll have no choice but to send you into another sleep," proposed Whisper. The three guards in the car looked at him in dismay.

"You have my word that, bar unexpected circumstances, I will not try anything until we arrive at the next destination," Kevin replied after a moment of silence. He awkwardly extended his cuffed hands to shake on the deal.

"Agreed!" replied Whisper, accepting the handshake and understanding that by 'unexpected circumstances', Kevin meant a rescue from MI6.

"Sir, I must protest! You can't honestly believe that he'll keep his word," said the guard who was sitting in the front passenger seat. Until now, Whisper had never heard him speak. He was just another unknown member of the team. Whisper wondered how many guards the the Consigliere actually employed.

"If I were you, I'd focus on teaching Mr Driver here the reason why our hostage picked up that the car back there now knows it has been seen," hissed Whisper. He did not trust these bunglers and hated having his orders questioned.

"What?" asked the same guard. Whisper didn't know his name either.

"I know you like to think that this is your team and you're probably not too happy that I'm giving the orders. Nevertheless, as far as I'm concerned, you are still accountable for their actions. So, I'm going to repeat myself for the last time: tell your driver what he did wrong!" The venom in Whisper's words was obvious. Why did he have to deal with such poorly disciplined people who try to sell themselves as being professionals?

The guards looked nervously at one another, unsure what mistake had been made.

"Kevin?" Whisper said scratchily.

"Sure. What Whisper is trying to tell you gents is that we have been switching lanes consistently at five minute intervals. By my count, we have now not done so for the last nine minutes. This tells the car behind us that something has just caused a change to our routine, which, if they are highly trained, they'll interpret as us having picked up on their presence," Kevin said promptly. "Very careless," he added. He hoped his disapproving tone would unsettle the guards and increase the rate of their mistakes.

"Sir, you said to keep it steady!" objected the driver, looking back at Whisper.

"That means not do anything different," responded Whisper who was feeling entertained by Kevin's speech.

"So what do I do now? Should I go back to changing lanes or stay in this one until the exit?" asked the driver. To give him his credit, he was able to set the personal criticism aside and was genuinely interested in learning from the two professionals in the back seat.

"Go back to the routine of switching lanes," replied the team leader quickly in an effort to regain from the temporary loss of reputation.

"Kevin?" asked Whisper.

"Sure," Kevin replied again. "Gents, if you go back to changing lanes every five minutes, a professional might interpret the difference as a temporary mistake by us or they'll guess that we are trying to return to our previous routine in an attempt to make it look like it was a mistake while possibly planning to act upon our discovery. However, if we now stay in this lane until the exit, we'll most likely just come across as a poorly trained team who have reached a comfort zone where we feel it's unnecessary to look over our shoulder so there's no need for us now to change lanes." As he spoke, he tried to make out any external sounds or smells that might come in handy later on.

"I don't believe this! We're taking advice from our hostage now?" snapped the team leader. He turned to stare directly at Kevin. "So, tell us, Mr Know-It-All, if the people in the car behind us are so professional that they can guess everything about us just from a change of routine, then why did they make the stupid mistake of giving themselves away in the first place?"

"Oh, please, Whisper, can I answer?" asked Kevin. It was probably just as well that with the hood over his head no one could see the big grin in his face.

"Be my guest," replied Whisper with a very thin smile. He really did not like this team and was wondering if the Consigliere knew how incompetent his goons were.

Kevin's smile widened. "What makes you so sure that the 'mistake' was not intentional? There are several reasons why the car behind might choose to give itself away. For starters, it could be to provoke a reaction in order to determine this team's level of expertise, which, by the way, is pretty obvious in this case. In case you hadn't figured it out, turning around to stare at a man eye to eye when he's wearing a hood is kind of pointless." He paused to register the affronted sound the team leader made at having his inanity so plainly stated. "In addition to seeing us no longer regularly changing lanes, the car behind has now most likely seen the front passenger sharply turn around to face in their direction. This is obviously an even a bigger mistake than not continuing to changing lanes." A nice level of tension was now building in the car. Kevin was quite satisfied, but also intrigued that Whisper was allowing it to continue.

"Listen, buddy, I've a gutful of..." But the team leader never finished his sentence. In one swift motion, Whisper reached forward and twisted his head. The sound of the snapping neck was clearly heard by all in the car. After killing the man, Whisper simply sat back in his seat as if nothing had happened. The two remaining two guards froze with no idea what to do next. Their eyes darted between the road ahead and the body that sat dead in the front seat.

"So that's why?" commented Kevin, as if to himself. The reason Whisper had encouraged Kevin to unsettle the team was now clear.

Yes. Thank you," replied Whisper. He knew Kevin understood the role he had played in he facilitating the elimination of a person that Whisper did not want around.

"But you are now one man short," continued Kevin.

It's true I could have waited," Whisper agreed conversationally. "But that would have meant that you or Beppe would have to travel in the boot. This was a good opportunity to deal with two issues at once." His revelation that the person trailing them was Beppe had been entirely intentional.

"Sir, we still have an unresolved matter," the driver spoke up. He was only mildly comforted by the thought that he could not be

Adrian Monico

killed whilst driving.

"Yes, we do. Kevin?" prompted Whisper.

"Young man, you will be pleased to know that Whisper here would be glad that, despite what just happened, you are keeping your focus on the mission. In terms of the unresolved matter about what to do next, the answer is to stay in this lane. The damage is done now and the person behind us is more experienced in this field than all of us combined. Right now, he is fully aware that this car contains Whisper, myself, a semi-experienced driver, a dead team leader, and an unknown fifth person. So, we might as well move pass the mistakes and focus on what happens now. Did I miss anything Whisper?" replied Kevin, playing along.

"Thank you, Kevin. I'd say you covered it all," grinned Whisper.

"Sir, how do you know who's in the car behind us?" asked the driver. There was so much he could learn from what were obviously two masters in their field.

"I used the mirror to first determine the number of people in the car behind us. The silhouette caused by car lights further behind helped with that. I then waited for us to pass a street light to try and make out facial and body features that might trigger recognition within my memory. As I know the person behind us extremely well, it was very easy to determine his identity," replied Whisper. Although apparently genuine, his motivation to coach the young kidnapper was really an attempt to assert himself as the new leader. The driver, not knowing any better, thanked Whisper for the explanation. If could manage not to get his neck snapped by this man, he might just end up being a lot better at his job.

Knowing that Whisper was in the car, Beppe's assumption was that the person sitting in the front passenger seat either upset him somehow or the plan had been to get rid of him all along. The next phase was to determine how they would capture him and what to do to ensure that the kidnap attempt would not "go south" and result in his own premature death. As there was little else to be done, Signor Beppe reflected as he drove on how he would go about the kidnapping if he were Whisper.

The duty officer knocked briskly on Beta's door and called, "Excuse me, sir. I have the latest SITREP." He waited for permission from Beta to enter the office and deliver the situation report.

"Come in, Charles!" replied Beta, glancing up distractedly. "Please leave it on the desk, thank you."

"Sir," Charles said in acknowledgement. He dropped the red folder on the desk as instructed before leaving the office. Although the encounter had only been brief, Charles felt exited by his first visit to Beta's office. The Head of MI6 had even called him by name!

Beta waited for Charles to leave, took a glance at the report and made a private call on his personal phone. As soon as the call finished, he took the micro SIM card from the phone and put it in his coat pocket. He would dispose of it later on.

"Aleks, you know that Signor Beppe might be too far away for us to do anything when the call for help comes?" asked Bernie. The two of them stood in the foyer of the villa while the teenagers assisted with sifting through the potential clues recovered from the scene by the MI6 team.

"I hear you, buddy! So, I guess that you've already figured out a way to babysit these two and help Signor Beppe at the same time?" replied Aleks, pleased that Bernie was reading his mind.

"I guess we were never told where we had to babysit," observed Bernie, breaking into a subtle smile.

"Nope! I'll go and get the car," called Aleks. He was already on his way back to the house when he heard Bernie's reply.

"I'll get the boys ready. We'll be behind you in five!"

After a quick stop to refuel the car, Chiara and Deepa were back in pursuit of Signor Beppe. The temporary halt in their pursuit did not cost them much time as there was nobody else at the petrol station. While Deepa was refuelling, Chiara went to the counter and waited to pay. Within five minutes, they were back on the road and accelerating to make up for lost time.

"You know that it might come down to just us?" asked Deepa, breaking a long spell of silence.

"In terms of being able to rescue Signor Beppe, you mean?" asked Chiara. With her eyes focused on the road ahead, she seemed completely distracted by another thought.

"Yes. I mean, Signor Beppe might need us to go and help him before it's too late," Deepa elaborated. She could not shake the feeling of concern she had for him.

"I doubt it'll come to that. After all, he wants us to simply keep track of him and, if the bug is found, simply move our closer to trail him at a visual distance. The only way we would need to go to his rescue is if the MI6 team can't make it," Chiara explained, finally managing to concentrate on the task at hand.

"Turn right at the second exit," ordered Deepa in response to the screen that showed Beppe's location. "Looks like they have gotten off the freeway." Suddenly Deepa's phone rang, startling both girls. The shock caused Deepa to speak louder than intended. "Simon!" she yelled. "I thought you understood the need for radio silence."

"Hi Deepa. Sorry, I thought that you should know that I'm with Stephen and, along with our two babysitters, we're on our way to help," Simon replied ignoring the reference about the radio silence.

Although this was not strictly in accordance with Beppe's plan, it was a relief for both girls to know they were no longer going to be alone.

"You are in luck. As the roads are empty, and thanks to Bernie's slick driving we are quickly gaining on you," Simon followed.

"We are glad to hear from you Simon. Chiara and I will keep providing you up-to-date locations of our whereabouts so that you can travel to us along the most direct route," replied Deepa.

Signor Beppe glanced at the dashboard display and frowned. It was not part of his plan to run out of petrol before he had the chance to be captured. He had been in pursuit of the car carrying Kevin and Whisper for hours now and there seemed be no end in sight. The sun was starting to appear on the horizon. Before long, the early morning traffic would thicken and risk getting in the way of everyone's schemes. Beppe turned down a small lane and came to a halt at a stop sign. He could not see the car ahead, but fortunately caught a glimpse of it turning left only a few moments earlier. Just as he reached the junction, the car ahead reversed suddenly back towards him, screeching to a halt and barely missing his bumper bar. Instinctively, Signor Beppe shifted gears from first to reverse, but before he could release the clutch, a metallic object rapped sharply on his driver side window.

"You know I won't miss! Please switch off the engine and get out slowly with your hands on your head," came the instructions from the man who had used the barrel of a pistol to knock on the window.

Signor Beppe looked up. Despite being confronted with the barrel that was pointed without wavering at his face, he felt a wave of happiness at being reunited again with Whisper. He followed the instructions and exited the car with both hands held high. Whisper silently proceeded to turn his mentor around and use plastic ties to handcuff his wrists behind his back.

"Ciao, Whisper. Despite the circumstances, I am happy to finally see firsthand that you are ok," observed Signor Beppe as he was guided firmly but respectfully to the other car.

Whisper ignored the comment and gestured for Signor Beppe to sit in the front seat. Although prisoners were usually transported in the backseat of a car, Whisper felt more comfortable having the prisoner in front of him rather than behind. As Signor Beppe was being helped into the seat, he saw Kevin sitting silently in the back with a black hood over his head.

"Looks like we are finally going to have that family reunion we never had the chance to arranged," joked Signor Beppe. It was an attempt to be heard by and perhaps also reassure his son.

"All we now need is a belly full of food and wine," replied Kevin, acknowledging Signor Beppe's presence and conveying to him that he was unharmed.

"It's funny you should say that," laughed Whisper. "That's exactly what we are on our way to: a family reunion. You wait and see who the guest of honour will be!" He laughed again. "Meanwhile, you will not need this," continued Whisper. He lifted Signor Beppe's feet from the car and removed first his shoes and then his socks. lifting them outside the car, where he was standing.

Signor Beppe watched in dismay. "Oh dear. Che dispiacere." He let the words slip out. 'Family', Whisper had said. What family members was he talking about? Beppe's family in Italy had no part in his espionage career. Had the Consigliere resorted to kidnapping them?

Kevin, too, had reacted to Whisper's hints. Oh God, he thought. Simon! A cold chill raced down his back.

"Displeased about what?" asked Whisper in response to Beppe's comment.

"La vita," sighed Beppe, slipping into self-reflection. "Life!"

CHAPTER 7 - Springboard

"Chiara, let's stop here. They're just down at the end of the next alley on the left. And they haven't moved in ten minutes," said Deepa, eyes fixed on the slow flashing dot that signalled Signor Beppe's position on a digital map on her phone. Chiara did as asked and pulled over. They decided to wait for another ten minutes. If the winking signal did not move in that time, one of them would be get out of the car and go for an inquisitive walk.

Meanwhile, the car carrying Simon and Stephen and their babysitters was only ten minutes away. The whole drive had been very quiet, broken only by the occasional comment from Simon repeating Deepa's SMS updates. He was really pleased to be in the company of Aleks again. Although a naturally reclusive person like Bernie, Aleks always tried to make Simon feel at ease by revealing the humorous and rarely glimpsed warm-hearted side of himself.

Aleks himself did not think much of the spy world and all the dirty jobs that came with it. Although in his career he had killed numerous times, it had always been in self-defence. He certainly did not condone the assassination orders that governments were often giving to their special services. He respected Signor Beppe and his career achievements, and once told him that he believed assassination was a coward's way to deal with conflict. Signor Beppe, as always, had responded diplomatically to the younger man's observation and simply ended by agreeing with Aleks. Still, if it came to the point and there were no alternative options, he hoped the 'termination' would be carried out by someone ethical and humane. Signor Beppe, although never troubled by any special remorse about the killing he had done, never lowered himself so far as to make his targets suffer, or worse still, to toy with their fear before delivering a clean death to them.

In the driver's seat, Bernie spent the journey replaying in his mind all the events that had occurred after his capture. Something was missing. He could feel it. That was why he was glad to be driving. It kept his body occupied and let his thoughts analyse over and over every detail of the past few hours in the hope of identifying some piece of intelligence that would give them an advantage in this mission, even if it was only slight.

"Aleks, what's your involvement in all of this? You obviously aren't part of the Secret Intelligence Service, nor do you belong to any of our armed forces. In fact, although you do a great job at mimicking someone from an English background, I'm starting to think that your Surrey accent is all an act," said Bernie. Was it something about his fellow babysitter that was bothering him?

Aleks took his eyes off the road for a second and gave Bernie an inquisitive look, trying to determine just how much he could trust the person he just met. "I guess it's only fair that I share something about myself," he conceded after a pause. "Especially as I got to read a synopsis of your dossier before we left the house," grinned Aleks.

"What? How?" were the only words Bernie could muster in response to the revelation that this stranger could gain access to such information.

"Don't worry, Bernie. It's part of my role to do some research about everyone I deal with. It helps to avoid any unnecessary surprises in the midst of a battle. Speaking of which, I'm pleased with what I read. We're going to get along just fine," replied Aleks blithely, returning his focus to the road.

Simon could not help but smile at the change of direction that the conversation had just taken. Aleks certainly went from the defensive to the offensive. He glanced across at Bernie who sat quietly, hands firm on the steering wheel, gaze fixed forward. Although appearing calm, Bernie was uncomfortable about the upper hand the stranger next to him just gained. As if sensing this, Aleks commenced without any further prompts to tell his companion about his background, from growing up in a hunting family, to spending his teenage years living in a hut in the Norwegian mountains, and starting his career in the Norwegian Army. This was followed by his time in the FSK Special Forces, his temporary secondment to the German Intelligence agency Bundesnachrichtendienst, and how he finally came to find employment protecting Signor Stefano, Signor Beppe's brother. Bernie found himself completely captivated by Aleks' stories. Although Bernie's own background was equally impressive, he acknowledged the talent Aleks had in storytelling. Even the two teenagers in the backseat were enthralled by the narrative.

"Any family?" asked Bernie genuinely interested.

"Bernie, if that was something that mattered to us, then you and I are in the wrong business. I've had various 'friends' during my life, but nothing longer than a few months. Usually I terminate the relationship before it starts getting complicated," Aleks replied honestly, reflecting briefly on a couple of his friends. "Not to mention that even if I wanted to be in a relationship, it would hardly be the kind that would result in marriage and kids," he added.

Bernie found himself startled by Alek's last statement. He wasn't expecting such frankness from such a seemingly reserved and private man. There were many ways to interpret this comment, but Bernie was too uncomfortable to follow up with any further queries. Just as well, for Aleks would not have answered any further questions on this matter.

Chiara stood at the end of the laneway looking down at the sock that was faithfully emitting the tracking the signal. Although the meaning of the discarded the sock was immediately clear to her, she stood and reflected for a few minutes about what to do next. Removing her mobile phone from her back pocket, she quickly dialled a number.

"It's me. He's been taken. I assume that this was your plan all…" Chiara broke off and listened as the person she rang interrupted her. "Sorry… Yes, I'm listening! Ok… Ok. Bye." She disconnected the call then turned and started walking slowly up the laneway to where Deepa was waiting. At the last minute, just before reaching the point where Deepa would see her, she broke into a sprint.

Deepa knew something was wrong the moment she saw Chiara skidding around the corner and sprinting to the driver's side of the car. Without hesitation, thinking that Chiara was being chased, Deepa stretched across towards the steering wheel and twisted the car keys in the ignition. As Chiara touched the door handle, the engine burst into life.

"What's wrong?" cried Deepa, eyes flicking between Chiara who was now sliding into the seat and the end of the laneway ahead of them.

"He's gone! They've taken him!" The words rushed in a faked panic from Chiara's mouth as she reached across for her seatbelt.

"What you mean? But the signal," replied Deepa looking down at the bleeping dot on her mobile phone as Chiara put the car into gear and stepped on the accelerator, leaving her companion to register the situation. "But how? How did they find the chip so quickly?" continued Deepa. Adrenalin was flooding through her veins, filling her body with fear.

"I don't know, ok! All I know is that all I found were his socks lying on the ground," Chiara yelled as she skidded hard left into the laneway.

Deepa, caught off guard by the sudden change of direction, reacted by seizing the door handle on the passenger side and trying to keep her balance as the car veered from side to side. Chiara accelerated down the laneway as fast as she could. Halfway down, Deepa could make out the isolated socks lying like two small icebergs in the middle of the Pacific Ocean. Deepa's eye locked on the socks and her mind simply froze. Chiara suddenly slammed both feet on the brake, locking all four tyres and forcing the car into a loud skid. The momentum of the vehicle carried them across the stop line, eventually bringing them to a halt in the middle of the adjacent street.

"Deepa, snap out of it! Which way?" demanded Chiara. They were already losing time in their pursuit.

"Let-let me think!" said Deepa, emerging from her mind freeze. "They're unlikely to go back to a main road or freeway as the traffic cameras would pick them up," she continued as she scanned the map on her phone. "Left," she decided. "Turn left. There's lots of suburban streets."

Chiara immediately punched her foot on the accelerator while leapfrogging both hands over the steering wheel in an effort to turn it as fast as humanly possible. The rear wheels clawed into the asphalt and the car jack-knifed to the left. At that exact moment, the phone rang.

"Hey, Deepa," came Simon's voice calmly. "What's up?"

Simon felt his pulse quicken in response to the news from Deepa. "Aleks, put your foot on it!" he called. "They've got Signor Beppe and Deepa says they must have found the bug too." He could almost feel the level of tension in the car rise as each of the four occupants grew suddenly more alert. "Yes I'm listening," he said into the phone. "Where? Ok... Yes I can still track you on my mobile... Ok, I'll make the call and request a satellite! And Deepa," he added, "be careful!"

"What's happening?" asked Stephen on behalf of the rest of the car.

"Hold five, Stephen," replied Simon asking to wait whilst scrolling through for the phone number of the MI6 control room and dialling it. "Hi, I need urgent connection to Sunray! Access code: TB33. Yes, I'll standby," Simon said into the phone as soon he was connected. "Hi... Yes I am. Signor Beppe has been taken. We've lost his tracking signal. I request immediate satellite coverage. Please use Deepa's mobile signal as the starting point of reference. Stephen, the assigned agents and I are in another car heading at speed towards the girls' location. We should be there in ten minutes. Deepa is Point for more details," Simon stated clinically. He had learned during his military training the importance of giving short, direct and calm orders. After a pause he said, "Thank you... Yes, I'm ok... Yes, we are armed... Yes, they both arrived at the house at the same time... Ok, I'll let them know... Ok, I'll report back in fifteen minutes." He disconnected the call and took a breath.

"Gents," he said to the car at large, "you've heard my summary to Beta. He has appointed Bernie as Lead. Satellite feed will commence in seven minutes. He also said that he is keeping Team 12 in country on a two minute Ready Stand By notice!"

"Bernie, your call," Aleks said.

"Stephen, how are you with a map?" asked Bernie, not wanting to waste any time.

"Great!" replied Stephen, a little too loudly. The sudden increase in tempo had given him a jolt of energy.

"Good," said Bernie. "Let's swap seats. I need you to jump in the front passenger seat and navigate. Simon, you and I need to go through every single detail that Deepa gave you. Right now, I need to understand everything there is to know, preferably without having to contact Deepa and Chiara." Privately he thought they had already lost the opportunity to find Signor Beppe immediately, but at the same time, he was not going to cause any further time or advantage to be lost.

Beta came back to his office from the control room and poured himself a glass of scotch. He sat at his desk, staring at the viscous, aged nectar for a few minutes. It was becoming harder to drink each time he poured it, triggering as it did conflicts within him, especially the dilemma of sacrificing friends for the greater good. Before finally wetting his lips with the liquid, he decided to make a quick call from his secure phone.

"Hi, it's me... Yes, I've heard. Just make sure they are treated with dignity... That's fine, I know what he has planned for Signor Beppe. I've accepted that. Even so, make sure it'll be humane... Call me as soon as you get there. And tell him that I expect him to call me within the next four hours."

He disconnected the call and found the glass filled with scotch staring back at him. The mere thought of lifting the glass containing the vile substance made him feel nauseous. Exasperated, Beta rose from his chair and walked from the office, leaving the glass resting, still full, on his desk.

Once Whisper hung up the phone, the car returned to absolute silence. Although the two hired guns wanted to know if there were any new instructions, both feared speaking out of turn. They certainly did not want to end up like their broken-necked leader in the boot of the car.

"Whisper, all of this doesn't make sense to me," Kevin said suddenly, breaking the silence. Whisper looked at him without responding. "I don't understand how you're comfortable with helping someone who obviously has a vendetta agenda against our family," continued Kevin, although he didn't really expect a reply.

"We welcomed you into our famiglia and I loved you like my own son," joined in Signor Beppe. He switched into Italian. "Per un bel tempo mi hai chiamato 'Papa'," he said, reminding Whisper that he used to call him 'Dad' during his younger years.

"Basta!" Whisper snapped abruptly, wanting his two prisoners to stop.

"We're not trying to use guilt to convince you to help us," Kevin insisted quietly. "We're trying to tell you that if the plan is for us to die, then you should walk away from this now before you end up with your family's blood on your hands."

"It's because of our family that I'm embroiled in this!" Whisper barked back. Instantly he regretted his use of the words our family. "I feel disgusted about this whole mission," he went on. "But at the same time, I finally feel vindicated."

Both Signor Beppe and Kevin were silent after this outburst, startled by the insight they'd just received about their kidnapping. Whisper too was quiet. He glared out of the window, frowning with sudden uncertainty.

"Left at the next turn," directed Deepa. The role of navigator felt to her like being a life raft in an ocean of despair.

"Should we check in?" asked Chiara, mindful of the time that had passed since their last update.

"I want to. But we were explicitly asked not to, remember?" replied Deepa. "Right at the next junction," she added, balancing the instructions with her response to Chiara's question. "I just hope we're heading in the right direction," she fretted. "I'm still thinking that if I was them I would want to use roads that were not under surveillance to lead me to an alternate vehicle. Hopefully this situation was unanticipated and they have no other car to switch to." She looked across at Chiara, desperately wanting to hear some confirmation of her thoughts. It was quick in coming.

"I agree. I'm just hating the fact that it feels like the rescue mission is solely comprised of two teenage girls who are completely out of their depth," observed Chiara as she grinded the gears. They both glanced momentarily down at the gearstick before looking up at one another and bursting into nervous laughter.

"Sorry, I actually thought that I was doing well at this, considering that I only started getting driving lessons a few months ago," admitted Chiara with some embarrassment.

"No sweat! My lessons have only been in automatic cars, so I'm the last person to comment. I'm so glad you are doing the driving." Deepa smiled for a second before realising in panic that she had taken her eyes off the electronic map. "Second on the left," she instructed after taking a few seconds to find their location again.

As Chiara swung the car around the corner, she reflected that really liked Deepa and her other two companions. In fact, she wished at times that her core mission could be abandoned and she was free to be a genuine member of the teenager training program. This was certainly not what she asked for when she approached Beta about joining MI6. She still recalled the day when Beta finally agreed to bring her in. Her first mission had been exciting and it put her on the right track to one day avenge the death of her dad. She now understood that it had all been part of her induction into a different, uglier part of the espionage world. Her initial task required her to locate herself in one of the more beautiful parts of the world. Under the pretence of being a waitress, she spent her days collecting and reporting data on a particular target. Little did she know that the individual in question would turn out to be a Director of MI6, who was also the father of a friend who had a crush on her and Beta's best friend.

In the six months since that mission, Chiara certainly felt that she had matured. Her time in Tuscany was no challenge when compared with what she was now being asked to do, yet even so, amid the exhilaration she experienced back then came bouts of high stress caused by her fear of being discovered as a spy in a foreign country. She recalled a secret visit to Pisa with Beta, during which she asked him how his agents sustained such constant high pressures. His response was that eventually there was little that would trigger fear. Her immediate assumption was that was because agents became used to it. She was partially corrected in this by Beta, who said that the chase for adrenalin would also predispose agents to ignore everything else. Now, as she wound the car through the suburban streets following Deepa's directions, Chiara could not help but reflect drift on that conversation with Beta. He had certainly been grooming her for greater risks, but until a week ago, she never truly understood what she had agreed to do, which was to be a double agent put in place by the head of the organisation she was lying to. When Chiara first agreed to work for MI6, never in her wildest dream she thought that she would be spying against the agency that hired her. And she certainly never thought that the day would come where MI6 would ask her to betray one of their agents.

Kevin sat silently replaying Whisper's last words in his mind: "It is because of our family that I am embroiled in this. I feel disgusted about this whole mission. But at the same time, I finally feel vindicated." His immediate thought was that he and Beppe had somehow implicated Whisper into this situation. That was certainly plausible, as there were plenty of enemies that Shadow and Signor Beppe had built over the years. It was very unlikely that whoever was behind this was one of Signor Beppe's enemies, as by now most of them were either in a grave or living it up in some swanky retirement home. It was therefore most likely something to do with Shadow's history. Kevin did give a passing thought to the drug lord who was supposedly was after Signor Stefano, but quickly dismissed the idea for there was no logic in kidnapping a family member. Killing would be the faster and cheaper approach to hurt Signor Stefano.

What Kevin also struggled to determine was what someone could have that would compel Whisper to be part of this. Since the first day Kevin found him near the Berlin Wall, Whisper was one determined person and nobody could get him to do anything unless he wanted to. Whisper had no other family, no valuable possessions and was not fearful for his life, rendering him largely immune to any kind of threat. Although his departure from the family was a sorrowful event, and one that Signor Beppe regretted to this day, it had happened a long time ago and Whisper could have easily come back for revenge. Kevin then wondered if something occurred along the way that completely changed Whisper. Based on their interactions since Kevin was kidnapped in South America, however, he sensed that there was still a strong bond between them. In the back of his mind was a constant fear for Simon. His son seemed to be the missing link. Years had passed and there had been no retaliation from their unknown captor, yet everything seemed to have started after Simon came to Italy. Not getting anywhere with his speculations, Kevin concluded that he would need to provoke more information out of Whisper.

Signor Beppe was also trying to make sense out of Whisper's last words. He hated the idea that his family had brought unhappiness to another of his sons, for he loved Whisper as he did all of his children. Although Whisper's departure was a very low point for Beppe as a parent, he never stopped loving him. In fact, after Lucca's death, he longed to mend his relationship with Whisper. Lucca's departure had also been bitter, although it was not violent like Whisper's had been. The other difference between the two of them was that Lucca was now dead and Signor Beppe would never be able to mend that relationship. But Whisper had let fall the cryptic words behind this kidnapping. A "family reunion", he had said. Was someone out to destroy his family all in one hit? If so, why now?

"Dio!" Beppe whispered to himself.

Kevin was contemplating what to say to Whisper when the silence was broken by his father.

"I am sorry."

Whisper, along with the two remaining members of his team, ignored these words.

"I again have somehow caused you pain," continued Signor Beppe. Could it be Whisper himself who wanted to destroy his family? He did not believe that Whisper was capable of that, but he had always been so unpredictable.

Whisper remained silent but felt his stomach twist into knots.

"A father should not make the mistake I made with you. It was unforgivable and I don't want things to end like they did with Lucca, where I will never be able to make amends," Signor Beppe confessed. He saw no reason not to say what was genuinely in his heart.

"That's a presumption." The words escaped, immediately regretted, from Whisper's mouth. Although he had spoken softly, Signor Beppe heard him and felt a sudden jolt of joy. He interpreted Whisper's outburst as indicating that he did still have a chance to make amends, unlike with Lucca.

Kevin, who got a different meaning entirely from Whisper's reply, felt a chill run up his spine.

"Hello," Bernie said into the mobile phone after accepting the incoming call. "Yes, we are a kilometre away from the girls, but I've decided to use alternative roads to go in the same direction. It widens our area of search," continued Bernie. He paused to listen, realising at the same time that everyone in the car was completely hanging on his words. "Ok, standby. Simon," he said, turning to the attentive teenager, "Sunray has asked you to pass me your helmet. Apparently he's about to stream satellite footage of this area into it." He looked down at Simon's feet where the helmet lay inside a carry bag.

"Ok. But shouldn't we give it to Aleks? It'd help him with navigation," replied Simon as he reached for the bag.

"Yes, but first I want to have a look and get a feel for the area," replied Bernie, pleased by the lateral thinking Simon had shown. "Sunray, have you got a team reviewing all of the local CCTV footage?" he said into the handset. "Bugger! They certainly thought this through. Ok... Yes... Out!"

"No cameras in the area?" Aleks asked.

"Zilch!" came Bernie's frustrated reply. "None in the next five kilometres along the whole north-south strip we're travelling along."

"But…" Stephen began, then stopped.

Aleks flicked a look across to him. "But what?" he asked.

"Oh, sorry. I was about to ask how we're supposed to find them then? I decided to refrain from asking because there didn't seem to be much point," Stephen lied quickly.

"Ok, I guess we need to stick with the current plan then," observed Bernie, ignoring Stephen's comments.

"Stephen?" Simon called softly.

"Yes?" he replied in a disinterested tone.

"Can you please turn around and look at me?" Simon continued in a polite undertone. Stephen pivoted around and faced Simon. "The Director is my father. I have never known him, as I grew up with just my mother under the belief that my father died when I was younger. I only learned who he was as he was leaving us in Barcelona. That means I haven't even had the chance to tell him that I know. And now…" Simon didn't finish his sentence. The words got stuck in his throat.

Stephen did not need to hear what Simon had intended to say. He knew that the way the events were panning out, Simon might never get to see either his father or grandfather again. He did not say anything but simply turned around and gazed at the road ahead. Regardless of was happening, Stephen hated Simon. This was not because who Simon was, but because, until now, he came across as a teenager who was brought up by parents who loved and spoilt him. To Stephen, Simon also represented the organisation that ruined his relationship with his own dad. That was what he had always believed about Simon. Until now.

Unaware of the effect of his revelation on Stephen, Simon sat in the back seat felt gutted and completely exposed. He sensed that Stephen might have thought of something that could help in their pursuit and had only confessed his secret in the belief that it might get Stephen to put aside whatever differences they had. As he gazed morosely at the road ahead, he realised this was not to be the case.

"Kid, are you ok?" Aleks broke the silence, peering at Simon in the rear-view mirror. Signor Stefano had confided in Aleks about the relationship between Simon and Signor Beppe, but finding out who Simon's father was took him by surprise. Simon made no reply and Bernie, who was also feeling for him, decided it was important get everyone focused back on the mission.

"Here, Aleks, put this on," Bernie offered, as he reached forward to slip Simon's helmet over Aleks' head. "You're in luck. Simon's head is larger than yours so it should slip on quite easily," continued Bernie. The car slowed momentarily as Aleks shook his head a little to settle the helmet. Simon continued his silent staring.

"I have an idea that might give us an advantage." It was Stephen who had spoken and his words instantly caught everyone's attention. "Pretty soon, more cars will be hitting the road as I'd imagine people who live this far out of the city would be early risers and early drivers in order to beat the peak traffic. That means our travel is about to be slowed down and it will become harder to spot the target vehicle. I'd also imagine that Whisper is aware of this. If I were him, I'd want to change the vehicle pretty soon. If they don't already have one waiting to jump into, they'll need to steal one. If they intend to break into a car, they need to do it pretty quickly before too many witnesses are driving around, and if I'm right, they will lose a bit of time in finding the vehicle and doing the switch. I've noticed in this area that most houses have a double garage, which will make it even harder to find a vehicle parked in the street." The words rolled out of Stephen's mouth.

"So, what are you proposing?" Aleks asked. He had already realised most of what Stephen had just said.

"I think that we, including the girls, quickly jump back on the freeway and race ahead. I've looked at the map. In the next seven kilometres, there are four entry points into the freeway and the next one is one kilometre away. I think we should get on the freeway there, as it'll allow us to race ahead and set up surveillance at any of the entry points. Hopefully, because of the speed, we can reach the freeway ahead of them. When you combine that with the time Whisper might lose in swapping a car, it would give us enough time to leap-frog them and set up a 'net'," Stephen concluded, still keeping his eyes on the road.

"Bugger me, kid! It's a simple plan and it's fraught with several obvious risks. Still, it could be the best option we've got right now," responded Aleks, feeling impressed with the teenager's reasoning and planning.

"Simon, call the girls and tell them to get back on the freeway pronto! Stephen, any idea how to mitigate the risk associated with choosing the two wrong entry points? And how are we going to spot their stolen vehicle?" Bernie followed on. Simon was already dialling his mobile.

"Well," hedged Stephen as Simon conveyed the plan to Deepa. "We could leave a mobile phone at the two entries we can cover and have them stream the video footage to us. In terms of the vehicle, I seem to recall that most people are not fussed enough about our environment to carpool to work, so I'm thinking that there can't be too many cars that have all the seats filled with people. I'm also thinking that Sunray might be able to tell us if there are any surveillance cameras located at any of the entry points."

"It could work," agreed Bernie, who was looking across at Simon.

"No!" snapped Chiara. Her tone was so sharp that Deepa almost dropped the phone in surprise.

"What?" she asked, regathering the phone that was set to handsfree mode.

"What?" echoed Simon, not realising that Chiara was also listening in on the call.

"Simon, don't tell the control room anything. We have been one step behind all along and I think it'd be prudent to keep this plan to ourselves," Chiara called loudly. She wanted to make sure she could be heard but was also feeling guilty about potentially compromising her own covert mission.

"Ok. Thanks, Chiara. Let me tell the guys here," replied Simon.

As Deepa sat waiting for Simon to speak again, she stared at Chiara, sensing that there was more to her vehement response and her caution. Chiara, aware of her companion's scrutiny, did not take her eyes from the road. A moment later, Simon's voice came through the phone again.

"Ok. I've been asked to direct you to the third exit. Be careful." He hung up without waiting for a reply.

"Chiara, is everything ok?" asked Deepa. Something wasn't quite right but she felt uncertain about how to address her concerns.

"Yes, why?" replied Chiara.

"I'm sorry if this comes out wrong, but your snap reaction to Simon's suggestion to call MI6 was, well, just a little too emotional. What is it? Why are you so against us reporting back?" Deepa inquired softly.

Chiara knew she had made a fatal mistake. But at the same time, deep within, she felt a small sense of relief.

"Deepa, now isn't the time. I need you to help Simon and the best way you can do that right now is to drop this conversation. Most of all, you can't say anything about this to any of the others." Chiara turned her head momentarily to look into Deepa's worried eyes. A flash of determination illuminated them in response to these words and Chiara realised her friend was even more motivated to dig further. Before Deepa had a chance to speak, she said in a heartfelt tone, "If you love him, you need to trust me."

"And if you care for him, you need to trust me!" Deepa shot back.

Chiara sighed and tightened her hands on the steering wheel. "Ok, I'll tell you. But I need your absolute word that you'll take it to the grave with you, unless I give you prior permission to tell anyone." Having already made one monumental error, she was about to make an even a greater mistake. At the same time, she realised that all her recent ruminations had led her to conclude that what was asked of her had been completely unethical and gone right against her moral fibre.

"Ok. I'll take it to the grave with me," Deepa promised. She had a gut feeling that her life was about to be shaken up once again. "What is it that don't you want anyone to know?"

"I've been thinking about a better solution to increase our chances," Aleks said into the first moment of silence after Simon hung up the call. "We split up. Young Simon and I find another car to use," he continued, knowing that the logic was unquestionable at this point in time.

"Yes. I completely agree," Bernie replied after a second of thinking about which of the two teenagers should go with him. He liked both boys, but Stephen's plan had impressed him.

It took only five minutes for Simon and Aleks to find, acquire and start driving a relatively new black Toyota Camry that looked to be in fairly good condition.

"I know I've asked you before, but are you ok, kid?" Aleks asked, as smoothly changed gears in the new car.

"Yes. Thanks. It's just that every time I get close to my dad, something drives an even greater wedge between us. I actually felt closer to him when I thought that he was dead," Simon reflected, aware that he was drifting into a despondent mood.

"It'll be ok. Your family is bulletproof. They always come out the other side victorious," Aleks said heartily in an attempt to cheer Simon up.

"You know what bothers me?" Simon asked. "About the mission, I mean." Much as he liked Aleks, he was not really in the mood for a personal conversation about his life.

"The 'bug'," Aleks responded in a flash.

"Yes! It was strange that Signor Beppe told the girls about it and then asked them to tell us. Unless…" He paused. "Unless it was a test."

"It was. And it worked," Aleks replied taking a quick glance at the teenager.

"It worked?" Simon's eyes widened with surprise then narrowed as he realised. "I see. It shows that we have a mole."

"Yes. And by the two of us splitting away from the others, it'll hopefully help determine which of the other teams has the mole."

"And you figured that I was a safe bet as I'm the only one who is related to the director and Signor Beppe?" reasoned Simon.

"Correct."

"But if there is a mole, then our current plan might have already been exposed!" The idea of this jolted Simon upright in his seat.

"That's true," conceded Aleks. "But I think I know what to do next to ensure that the odds are still on our side."

It didn't take long for Chiara and Deepa to reach the entry to the freeway. They drove onto it and, by a stroke of luck, found a petrol station one hundred metres ahead. They took advantage of a few parked trucks and hid themselves between them. This gave them some degree of disguise while still allowing them to maintain a clear view of the freeway. As they waited, Chiara continued explaining her situation to Deepa.

Stephen and Bernie decided that parking on the side of the freeway would not be the best way for them to remain hidden. Instead, they found a side street that had good visibility of the freeway entry ramp. Once parked, both remained silent, eyes focused on the ramp.

"What happens if they don't come this way?" Simon asked. Aleks' plan was not a bad one but Simon still felt nervous about it.

"Your world, kiddo, seems to always come down to quick analysis and then a flip of a coin. Hopefully the choice you make will give you greater odds, but it still comes down to having a bit of luck."

"And you still think here is where we get the greater odds?" Simon asked, not convinced.

"Well, the freeway is pretty much covered. Even if we don't cover one of the entry points, the next two are now being watched. This means that in a worst case scenario, we might have missed the kidnappers driving onto the freeway earlier on, but eventually they would drive past the other two teams. However, if the kidnappers decide to take another route, then hopefully we'll get them caught in our net," Aleks replied. The odds were low but he was confident with what he'd worked out.

The chirp of an incoming SMS broke the silence in the car. Whisper looked down at his mobile phone and thought for a few minutes.

"Turn back!" he ordered at last. The driver immediately looked for some space to perform a U-turn. "A couple of hundred meters back, I saw a sedan parked in the street. We'll swap it for this car," continued Whisper. If it came to a choice, he'd rather be chased by the police in a stolen car, than by MI6 in a known one.

"Signor Beppe, did Lucca have anyone in his life when he was killed?" Kevin asked. He chose to address his father formally so as to avoid giving the other guards any more information about their relationship.

"I think he once mentioned to his mamma that he met a girl on a trip to Germany, but I am not sure if it was serious. At the time, he was angry with me and mostly spoke to his Mamma," Signor Beppe replied after a very long pause.

Whisper felt an urge to end the conversation, but his curiosity permitted it to continue.

"Did he go to Germany often?" Kevin continued.

"Non so! At the end, before he was deployed to the Middle East, he did spend more time away. Weeks at the time. But the answer to your question is that I do not know."

"And his body?" Kevin asked. He always assumed that it was flown back to Treviso, but had never wanted to go and see the grave for himself.

"It's still there. Somewhere. I tried and tried to have it returned, but 'they' told me it was too dangerous to go and get it. I still hope that one day my Lucca will be sent back home to me."

Almost reluctantly, Whisper felt deep within him sorrow for Signor Beppe. Although he still held small pockets of resentment from the time when he left this family behind, over the years his other memories of that period of life had grown more positive. This conversation hit a soft spot with him, as one of the reasons Lucca ran away from home was that he was jealous of the time Signor Beppe spent with Whisper, training him to be a spy. In a way, Whisper had been the seed that led to the family feud. Maybe that went some way to explaining the truth behind his acceptance of this mission?

Determined to avoid hearing anything else that might lead him further down a self-reflective path to guilt, he suddenly gave the order for silence.

"Are you angry at me?" Chiara asked. While ashamed of her actions, she felt at the same time as if a heavy weight had been lifted from her conscience.

"No. Although part of me feels betrayed, the reality is that you were just following orders from the same organisation that I also report to. So although you being ordered to go against us is completely insane, you are in fact following MI6 orders as well, "Deepa replied after a moment, feeling somewhat confused.

"Am I? I mean, am I really following the orders of MI6 or simply the orders of an individual within MI6? After all, if my orders to assist with Signor Beppe's kidnapping were genuinely 'official', then the only plausible reason that I can think of for being asked to work against you all is that this is some mock mission that has been set up up to train us. The problem is that this does not seem at all like a training mission. It's too complicated and there's too much risk placed on all of us. I mean, this could be really psychologically harming for Simon." Chiara's analysis brought a frown to her face.

"Mmm, I agree with you," Deepa followed on. "Not to mention the fact that Simon called out the genuine casualties that resulted from the clash at the villa. Would MI6 sacrifice people's lives for the sake of training four teenagers?".

"I've thought about that, and the only sane way to explain it is that they actually did not die, and that too was a clever trick of some kind," Chiara proposed, but her tone indicated that she did not really believe it.

"MI6 could have not predicted Simon's spontaneous actions. Besides, the way Simon described the events at the house, I reckon the death of those people were real. I think the reason we're trying to justify this is a training exercise is that the alternate is too horrible to comprehend," Deepa added.

"So Beta is a double agent!" Chiara called out, as the realisation of the truth hit her.

"Maybe," conceded Deepa. "Either way, you need to springboard yourself out of this predicament and help us, help Simon, to free the Director and Signor Beppe." These last words were spoken with genuine conviction.

"You are right! I hate myself for having been so easily fooled. And right now I feel completely alone for having betrayed myself and you guys too. I need to snap myself out of this! 'Springboard' into redemption it is," Chiara responded, trying to inject positive energy into her words and herself. The frown, however, remained on her face.

Simon and Aleks sat silently in the car. Mindful that leaving the vehicle running would cause smoke to be visible from the exhaust pipe and could also use fuel that they might need later on, Aleks decided to switch off the engine while they waited. Unfortunately, this meant the car heater was off and it wasn't long before the chill of the morning seeped into the car and engulfed them. Simon kept rubbing his hands together and blowing warm air into them. His adrenalin rush from his earlier battle had now completely worn off and he struggled against the tiredness that his training had warned him would follow the rush. Aleks, feeling the cold as well, ruefully recalled the new pair of leather gloves lined with Merino wool that reposed comfortably in his travel bag back at the house. He gave himself a swift, mental kick for leaving without them and glanced across at Simon who was, he saw, minutes away from falling asleep. Although the extra set of eyes would come in handy, Aleks knew Simon needed to recover from his earlier battle, as there was sure to be more action to follow in the coming hours. His gaze returned to the windscreen and within minutes, Simon was out like a light.

Kevin was puzzling over the SMS Whisper received earlier. His brother's immediate reaction had been to turn the car around. That meant that whatever the message said, it most likely indicated that it was a lesser risk to retrace their route back towards those chasing them than it was to continue going forward. Signor Beppe also had the same thoughts. His conclusion was that MI6 had somehow set up an ambush ahead, but that Whisper had been alerted to it.

"Guardian angel in MI6 looking after you," Kevin called out, trying to provoke a response. None came, so the Director continued. "Not that the idea of a mole within MI6 upsets me," he said. "After all, double agents have been around since men humans started rubbing sticks together to start make a fire. I am surprised, though, that it has taken MI6 this long to smoke the agent out," Kevin went on after waiting again for a reaction from Whisper. "Over the years, Beta has certainly built a great team of Hunting Dogs."

This was the nickname given to a small, specialised counter-insurgency team. Their main role was to find out foreign spies on British soil and act accordingly. Sometimes, these 'Dogs' covertly influenced foreign spies to operate against their own nations without knowing it. At other times, they turned them into double agents or would arrest them, and on a few occasions, they 'neutralised' them. Among the agents used for the latter purpose were the Director, Whisper and Signor Beppe.

"To be frank, I'm amazed you've lasted this long," Whisper hissed at last. "You still jump to conclusions influenced by limited lateral thinking." He knew Kevin was simply trying to draw information from by using provocative statements. Although unsure of the reason for this, Whisper was enjoying this situation, and intentionally giving away only the smallest snippets of intelligence. Both Kevin's and Beppe's brains snapped into overdrive and instantly commenced analysing this reply.

"I guess I had a lot of luck on my side. It might even be a family trait – one that most likely rubbed off on you as well," Kevin joked in an attempt to keep the conversation going.

"I certainly have picked up a lot of things during the years, but 'luck' isn't one of them," Whisper replied. His mind flew briefly to the years of training he received under Signor Beppe. "Trust is also another thing I did not pick up. This is sadly also another trait of your family," he continued with a slight smile.

"Trust? I guess so. But that's really only a privilege I grant to a handful of people in this world: you being one of them. Which, I guess right now, is not really looking like it was a wise decision," Kevin observed. A taste of bitterness washed through his mouth as he spoke these last few words. Whisper reacted too, feeling his stomach tighten as Kevin's reflection hung in the air.

"It's still so!" insisted Signor Beppe suddenly. "This is just a small tear in my heart." Unknown to each other, both Whisper and Kevin felt a pang of guilt for taking their discussion down this path. It had obviously unsettled their father. "Figli miei, I feel like I am watching the chess games that you two used to play for hours. You spent most of it psyching each other out with words, but not moving many pieces," Signor Beppe continued. Again, both brothers responded independently but simultaneously. Each smiled in the recollection of the times they spent carrying out their "word duels" between very infrequent chess moves.

"Sir!" the driven suddenly called out, pointing down a street to their right. Whisper's gaze snapped in that direction. He saw immediately what had alerted the driver's attention.

Simon jolted into his seat as he heard the tires of a car suddenly clawing into the road. Aleks, upon seeing the car containing the five men, started the engine and dropped the clutch in a few split seconds.

"What's going on?" called Simon, feeling panicked by the sudden take-off.

"We've caught ourselves a big fish, my young man!" replied Aleks, full of excitement that his hunch had proven true.

Simon's excitement was more tempered as the realisation set it. "Oh my God! You were right! One of the other four is working against us." His thoughts went immediately to Stephen.

CHAPTER 8 - The Switch

Chiara and Deepa sat quietly with their eyes glued to the road. There was a lot more Chiara wanted to tell Deepa, but she realised that now was not the time. One single blink could be all it took for them to miss their target driving by.

"We should at least check in," Deepa said at last.

"Yeah," was the single word that came back as a response.

Deepa, without taking her eyes from the road, picked up the mobile phone lying beside her and lifted it up to call Simon's number. "What?" she cried in response to what she saw on the small screen.

"What is it?" asked Chiara, casting only the briefest of glances across at Deepa, as she found herself, like her friend, unable even for a split second to look away from the traffic speeding by.

"I had the electronic map left on and it shows Simon is travelling through the backroads away from here," replied Deepa, her voice betraying her uncertainty and concern.

"Are you sure that it isn't just the software playing up?"

"No. Look! The signal is clearly showing that Simon is moving away from us and retracing the road that we travelled on earlier."

Chiara's eyes flicked to the screen only long enough to confirm Deepa's words. "Is Stephen's signal also visible?" she queried.

"I can't see it," frowned Deepa, peering more closely at the small, glowing screen. "Maybe Simon's marker is superimposed on Stephen's?" She tried to focus on the edges of the green dot reflecting Simon's phone.

"Ok. Where are they in reference to us?" Chiara was already planning for the worst and thinking about how they might catch up to Simon.

"Hold on, let me zoom out," replied Deepa, using the touchscreen to enlarge the map. "Here we are. Looks like if we have to catch up to them, it'd be best to drive back via the freeway," she observed as her eyes scanned the growing distance between Simon's green dot and their own yellow one.

Chiara glanced down again. "What's this?" she demanded, pointing to a blue dot that was flashing a few kilometres to the south of their one.

"That's Stephen's mobile. I don't understand. They appear to have separated." The concern was now obvious in Deepa's tone.

"Call Simon!" advised Chiara abruptly. The whole situation was making her feel uneasy, especially the bit about having been kept in the dark. Instinctively, she wondered if the other teams had somehow found out about her secret role.

At first Simon did not hear the phone ring. The speed at which they were flying down the road consumed most of his senses. Once the car ahead had spotted them following behind, it instantly charged off, turning the pursuit into a high speed chase.

"Simon! Mobile," Aleks called when he realised the teenager was not answering.

"It's Deepa. Should I answer it?" asked Simon after looking down at the caller ID information.

"Of course! You're all on the same team," replied Aleks as he made a sharp handbrake turn to the left and raced along a side street.

"But we've got a mole amongst us," observed Simon. Secretly, he was already convinced that person was Stephen.

"Listen up, kid," said Aleks, keeping the pedal to the metal and his eyes fixed on both the road and the car ahead. "Firstly, we don't actually know if there is a mole in our team or if simply someone is being duped. Secondly, we need all the help we can get, so getting the other cars to work with us to set a trap up ahead is a good thing. Thirdly, even if we did have a mole, we are right now in pursuit of the "bad guys", so I think our enemies already know exactly what we're up to. Just answer the phone, ok?"

"No answer!" cried Deepa, as the phone rang and rang. "What do we do?"

"I don't know," fretted Chiara. "I want to go to them, but our mission is to stay here."

Suddenly a distant voice called out through the mobile handset. "DEEPA? DEEPA!"

"Simon!" Deepa replied in relief.

"Yes. Listen. We found them! We are currently in hot pursuit of the kidnappers and heading back the way we came. I need you to call Stephen and Bernie and tell them to race ahead via the freeway to set up an ambush. You all need to make sure you can find a position to shoot at the tyres. Have you got that?" yelled Simon over the roar of the engine as he bounced around in his seat.

"Simon, hold on! Chiara, back down the freeway as fast as possible! Simon, we don't have any weapon to take out the tyres. I only have the mosquito pistol and the needles will just bounce off the tyres." Deepa's response poured from her in one single breath.

"You'll have to think of something. Just stop the car in front of us. Gotta go!" replied Simon who was unable to think come up with any clever solution himself.

As the call cut out, Deepa thought for a moment she heard the sound of pistol shots coming through the phone, but that couldn't be right. Brushing the idea aside, she immediately called Stephen.

"Are you ok?" shouted Simon, instinctively ducking as the sound of the pistol whipped the air.

"Yes, kid! They only fired a few random shots to scare us.

They were not aimed directly at us," observed Aleks. To Simon's wide eyes, he appeared to be remarkably calm.

"What's the point of that?" Simon demanded, sounding slightly aggrieved.

"Well, I guess that whoever is shooting doesn't want to harm us or, most likely, you. Even so, most people in pursuit of a car would drop back if they were fired upon, which is handy to know if you want to create opportunities get away by using a greater separation between the vehicles," Aleks called back. It seemed a curious time for a lesson, but he figured he might as well use the situation to teach Simon.

"But wouldn't a greater distance allow us greater reaction time to respond to whatever they do?" Simon asked, remembering the motorbike chase between himself and Stephen, during which his split second turns resulted in Stephen's inability to react quickly enough.

"That is also handy," agreed Aleks, recalling missions in which he had used those exact tactics. "However, if you think back to all those Hollywood action movies, you might recall how the cars just get across the railway tracks before a train comes along and cuts the pursuer off, or you have the chased car driving through a red light and just making it through between the traffic, or the car that takes several sharp turns to then hide in a back alley or a garage?" Simon nodded. He'd seen plenty of movies with scenes just like the ones Aleks described. "The point is that the distance is an advantage to the car in front."

"Ok. So, why are we not ramming them down? Wouldn't this be the same as an ambush?" asked Simon, moving rapidly on from the topic and focusing his attention on their next action.

"Your idea about shooting the tyres is spot on for this scenario. Firstly, if we stop them now we would be outnumbered three to two. However, if we use the other two teams to shoot the tyres, there would be six of us against three of them. That's better odds, even if you kids only carry mosquito pistols," replied Aleks. He too was starting to analyse the next possible situation.

"And Mosquito hand grenades," interjected Simon.

"Ok, those too," agreed Aleks before resuming his list. "Secondly, I'm hoping they will take a few more pot shots at us, thus reducing the number of rounds available to them if – or more likely when – we eventually get into a gunfight with them. Thirdly, it's been a while since I was the one chasing rather than being chased and I don't want to end the fun too quickly," Aleks ended with a grin and a wink.

"Should we call Control for support?" Simon asked.

Aleks remained silent for what felt to Simon like hours.

"Dammed if we do, dammed if we don't," Aleks eventually replied. He paused again and then spoke decisively. "Make the call. Just don't tell them about our plan." Simon immediately began dialling the phone.

"Sir! We just received a call from Montenegro asking for direct support. The recruits have re-engaged the target and are in hot pursuit. Team 12 is still in the area. Request approval to assign them to the mission," Charles the duty officer announced the moment he received permission to enter Beta's office.

"Approved. Keep me posted," Beta ordered. Displaying no emotion, his mind raced ahead to work out his next step.

"Thank you, sir!" Charles responded as he turned and walked briskly back to the control room.

Whisper answered the phone without looking at who was calling him. "I imagine you've heard about the change of events," he said without letting the other person speak.

"I'm actually calling to let you know that Team 12 will be there in fifteen minutes," Beta replied.

"Can't you hold them off?" Whisper asked, although he knew that doing so would expose Beta as the mole in MI6.

"I don't have time for silly questions!" Beta snapped. "There is a small multi-level car park at a shopping centre nearby. There is a change of car and someone waiting for you on the second level," he continued, frustrated with the mess that had evolved.

"Ok," replied Whisper and hung up.

"Five kilometres ahead there's a set of lights. Turn left and drive until you see a small shopping centre. Head into its multi-level car park," Whisper instructed the driver, who acknowledged the orders with a small nod of his head.

Kevin listened closely to everything Whisper said in an effort to keep apace with developments and perhaps find some way to leverage their current situation. "You know that if you let one of us go along the way, it'll buy you time as the car behind will stop to rescue us," he observed casually. "Since Signor Beppe is old and slow, he would obviously be the ideal candidate."

"Nice try, Kevin. You already know that this is really all about Signor Beppe. So, if I were to let anyone go, it'd be you. That would also mean that I don't have to put up with you" replied Whisper, giving the suggestion enough acknowledgment to show that it could actually be a viable option.

A metallic blue van entered the multi-level car park. The driver was a very tall and extremely skinny local whose appearance bordered on the anorexic. His face was gaunt and his complexion extremely white. His eyes were buried in dark sockets, his hair was cut in military style and his fingers were long and bony. Thanks to his looks and his employment, he was referred to as the Reaper. As instructed, he drove the van to the second level and parked. He then proceeded to pick up his high powered sniper rifle and walk to the edge of the car park on the side he had been briefed the two cars would be coming from.

"How far are we?" Chiara asked, checking in the rear-view mirror for the car carrying Bernie and Stephen.

Deepa looked down at the map on the phone. "It's the next exit."

Chiara drew in a breath. "So, let me get this right. At the exit, the car behind will overtake us. Bernie will drive on ahead and set himself up with his pistol to try and shoot the driver of the car we want to stop. Meanwhile, we are to find a driveway from which to side ram the car in the event that Bernie fails and the kidnappers get past him."

"Yeah, I know," said Deepa. "Not the best of plans. But it was the best we could come up with." She wished she could quell the feeling butterflies in her stomach.

"Are we going to make it in time to set ourselves up?" worried Chiara.

"It'll be close. Looking at Simon's current location, we're about to just overtake them. I'm hoping that by the next exit, we'll have gained enough of a lead to get off the freeway and arrive at the junction with sufficient time to set up the ambush." As she spoke, Deepa imagined the sequence of events. Chiara nodded once and pressed the accelerator a little harder.

"You! Swap places with our backseat guest," Whisper ordered the guard sitting across from him. Kevin knew immediately what Whisper was preparing to do, but said nothing. As if reading his thoughts, Whisper said to him, "I see that you're not talking. It's not a done deal. But I'd like to be ready, just in case." He watched as Kevin and the guard swapped seats. The exchange was made more difficult by the fact that Kevin was still blindfolded and handcuffed. "You know," said Whisper unexpectedly, "I always secretly wanted to one day operate with the two of you. Funny how life has made that happened, but with its own interpretation." He opened the window once more and took a random pistol shot at the vehicle behind them.

The bullet ricocheted off the car bonnet and struck the centre of the windscreen at high speed, half-penetrating the reinforced glass. Simon threw himself forward, trying to get below the dashboard height while also turning his head towards Aleks, who seemed, as before, to be unperturbed by the risk of getting shot. After a few seconds during which no further pistol shots were heard, Simon sat again back up in his seat, feeling his blood drowning in adrenalin.

"Aren't you scared of getting shot?" he asked, astonished that Bernie could remain so cool.

"Of course, kid. After all, I don't really enjoy being a sitting duck. But the time to react is actually before the bullet is fired. Once the round is shot, it's already too late, as with most current handheld weapons, the bullet travels faster than the sound," Aleks explained, cracking a small smile at Simon's look of admiration. "It's true what they say. You won't hear the bullet that hits you."

"But wouldn't you react anyway to make sure the next round is not adjusted to hit you?" Simon asked, still unable to comprehend Aleks' calmness.

"Absolutely! But we already know that the person in the car ahead is only firing single, random shots. If he wanted to actually kill us, my bet is that he would be double tapping and the bullets would be in perfect line for either you or me."

"And you'd bet your life on that?" Simon questioned doubtfully.

"Ha ha! I guess not," Aleks laughed. He realised that he must sound alarmingly blasé to Simon.

"I honestly struggle to understand how all of you are so unaffected by these events. You, Signor Beppe, Whisper, D-dad," replied Simon. The last slipped out accidentally. He tried to recover his error by whispering it.

"I guess our careers have shaped us this way. Even the hardest rock gets shaped by water. It really is something that happens over a very long time and with such small, incremental changes that it's unnoticeable for years," stated Aleks, reflecting on how many years it had been since he used to think and react in ways similar to Simon. His own upbringing had been more shady than the teenager's, so perhaps he had been more prepared for the dangers he had to face as a spy.

Simon just shook his head, relieved that Aleks appeared not to have heard his mention of his father.

"Ok. Time to switch," Chiara called out as she started driving down the freeway exit. Stephen and Bernie, who were also taking the exit, maintained their speed while Chiara slowed down. Within a few minutes Bernie's car overtook Chiara's. Before long, both cars arrived at the ambush site. Bernie decided that he and Stephen would act like pedestrians at the traffic lights. He would stand a little further apart from Stephen, so as not to seem too obvious. Chiara and Deepa would stay in their car at the first driveway past the junction. Bernie was conscious that there were a few aspects to their plan that would make the difference between success and failure.

For one thing, he would have to be accurate with his shooting. Then, if he failed to shoot the driver, the get-away car would need to continue on in a straight direction in order to line up with the girls' car. If the car with the hostages turned either left or right at the junction, then the second part of the ambush would also fail. To increase their chances of success, Bernie assigned Stephen to stand by the pedestrian crossing and be ready to trigger the red stoplight as soon as they saw the car's lights in the distance. Although Bernie had limited details of the targeted car, there were still very few vehicles on the road, so he was willing to take a guess. This would most likely not be too risky, as he doubted there would be any other cars in the area travelling at such high speed. Bernie did ponder whether he could shoot the tyres instead of the driver. However, he decided he was not confident that the bullet would successfully puncture the hard tyre rubber. Better to stick with the original plan, he reasoned.

Stephen's mobile rang. "Hey. Ok. Thanks. Ok. Bye. Wait! Um... Be careful," he said into it, before hanging up and turning to Bernie. "That was Deepa calling to warn us that the cars are only a kilometre away."

"Thanks, kid. Get ready. Remember, you have a tranquilliser pistol, so don't hesitate trying to work out who to shoot. If I manage to stop the first car, fire at will. We can apologise later to Kevin and Signor Beppe," Bernie instructed the young teenager.

"Here they come!" Stephen called, pointing to the car lights now visible in the distance.

"Ok. Press the pedestrian lights in ten, nine, eight, seven... Now!"

"Deepa, I'm scared," Chiara said out of nowhere.

"Me too," replied Deepa immediately. She had been quietly trying to suppress her fears and felt strangely relieved by her companion's admission. "I never thought that I'd find myself in such situations. I thought that we'd spend be doing surveillance."

Chiara shook her head. "That's not it. Although I do have fear about myself, I'm actually scared that my role as a mole might lead to one of you dying." Images of her friends lying dead on the cold road filled her mind and would not leave.

"I'm sure it wont come to that. Remember, if the car gets through the lights, as it probably will, we'll ram into it from the side and then quickly reverse away from what is most likely going to be a gunfight. Bernie and Aleks will take care of the rest," Deepa replied in an attempt to get their minds back on the mission.

"Thanks. You've been great," Chiara responded with genuine feeling. "It was good to finally unburden my… doubts."

"That's ok. It's what friends are for," replied Deepa. She couldn't help noticing Chiara's hesitation before saying the word 'doubts'.

"And you're a great friend," said Chiara with a big smile.

"Turn coming up, sir," the driver called out to Whisper.

"Ok. Let's try to distract them at the last minute before you make the turn," Whisper responded. He opened the passenger window and prepared to fire another random shot.

"We're coming up to the ambush site," Simon reported, looking down at the flashing signal of Deepa's mobile phone on his digital map.

"Ok. Get my pistol from the left holster. You'll most likely need to use it as it might get tricky for me to do it and focus on the driving," Aleks instructed.

"I have my Mosquito pistol," Simon responded, his tone a little subdued.

Aleks heard the words he didn't say. "Sorry kid, but won't do. Look, I know you don't want to kill anyone, but if we get into a gunfight, I promise you'll not have the moral dilemma that you're having right now. This isn't about killing someone. It's about giving you, me, your friends and your family the best chances of surviving. In a gunfight, people take cover behind hard and preferably bulletproof objects. My pistol has enough punch to get through a car door, but your tranquillising needles don't," explained Aleks in as reassuring a tone as he could manage.

"Ok," replied Simon. Hesitantly, he reached for Aleks' pistol.

Stephen watched the whole event unfold as if in two distinct timeframes. The period from when he first saw the cars in the distance until the moment they reached the traffic lights seemed to flash by. Using all of his concentration and willpower, Stephen focused on trying to slow the movement down in his mind. He felt like he had his foot stuck in the tracks of a railway crossing while a locomotive accelerated at high speed towards him. He felt full of trepidation, frustrated by his inability to freeze time and thereby give himself the opportunity to avoid the inevitable.

The second timeline started from the moment the car reached the traffic lights. Then, everything seemed to happen in slow motion. He found he could observe even the minuets of details. The car commenced a handbrake turn to the left, heading away from him. As it swung past him, he stared directly for one long moment into the eyes of the driver. Then he saw the bullets spewing out of Bernie's pistol, slowly floating across the air. After what seemed like an incredibly long time, he saw them eventually entering the car through windscreen and embedding themselves into the shoulder and chest of the driver.

At the same moment, a blonde haired man with a pistol held out through the open window was firing at the car behind him. His bullets were also crawling through the air until they finally penetrated of the windscreen of the car behind. Stephen could also see his own hand bringing the mosquito pistol up in line with the blonde gunman. In what felt like an out-of-body experience, he felt as if somebody else's finger was pulling on the trigger, sending thickets of sedative needles travelling more like paper planes then subsonic projectiles towards the open car window. As the car drifted to the left, Stephen felt defeat creeping into his mind. Although the stunt turn was occurring in slow motion, he was incapable of doing anything to stop its successful getaway.

Just as the car lined up perfectly with the perpendicular road after drifting 90 degrees to the left, as the tyres finally seem to claw into the road and be about to project the vehicle forward, at the last possible second, something invisible force gave an extra push to the car, causing it to lose control and continue on the parabolic slide that the driver had intentionally initiated. Stephen watched the driver's eyes widen with the realisation that he had lost control. The car skidded until it was travelling backwards, now facing in the same direction it had come from. Bullets were now flying past Stephen and floating towards the target car. He slowly peeled his eyes away from the injured driver and retraced the floating bullets back to their source. Simon was hanging out the window of a car, holding a Glock pistol in his hand and firing it as fast as he could. On the opposite side of the road, Stephen saw Bernie holding a pistol in each hand. He was slowly walking towards the car and showering it with bullets. One pistol seemed to be aimed at the car radiator, while the other was trained on the driver.

Kevin heard only the first bullet as it penetrated the windscreen and embedded itself in someone's flash. The next sensation he felt was a small prick on his cheek, then all went black as Stephen's tranquilliser needle took immediate effect. Signor Beppe had spotted Bernie and Stephen at the intersection well before anyone else in the car. The second he saw Bernie's pistol spewing red hot suppressed gas from its barrel, he instinctively slid down the seat and folding onto his knees, almost touching the floor with his head below the dashboard. He watched the rest of the encounter from a child's perspective: looking up.

At the moment Bernie launched the ambush, Whisper was too occupied with looking back at the car that was following them to foresee the events that were about to occur. Just as he pulled the trigger to fire, the car he was in began its drift to the left. The explosion of Bernie's first bullet coincided with Whisper firing his second round, leaving him was completely unaware that his driver had been hit. The first realisation Whisper had that it was all about to go wrong was the moment when he withdrew his pistol from the window and pivoted in his seat to face forward again. As he swung his body around, he found himself staring at his young apprentice who was standing on the side of the road firing a Mosquito pistol at him. For Whisper, as for Stephen, this moment seemed to grind into a slow motion with both of them staring into each other's eyes as the tranquillising darts floated towards Whisper's face, barely missing his cheeks as they continued their flight past him. In Whisper's case, however, the slow motion effect only lasted a split second. What happened next was

Simon Eady - The Teenage Spy

time catching up to reality at the speed of light.

He was unexpectedly thrown sideways by the car spiralling into a reverse spin then slamming into a shopfront. Whisper found the force too strong to counteract and he felt his body being crushed against the back seat, his pistol flying out of his hands. It crashed into the back windscreen. Before he could peel himself away from the seat, he watched horrified as a special agent walked towards the car firing two pistols simultaneously. Before he could react, the guard sitting next to him launched himself between the two front seats and over the lap of the driver, landing head first onto the car accelerator. His intent was immediately clear as the car suddenly pounced forward towards the approaching gunman.

Simon had known the ambush was set at the upcoming traffic lights. He sat in his seat unsure about what he should do next. However, in the moment that he saw the pistol in Whisper's hand protruding from the side window, his body simply reacted. His left hand reached for the automatic window control. As the window began to lower, he started edging his body through it. First his right hand that was holding the pistol slid through, then his whole right arm, followed by his head and eventually the rest of his upper body. As Simon slid out of the window, his finger kept flicking the pistol's trigger, sending a wave of bullets toward the shooter in front of him. All throughout the firing, Simon was completely numb to whatever else was happening around him. His mind had contracted into tunnel vision on the person firing back at them.

Aleks saw the car they were trailing initiate a handbrake turn to the left. He likewise dropped his right hand immediately to the handbrake and prepared to trigger a drift turn. However, just before the initiation of the turn, he realised that the targeted car was about to lose control and rotate into a reverse spin. He snapped his hand back from the car's handbrake and groped towards Simon's body, grasping the first section of clothing he touched.

Chiara and Deepa both watched in horror as events unfolded like they were spectators on the set of an action movie. For them, it seemed the events all happened in seconds: Bernie shooting at the driver of the car, Stephen firing into the open rear window at someone firing back at him, Simon half hanging out of the passenger window also firing at the car, and then the targeted car doing a 180 degree turn and slamming backwards into the shopfront. Chiara had already the car in first gear and her foot was ready to drop the clutch, however, nothing in front of her was going according to their plan. Not knowing what else to do, she suddenly dropped the clutch and made the car rocket towards the gunfight.

The pistol in Bernie's left hand was the first to run out of bullets. In a blink of an eye, he depressed a release catch and let the empty magazine drop to the ground. Then, as his right hand pistol also ran out of bullets, he repeated the action, but used this hand to reach down for two fully loaded magazines located in special pouches attached to his belt. Although his reloading of his weapon was carried out smoothly, there was a split second in which Bernie dropped his eyes from the out of control car. It was in that same second that the guard dived onto the accelerator and launched the car directly at Bernie. When he lifted his eyes and saw what was coming, Bernie instantly knew he had nowhere to go. No bullets were going to stop the inevitable. He closed his eyes and tried to prepare his body for the impact.

Suddenly, he felt a blast of wind coming at him from behind. It almost threw him over. Then, just before he was rammed down and swallowed beneath the oncoming vehicle, Aleks' car brushed passed him and slammed into the other one car with a thunderous metallic boom. Simon had no opportunity to react. One second he was hanging out of the vehicle and the next he found himself staring at the harrowing collision unfolding before his eyes. Fortunately, Aleks had used his grip on Simon's clothing to yank him forcefully back into the vehicle as the bumper bars of the two vehicles melded themselves together.

Bernie's relief was short-lived. Although the oncoming vehicle stopped centimetres from his knees, the force of the collision caused the rear of both cars to swing into a scissoring that mashed the panels into one another. The rear end of Aleks' car hit Bernie from behind, flinging his tall body over the boot as if he were nothing more than a stuffed toy.

The guard, still with both hands on the accelerator, felt the impact of the collision but remained conscious. He did not know what bought the vehicle to a halt, and simply presumed that he must have hit the gunman and crushed him into the building on the other side of the street. After a brief and eerie silence, during which even the gunfight seemed to have gone dormant, he heard the vehicle's driver softly calling out, "Reverse." Without attempting to interpret the instruction from his semi-conscious colleague, he used one hand to press down the clutch and reached back with the other to move the gear stick into reverse. Then, without missing a beat, he used both of his hands to drop the clutch and press on the accelerator.

Aleks, still stunned and trying to register what had just happened, looked across to his right and stared directly at the target vehicle that was almost perfectly aligned alongside him. However, before he could react, he realised the vehicle was accelerating away from the junction in reverse.

Whisper, too, had registered what the two guards had initiated. He instinctively jumped towards the front seat and grasped the abandoned steering wheel. Although not in an ideal driving position, he managed to squeeze himself between the two front seats and keep hold of the steering wheel while looking back over his shoulder. In this way, he gained some control of the vehicle, reversing it at high speed.

Chiara skidded the car to the right in pursuit of the target vehicle. As she swung into the junction, she saw Aleks looking back at the rear of the kidnappers' car while trying to unsuccessfully restart the car. Completing the turn and lining up towards her prey, she could see from the corner of her eye Bernie's body lying motionless on the ground near the rear end of Aleks' car.

"We need to change directions! We can't outrun them in reverse. On 'three' I need you to press the clutch so I can use the handbrake and steering wheel to make a 180 degree turn," Whisper shouted as the new car appeared in pursuit of them. "One, two, three!"

The guard used his hands to press the clutch and release the accelerator. When he heard Whisper's call to drop it, he executed the opposite motion. The manoeuvre worked. The vehicle spun once again and ended up facing forward.

Up in the car park, the Reaper watched the pursuit through his high-powered rifle scope. At first, he focused the crosshairs on the faces in the first car, then moved them to the second car, where he finally rested them on Chiara's face.

Adrian Monico

Whisper was worried. The steam and smoke spiralling up from under the bonnet looked ominous. He knew the car could not travel much further, and hoped that it would not explode into flames before he reached the car park. Suddenly his mobile phone started vibrating in his pocket.

"Speak!" Whisper shouted, paying close attention to the voice in his earpiece.

"I have you and the vehicle behind in range," came the reply in a deep, smoke-damaged tone.

"Roger that. Our car might not make it. You'll need to take the rear vehicle out right now! It could give us time to cover the last few hundred meters," Whisper ordered. He flicked a quick look at the car park that was still a kilometre away.

"You want the occupants in the car to be taken out too?" the sniper asked, although he would have preferred to just take the initiative.

Whisper looked down at Signor Beppe, still crouched between the passenger seat and the dashboard. The old man was staring back at him as if he had somehow heard the question. "No," he decided. "Let them go. Just stop the car." Whisper knew he was doing this to please Signor Beppe rather than from any actual concern about the girls' lives.

"Any friendly casualties?" the husky voice asked.

"Yes. Driver," Whisper replied, knowing exactly what he had just ordered with this reply.

Without further discussion, the gunman shot two clinical rounds into the second vehicle's engine block. Then, as the car started swerving from side to side in an attempt to become a harder target and avoid the bullets being fired at it, he placed a well-aimed shot into one of the front tyres. The 50 calibre round found its mark and blew a section of the tyre completely off, causing the car to lose control and slam into a light pole four hundred metres from the car park. The sniper then moved his rifle's crosshairs onto the next target.

Although Whisper was expecting what happened next, he still felt a jolt when he heard the bullet smash through the windscreen and erase the driver. But before he could abuse the gunman for not waiting until they arrived at the car park, flames and thick black smoke erupted from underneath the bonnet.

"Break!" Whisper shouted to the only surviving guard.

The car skidded to a halt only one hundred metres from the car park. Whisper and the guard both slid back into their seats and scrambled for the rear passenger doors.

"Get Signor Beppe and run towards the car park!" barked Whisper. He grabbed Kevin's unconscious body and dragged it out of the car and onto the front lawn of someone's home. Although Whisper had been ordered to get both prisoners to the Consigliere, the reality was that Signor Beppe was the priority was and Kevin simply a bonus. As Whisper walked away from Kevin's body, he looked back along the road and saw the two girls running towards him. He was impressed by their tenacity.

"No!" he snapped at the voice in his earpiece. "I'll take care of it. You just worry about the package."

"Aren't we too exposed?" panted Deepa, mindful that they were running in the middle of the street towards someone who had shot their vehicle to a halt.

"Yes. But I'm hoping that for the same reason they shot the vehicle instead of us, they won't shoot us now!" replied Chiara.

"Chiara, you can't trust whoever it is. They could turn on you just as easily as they turned on us."

"I know," snapped Chiara between gasps. "I no longer report to Beta. But he doesn't know that!" They ran on, steadily gaining on their targets.

A little way ahead, the three men entered the car park. Whisper looked back and started formulating a plan to deal with the two girls who were now closing in on him. He slipped into the shadows of the large concrete structure.

Chiara and Deepa both came to a sudden halt at the entrance of the carpark. They raised their Mosquito pistols and held them with two hands. Chiara silently signalled to Deepa, who was standing on her right, to cover the left side of the entrance as she would cover the right side. Then, they took a few cautious steps into the car park and were swallowed by the looming darkness. Whisper, knowing the girls were unaware of his proximity, slithered between the dark dank shadows. Deepa and Chiara, remembering their training and having now cleared the entrance, both swung their pistols to cover the perimeters while backing closer together so they stood almost back to back.

"Ready?" Deepa whispered.

"Born ready," Chiara whispered back in a nervous attempt to quash with her fear with humour.

Both girls progressed slowly towards the ramp. With each step, Chiara positioned herself slightly behind Deepa who was scanning the area ahead in a wide arch. Chiara was doing the same in the direction that they came from. Whisper watched their movements, noting the level of professionalism shown by the young recruits. He permitted himself the merest moment of admiration before springing into action.

Deepa never heard Whisper approach. Nor did she know Chiara had been knocked unconscious just two metres behind her. Her first sense that anything was wrong was the feeling of a pistol's barrel pressing firmly against her head. She reacted by slowly raising her hands.

"Good girl," approved Whisper. One arm was fully outstretched towards Deepa's head while the other extended toward the body of the unconscious girl at his feet. "Now, please reach back and pass me the pistol while ensuring that the barrel still points forward. Be very careful about this. Your pistol has a very sensitive trigger."

"Is she ok?" asked Deepa, more concerned about Chiara's wellbeing than her own.

"She's fine. She'll wake up with a bad headache though," Whisper smiled.

"Now what?" Deepa asked, following Whisper's instructions and passing the gun back behind her.

"I need you to move your young friend some place where she'll not get run over," Whisper instructed. He checked towards the entrance, mindful that his time was running out.

Deepa turned slowly and gathered Chiara's limp body by her arms. As she dragged her from the path of any oncoming vehicles, Whisper called the sniper and told him to drive down to the entrance.

"Ok," he said to Deepa, once she had placed Chiara gently on the ground. "You're about to come for a little ride with Signor Beppe and me. This is solely as protection, you understand? I have no need of you and if you play your cards right, I'll let you go unharmed," he explained as he considering whether or not to handcuff girl.

The van approached and came to stop beside them. Whisper gestured for Deepa to get in the back. Her legs were shaking so badly that she had trouble climbing into it, but within a few moments later, both she and Whisper were seated next to Signor Beppe and the surviving guard.

"Dear girl!" said Beppe with some alarm. "Are you ok? Where is Chiara?"

Deepa, relieved to see the old man was unharmed, tried to reassure him with a shaky smile. "I'm ok. Chiara is too. She's knocked out, that's all. Are you alright? I'm so sorry about what's happened." She blinked quickly, fearing that her eyes might fill with tears.

"It's not your fault. And I'm fine. It will all be ok," he promised.

"Enough," barked Whisper and a strained silence fell over the van.

Team 12 arrived at the ambush site a few minutes after Chiara and Deepa were seen driving off into the distance. Aleks, along with Simon, Stephen and very bruised but conscious Bernie, were loaded onto Team 12's helicopter which flew at high speed along the road the target vehicle was believed to have raced down. Less than a minute later, they found the two damaged vehicles, one of which was still swathed in thick black smoke from the fire that was now consuming the vinyl seats. Looking ahead, the pilot spotted a man carrying a pistol entering a shopping centre carpark.

"Get ready! Alpha 1, you will be dropped at ground level. Alpha 2, you will be deployed on the roof top," the team leader ordered his two sections. "Sir, I suggest your team waits in the helicopter," he added to Bernie.

"Ok. Thanks, chief," Bernie responded, wincing and looking at his beaten up colleagues.

"Be careful, we have four potential friendlies in there," Aleks called.

"Yes, sir. We received photos of you on our way here. I can see who's missing," replied the team leader.

Adrian Monico

A few moments later the Sikorsky HU-60K Black Hawk landed in the middle of the road and offloaded four Special Forces agents. Moments later, the helicopter was hovering over the roof of the car park from where the rest of Team 12 rappelled using ropes. It only took eight minutes for Team 12 to clear the whole car park, but to Simon it felt like much longer.

"They've found one of your guys. He's ok and is being escorted toward the entrance," the pilot yelled over the noise of the turbine engine.

"Anyone else?" Aleks asked.

"No. Wait. Standby… Ok, they've now cleared the building and have found an unconscious girl. She seems to have been sedated. Standby." The two agents and two teenagers looked anxiously at the pilot, awaiting his every word. "Ok, I'm getting the chopper down to pick them up."

When the helicopter landed, Team 12 came running out of the car park entrance, accompanied by the Director who was carrying Chiara in his arms. As he reached the helicopter, he passed the unconscious girl over to Aleks.

"Thanks, team," Kevin called to all the passengers in the back of the helicopter as the last member of Team 12 jumped aboard.

"Where to next, sir?" the leader of the Special Forces team asked Kevin.

"Let's get in the air and scan the area for any travelling vehicles. Bernie, please get in touch with Control and ask them for the surveillance footage of the car park. I also want satellite feed right now."

Aleks was checking Chiara's vital signs. "She should be ok, but we need to head to a hospital the second things change," he reported. "Stephen and Simon, are you kids ok?"

"Yes," both boys replied. Simon was struggling to hold back his tears. Even now, face-to-face with his dad again, he was unable to say anything.

Sensing something was wrong with his son, the Director looked at him sharply. "Simon?" he queried.

The helicopter rose directly into the air before dropping its nose and projecting forward at high speed.

"Sir, Control just sent through a photo of a metallic blue van seen leaving the site eight minutes ago," Bernie called out, looking at the image he had just received on his phone.

"Right! Team, you know what to look for. Bernie, how long before the satellite feed?" Every minute was essential and Kevin could feel them sliding by.

"Four minutes," Bernie replied, casting his eyes toward the road ahead.

"Simon?" the Director asked again.

"I know!" was all that Simon could muster as a reply.

"Know what?" Kevin asked, though his heart skipped a beat in anticipation of the answer, but Simon could not speak. He was barely managing to hold the tears back. Kevin no longer needed to hear any words. He could see the truth in Simon's eyes.

"How did you work it out?"

"Your comment to Deepa about her fear of sharks. It's the same advice you gave me when I was little, when you and I were confronted by a shark," Simon replied, still looking for a final sign of confirmation that the man staring back at him was indeed his father.

Kevin simply smiled. He was proud of his son's bright mind and felt an old load finally being lifted from his shoulders.

"Are you?" Simon murmured, almost to himself.

Having lip read Simon's last two words, Kevin nodded.

"Contact!" the co-pilot suddenly shouted.

Everyone reacted by trying to get a view of the road ahead. Several Team 12 members leaned out of the helicopter where the rear doors were once present, holding on with one hand and pointing their rifles in the direction of the speeding van with the other.

"Right, men. You know the drill. Alpha 2, you and your guys will get the first exposure. Be ready for a hot one!" the team leader called to a red haired section leader.

"Roger that!" Alpha 2 acknowledged, as his men wedged their carbine rifles back against the shoulders while edging toward the side entrance of the helicopter with their feet hanging in mid air.

The helicopter overtook the van, barely missing its roof. A hundred metres ahead, the pilot flared the machine to a halt by lifting its nose almost vertically above its tail, which itself was only a few metres away from scraping the road. As the helicopter stopped its forward travel, the nose dropped to be level with the whole frame and then pivoted anticlockwise to expose its left side, revealing four black uniformed men, all aiming their rifles at the oncoming van.

The driver of the van, although startled by the helicopter's close overpass, remained calm and slowly brought the vehicle to a stop. He then put the vehicle in neutral and lifted his hands from the wheel to signal that he was not a threat to the four men, who were now quickly moving in his direction in two single files a few metres apart. As the men neared the van, the helicopter pivoted on the spot to expose its opposite side, where the remaining members of Team 12 were ready to fire their rifles in between the gap that had been intentionally created by the disembarked team members.

"Sir, we need you to get out of the vehicle while keeping your hands up!" Alpha 2 called out, hoping that the driver actually spoke English.

"No problem," the driver replied with what sounded like a Dutch accent.

"Now, slowly turn around, place your hands high against the van and spread your legs. We're going to search you!" Alpha 2 ordered as the driver got out of the van.

Two of the men had positioned themselves at the rear of the van, ready to open the doors and contend with whatever they might find. The fourth team member covered Blue as he commenced searching the driver for weapons.

A few minutes later, Alpha 2 was moving back towards the helicopter. "He is clean, sir. There's nobody else in the vehicle and no evidence of foul play. The driver is just some backpacker in the wrong place. His breath stinks of alcohol!" he reported with a disgruntled shake of his head.

"Ok. Thanks, Alpha 2. Call the team back!" the Team 12 leader ordered, ready to ascend again and continue the search for the kidnappers' vehicle.

Pleased with himself for fooling the MI6 special team, the sniper got back in his van and continued toward the RV point.

"Get yourself comfortable. We'll be here for a little while," Whisper advised Deepa and Signor Beppe, who were sitting on a hard seat at the back of a helicopter.

"Sir! Incoming call for you on Channel 2," the pilot called out, not moving her gaze from the direction they were flying.

"Thanks, Pearl!" Whisper replied, calling the pilot by her codename. He then spoke into his headset. "Whisper here... Yes... No, I had to let Shadows go... Don't threaten me! It's your messy family affair... Before you lecture me, keep in mind that instead of hiding in the shadows playing dead, you could've taken care of this yourself... I'll see you in just over an hour!" He removed the headset and hung it on a metal hook before the caller had even finished talking.

"Family affair?" Signor Beppe asked with an inquisitive stare at Whisper.

"You are in for a treat," Whisper replied. He moved forward and took up the co-pilot seat, leaving Beppe and Deepa wondering what on its way next.

CHAPTER 9 - Awoken Into A Nightmare

Deepa had no idea where they were. While European geography was not her forte, Signor Beppe could be fairly confident to mark their location accurately on a map within a ten kilometre radius. He knew Serbia well and guessed where they were heading a full ten minutes before he recognised, in the distance, the village of Brodarevo. It was time for him to act.

"Whisper, my destiny is obviously sealed with this one way flight. But this young lady has nothing to do with whatever this is about. Please let her go," he said.

"What makes you assume it's a one-way flight?" Whisper asked.

"You know that I know this area well. You haven't bothered with blindfolding me, which means that you are not worried about me escaping. Usually the best opportunities for escape occur while prisoners are being moved between locations, particularly when switching from one mode of transportation to the next. So, I am thinking that we are currently on a direct flight to whoever is behind all of this. And looking at the risks and investment that have been involved in my capture, I'm not thinking that it is just for afternoon tea. My time is obviously coming to an end." Beppe's observation held neither fear nor regret. He had lived a long and exceptional life.

"Perhaps there was no need to detain the girl, but what's done is done. We don't have the time to land her somewhere, and I certainly have no intention to let her race off and call for reinforcements. Perhaps if you and she play your cards right, then once all of this is over, I'll make sure that she is returned safe and sound," Whisper proposed, feeling somewhat surprised by this uncharacteristically humane offer.

"Do I have your word?" Signor Beppe asked, even though he did not trust it. This was all he could ask for in the present situation.

"No!" Whisper snapped back, already annoyed at himself for having made the offer in the first place.

"Call it one of my two dying wishes," Signor Beppe insisted.

"What's the second one?" Whisper asked, wishing himself that Signor Beppe would not keep talking about dying.

"Make amends with your family. You are still my son and we all miss you."

"What?" The word burst unintentionally from Deepa. She could make no sense of how this brutal, cold-hearted kidnapper could possibly be Signor Beppe's son.

"I see that the young lady is confused," Whisper observed, grateful for the interruption. He peered back at Deepa, fixing her with an emotionless stare. "You, see young lady, your Director, who is also Signor Beppe's son and father to your friend Simon, found me as a teenager lying half dead just outside the Berlin Wall. Signor Beppe here trained me up to be the agent that I am today. However, despite him now calling me his much beloved son, he beat me up to a pulp and threw me out of the house many years ago. I guess that back then, he didn't really love me like a true son." The sudden change of colour on the teenager's face as she listened to his explanation gave Whisper a flash of cruel satisfaction. "Shocked?" he taunted her. "Well, that is just the start of it. The whole sordid affair surrounding this family is even more messed up than what I've just described." He gave a harsh smile, knowing that Signor Beppe himself would very soon be as shaken as the teenage girl.

"Fifteen minutes out," the pilot reported. Whisper turned back to stare at the city they were rapidly approaching.

Team 12's helicopter landed back at Podgorica Airport. Waiting for Kevin was a Learjet with engines already running.

"Are you going to be ok, sir?" the team leader called out to the Director as he was about to step off the helicopter.

"Yes, gunner. Thanks for the lift. Please take care of this crew," Kevin replied, looking back into the faces of those seated at the back of the Blackhawk.

"Yes, sir! We'll refuel and then take off. I've also requested the flight records in case you are right about a helicopter pickup having whisked our target away," the team leader shouted over the turbine noise, while attempting to hide his surprise that the Director knew of his entry into the army as an artillery gun crew soldier.

The Director waved, then paused for a moment, looking into Simon's eyes. He winked, smiled and turned to walk away from the helicopter. Simon looked as his dad once again walked away from him. He sat on the helicopter floor, feeling every part of his body screaming to jump up and run to his father. Unfortunately, his pride was getting in his way. That and being scared of embarrassing both his father and himself with his childish behaviour. As he sat and wondered what to do next, he heard the rotors increase in speed. They were about to take off again.

"Dad!" Kevin suddenly heard from behind him. He quickly turned and saw his son running towards him. Simon sped the few meters from the helicopter and came to a halt just beyond arms' reach of his father. For a long, slow moment, both Simon and Kevin stood staring at each other, neither one knowing what to do next. Kevin was the first to break the silence.

"Simon, I know how hard this is for you, now that you've found me. But I need to go to the UK, as it might be the only way to save Signor Beppe, my father. So, please, please just let me go. We will have time together, I promise. All three of us will finally celebrate being together again," He reached out with his right hand and tentatively grabbed Simon's left shoulder.

"I… I understand." Simon dropped his gaze to the ground. Then, feeling his dad's warm hand lift from his shoulders, he instinctively stepped forward and wrapped his arms around him. At first, Kevin was startled and simply left his own arms hanging. But as Simon's warmth started permeating through his body, he too moved to circle his arms around the teenager. It had been many years since he had held his son like this.

"I love you Simon," he whispered into the boy's neck. "And I've been dreaming of this moment for the longest time. After this mess is over, we will have time to get to know one another better. But right now, we have a family member in trouble. He needs both of us to give it our best. We can't lose out focus." With a final squeeze, he let go of Simon and hesitantly stepped back.

"I love you too, Dad. I understand," Simon said a second before turning back to the helicopter. It was his last means to prevent the pent up tears from streaming down his face. Kevin stood, proudly watching his son return to the helicopter moments before it took off.
"Sir, I'm Captain David Richards," a uniformed man announced from behind Kevin. "The jet is ready whenever you are."

"Great. Let's get cracking," the Director replied as he turned to look at the pilot.

Ten minutes later, the Blackhawk was flying at high speed back to the search area."

"Sir, this just came in," Blue called. The Second In Command (2IC) of Team 12 was an angry man, who seemed to have found the one role in life that permitted him to legally explode in anger and cause devastation. His nickname 'Blue' was bestowed on him because of the thick red hair he had in his younger years. Most of this was no longer visible, as some of it had fallen out and the rest had been shaved off. Physically, Blue was smaller and slimmer than the rest of his colleagues. However, his lack of physical strength was more than compensated by his speed, both in running and unarmed combat reflexes. It was these qualities that enabled Blue to become one of the most deadly troopers in the SAS and eventually get the attention of MI6.

"Thanks, Alpha 2." The team leader glanced down at the list of flights that had been in the area at the time of the 'disappearance'.

"Sir, I already had a squiz at it and spotted this," Alpha 2 replied, pointing to a specific item on the list.

"I'll be dammed," the team leader replied. He turned to the large man sitting on the cabin floor. "Bernie, looks like the Director was right! There was another helicopter in the area. Looks like it headed into Serbia." The two men knew each other, having previously served together in the Special Air Service (SAS).

"Ok. Let's get going, Trace," Bernie replied automatically, whilst doing his best at hiding the pain caused by being run over by a car. Only after the words left his lips did he realise it was possible that nobody knew of the team leader's nickname, and certainly not the reason behind it.

"Alpha 2, who Alpha 1 would usually call him "Blue" outside of operations, you take the lead. Let the pilot and crew know we are heading into Serbia," Trace ordered, before stepping around several people sitting on the cabin floor and making himself comfortable next to Bernie.

"So, how've you been, NIG?" Trace asked, loud enough to be heard only by Bernie.

"Please, still using that nickname? Haven't you grown out of it yet?" Bernie replied.

He thought back to the time when had first met Tim and recalled the reason he ended up with that particular nickname. Bernie not long just got off the bus as a recently recruited soldier, who was selected to serve in the 29th Commando Regiment. At first, he struggled with the unfamiliar terminology. During his basic training, all language was associated with infantry units – battalions, company, privates, corporals and so on. Then, as part of his gunner basic course, the terminology changed to names like regiment, battery, gunner and bombardier, with soldiers in the artillery starting at the rank of gunner. He got to know Trace almost immediately. Trace, then known as Bombardier Tim Thompson and now Alpha 1, was the person ordered to get the new intake of gunners settled into their accommodation before the Commanding Officer (CO) met them. Bernie never forgot the words the Bombardier used to introduce himself.

"Welcome to the 29th," he had said. "I'm Bombardier Thompson. I will make sure that in the next few days you settle into this unit. You might refer to me as Bombardier Thompson, Bombardier, or Bomber – I don't mind which. I will refer to all of you as NIG - New Intake Gunner. For the rest of your career, you will continue to be my NIGs. Even if, by some freak act of God, you one day outrank me, you will still be my NIG, so get used to it. Now, get your bags, form up into two ranks, and I'll march you to your new accommodation!"

"How's life treating you, Trace?" Bernie asked, feeling pleased to have a quick catch-up with his former bombardier. He was not a man who really had close friends, but the closest he had to one was Trace.

"Life's great!" came the enthusiastic reply. "I was rapt to see you back at the house earlier on. I was going to come and say hello you did another disappearing act on me before I got the chance."

"Yeah, sorry about that. You know how it is."

"Well, at least I now know what happened to you. One minute we were in Afghanistan avoiding a shower of bullets in a lovely little spot behind a rock and the next thing I know, you got on a chopper, without a good-bye mind you, and left never to be seen again. It's reassuring to at least know that you didn't meet our maker and simply became a spook instead." Trace's jovial tone belied the relief he felt upon knowing his friend was ok.

"They made me sign a piece of paper that wiped everything about my life," Bernie apologised.

"All good, NIG," grinned Trace. "Not here to bust your chops. Just simply glad to see you again."

"Funny how it turned out, though," Bernie mused.

"Yeah. You joined the 29th as my NIG, I then managed to get accepted into the 22nd SAS where two years later, there you are again, lining up as one of my newbies. Then you disappear and shortly thereafter, I get an offer to join a special team that is under the command of MI6, only to find out that you are operating as one of their spooks! Talk about military serendipity."

"Don't get all sentimental on me, Trace. I know that you're almost female, but there is no need to get all lovey dovey," Bernie shot back, reminding Trace of a drunken night during which he had tried to sneak back late into the military base by jumping the perimeter and ended up leaving a testicle hanging on the barbed wire.

"Thanks for the reminder, NIG. That certainly was a memorable night," Trace said, adjusting his seat slightly. "What I still find funny, though, is that you nicknamed me 'Trace'. You always claimed it was a more befitting name for someone who accidentally become half a man. It wasn't until later on that I worked out it was an abbreviation of the word 'Tracer'."

"Lucky thing that you were already known for putting two tracer rounds near the end of your rifle magazines so you knew when you were about to run out," Bernie observed, referring to the bullets with a small pyrotechnic charge at their base that burns brightly when the round is fired, allowing the shooter to adjust the firing by following the bullet's trajectory. "Your nickname was interpreted as a reflection of that behaviour." It was signs of such talent that had prompted Bernie recommend Trace for a role in the ultra-secretive Team 12.

"So, what next?" Trace asked, returning to the job at hand.

"You know, Trace, all of this smells suspicious to me. I feel like every time I do something, it's already known by the enemy. I just got rescued from having been kidnapped, and I swear they knew I was coming. It's like walked into a trap," Bernie reflected. He knew enough to trust his gut instincts and still felt annoyed about the betrayal.

"Got a clue as to who the mole is?" Trace asked, looking around at the strangers in the helicopter. He too felt uneasy about the situation and was glad to hear that Bernie felt the same way.

"Nah, man! For all we know, they might be inadvertently providing intel to the enemy, but I think it's someone back at Crystal Palace." There were too many 'unknowns' in MI6 headquarters for Bernie's liking.

"Ouch! You know, I'm not happy knowing that I'm now also a pawn in this game you're part of," Trace said suddenly, aware of his responsibility for his team's wellbeing.

"I guess we just need to keep following the crumbs. Stick to the mission and hopefully, along the way, we'll expose the mole," Bernie replied as he glanced down at the flight manifest details.

"Good call, NIG. Let's see if we can find this sucker! I've already got MI6 plugging into the airspace radar to see where that getaway chopper is," Trace said. If the theory about the mole were true, however, he knew a diversion the chopper would right now be flying away from the site where the kidnapped people were dropped.

"Hey, Trace, do air traffic control towers keep historical data of recorded flight paths?" Bernie asked, having just had the same thought as Trace.

"Good question. Let me make a call and see what I can dig up."

At the back of the helicopter, Chiara sat with her eyes closed. Her head was still quite sore from the drug that was used to knock her out. As she was recalling the event that led up to Deepa's capture, she heard Bernie's words to Trace loudly enough for them to register in her brain. She was particularly alerted by the word 'mole' and felt relieved to hear that Bernie did not think the mole was one of them, and was instead convinced that it was someone at MI6 HQ. She, of course, knew who that person was. However, she did not know whom to trust with this information and felt guilty for not having told the Director when she had the opportunity. Her urge to call him now was so strong that she reached for her phone but stopped. It really would look too suspicious if she made a call right now.

"Hey, are you ok?" Simon suddenly called to her, placing his hand on her arm to gain her attention. "Don't sweat, we'll find them."

"Thanks, Simon. I feel so guilty. I'm making everything go from bad to worse," Chiara replied, uncomfortably conscious of all the actions she carried out in the past week to work against her team.

"You know, I do believe in new beginnings. So, even if that was true, which it isn't, we can brush it off and do better the next time. It's never too late," Simon replied. He did not understand why Chiara felt guilty and wanted to make her feel better. She, like the rest of them, had done her best. Perhaps her guilt was because she was free while Deepa and Signor Beppe were now hostages?

"Thanks, Simon," Chiara said again. "They are nice words." She wished she could believe them.

"They're not mine. Signor Beppe said them to me, except he ended them with a 'capisci?'," Simon added with a grin at his attempt to mimic Signor Beppe's accent.

"Capisci? As in asking if you understand?" Chiara asked. She did know the meaning of the word, but her brain was struggling to stay focused and suppress her feelings while still dealing with the after-effects of the drug.

"Yes. Anyway, anything I can do to make you feel better?" Simon asked. There seemed to be such pain in Chiara's eyes.

She remained silent for a long time. Simon had almost given up on expecting an answer, when suddenly Chiara whispered, "Can you get our Director to call you back on a secure line? I'd like to talk to him directly, but I don't have my mobile on me. I think it was stolen by the kidnappers," Chiara lied as she was concerned that her phone was bugged.

Adrian Monico

"I can, but why?" asked Simon, feeling surprised by her request.

"I don't want to burden you now with the reason," Chiara replied uncomfortably. "It's too long and complicated. Please don't be offended." She wanted Simon to trust her and would confide in him when she had more time to explain.

Simon took his mobile phone out of his pocket and took a moment to think how to make a secure call. Not having a clue about this, he instead decided to send an SMS to his dad, asking him to call back urgently on a secure line. The call came within a minute.

"Hey, Simon, are you ok?" Kevin's voice sounded concerned.

"Yes. It's not me," Simon replied. "Chiara has asked to talk to you in private. Here she is." He handed the phone over to her.

"Hi, sir. It's Chiara here." She tried covering her mouth and handset with her spare hand to disguise what she was doing, however, just about everyone in the back of the helicopter could not help but be aware that both Trace and the teenage girl were on a phone. Even with the turbine noise, Chiara did not want to risk being overheard or having her lips read. The call was too important and risky.

"Hi, Chiara. What's on your mind?" Kevin asked.

Without any preamble, Chiara blurted out her message. "I-I know who the mole is. It's Beta." An instant feeling of relief washed over her.

"I know," came the Director's calm response. "And he was using you as an insider. Most likely, he told you that you were operating for MI6 purely as an internal observer of the team's performance."

"Yes," gasped Chiara as a chill went up her spine. "But how did..."

"How did I know? Let's just say that he made a few mistakes and something that was said while I was kidnapped opened my eyes. In terms of your involvement, it's a basic tactic to turn agents into double agents by making them believe that they are still on the same side and just being privileged to have been selected for a higher calling," Kevin explained.

"I see," Chiara replied in a small voice.

"Don't take it personally," Kevin advised her. "Throughout history there have been exceptional spies who have fallen for the same trick. And if you think about it, you were tricked by the highest ranked and smartest spy that has been part of this organisation to date."

"What happens now?" Chiara asked, unsure if any punishment would be forthcoming.

"You've been incredibly brave to speak up. I now need you to brush this aside and look after Simon and Stephen. Those two are going to continue clashing and you are the only person who can keep them focused on the job at hand. Neither of the boys has had the easiest life. Stephen is also not out of the storm as yet. He'll need a good friend in the weeks to come, which means you have also got to be careful about Simon," the Director replied. Giving away that very small piece of intelligence was a subconscious way to test Chiara.

"Ok. Can I know more about the first person?" Chiara was intrigued, but very intentionally did not mention Stephen's name aloud.

"Sorry, not yet. It is just a hunch. I'm currently gathering data to prove it. In terms of Simon, you already know that answer."

"Jealousy," Chiara replied. She felt a tad silly for saying it.

"I don't want to come across as condescending, but I'm proud of you Chiara. You don't give yourself enough credit. Are you going to be ok?" the Director asked. Although the voice encryption software he used was state of the art, Kevin still lived by the discipline of keeping phone calls to under a minute in length.

"Yeah. I'll be fine. And thank you for your kind words. I haven't had too many of them."

"Ok. Gotta go. Remember, look after them." He disconnected the call before Chiara had a chance to say goodbye.

Kevin sat in the jet, pondering the best way to deal with Beta. They had been friends for so long that the idea of having been betrayed by him was giving the Director heartburn. His first few thoughts were about going directly to the Minister and exposing the Head of MI6. Then his plans went down the path of personally arresting Beta, although this could be risky, as no one else in MI6 was aware of Beta's betrayal and he might simply convince everyone that Kevin himself was the actual double agent. His next speculations were about leaving Beta in place and simply feeding him false information that would help with the liberation of Signor Beppe and Deepa. Unfortunately, this would take time to put in place and Kevin did not have that time. Thinking about Signor Beppe and Deepa, he wondered if perhaps he could kidnap Beta and arrange an exchange. This last plan certainly had lots of merit, with the exception that getting Beta out of the MI6 building without an escort would be very tricky. His ideas rolled on as the plane roared ahead. Despite coming up with several other plans, Kevin dismissed all of them as being far from ideal.

"NIG, we're in luck. Look at this," Trace called, pointing to an SMS he just received. Aleks, who had left the two men alone during their conversation, now moved closer to see what Trace had discovered. At first, the former bombardier hesitated in showing Aleks the SMS, but one nod from Bernie and he relaxed.

"Gents," he said, "I just got sent the flight coordinates of the helicopter that we're looking for. It's not much to go on, but have a look halfway down the list." He held his phone between the three of them so all could see the list of coordinates and correlating timestamps.

Aleks was the first one to spot what the team leader was highlighting, but Bernie was the fisrt to speak. "I'll be dammed! There is a duplicate entry."

"It's a long shot, as these entries have a ten minute separation between them. But given we have nothing else to go on, it looks right now like the helicopter was stationary for at least ten minutes at this coordinate," Trace observed. He looked around the helicopter. "Yo, Bill," he yelled across the cabin to the man he was about to give an order to. "I want you to map the following coordinates. Pass them on to the pilots as well."

"Send, boss!" the newest Team 12 recruit called as he whipped out a green covered notebook.

Trace began reciting. "It's 43.24'32"N 19.47'33"E. Got it?"

"Got it, boss!" Bill called back. He rapidly entered the coordinated in his electronic map. "Boss, the coordinates point to Mountain Zlatar near a town called Nova Varos in Serbia. Been there before?"

"I went skiing there once," Aleks interjected. "Very picturesque. Lots of lakes, a great river called Uvac, alpine style housing, and I think they have a famous rehabilitation hospital. I stayed in a beautiful hotel called the Panorama."

"Ok, I can see the rehab centre," Bill said, peering at the map. "What's next boss?" he added as he looked back at his leader.

"Let's get there. We'll need to look around and hopefully pick up something 'unusual'," Trace responded, also seeing Aleks nodding as a sign of agreement.

"Should we call it in?" Bill asked.

"No!" Bernie and Aleks both called simultaneously. They glanced at each other. Neither wanted a call of this nature made back to MI6 headquarters.

"Ok, then, I guess that's a 'no'," Trace said after pausing for a second and trying to read the two men's minds.

"Roger that!" Bill called as he turned to brief the pilot.

"All right, gents. Let's have it. What's with the a capella performance?" Trace asked, using the Italian word for singing in tune without music accompaniment.

"I guess Aleks and I have to compare notes. It seems we both have an inkling about a possible mole," Bernie said. He'd been surprised by Aleks' response to Bill's question.

"I guess we do," Aleks agreed.

"Obviously HQ can see us, but my guess is that they don't yet know where we are going," Trace went on, as Aleks moving closer to him and Bernie and the conversation continued in lowered tones.

Nearby, both Simon and Chiara sat quietly, acting like they were unaware of the discussion between the three men. Simon did not really know too much about it, but he recalled his earlier conversation with Aleks and had overheard Chiara's conversation with his dad. He looked across at her then away again. Whatever else happened, he did not want to get Chiara into trouble.

"Please make yourself comfortable. Our guest of honour is running a tad late. Anything we can do to make you more comfortable? Something to eat or drink?" Whisper asked.

Tired, angry and afraid, Deepa snapped back. "You can shove your food and your drink!"

"Si, grazie," responded Signor Beppe calmly. "We both will have some food and drink." He looked compassionately at Deepa.

"You have a good coach, young lady. You might not realise it, but it's essential that you always keep your energy levels up and stay well rested, as it might be the only difference between a successful or failed escape attempt," Whisper observed with a very slight smile in Signor Beppe's direction.

Deepa was surprised by his insight and immediately felt a bit silly about her reaction.

"Figlio mio, how long before this guest arrives?" Signor Beppe asked.

"Please don't refer to me as your son. And to answer your question, it looks like you'll be waiting for approximately an hour," Whisper replied. "I'll see what provisions we can rustle up," he added as he left.

The room they were in was located in the underground section of an old stone house. It contained a couple of chairs, a sofa bed and a desk. It had all the appearance of having previously been used as some sort of office. The floor was covered in a very dark timber and the inside walls were comprised of various large, exposed stones. What they had seen of the house itself resembled an Austrian Alpine hut with its black window frames and roof beams. Signor Beppe mentally noted that this was just a holiday house and had none of the special security measures that were usually to expected with 'safe houses'.

Once they were alone, Signor Beppe turned to Deepa. "You know, my dear, you must always keep calm and professional. A hostage who stands out tends to be at greater risk. So never act out in anger, nor in fear. It is hard, but I know that you can keep a cool head, si?"

"Signor Beppe, I never expected this," fretted Deepa. "I always imagined that I would spend my time looking at places and people of interest from afar and the most dangerous aspect of my work would be getting paper cuts from the pages where I would be taking notes." She was genuinely regretting ever having asked to join MI6.

"My dear young lady, I don't believe you ever thought that far. I think you were driven by love and you have the brains that enabled you to pursue him into the espionage world," Signor Beppe said, softening his observation with a warm smile.

"Am I that transparent?" Deepa blushed.

"No. But I am alive today because of my ability to read people."

"I guess that I am a fool for following him," Deepa conceded. She avoided saying 'his' name, just in case Signor Beppe could not completely read her.

"Simon is a good boy," said Signor Beppe, making it plain that her subterfuge was useless. "And in his next few years, if not for the whole of his life, he will be mostly invisible to the world. I think you knew that and you chose to do just what I would have done at your age." He spoke with genuine admiration for the teenager's actions.

"I feel so silly. And now I might actually die because of it," Deepa shuddered. Since feeling the cold metal of the pistol barrel against the back of her head, she had been afraid of what might happen to her. Now, a strange sensation brewed deep within her that she might not survive this ordeal.

"Italians do many illogical things just for a bit of love. Many times I have defended my childish behaviours by calling them out per amore e patria" Signor Beppe admitted.

"Sorry, Signor Beppe, my Italian is not that great. For love and what?"

Adrian Monico

"Country, my dear. For love and country," Signor Beppe explained with a laugh. "Signorina, I would not be worried about your death just yet," he continued in an attempt to reassure Deepa. "They want just me. They will let you go. You will see."

"Thank you," Deepa whispered, but she remained afraid. Every instinct in her was screaming. She shivered and stared blankly at the thick wooden door that was the only way out of the small, cold room.

"Hello, Prime Minister," Kevin said into the inboard phone. "I'm sorry to trouble you. I'm not sure if you remember me, but we met a few months ago when discussing starting up a spy academy."

"Kevin isn't it? Yes, I do remember the meeting with you and Beta. And I know how much this great country of ours owes you for all you have done," Calum Lloyd, the Prime Minister, replied. He recognised the voice on the phone and vividly remembered both the man it belonged to and his impressive dossier. "Now, what do I owe this unexpected call?"

"Well, sir, I have troubling news. Before I act on it, I wanted your consent."

"Apologies for my bluntness, but shouldn't Beta be the one having this discussion with one of my ministers?"

"That is just it, sir. What I'm about to tell you is so sensitive that it goes above Beta and I don't want to trust anyone else with it but you."

"I see. You have me intrigued, not to mention completely alarmed. Please go ahead and tell me this news," the Prime Minister requested.

"Sir, although this is a secure line, I would prefer to tell you in person. It is ok for me to come to your office?" Kevin requested. Although he tried to sound confident, he was unsure about how his news would be taken, particularly as he himself could be seen as a rogue spy.

"One second, please," the Prime Minister requested. "Where are you now?"

"I'm on a private jet, thirty minutes out of Heathrow."

"I'll send a helicopter to pick you up," the Prime Minister agreed, having already formulated a way to meet with Kevin face-to-face.

"Thank you, sir," said Kevin. "And sir, if you are going to tell anyone about this call, please bring them with you. It would be preferable if we have no leaks for the next few hours."

"I understand. See you shortly." The line went dead and Kevin stared out the window, still holding the receiver in his hand.

"Excuse me, sir! I have the latest SITREP for Team 12," Charles the duty officer called from Beta's office door.

"Sure, sure! Come in," said Beta with a cordial wave of his hand. "What do you have for me?"

"Well, sir, the honest answer is lots of uncertainty," the officer replied as walked towards Beta's desk with a yellow folder extended ahead of him.

"Oh? Tell me more." Beta stopped writing and lowered his pen, alerted to the tone in the young officer's voice.

"Sir, shortly after Team 12 searched the van, they flew to Podgorica Airport. This was reported in as a refuelling stop. Since then, they have gone to radio silence and have failed to respond to any SITREP requests," Charles explained.

"Ok. They obviously needed to refuel to continue their search. And they are a secretive bunch of loners who we know don't like getting on the blower," Beta observed. So far there was nothing in the brief to get alarmed about.

"Sir, when we first sent them on the support mission, they had just refuelled the Blackhawk, including having four full external tanks. They had enough fuel to continue flying for hours. When they stopped the van, they were only minutes behind whatever getaway car the kidnappers had switched into. I'm puzzled about why they decided to abandon chasing down a hot trail to go back and refuel when there was no need to do so," said Charles.

"Yes, I agree that it is unusual, especially when looking at the situation from back here. But these guys don't do random or illogical actions. They most likely had a reason. Where are they now?" Beta asked. A slight prickle of concern about his clandestine mission was beginning to make itself felt in his mind.

"Sir, I looked for the transponder signal on the local air traffic controller radar, only to find that our pilot switched it off minutes after taking off from the refuelling stop. I then used our satellite to see if we could spot the helicopter from above and struck it lucky by spotting them at the edge of our range," Charles responded. He placed a terrestrial map on Beta's desk and pointed at a red cross marking a point in the middle of the map. Beta nodded once, indicating that he understood and the officer should continue with his report. "Sir, I then did a random search of traffic and security surveillance cameras in the area, in case that we could spot the helicopter on the horizon. We were in luck again and spotted this." He placed a black and white photograph on the desk. It showed the main road of a town with a small helicopter just visible on the horizon.

"And where were they?" Beta asked. He was impressed by the officer's lateral thinking.

"Actually, in the first photo, they appear not to be too far from the shopping centre where the original getaway car was abandoned," Charles replied, pulling out a permanent marker and drawing an arrow on the map. "The arrow shows the direction that they were heading. North west, sir." He was preparing to reveal the last, vital bit of information.

"Ok. That's good, right? That's where we expected to find them," Beta replied, already anticipating that the young officer had kept the best news until last.

"Sir, this is the next surveillance photo I've found," explained Charles, as he placed two more photos side by side on Beta's desk. "This one basically shows a black dot in the sky," he said, tapping the first image. "The next photo is an enlargement that I got one of my staff to work on."

Beta held both photos up and compared the two images.

"Sir, this photo shows the helicopter here." Again the officer again drew an arrow on the map, this time pointing directly east.

"I'm seeing nothing unusual about this. They are obviously searching the area," said Beta. The prickle he had felt earlier was settling down and he was becoming bored with the laborious explanation.

"Yes, sir," responded Charles, who could sense that his brief was about to come to an abrupt end. "But, if I could just impose on you for another minute to propose a theory?"

"Ok, let's hear it," Beta sighed.

"Thank you, sir. If these photos were taken immediately after the van was searched, I would have simply accepted that Team 12 was widening the search area. However, they went back to the airport to refuel. This tells me that they were considering temporarily abandoning their pursuit in favour of another plan. Next, if we compare the height of the Blackhawk from the horizon between the first and second photos, you'll notice that it has quadrupled. I believe that the height in the second photo is not ideal for area searches, but it is the height needed to clear mountains in the area. My interpretation is that the helicopter is aiming for a specific location that requires extra altitude to reduce the time wasted by travelling closer to ground level. Thirdly, if I may..." Charles stopped speaking and pointed to Beta's diary.

"Sure," Beta replied, realising that he was asking permission to use the leather bound diary that was there purely for show.

The officer used the edge of the closed diary as a ruler to line up the two arrows he had previously drawn. He then used the permanent marker to draw a line from the first arrow to the second, continuing it to the end of the diary's edge.

"Sir, I believe that they are heading into Serbia. You know that unless otherwise arranged, they are to get clearance from this office before they enter another country's airspace. That crew, including the two pilots, are the best we have. They don't make mistakes like forgetting to get appropriate flight permission. So what is it that could possibly drive these highly professional soldiers to disobey an order that comes directly from the Foreign Office?" He paused to allow Beta time to absorb this information.

The Head of MI6 kept his face carefully blank despite his rising feeling of alarm. "Theories?" he asked.

"I hate to say it, sir, but I think they are trying to keep whatever they're planning to do secret from us. They have discovered something that has them flying into Serbia, but they don't want us to know what it is." Emboldened by his reception so far, Charles rushed on. "Sir, when Agent 2C was captured, we had one of the directors making us do some unusual research. Since then, I've gone back and re-examined what he requested. I now believe that director spotted Agent 2C using a very old field hand signal that essentially alerted us that the kidnappers were expecting him, which I read as us potentially having a mole. If I now come back to the secretive behaviour of Team 12 and their guests, I'm of the impression that they too might have identified something that leads them to the same conclusion." He took a breath and waited, unsure of how his speculation might be taken.

Beta paused before responding. "I commend you for a great piece of investigation, Charles" he said after a moment during which the duty officer wondered if he had delivered his last report. "However, there are a few bits of the puzzle that I can fill in for you. First, both Agent 2C and the Director that you are referring to are currently with Team 12. So, this theory about a mole, which I'm secretly investigating as I don't want to alarm our staff, is really just coming from the same source and not from two different groups. Secondly, both Agent 2C and the Director just went through a kidnapping experience, so they might be still shaken by the event. Both men outrank Team 12's leader, which makes me think that the radio silence is the result of a direct order, perhaps driven by their recent psychological trauma. For now, I would ask you to cut them a bit of slack as they are, after all, highly decorated and reliable colleagues." He gave the officer a reassuring smile.

"I understand, sir," Charles said apologetically, although it bewildered him how a director of MI6 could be so psychologically traumatised by what had seemed to be a fairly innocuous kidnapping that he would forget direct orders from the Foreign Office.

"Meanwhile, for your great display of initiative and sound analytical work, I'm going to make an entry in your performance records," continued Beta.

"Thank you, sir. That means a lot." He started collating the photographs and other documents and placing them back in the yellow folder.

Beta lay one palm on the pages and smiled. "Actually, do you mind if I keep these and use them as examples in future training sessions?"

"I'd be flattered," replied Charles, instantly forgetting his misgivings.

"And with regard to the mole hunt, I know I can trust you to keep it to yourself. We don't want to panic people or send them on a witch-hunt. Worse still, if there really is somebody in this organisation working against us, you wouldn't want to give him or her a whiff that we are on to them, would you?"

"Yes, sir. I mean, no, sir," the young man said eagerly. "Unless you tell me otherwise, I'll keep this information to myself."

"Clever lad," Beta replied. He picked up his pen again to resume to the work he was attending to before the duty officer walked in. Charles took the cue, thanked Beta and left the office feeling more confident about his future in the organisation than he had been half an hour before.

The moment he was alone, Beta placed a call on his secure phone. "How long before you get there? You have company heading your way!" he yelled as soon as the call was answered. "Don't know," he said after a short pause. "They might simply be heading into the area, but I don't want any more hiccups." He paused again. "No more shenanigans, you hear me? I have given you more than enough latitude on this affair. Get it over and done with now!" He hung up before a response came back.

Beppe and Deepa had just finished their club sandwiches when Whisper returned. He moved a wooden chair into the middle of the room and placed a second one directly beside it. He then signalled for both the hostages to sit on the chairs and bound their wrists to the back of their chairs with sturdy nylon restraints.

"I guess now we finally meet the person behind this, si?" Signor Beppe asked while maintaining constant eye contact with Whisper. "You remember my last two wishes?"

"Signor Beppe, I-I'm scared," Deepa whispered. She kept staring at the door, expecting at any moment that her executioner would walk through it.

"It is ok, my dear," Beppe reassured her. "You will be ok. Remember to stay professional." He was feeling worried about their sudden need to be handcuffed. "Whisper, at least take Deepa to another room," he implored. "She has nothing to do with this and she does not need to be part of whatever is coming next."

Whisper paused for a second and looked at both hostages, his gaze lingering on Deepa.

"She is just a child. You know what I'm asking is the right thing for you to do. Remember my teaching. Never children!" Signor Beppe insisted.

"Ok, old man. I'll see what I can do. Now pipe down!" Whisper walked out, leaving the door open.

Neither hostage saw what happened next. They were both looking down at the floor, awaiting came next, when the Consigliere quietly slipped into the room and stopped a few metres short of them.

"Ciao, Papa," he said.

Signor Beppe looked up. His mouth instantly went dry and his tongue felt paralysed so he could not speak. Tears flooded his eyes and ran down his cheeks.

"Hello Signorina. Whilst my father here takes a second to compose himself, allow me to introduce myself. My name is Lucca. I'm one of this man's four sons. I believe that you have met another two of them. One is your so-called Director, and the other is your host, Whisper." Lucca's words were sarcastic and he cherished the bewilderment in Deepa's face.

"But... But then..." Deepa found herself unable to finish her sentence.

"Ah, yes! I'm assuming that you are about to deduce that I'm Simon's uncle. That is correct," Lucca replied, pausing for a second before bursting into a mocking laugh. "I guess it must be rather startling for you to discover that the person behind this inauspicious situation is your sweetheart's uncle. And I haven't even pulled out the ace out of my sleeve yet."

"The ace in your sleeve?" Deepa echoed, without fully realising she had spoken the words.

"Let's see if you can work it out, my dear. I am Signor Beppe dead son. Whisper is sort of an adopted brother to me and your Director is also my brother, which makes me Simon's uncle. I am also the orchestrator behind Chiara's role as double agent, and... Come on now, have a think. Who have I yet to mention?"

"Stephen," Deepa murmured softly.

"Bingo! I am Stephen's dad," Lucca laughed aloud, delighted with his game.

"Figlio mio, what has happened to you? Why are you like this?" Signor Beppe asked, feeling parts of himself dying inside.

"This is who I am!" Lucca roared back. "And I like it. I have become a far greater professional than you ever were and I did it all on my own." He looked at Deepa again, swallowing back on the bile he tasted in his mouth. "You see, young lady, I was the youngest in the family. I grew up with parents only admired and respected my older brothers. My eldest brother was the intellectual star who gave my parents a lot of pride in his academic achievements. Then there was daddy's dear Kevin, who achieved outstanding results in athletics and always, always stood up for the weaker person. He just embodied goodness and could do no wrong. Even Whisper was at first loved and admired by my daddy dearest more than me." His voice descended to a snarl.

"Lucca, this is exactly why I did not train you," Signor Beppe said in a strained voice. "I loved you as much as the rest of them, but you always struggled to control yourself in certain situations. You mother and I had concerns about your temperament. We were afraid for you if you entered into such a violent career." As he spoke, he remembered thinking that something was wrong with Lucca from an early age.

"How ironic!" scoffed Lucca. "You didn't want me to follow in your footsteps, but in the end, both you and Kevin ended up working from me without even realising it. You fools have no idea how much I have controlled your lives." So many times he had sent his father and brother to assassinate his enemies, making them believe that they were all legitimate MI6 missions.

"No," whispered Signor Beppe, struggling to keep his heart from falling into an abyss of darkness. "This is not you!"

"Open your naïve eyes, Daddy Dearest. Wake up to the fact that your 'psychotic' son has been your puppet master," Lucca gloated, labelling himself with what he believed his parents most likely thought of him through all those years. At that moment, Whisper walked back into the room. Lucca swung to face him. "Ah, there you are, Whisper. Come on in and join the family reunion. Of course, if it wasn't for your mistake, we might have also had our dear brother in the room, but no matter. I just had a moment of great entertainment with this young lady." He gestured towards Deepa who was still struggling to understand the intricacies and vicious tension of the situation.

"Consigliere, I have set up another room for the girl. I was intending to move her there and give you and your father some privacy," Whisper said, ignoring Lucca's attack.

"But why? This is such fun," Lucca objected. He turned again just in time to intercept a look being shared between Signor Beppe and Whisper. "Ah, I see!" he said. "Dear Dad's old rule about women and children. Well, caro padre mio, I don't live by his stupid rules. It's one of the reasons behind my success." These last words were snarled in Signor Beppe's face.

"You are my son. You might be very angry with me. But it does not change who you are," Signor Beppe insisted, his voice growing stronger and more determined.

"Really?" Lucca asked. Without any further comment, he reached into his Armani suit and withdrew a Glock pistol. In the same fluid movement, he pointed the gun at Deepa's forehead and pulled the trigger.

CHAPTER 10 - Change Of Guard

As soon as the Blackhawk helicopter reached the target area, it commenced scanning the region using a thermal imagery device that was capable of identifying human body signatures within most buildings. The helicopter crew and its passengers were looking for suspicious buildings and vehicles using various optical magnification devices.

"Sir, we are going to start from the given coordinates and commence circling in an increasing radius," the pilot called to Trace.

"Roger that," Trace called back before addressing his team. "Right, all eyes on deck! We're looking for anything out of the ordinary: guards posted outside a residential house; one or more cars, or most likely vans, parked outside isolated houses; a helicopter pad; areas of cleared vegetation from a helicopter down force; buildings with vegetation clearance that looks like a firing range or has markers; suspicious behaviours by people who spot our helicopter; or houses with state of the art surveillance equipment." He raised a set of high powered binoculars and peered down at the ground.

"Bernie, thermal satellite imagery is now being fed to my mobile phone," Aleks said to his colleague while adjusting the resolution on his screen.

"I thought the satellite would not be in range for another thirty minutes?" Simon said in surprise.

"Kid, that was the NATO satellite," Aleks grinned. "Let's just say that Signor Stefano has many friends who are, for a price, happy to 'share' their toys." He noticed Bernie was also paying attention to his answer.

"Do we have anything on board searching for Signor Beppe's or Deepa's or even Whisper's mobile phone?" Chiara asked, looking around at all the electronic devices that were being held by various individuals in the helicopter.

"Kid, I sincerely doubt that the people we are looking for are that stupid," one of the Team 12 members remarked.

"I understand that! But are we going to be stupid enough not to have some form of monitoring just in case the kidnappers make a mistake? Suppose that Deepa or Signor Beppe manage for a split second to turn on their mobile phones during an escape attempt.

Wouldn't we want to be ready for that?" Chiara replied, trying to hide her annoyance.

"Yes, we do," Trace said firmly. "Get on it," he ordered, giving a stern look to the team member who had spoken. "And please forgive Clarence for his condescending reply," he added to Chiara.

Beta needed to think. He had gone up to the building's rooftop for some fresh air. Although he accepted that he devoted his life in the service of world that often demanded the termination of certain people, he still felt his stomach churn whenever an unnecessary death occurred. His job was, after all, predominantly about saving lives, not taking them. The call from Whisper still disturbed him. Not only was he the head of a clandestine organisation that just killed a teenaged girl, but that girl was a member of his own MI6 team. He inhaled deeply but the breath did not assuage his guilt. Beta was now hoping that after a glass of single malt whiskey, he would be able to put the girl's death aside until such time that an appropriate opportunity for punishment would present itself. For now, he needed to move on.

Returning from the rooftop, he slowly entered his office and walked directly to his desk for the desperately drink. He walked around the desk and opened a side door in it. To his dismay, the scotch was gone. He stared for a few seconds at the empty place, trying to think where he could have left the bottle. Just as he lifted his gaze to his couch, Kevin spoke.

"I've already poured us a glass. Apologies for breaking into your office, by the way, but I promise I wasn't going to start without you." He sat back and pointed to the open bottle and the two glasses.

"Kevin. You startled me," Beta replied. It was not only the shock of seeing Kevin in his office, but also the fact that Kevin had secretly abandoned the search for Signor Beppe and flown back to the UK.

"You must be the only person in this world I trust with my thirty year old scotch," said Beta, as he moved towards the other couch and extending a hand to his old friend.

"Then our first toast should be to 'trust'," Kevin proposed, accepting the handshake.

"Trust it is," agreed Beta. "Cheers!" He picked up the glass and gulped the content down in one swallow. Kevin did likewise.

"Another?" Beta asked even though he already commenced pouring the liquid into their glasses.

"At least! I've had one of the worst days and it's only going to get worse," Kevin replied. He looked directly into Beta's eyes. It was the first moment in just over an hour that Deepa's death was not the primary thought in Beta's mind.

"Let's have it, my friend," he said, giving Kevin the opportunity to explain.

His explanation was simple. "You are our double agent," Kevin said and leaned back with his refilled glass.

"I see," Beta said as he watched the longest friendship he'd ever had vanish before his eyes. "What else have you learned?"

"I have learned that my long trusted friend has been working against his own organisation and that he is the reason I was kidnapped. He is also the reason my father has been kidnapped." Kevin replied. He was trying hard to suppress the anger that was building within him.

"I'm sorry, Kevin," sighed Beta. "Although with some of these events, I had no choice, I have sadly had my hands in both of those incidents."

A few moments of silence passed. Both men looked from one another to the untouched glasses in their hands and back again. Kevin was first to break the silence.

"Tell me," he pleaded. "I can't understand it. Why have you betrayed me, your oldest friend? And how could you have betrayed all that we stand for?" He realised as he spoke that he still held out hope that it was all somehow a mistake.

"How far back should I go?" Beta asked, unsure where begin and how much he could tell Kevin.

"Start from the point where the Head of MI6 betrays his own country. Then, maybe tell me how you got away with your duplicitous behaviour. And while you're at it, you could say if we ever truly were friends. No," he corrected himself quickly. "Don't answer that. A true friend doesn't want to see his own friend dead and his family destroyed!" He gulped down the contents of his glass and leaned forward to pick up the bottle again.

Adrian Monico

Before responding, Beta too drank his glass in one mouthful and leaned forward to have it refilled by Kevin. "Many years ago," he began, "just before you were officially hired by me, I discovered a clandestine organisation that was run and funded by several extremely wealthy individuals. Back then, I had only been in this job for a few years and I instinctively disliked secret societies and anyone working outside the law. I decided to look into this organisation and eventually my secret investigation became known to its leaders." He paused, giving Kevin time to have another sip of the scotch.

"What is the organisation known as?" Kevin asked.

"I'm sorry. But I can't tell you that."

"Ok. We'll come back to that later," Kevin replied. "Go on."

"I was investigating large quantities of bonds being shipped into the UK. After sending an agent to France and then Germany, I became suspicious about this organisation. A few months after I commenced the investigation, my agent disappeared. At the time, I still got my hands dirty from time to time, so I flew into Spain to investigate firsthand. It didn't take long before I was captured and taken to an underground facility in Madrid. I remained captive there for five days, during which time my kidnappers – or they were more like hosts really – essentially recruited me into their organisation. Their initial request was very simple. They wanted to be kept informed of any activities that might appear as 'illegal' and I was not to meddle in their affairs. In exchange, they would give me access to their organisation's resources for any governmentally sanction mission. I simply agreed to it up front so that I would be freed and have the opportunity to came back here and shut this organisation down. But after I got back home, the organisation vanished." Beta stopped his narrative again and slowly refilled both glasses.

"What happened next?" asked Kevin, whose anger was slowly being overtaken by his curiosity.

"Actually, you did," Beta replied. He glanced down at his glass, recollecting the moment when he needed this organisation's help. Kevin sat silent, confused by this reply.

"You and I hit it off almost from the word 'go'," Beta resumed. "If you recall, I was the youngest MI6 Director in history. But that also meant that I had to work bloody hard to prove myself to the old timers who most likely thought that one of them would get the job. My peers and staff were also not convinced that I would succeed. At the time I was given the role, basically everyone around me was giving me the cold shoulder. Everyone, that is, except you. When I first recruited you, it was mostly because of your achievements while working as an independent. I was at a low point in my life, completely alone and miserable. That changed when you and your father walked through that door and made me feel part of your family. If you recall, shortly after you two started working for me, you often invited me on holidays with your family and you regularly had me over for dinner whenever we were in the same city."

"That's why I'm so bloody confused about you, of all people, betraying Dad and I!" Kevin interjected, his anger rising again.

"Yes. I understand, Kevin."

"Do you? Then make me understand too," he shouted back.

Beta sighed again and resumed his tale. "Over time, I become closer and closer to your family. I witnessed Lucca becoming angrier and angrier at the fact that Signor Beppe didn't want another son of his placing his life at risk like the two of you did. I also remember when you met Candice. You two were so in love." He smiled briefly. "I cared so much about your blossoming relationship that I was looking for ways I could transition you to a desk job. Unfortunately, by then, Shadow's reputation was global. You were in high demand from other government agencies. That was the time when I had to make the deal that got me here today." He took another drink.

"Go on," Kevin instructed again as he proceeded once more to fill their glasses.

"If you recall, you found threatening photos of you and Candice. You were quite upset by it and pleaded with me to help you. At first, I sent you two to Australia. That was only meant to be until such time as I found the source of those threatening photos. Unfortunately, the only discovery I made during that period was how dependent we had become on Shadow. I had several missions fail on me. I was also put on short notice by the ministers that if things did not improve, I was out of a job." Beta took another sip of his scotch and paused a second to savour the burning sensation of the alcohol clawing its way down his throat. "One afternoon, I walked into my secret apartment and found myself staring at the same four gentlemen who had 'hosted' me back in Madrid. They had a new deal for me. They would put me in charge of their operations branch, help me recover my reputation in MI6 and find whoever was threatening your wife."

"What was the catch?" Kevin knew it would not be that simple.

"The catch? I had to keep myself employed as Head of MI6 and I had to accept that you, Candice and young Simon would be forced to separated and live unconnected lives."

"I don't understand. Why would they care about my family?"

"They just you, Kevin. Like a collectable in their glass cabinet. So I acted selfish and agreed."

Kevin's mind was churning. "Did I ever get ordered to carry out missions on their behalf?"

"Yes. Often," Beta replied, knowing how Kevin would feel as a result of that answer.

"How many people did I kill who didn't need to die?" Kevin asked in a quiet tone that failed to disguise the anger that was escalating.

"None. I had three assassins working for me. You, Whisper and one another. The last two were used for missions that were of common interest to the organisation and Britain."

"Was that last person my father?" Kevin asked, still desperately wanting to believe that his missions were sanctioned by his government, even if they also brought benefit to another organisation.

"No," said Beta firmly. "I left your dad completely out of this."

"Why?" demanded Kevin. Even now he was suspicious about what Beta was saying.

"Various reasons. But somehow, I was always a little wary of Signor Beppe. He could always see through people." Beta smiled lightly, trying to break the tension.

"Good," Kevin said, swallowing another mouthful of scotch.

"The reality was that I could not face him because of my guilt," Beta admitted, swallowing the contents in his own glass.

"Guilt?"

"Yes. As you'll remember, Lucca wanted to follow in yours and Whisper's footsteps, but your dad forbade it. In fact, he asked for my word that I would not recruit Lucca, as I had done with you and

Whisper."

"I remember. Poor Lucca. He wanted it so badly that it got to the point that he was approaching anyone who would give him the chance," Kevin observed. An image of the smiling face of his kid brother came to his mind. "That's why Dad and I were so relieved when he finally got himself accepted into the army. Up until he lost his life, that is. Dad is still wracked with guilt about that. Since Lucca's death, he has convinced himself that maybe his son would still be alive if he had been helped to get into this profession."

Beta paused for a second then asked, "You know how I said I had two other assassins?"

"Yes. Whisper is one of them."

"And Lucca is the other," Beta revealed.

The realisation sank into the Kevin. "You mean that Lucca was actually working for this organisation, and you, when he died?"

"No," said Beta. Then, as gently as he could, he added: "Lucca is alive."

Kevin sat back in shock, as Beta went on. "When I was given the head of operations role by the clandestine organisation, Lucca was, unlike you and Whisper, already working for them. As part of the deal, I was specifically asked to maintain his cover story. You see, Lucca started out as one of their assassins. But over a few years, he worked himself up to being their senior leader."

"What do you mean?" Kevin could not help get drawn into Beta's story, despite struggling to accept that his brother was alive.

"The four gentlemen have three branches in this organisation. One is the operations unit, which I lead. One is a philanthropic unit, and I'm sorry, but I cannot reveal who the manager of that is, although it would shock you. The last is in essence their revenue generation unit. Your brother is the executive director of that one, although he refers to himself with the title of 'Consigliere'."

"Consigliere? But that is the 2IC of the drug lord we are scavenging the world for! That's the same drug lord that has been trying to harm my family, the family that has made you a part of it," Kevin yelled.

"Well, yes and no," hedged Beta. "Their revenue generating unit is a blend of legitimate and illegitimate businesses. Most have CEOs in charge who report to boards and have no idea at all that they belong to this organisation. The less legitimate businesses, including a special operations unit, all report to the Consigliere, who answers directly to the board that comprises these same four gentlemen. There is no drug lord. That was a fictional person that Lucca invented as extra personal protection from his enemies. In terms of the drug business, this organisation's involvement with that is solely as a shipping service. Once in a while, amongst the various illegal shipments that occur around the world, drug companies approach this organisation for their services. And before you ask, many governments are happy to turn a blind eye to it, as they too use the same services for their clandestine activities."

"You are kidding, aren't you?" Kevin demanded. "The Consigliere is a dangerous, violent drug lord. Either you are a fool or he has outsmarted you." Before Beta had a chance to respond, Kevin charged on, impatient to get to the end of the story. "This is all fine and dandy, but why has my family been kidnapped?"

"It comes down to a stupid family feud. It's all about Lucca and your dad."

"That's insane," retorted Kevin. "How can that be possible? How can such an organisation allow this situation when it's now placed the secret of its own existence at risk?"

"Lucca makes a lot of money for the board. He has tripled their power in the last five years alone. The most senior member of the board is his mentor. When Lucca asked permission to pursue this, shall we say 'personal vendetta', he was given the authority to do as he pleased."

Kevin remained silent for a few moments, letting the last piece of information sink in. "Ok. But how could you allow this situation to continue? You have a moral obligation and responsibility to protect your country, its people and those who every day devote themselves and risk their lives to follow your orders. They, we, believed that you, above all people, embody the oath we all took. You have betrayed all of them, not just me and my family!"

"Kevin, I am tired of being subjected to failures. Seeing people die or being victimised because my hands are tied by politicians who are more motivated by votes rather by than doing the right thing. To you I might come across as a traitor. But let me tell you this: as head of operations for the clandestine organisation, I have achieved more good in this past year than I have in my whole career of sitting in this office. You think that chasing down other spies, playing war games with other nations, listening in on phone calls from mums and dads is making any difference? Other governments are not the threat to humanity, nor are the criminals who make a living by stealing pennies from one another. The foremost threat to humanity and its freedom is the handful of powerful men that are in alliance and ready to take over the world." Beta was warming to his topic, speaking forcefully and staring intently at Kevin.

"There are two major secret societies in this world," he explained. "Both are in a race to overpower the other. Both are generating wealth and power by involving themselves in illegal affairs. Both are corrupting politicians, laws, judges, police, military forces and anyone else that they believe will succumb to their supremacy. The only difference between the two is that the one that I'm part of is fundamentally built on a better humanitarian principle."

Kevin stared back at Beta, astonished and appalled. "Seriously? You really believe all that crap? This is just some attempt at justification for your actions. Greed is your only motivation. Greed for power, just like the rest of them. A 'humanitarian principle'? Don't make me laugh! You know that it's just smoke and mirrors hiding their true intent, which is power. There is nothing noble about this and you know it! You're head of MI6. You can't be that stupid. You're only making excuses!"

"I realise that I might come across as naïve," Beta conceded. "But this organisation is the only means by which the other can be opposed. And in terms of the humanitarian principle, believe it or not, this organisation was founded five hundred years ago by Druid priests." He realised after saying them that this last observation might not actually help his case. Judging from the look on Kevin's face, he was right.

"Naïve? Is that what you think I believe you are? No, Beta, there are too many questions. This is not some kind of Da Vinci Code or Angels and Demons book you're talking about. We're dealing with real life criminals here. You can't honestly think that any organisation like this, whoever founded it, is the lesser evil just because some other one was founded by someone else? They're all criminals and it's our job to stop them. All of them! So please, spare me the whole 'they are not really that bad' act."

Kevin had spent too many years of his life without his wife and son. Now his father's life was on the line. He wanted to strike out at Beta, but it would only give him a moment's satisfaction. He had be smart if he wanted to get to the bottom of this dangerous game, so he took a deep breath to calm his anger. Both men stared into their glasses, lost in their own nightmares, neither knowing what to say next as each realised that their many years of friendship had now ended and they were standing on opposite sides of no man's land.

"So what's next?" Beta asked, knowing that Kevin always had a plan meticulously worked out.

"You have two hours. After that, you will be hunted down as a traitor. You will also know what it's like to be on the run." Kevin's reply was angry.

"This has been sanction from above?" Beta asked.

"Everything but the two hours' lead. That head start is just me."

"You know they will come down hard on you for letting me go," Beta observed.

"I can take care of myself," shrugged Kevin. "But don't kid yourself. You'll be known as a traitor to all and your life will become a living hell. You'll never know who is waiting for you and who can trust. You'll be back to square one, no family or friends." His voice dropped to a menacing tone. "And you had better pray that nothing happens to my dad or to Simon or the shadows will become your incubus."

"In that case, I better get a wriggle on." Beta stood up, looking around his office for the last time.

Both men walked to the office exit door and stood a moment, watching at each other silently. "Who is assigned to look after this place?" Beta asked, surprised to find he was curious about this matter.

"Until they find someone else, I will be minding the agency," Kevin admitted. He was a little at having been appointed to the position under these circumstances.

"I am happy to hear that," Beta said with genuine emotion. "Look after the people here. They are a good lot."

"Better than you, I hope. In terms of a handover, I'm assuming that you have not changed the combination for the safe and that you still keep a ledger of your current activities?"

"Yes to both. Well, my friend, I guess this is it." Beta offered his hand but this time, Kevin did not take it.

"I'm not your friend. You betrayed our friendship a long time ago. From now on, we will certainly be on the opposite sides of the law. The only difference this time is that it will be obvious."

Beta withdrew his hand before turning his back on his friend, his office and his life.

"Done," Whisper said as he re-entered the house with a shovel in hand.

"I really don't get you," mused Lucca, giving him a withering look. "You have killed more people than anyone else in your profession, but here you are, upset by the killing of some nobody. I hope that digging her grave yourself will now allow you to get your mind back on the job."

"Her death was unnecessary. You ignored my request to leave her unharmed," Whisper retorted. He leaned the shovel against the wall.

"Fine! You have my apology. Can we please now move on? This conversation is boring me," Lucca snarled back. With an impatient gesture, he turned and started walking back towards the basement where Signor Beppe was held, now alone. Lucca's phone rang and he paused to read the number on the screen. "Do me a favour, Whisper, and take lunch down to our dear father. I have to take this call."

Whisper collected the tray of food. As he left the room, he heard Lucca speaking into the handset. "Yeah, what? ... You're kidding me! Well, well, well... They will not be happy with you!"

Downstairs, Signor Beppe sat on the wooden chair, hands still bound behind him. He was struggling to clear the image of what happened to Deepa from his head. Almost more shocking to him than her sudden death was seeing his beloved son come back from the dead as a different person, a cold-hearted killer who had just slayed without thought or mercy an innocent teenage girl. The horror of what he just witnessed still shook him. Even when Whisper entered the room and carried the tray of food to a small table, Signor Beppe did not shift his gaze from the place where Deepa had sat when she was killed.

Whisper placed the tray down on the table and then moved behind Signor Beppe. He took a butterfly knife from his inside jacket pocket and flicked it open. After cutting Signor Beppe's hands free, he helped him to his feet and guided him to the table. Signor Beppe's mind was blank, completely consumed by the events that occurred within the last hour. He struggled to refocus and simply moved to the table with Whisper's help and slowly sat down. He stared at the food, not really seeing it, nor anything else except the execution that kept replaying over and over again in his head.

"Please eat," Whisper said. He sat at the second chair that was located near the table. "I'm sorry. Her death was unwarranted." Signor Beppe did not move or speak. Whisper went on. "I'm also sorry that I was unable to keep my promise to you. But you need to let it go and keep your energy up." Still Beppe did not reply. He continued staring at his plate.

"Please..." Whisper said again, but this time he placed his hand, almost inadvertently on Signor Beppe's shoulder. The warm sensation of Whisper's hand at last prompted the old man to look up.

"Where is she now?" he managed to ask in a hoarse moan.

"I've buried her near the forest, overlooking the valley. It is a good spot," Whisper replied.

"Grazie, figlio mio," Signor Beppe muttered softly.

"Why do you insist on calling me your son? I am not your son," Whisper said with tired irritation.

"You are," Beppe said sadly. "You are. You might not be my flesh and blood, but I love you just the same as my other children."

"You say that, but at the first instant you thought that I'd be a threat to your own children, you beat me up and kicked me out."

Signor Beppe looked at Whisper from a face lined with pain. "You are right. I have been a terrible father. I'll regret that to the day that I'll die. I would do anything to go back and change things. But no matter what has happened, te se il mio figlio e ti voglio bene." He gazed at his son, reconfirming his fatherly love. Whisper's eyes narrowed and he felt a clenching in his chest.

"Eat your food," he said abruptly and turned his face away, unable to stand the man's grief any longer.

"Sir, you will not believe this! We've picked up one of the mobile numbers." The call came from one of the Team 12 professionals.

It was made in Bernie's direction, although he was not the first to respond to it.

"Let me see!" Simon cried, lunging between several people to see which number had shown up. The soldier, seeing Simon's concern, turned the small electronic device towards him to reveal the number that appeared.

"It's Deepa," Simon said excitedly.

"Miss, looks like I owe you an apology," the soldier holding the device called to Chiara. She simply smiled back at him.

"How far?" Trace asked.

"Ten minutes. Do you want to do a hot landing?" Aleks replied, peering over Simon's shoulder at the screen.

"No. A hot landing might result in too many casualties. Let's sneak up on them," Trace replied as he checked the map.

"There," said Bernie. He tap a spot on the map with one firm finger. "That clearing's ten kilometres out from the signal. Those hills might help shield the sound of the helicopter."

"Are we ok with the two hours hike?" one of the soldiers asked with a doubtful look at the teenagers.

"I think you'll find that these kids are fitter than you," retorted Aleks.

"Relax, Aleks. He was talking about me," Trace replied, making everyone laugh. "Ok, let's take only the essentials. We don't want the extra weight. You know the drill. Kit up!"

"What are you carrying?" the same soldier asked and pointed at his rifle.

"Mosquito pistols," Stephen replied. They were the first words he had spoken in over half an hour.

"Ok. Behind you there is a small set trunk. Open it and help yourselves to anything that catches your fancy. The Mosquito pistols are great and all, but you might need something with more penetration power behind it," the same soldier said.

All three teenagers turned and looked into the trunk. Chiara elected not to swap her pistol, but Stephen and Simon both reached for the assault rifles.

"Looks like you kids will be the first in our team to try those SCAR-L puppies out," Trace noted. "We just received a couple on loan from our stars and stripes friends. We often swap weapons with them to get an independent view of any trialled rifle. We've had those ones for a month now, but none of us want to part with our own guns."

"SCAR-L?" Stephen asked. He was unsure which rifle Trace was referring to as he now held one in each hand.

"Stands for Special Operations Combat Assault Rifle (SCAR). The 'L' is for 'Light' version. It's the rifle you're both holding," Trace explained.

"You boys carry your Mosquito pistols too, please," requested Bernie. "They may come in handy."

"No probs. We were going to take them anyway. They were custom made and factory calibrated specifically for our individual requirements. The Director ordered us never to part from them," Simon replied.

"Factory calibrated?" Trace asked, finding himself intrigued by Simon's use of the words.

"Well, for instance, when I fire my pistol, I tend to pull back too much. So although my grouping is less than ten centimetres, the rounds hit consistently ten centimetres higher. They remoulded the pistol for me so that the weight distribution helps keep it steady. For Stephen, they adjusted the trigger to only require a faint breeze to release the firing hammer." He looked across at Stephen for a nod of confirmation but Stephen ignored him. "I think he likes the idea that one day he'll be in a Magnificent Seven pistol duel," Simon finished.

"Wow! Ten centimetres at twenty-five metres is great shooting. Bob, that's four inches for us old fellas," Trace observed.

"That's at fifty metres in an indoor range," Stephen corrected him. "There were no weather conditions influencing the needle's flight."

Trace shook his head. "I'm sorry, kids, but that's hard to believe. You mean to say that at fifty metres, you can just about hit my hand with every shot from your pistol? I don't know what the Olympic standard is, but I'd be surprised if Olympians have that level of accuracy."

"Trace, the Mosquito pistols have essentially no recoil and in an indoor environment the needle's trajectory is affected by solely gravity. What the boys are telling you is quite possible. The problem is what happens when they're fired outdoors. Stephen?" Aleks interjected. The teenager had explained this to him during the car pursuit earlier on.

"That's correct," Stephen said promptly. "Outdoors, from fifteen metres onward, we need to aim for the body. Even then, with a slight wind, we have a success rate of only sixty per cent."

"So why use it? I mean, you need a weapon to deal with both outdoor and indoor conflict scenarios," Trace asked.

"For outdoors, the Mosquito rifle is issued. Where the pistol's needles are only subsonic, the rifle's ones can reach supersonic speeds. So, in a range of up to six hundred metres, in most weather conditions, they'll have the same accuracy as your assault rifle," Bernie replied. He was rather enjoying the conversation as it provided a break from his mission planning.

Other members of the Team 12 crew were also listening in. "How much do the pistols weigh?" one asked.

"Loaded it's 395 grams. Here, have a hold." Simon offered his pistol to anyone who wanted to feel its weight.

"The added benefit to its weight and accuracy in close quarter combat is that it is quieter than a nine millimetre standard pistol mounted with a silencer. The magazine also comes with forty-five needles," Bernie continued.

Trace whistled as he held the pistol and pointed it through the helicopter window while looking into the sight.

"Any special attachments?" another team member asked, speaking for the first time since the helicopter left the airport.

"It does come with a small laser designator. But the Director was telling me earlier on that he wants these kids to become instinctively accurate and not be dependent on the laser. Apparently, until this mission got them away from their training, they were firing close to eight hundred rounds a day each," Bernie replied. He suppressed a small twinge of jealously at of the amount of shooting practice the teenagers were enjoying.

"Five minutes to the landing point," one of the pilots called.

"Ok, boys and girl, let's get our minds into gear. We free our two hostages and get back in time for supper and a nice British Ale. First round's on me," Trace said, as he had done so many times before.

Signor Beppe ate his dinner silently. Although he could not taste anything but bile, he knew he needed to take his own advice and keep his strength up. Dutifully, he kept putting food into his mouth and chewing it. The difficult part was trying to swallow each dry mouthful. The painful, rasping sensation in his throat reminded him that this hellish nightmare was no dream. Every once in a while, he looked up at Whisper. But for most of the time his mind was repeatedly replaying Deepa's execution in slow motion. Whisper also sat quietly. He was feeling conflicted about the whole situation. An unfamiliar feeling was creeping over him. It took quite some time, but eventually he recognised it as guilt. The sound of Whisper's phone ringing sent a jolt of shock through both of them.

"Yes?" he said when he answered it. "Are you sure it's them? … How long do we have? … No, it's ok." He hung up.

"Company?" Signor Beppe asked, abruptly coming out of his reverie. Even in his drained state, his mind was finely trained to focus on a potential escape opportunity.

"The consequence of a foolish choice I made earlier on," Whisper replied. "And the prelude of another foolish decision that I've recently made. Nothing for you to worry about," he concluded while trying to plan his own exit from this whole mess.

"You don't make foolish choices. Everything you do is calculated. That means these two choices of yours were too," Signor Beppe observed. He meant it as a compliment.

"Whisper, I'd like some time alone with dear Dad," Lucca interjected. Neither man had seen him approach and stand in the doorway.

"Sure. I have an errand to attend to anyway. I'll see you in a few hours," Whisper said. He stood up, still gazing at Signor Beppe and keeping his back to Lucca.

"Errand?" Lucca asked.

"Yes. I need to call some clients. But to keep this position's secrecy intact, I'll drive an hour or so away from here and then make the calls." This time Whisper turned to look Lucca in the eye. Lucca nodded briefly, trying to act as if his brother needed his permission.
"No problem. You can go," he said. But Whisper had already brushed past him.

As soon as the helicopter touched the ground, the rescue team quickly moved to the cover of the nearby pine forest. As they started to climb the first hill, they could hear the helicopter rotors winding down and the engine switch off.

"Why is it not taking off?" asked Simon in a low voice. He had envisaged a military style landing in which troops get dropped off and the helicopter immediately flies away again.

"We might need it. As it needs to remain in the area, we're better off keeping it on the ground. Also, the sound of the engine is louder on take-off. It might carry to the target area and give us away," Trace explained quietly.

"They probably know we're coming anyway. We might as well have gone for a hot landing and cut off any attempt at escape," Simon observed. He was frustrated that every move they had made to date had been foreseen by the double agent.

"I know how you feel," Trace said, correctly interpreting Simon's unspoken implication. "But if you're right and we flew straight in, they'd chop every one of us into pieces with machine guns. That helicopter back there would effectively become a flying coffin. I lost two of my best men only a few weeks ago for that reason," he added, remembering the faces of his two dead friends. "I rather keep the rest of them alive for as long as possible."

"I understand. It's just that the only times when we have had some wins have been when I went against what was expected of me," said Simon. His impromptu break in at the mansion and the decision not to set an ambush on the freeway again to his mind.

"Kid, with that thinking, you either get yourself killed or become a hero. I'm betting the latter. But unless you operate on your own, the latter will also get those around you killed. One day, you might become a team leader, and when that happens, you'll have to put your people first. Such bold risks might pay great dividends, but they come with a body count," Trace warned.

Simon acknowledged the lesson. "I understand."

"Now, how are your military field hand signals?" Trace asked, raising his voice so that the other two teenagers could hear him.

"Good," Simon replied, although he unsure what the question was leading to.

"Ok. From here on, we are going silent. Field hand signals only," Trace instructed.

Chiara gave a silent thumbs up in an attempt to make a joke of the fact that she had received no military training to date. Trace smiled at her gesture and flicked his own thumb up in reply. Then he gestured for the team to be silent and continue their cautious advance.

"Where about are you?" Whisper asked into the mobile phone while looking for a parking spot.

"Five minutes out," came the response.

"Ok. I'll find a quiet coffee shop where we can meet."

"See you in five," Beta replied.

Trace looked at the map then tapped his watch and extended one finger. His team members immediately repeated the signal to one another in an acknowledgement that they had one hour to go. The teenagers also repeated the signal, including Chiara, who despite the seriousness of the situation could not help but find the silent charades amusing. She hid her grin and kept moving.

"Yes, sir?" Kevin said into the mobile, having recognised the number of the Minister for Defence.

"Settled in?" the minister asked.

"Yes, sir. I'll brief the staff in an hour. I'll inform them that Beta had to make an immediate departure for personal reasons. I figure that those who need to know the actual truth will be briefed at a later date," Kevin replied.

"That's fine. But Kevin – or should I address you as the new Beta? – I want this situation wiped from the history of MI6. Understood?"

"Completely," Kevin replied. The minister didn't need to know that Kevin did not intend to follow this order to the letter.

"How are you going to catch Beta?" the minister asked, his voice only slightly betraying the irritation he felt about having to go along with Kevin's plan.

"I have slipped a micro-tracking device into Beta's drink. With a bit of luck, it should remain in his body for the next few hours. Don't worry. He will pay for what he has done to us!"

"Fine," the minister said again, ending the call without another word.

"So, why here and not in the house?" Beta asked as he sat at the table in the coffee shop where Whisper was waiting for him.

"The house has been compromised. I figured you'd prefer to keep at bay. I ordered you an espresso," Whisper answered, hoping his last statement would shift the focus from the first.

"Thank you. Tell me about the house being compromised. Does Lucca know?" Beta asked, clawing the topic back.

"To be honest, I don't have the patience to go through it all. But the fact is that in about fifty minutes, the house will be under siege. Signor Beppe, if he is still alive then, will be freed. Lucca and his small posse of guards will be either captured or killed, and you will have the opportunity to bring forward your plan and step into Lucca's role. Is that enough detail?" Whisper took a moment's pleasure from the revelation that he knew about Beta's plan.

"I see. I guess that by that I can also conclude who gave the house away?" Beta noted.

"Turned out to be the teenage girl, I'm afraid, who Lucca has killed for no real reason," Whisper said. It was only a slight bend in the truth, after all.

Team 12 were moving through the forest in an arrow formation. Trace and Bernie were in the centre, with the teenagers at the tail end of the two rear points. The leader of this formation, the scout, was the person responsible for being the eyes and ears for any foe that might be encountered. He was called Neil and he was the newest member of Team 12. When he suddenly dropped to one knee and raised an open hand, everyone halted, passing the silent hand signal on to one another. Neil turned to his closest colleague, tapped three fingers on his opposite bicep, then opened the same hand and tapped his forehead a few times, finally pointing one single finger straight in the air. The next team member repeated the signal, until eventually every person got the message. In response to the signal, Trace moved forward.

Chiara, not sure what to make of it all, moved forward slightly until she was next to Aleks. "What was that?" she whispered. Her voice was so soft he could barely hear her.

"Three fingers on the bicep represent the rank of sergeant. The open hand tap on the forehead means to go or come to. The single finger represent the team subgroup. So the message is for the sergeant to go to the scout," Aleks replied with equal softness. His eyes scanned the area ahead as Trace reached the scout and kneeled beside him, facing in the same direction.

"What's up?"

"Sir, the signal is coming from two hundred meters up the hill. Best if I leave the team here and have a peek on my own," Neil proposed.

"Ok. We'll stay put," Trace acknowledged. He turned and made straight for Bernie to provide him an update.

"So, are you going to kill me?" Signor Beppe asked, breaking into Lucca's story of how powerful he had become.

"Don't interrupt me, dear Dad," Lucca snarled back. "I'm just getting to the good bit."

"You talk of how bad a father I am, but you are no different," Signor Beppe continued, switching now to Italian.

"On the contrary, Stephen has always got everything he ever wanted," Lucca said proudly, also speaking in Italian.

"Really? The boy behaves like someone who grew up feeling neglected and unloved. You probably sent him to boarding schools all his life and only saw him once a year, if he was lucky," Signor Beppe guessed.

"Shut up! You don't know what you are talking about. I did all of that because I love him," Lucca snapped.

"Love? I somehow doubt Stephen shares your view of feeling loved." Deep down, he felt proud of his newly discovered grandson. His heart ached, however, for the boy's childhood pain. So much sadness, he thought. Always, there is so much sadness.

The scout was heading back to the team, but instead of returning to his position at the arrow's head, he moved directly to Trace. When he reached him, he whisper the update into his leader's ear and handed him an object. A few moments later, Trace's gaze scanned across to the three teenagers. He pointed at each and tapped his forehead. All knew the signal, including Chiara. She, Aleks, Bernie,

Stephen and Simon, and Chiara quietly moved towards Trace. When they arrived, they forme a small circle around him and knelt down.

"Kids, what I'm about to tell you isn't pleasant. I need you to toughen up and channel the emotions that are about to overwhelm you into the success of this mission," Trace whispered. He paused; making sure everyone understood his request. They all nodded. "Neil has found the mobile phone that led us here," Trace continued, holding the small device into in the middle of the circle for everyone to see.

"It's Deepa's," Chiara heard herself say.

"The phone isn't locked by a pin code, so I activated it. I found the draft of an SMS," Trace said. He was speaking slowly, pausing between statements to allow the teenagers enough time to register the information and not be too overwhelmed by it.

Aleks frowned down at the message on the screen and read the words aloud. "Sorry, Simon. I tried to stop this. W."

"'W'? Is that from Whisper? Stop what?" Simon asked. A pounding sensation was beginning to reverberate in his chest as he looked at Trace for answers.

"Kids, take a deep breath," Trace whispered, knowing that there was no easy way to break the devastating news. "This phone was found resting on top of a freshly dug grave."

"But that doesn't mean that the grave is Deepa's. You're making a baseless deduction and just upsetting us for no reason. You're sadistic!" Chiara snapped, barely managing to keep her voice down. She started trembling and looked to Simon and Stephen to back her up. Their faces were pale, jaws tight. No one spoke.

A sudden wave of bile came up Stephen's throat. Without any ability to stop himself, he impulsively arched forward and emptied the content of his stomach. He lost Deepa. The only person that showed him any care, was now gone. This had to be a mistake. Deepak could not be dead. Someone had to pay. He would devote his life seeking out the people responsible for Deepa's death. Why did she join in the first place? She deserved better than a life in MI6. And then, just as quickly as desperation set-in, Stephen became focussed; he looked up at Simon and knew who was to blame.

Simon was in a trans; he felt completely empty and was oblivious to the hatred look Stephen was casting in his direction.

Aleks and Bernie exchanged a glance. They waited, giving time for the three teenagers to come to their own conclusions.

"Can we see the grave?" Simon asked at last. Chiara saw he was struggling to keep control of his emotions.

"Yes. But it'll have to be after we finish the mission. The grave is at the edge of the forest on the crest of the mountain. Unfortunately, it's clearly visible from the house. We need to keep following the line of trees and approach the house from the opposite side. Once we clear the house, we can then go back to the grave. I'm sorry, kids," Trace replied. There was genuine empathy in his voice. He understood the loss of someone close. Reaching out, he laid a hand on Chiara's shoulder but she brushed him off.

"Let's just get this over and done with," she said, feeling her sadness suddenly swinging into an upsurge of anger.

"Sir, Pearl just called in. She'll be back with the helicopter in twenty minutes." A guard reported the message to Lucca in the room where he was talking to Signor Beppe.

"Contact Whisper and tell him to get his butt back here or we'll leave without him," Lucca ordered without looking at the guard. He was still annoyed by Whisper unexplained departure.

Trace looked across at his extended team and waited for everyone to signal a thumbs up to reflect their readiness for the assault. The team stretched in single line along the forest edge just behind the house. As planned, Simon, Stephen and Chiara would remain in the forest until the house was cleared. Just as Trace was about to give the signal to stand and move towards the house, a guard appeared from the rear door. It was usual on a mission like this for the team sniper to neutralise any roving enemy guards, but the sniper in this case did not have a silencer on his weapon and the rifle shot would give the assault away. Trace made a snap decision and signalled that they would wait for the guard to return into the house. He realised within seconds that this might take a while, as flicker of orange light revealed that the guard was lighting up a cigarette.

"Filthy habit," Trace muttered to Stephen who was lying next to him.

"How far would you say we are from the guard?" Stephen whispered.

"Around seventy-five metres. Too far to throw a knife, that's for sure," Trace replied, automatically thinking of ways to neutralise the guard. As he watched the man blow a lazy stream of Page: 248

smoke, he noticed from the corner of his eyes the barrel of a black pistol. Turning, he saw Stephen beside him holding the Mosquito pistol at the end of his outstretched arms.

"What do you think you are doing?" Trace whispered in alarm.

"The pistol shot won't be heard by the guard. If I miss, it's very unlikely that he will detect the needle. The air is completely calm with no breeze. I've never shot from this distance, but I think I can lob the needle into the guard, as long as I have the right trajectory and keep a steady hand. The manual says that at 45 degrees, the needle can travel up to one hundred and eighty metres. So, if I've got my sums right, that means that for seventy-five metres, I should try to get an angle of approximately 18 degrees," Stephen explained to an astonished Trace. "Of course, most manuals often are sales catalogues and have a tendency to oversell. I reckon I'll go to 25 degrees. I'll need you to be my spotter and look through the binoculars to see where any missed needles land," he continued while trying to estimate what a 25 degree elevation actually was.

"Kid, you have completely lost me. I joined the military because maths was not my best subject. But you sound confident, so I'm going to I trust you. Ready when you are," Trace replied, as he moved his binoculars to his eyes.

Stephen took a breath and fired the first needle. It travelled up into the air for half of the distance before starting to come down. He had no idea where the needle was heading and lay silently beside Trace, waiting for him to call out spotting instructions.

The guard was leaning against the wall of the house, smoking and staring vaguely into the forest. He was daydreaming and clearly not keeping watch for any attack. Glancing down at his shoes, he heard a tiny tinkling sound. Curious, he first looked to his left and then up at the roof, thinking perhaps something had fallen. Then he saw something unusual. Embedded in the wall a few centimetres from his head was a small needle. He propped the cigarette in his mouth and reached to pull it out of the wall. It was odd, he thought, that he had not seen it before today. After all, this was his regular smoking spot.

"Crap!" Trace swore. "He's spotted the needle. The angle was good, although maybe we should drop down a fraction, but the line was slightly to your right. Actually, shoot the same line now," he advised Stephen. "The guard has conveniently positioned himself in the right spot."

Stephen, who had frozen in place after his previous shot, lowered the barrel of the pistol slightly and fired again. This time he reeled off three shots in quick succession. The guard felt a small prick sting the back of his neck. The sedative took rapid effect and he slumped to the ground before he had the chance to feel the next two needles hit their target.

Trace immediately signalled for his troops to get up and advance toward the house. "Good shooting kid," he whispered to Stephen as he moved out into the open area. "I'm very impressed."

As soon as the soldiers had moved away, Simon and Chiara scurried over to lie down next to Stephen. "Great shooting," Simon complimented him, momentarily forgetting about the past clashes between them. "I doubt that any of us are as accurate as you."

"Are we now supposed to just lie here?" Chiara asked. Hot tears still blurred her eyes every time the thought of Deepa crossed her mind.

"I'm not happy with this either, Chiara," Simon replied quietly. Inside, he was burning for revenge.

The three teenagers watched as Bernie, Aleks and Team 12 lined up along the side wall of the house, with half on either side of the back door. Trace stooped and quickly checked that the guard was completely sedated. He was impressed to observe that all three needles were embedded only a few millimetres apart on the back of the man's neck. He then nodded to his team scout Neil to open the door and allow all of them to slip into the house. Inside the kettle was boiling. One of the guards was making himself a quick cup of tea before heading out for his last patrol. As he approached the kettle, his world turned black. He had not even heard Neil slip into the room and fire a round into him from a pistol fitted with a silencer.

Lucca and Signor Beppe were in the midst of another argument when they heard the soft thud above them that was caused by the guard collapsing on the wooden floor. Most people would not have heard it or would most likely have assumed that someone had merely dropped something by accident. However, both Lucca and Signor Beppe immediately stopped talking and looked up at the ceiling.

"Looks like we might have company," Lucca whispered as he drew his pistol from the jacket holster.

"You are paranoid," Signor Beppe replied in Italian.

"We both know what that sound was from. Don't try to distract me," Lucca replied as started moving toward the door, still glancing at the ceiling and awaiting the next sound. When he reached the door, he pointed the pistol directly at it and moved his other hand towards the handle. Then, without warning, he felt a crack in his head and collapsed. Behind him, Signor Beppe held the remaining pieces of the chair he just smashed down on his son's head. As he reached down to check Lucca's pulse, all hell broke loose.

On the floor above, two guards encountered Team 12. Immediately, both sides opened fire. Within a few seconds, explosions from rifles and stun grenades rebounded off the thick walls of the house, turning the small space into an ear-piercing battleground. The noise was so loud that nobody in the fight heard the helicopter landing just a few metres outside. Most of the team members and the guards were firing at each other from the various doors that provided access into a common area in the house. The stone walls of the building provided great protection from the bullets for both sides. Downstairs, having satisfied himself that his son was still alive, Signor Beppe reached down and took Lucca's pistol from him, before moving carefully towards the stairs just outside the room.

The teenagers, listening to the gunfight that had erupted inside the house, were the first to spot the helicopter. Without any words between them, all three stood to run and stop anyone who may attempt to escape.

"Wait!" Simon yelled. "Looks like the helicopter is going to land on the opposite side of the house. Chiara, take my rifle." He held it out to her. "Run along under cover of the forest to your right until you can get yourself into a good firing support position covering the ground between the house and the helicopter. Stephen and I will run down to the house and then go around it to try and overrun the helicopter. If it tries to take off before we get there or if we get into trouble with anyone coming out of the house, you take them out!" he ordered.

"No, Simon! You're the best shot with a rifle. Stephen and I will go down to the house," Chiara barked back, annoyed that Simon had tried to sideline her.

"Now is not the time, Chiara," Simon snapped back, not wanting to place another person he cared for in mortal risk.

"Chiara, it's not because we're boys," Stephen interjected. "The two of us have had several years of unarmed combat training and you haven't. The reality is that in a close quarters fight against those guys, even Simon and I will most likely end up in trouble. Besides," he added, trying to end with a joke, "I trust you more than Simon with a rifle."

"Ok, ok," Chiara agreed reluctantly. "Go!" She raced off, still annoyed with the decision, trying to find a better angle to cover the opposite side of the house.

Signor Beppe eased himself up the stairs with the pistol ready to neutralise anyone he encountered. Although he suspected that the firefight was between Lucca's guards and his rescuers, he was not going to take any chances.

Back in the room below, Lucca, although nauseous from the knock on his head, fluttered his eyelids as he started regaining consciousness.

Simon and Stephen reached the door of the house where the sedated guard still lay motionless. They veered to the left, dropping below the window line, and moved expediently around toward the front of the house.

Pearl, the Irish helicopter pilot, was excited to be seeing Lucca again. Over the years, the two of them had enjoyed on and off encounters, and each time she found herself growing fonder of him. Between fantasising about another 'on' encounter with her boss and focusing on landing the chopper, she did not notice the slight movement at the edge of the forest in front of her.

Chiara dove to the ground to avoid being seen by the pilot. She snapped open the bipod attached to the rifle and settled herself into a comfortable firing position.

The room blurred a little as Lucca stood up. Although still dazed, he managed to reach for his spare pistol and get himself to the door. He walked into the corridor and paused for a second before throwing up the meal he had eaten earlier. After taking a few seconds to recompose himself, he started zigzagging unsteadily towards the stairs.

By this time, Signor Beppe had slithered to the top of the stairs. He paused, wondering whether to head for the open front door and escape or to turn right and move to the side of the house where the gun battle was still in full swing. As he squatted pensively at the top of the stairs, a guard came running past, heading for the front door.

At the corner of the house, Stephen and Simon paused to see if anyone was moving towards the helicopter. "I'll take the front door, and you take the helicopter," Simon said. It was meant to be a suggestion, but came out bordering on an order.

"Ok. Go!" Stephen agreed, before quickly moving towards the rear of the helicopter.

Simon also moved quickly, pistol fully extended, towards the entrance of the house. Once he reached it, he placed his hand on the door handle and took a breath to get himself ready. Just at that moment, the guard who had charged past Signor Beppe reached to the front door and hastily swung the handle. He was in such a rush to escape the firefight and save his own life that he almost failed to stop before the door. He yanked it open with full force and was momentarily blinded by wall of bright light him as he stepped out into the open.

Surprised by the door suddenly opening, Simon was caught off balance. He stumbled, dropping his pistol in an effort to keep his balance. As he hit the ground, he saw the guard appearing from behind the door and looking momentarily dazed. He had time to notice the guard raise his had to shade his eyes and realised that the man must be temporarily blinded by the unexpected glare. Without wasting the opportunity, Simon jumped his feet and launched himself with full force at the guard.

Stephen was almost at the helicopter. He glanced back at the house and saw Simon tackle the guard to the ground. He paused for a second, unsure if he should continue towards the helicopter or go and assist Simon. Although not really sure if Chiara was watching him, Stephen signalled into the forest for her to keep her eyes on the helicopter as he ran back towards the house.

The sudden burst of light from the front door also partially blinded Signor Beppe. Against the glare, he could make out the silhouette of a person tackling the guard. He interpreted this to mean that some of his rescuers had surrounded the house. With the understanding that his captors were about to be overpowered, Signor Beppe moved up the stairs and turned right to go and help those in the gunfight inside the house.

With every step, Lucca was getting more of his senses. He reached the bottom of the stairs and started climbing.

Chiara, looking through the high powered rifle scope, kept scanning between Simon's fight with the guard and Stephen approach to the helicopter. Having switched her glance to Simon, she missed Stephen's hand signal and was startled to see him suddenly change direction.

Simon and the guard were now wrestling each other on the doorstep. Both took swings at one another and tried to grab the other in a lock as they rolled over and over on the ground.

Signor Beppe reached the first door and peeked around the corner. He spotted three guards, all taking cover behind walls and firing through various doors each time a wave of bullets came flying at them. After fixing the location of the three guards, Signor Beppe stepped forward and pulled the trigger precisely three times. In a moment, all three guard were dead.

"Clear!" Signor Beppe called out loud enough to be heard by those back at the guards. He then turned around to check that nobody was sneaking up behind him.

Lucca had almost reached the top of the stairs that led from the room where the prisoners had been kept. Like the guard and Signor Beppe, he felt momentarily blinded by the sunlight pouring through the front door.

After reaching the pair who were still struggling on the ground, Stephen drove the back of his pistol into the guard's head at the first opportunity, immediately knocking him out.

"Thanks," gasped Simon. "But I was ok. I was completely on top of the matter." He grinned, heaving under the dead weight of the unconscious guard.

"No doubt! Once you've finished with snuggling up to your new friend, would you mind getting up and getting back to the mission? You two can have your deep and meaningful time together later on," Stephen joked back, not realising this was the first time he had shared any humour with Simon since they started training together.

It was his own training and familiarity with the teenage boys that enabled Signor Beppe to recognise

Stephen's silhouette at the door. He moved towards the door to greet them, not noticing Lucca coming up the stairs to his left.

Almost at the top the stairs, Lucca, too, spotted a silhouette at the door. Not wishing to take a chance while he was impaired by a likely concussion, he lifted the pistol and pulled the trigger.

Unable to stop himself from laughing at Simon's attempts to roll the heavy guard off him, Stephen looked into the house and saw his father pointing a pistol back at him.

Signor Beppe was almost at the door when he saw Stephen looking into the house and smiling. At first he thought the boy was smiling at him. Then realised that Stephen's gaze was slightly to his left. He turned his head in time to see Lucca raise his pistol.

Everything happened lightning fast.

Signor Beppe instinctively launched himself at the teenager just seconds before Lucca pulled the trigger several times. With each flash, a bullet flew out of the barrel. The first hit Signor Beppe between the shoulders as he reached the doorway. The second and third bullets found their way through the left side of his upper back, penetrating his lungs as with his final burst of energy, he launched himself at Stephen. Caught by surprise by Signor Beppe's sudden appearance from the darkness, Stephen was unprepared to maintain his balance when the old man launched himself at him. The impact of the collision propelled both of them to the ground. Stephen and Simon were in shock, unable to comprehend what had just occurred.

Lucca approached the door but held back a second to allow his eyesight to adjust. He then pointed the rifle down at the person he had seen falling with Signor Beppe, ready to kill him as well. Then he stopped.

"Stephen? What are you doing here?"

"You… you killed him! You fired at me and you killed him!" Stephen screamed in complete disbelief.

"Son, it was an accident. I didn't know it was you at the door. Are you ok?" Lucca replied, concerned but also mindful that the intruders would soon be making their way towards the front of the house. "Are you hurt?" he asked again.

"I-I think so," Stephen replied, looking down. Signor Beppe lay still with his head resting on Stephen's chest. Simon watched the exchange without moving. He did not know what to do.

Still feeling nauseous, Lucca suddenly became aware of the other two bodies to his right and swung his pistol towards them, ready to shoot.

"Don't!" Stephen screamed as he realised what was about to happen.

Lucca, with the pistol levelled at Simon, held his fire. The boy, still trapped under the guard, raised his hands as a signal of surrender.

"Stephen, get up! We're going to the helicopter," Lucca instructed as he started to move between the two teenagers.

Stephen rolled Signor Beppe off him, holding his trainer's head gently and lowering him to the ground. As he started to get onto his feet, he thought he saw Signor Beppe's fingers move. Stephen immediately dropped back down next to Signor Beppe and checked for his pulse.

"E' il tuo dest…" Signor Beppe whispered.

"Please don't talk. Someone will come to help you," Stephen replied, laying a hand against Signor Beppe's cheek.

"E' il tuo destino…" Signor Beppe said again, and with these few words he took his last breath and closed his eyes for the last time.

"Stephen," yelled Lucca, already a few metres away "Now!"

"E' il tuo destino? What does it mean?" Stephen asked of Signor Beppe's lifeless body.

"It means that it is your destiny," Simon replied. He was now sitting up, free of the guard, with tears streaming down his cheeks.

Stephen paused for a second, thinking about those words. He knew what they meant. He heard his father call his name again as he continued moving towards the helicopter.

Chiara had no idea what to do. She had seen most what had occurred through her high-powered scope. She did not know who the man walking briskly towards the helicopter was, and that did not help with her current decision about whether to pull the trigger and kill him. She kept the crosshairs of the sight fixed on him and let her finger rest on the rifle trigger.

"Sorry, Simon. I have to go. He's my father and even if I hate him with every cell in my body, he is still my dad," Stephen called out with a voice full of shame.

"He-he killed Signor Beppe! You-you didn't. Signor Beppe died to save you! Doesn't that mean anything to you?" Simon demanded. He was now on his knees, crawling towards his grandfather.

"Sorry," Stephen said again before turning to run towards the helicopter.

Simon collapsed on top of Signor Beppe and wept.

Chiara watched Stephen run towards the helicopter with a pistol in hand. She knew then that she had to put aside her hesitation about killing a human being and pull the trigger. As she applied pressure to the trigger, the explosion of the firing cap igniting the gun powder caused a huge recoil against Chiara's shoulder. She had finally found the courage to pull the trigger, but still she closed her eyes at the last second. She did not want to see the destruction her rifle shot was about to cause.

As Stephen neared his father, who was now a few metres away from the helicopter, he heard the distant explosion of Chiara's rifle. Before he could react, his father collapsed. Lucca howled in pain and he looked down at the bullet wound in his leg.

"Stop!" Stephen yelled at the top of his lungs, racing to place himself between his wounded father and Chiara's firing position.

"What have I done?" Chiara wondered to herself. Stephen's reaction surprised her but she felt a deep sense of relief upon realising that she had only wounded the man.

"Come on, Dad," Stephen called out, as he moved to assist his father onto the back of the helicopter, startling Pearl who was not expecting to see her boss wounded and in the company of a teenager.

"Hey, Pearl, this is my son Stephen," Lucca panted, loud enough to be heard above the noise of the helicopter's engine and rotors. "Now, be a good pilot and get us the hell out of here!"

Stephen helped Lucca to lie across the back seats. "Come on, son. Get in," Lucca shouted, mindful that the person who shot him in the leg could fire again at any moment. But Stephen stood just outside the helicopter, unable to move.

"Come on!" Pearl yelled, seeing men emerging from the front door of the house.

"Sorry, Dad. I'm not like you. I don't want to be like you!" Stephen said, starting softly but finishing with conviction behind his words.

"What? I don't have time for this. Get on board now!" Lucca ordered.

"Go!" Stephen yelled at Pearl, as he started stepping back from his helicopter.

"Stephen, what are you doing?" Lucca yelled. He pressed his hand against the wound in an attempt to stop the bleeding.

"I'm freeing myself from your toxic family war. It has bought me nothing but misery. I no longer want to follow in your footsteps. I choose the footsteps of the person you just killed – your own father," Stephen said angrily, still edging away.

"Stop this nonsense and get into the chopper right now!" Stephen shook his head. "You killed you own father. And you killed Deepa, the only person I have ever..." Stephen started to reply.

"Sir, we need to go!" the pilot called. Their attackers were now running toward the helicopter.

"I'm freeing myself from you," Stephen shouted. "I choose my own destiny. Good bye, Dad!" He stepped back further as Pearl pulled on the throttle and the helicopter sprang into the air. Stephen stood looking into his father's eyes for as long as he could before the helicopter's ascent blasted him with a wave of dust.

The helicopter tilted away from the house, gaining altitude rapidly. The soldiers of Team 12 members commenced firing at it with everything that they had at their disposal. Several bullets found their way into the belly of the helicopter, but none caused sufficient damage to bring the machine down. Within moments the helicopter speeding away, beyond reach of bullets, leaving Stephen and the members of Team 12 far below.

"What is the matter with you, kid? Get your head back in the game! People's lives depend on you. Our lives depend on you being in the game," Trace yelled at Stephen. He grabbed the boy's arm and swung him roughly around to face him nose to nose.

Stephen did not respond. His mind echoed with the words he just said to his father. I don't want to be like you. I'm freeing myself from you. I choose my own destiny. He shook himself free of Trace's grip. Without a word, he turned and walked toward the place where Deepa was buried.

Twenty-five minutes later, Chiara and Simon stood by Stephen's side looking down at a mound of dark, freshly dug soil that was marked by a small makeshift cross made from two pine branches.

"Let's finish this. We cannot have Deepa and Signor Beppe's lives been taken away for nothing," Stephen said suddenly. His silent tears were at last beginning to dry up.

"Are you sure? Do we really want to risk losing more lives for what is simply a stupid family feud?" Chiara asked. Her own tears had not stopped falling since she left her rifle post and joined Simon on the walk up the hill to her friend's grave.

"Their deaths cannot be for nothing," Stephen insisted, unable to take his eyes off the mound. "Her life cannot have been taken away for nothing."

It was Simon's turn to speak. "Stephen, don't get me wrong. I want revenge more than anyone one else. But Chiara is right. You know this is likely to get worse than it already is."

"I know!" Stephen said with irritation. "Either my father kills one of you two or he gets killed himself. Either way, we all need closure."

"We do," Simon agreed quietly.

"What time is the helicopter coming back for us?" Chiara asked looking down at her watch.

"About twenty-five minutes," Stephen replied, hating what needed to be done before then.

"Ok, then. It's not going to get any easier for us. Let's get over and done with it," Simon said as he passed the shovel and pick to his teammates.

"We have to do this. Inspector Lau would want her body brought back. She would want it too," Chiara said, in an attempt to build up her own courage.

"Let me start."

All three jumped, startled by sound of a man's voice behind them.

Simon stood frozen, looking into the eyes of the Director. After all these years, he did not know how to greet his father. Kevin, also feeling unsure what to say, simply moved forward and placed his arms around Simon, who accepted the warm embrace and buried his teary face into his father's shoulders. After several minutes, Kevin placed a hand on Simon's arm and stepped back to look at the three teenagers.

"It is a tough gig," he said. "But we need to take Deepa back to her family. Let me start." Kevin took the shovel from Stephen's hand and started digging. No one spoke for a while and the only sound was the swish of the shovel as it lifted the soft earth. Then Kevin interrupted their sad thoughts. "So, Stephen. I've just learned that you are my nephew. Welcome to the family. As you can see, we're a bit of a lost cause… so you should have no trouble fitting in." He grinned and winked at Stephen.

"What?" both Simon and Chiara called simultaneously. The Director's statement had completely ambushed them.

"Don't be harsh on poor Stephen. I'm thinking that a lot of this is news to him too," Kevin diagnosed, observing Stephen's white face. "So, how about we all start from the beginning and see if amongst the four of us we can connect all of the dots?" he continued. The discovery that his brother Lucca was alive, who had just shot and killed their father, had deeply unsettled him. However, he needed the team to start thinking of something else, lest their despair over the deaths became dangerous.

"It's a complete mess," he admitted. "And I overheard you three saying this affair needs closure. But before we can do that, I think we need to understand how we got here. That includes your involvement, Chiara." With an effort, he set his own grief for his father aside.

"I'd like that," Chiara replied.

"Me too," Simon followed almost immediately.

"How about you Stephen?" Kevin asked, after a few moments passed in silence. All three looked at him.

"I'm sorry," he said at last. "I never thought my actions would result in this." Guilt filled him over the loss of the first girl he ever loved and the death of a grandfather he never knew he had.

"Stephen, this isn't your fault. You were simply caught up in this feud because of your parents. Same goes for you Chiara and Simon," Kevin said firmly.

"How are we going to find them again?" Chiara asked, as another wave of sadness about Deepa rose sickeningly within her.

"I slipped a micro tracking device into a certain someone's drink. We have about four hours left to get back in the race," the Director replied.

"In that case, please start from the beginning," Stephen said.

"It started when I was a teenager," Kevin began, then he stopped. "No, actually, let me go back further than that. It really began with Signor Beppe…"